DEAD WITCH WALKING

By Kim Harrison

THE GOOD, THE BAD, AND THE UNDEAD
EVERY WHICH WAY BUT DEAD
A FISTFUL OF CHARMS

DEAD WITCH WALKING

KIM HARRISON

HARPER

Voyager

Harper*Voyager*
An Imprint of HarperCollins*Publishers*
77–85 Fulham Palace Road,
Hammersmith, London W6 8JB

www.harpercollins.co.uk

Published by Voyager 2006
6

A catalogue record for this book
is available from the British Library

ISBN-13 978 0 00 723609 1
ISBN-10 0 00 723609 3

Printed and bound in Great Britain by
Clays Limited, St Ives plc

To the man who said he liked my hat.

Acknowledgements

I'd like to thank the people who suffered through me during the rewrites. You know who you are, and I salute you. But I'd especially like to thank my editor, Diana Gill, for her wonderful suggestions that opened up delightful avenues of thought, and my agent, Richard Curtis.

DEAD WITCH WALKING

One

I stood in the shadows of a deserted shop front across from The Blood and Brew Pub, trying not to be obvious as I tugged my black leather pants back up where they belonged. *This is pathetic,* I thought, eyeing the rain-emptied street. I was way too good for this.

Apprehending unlicensed and black-art witches was my usual line of work, as it takes a witch to catch a witch. But the streets were quieter than usual this week. Everyone who could make it was at the West Coast for our yearly convention, leaving me with this gem of a run. A simple snag and drag. It was just the luck of the Turn that had put me here in the dark and rain.

"Who am I kidding?" I whispered, pulling the strap of my bag farther up my shoulder. I hadn't been sent to tag a witch in a month: unlicensed, white, dark, or otherwise. Bringing the mayor's son in for Wereing outside of a full moon probably hadn't been the best idea.

A sleek car turned the corner, looking black in the buzz of the mercury street lamp. This was its third time around the block. A grimace tightened my face as it approached, slowing. "Damn it," I whispered. "I need a darker door front."

"He thinks you're a hooker, Rachel," my backup snickered into my ear. "I told you the red halter was slutty."

"Anyone ever tell you that you smell like a drunk bat, Jenks?" I muttered, my lips barely moving. Backup was unsettlingly close tonight, having perched himself on my ear-ring. Big dangling thing—the earring, not the pixy. I'd found Jenks to be a pretentious snot with a bad attitude and a tem-per to match. But he knew what side of the garden his nectar came from. And apparently pixies were the best they'd let me take out since the frog incident. I would have sworn fairies were too big to fit into a frog's mouth.

I eased forward to the curb as the car squished to a wet-asphalt halt. There was the whine of an automatic window as the tinted glass dropped. I leaned down, smiling my prettiest as I flashed my work ID. Mr. One Eyebrow's leer vanished and his face went ashen. The car lurched into mo-tion with a tiny squeak of tires. "Day-tripper," I said in dis-dain. *No,* I thought in a flash of chastisement. He was a norm, a human. Even if they were accurate, the terms day-tripper, domestic, squish, off-the-rack, and my personal fa-vorite, snack, were politically frowned upon. But if he was picking strays up off the sidewalk in the Hollows, one might call him dead.

The car never slowed as it went through a red light, and I turned at the catcalls from the hookers I had displaced about sunset. They weren't happy, standing brazenly on the corner across from me. I gave them a little wave, and the tallest flipped me off before spinning to show me her tiny, spell-enhanced rear. The hooker and her distinctly husky-looking "friend" talked loudly as they tried to hide the cigarette they were passing between each other. It didn't smell like your usual tobacco. *Not my problem, tonight,* I thought, moving back into my shadow.

I leaned against the cold stone of the building, my gaze lingering on the red taillights of the car as it braked. Brow furrowed, I glanced at myself. I was tall for a woman—about five-eight—but not nearly as leggy as the hooker in the next puddle of light over. I wasn't wearing as much makeup as she was, either. Narrow hips and a chest that was almost flat didn't exactly make me streetwalker material.

Before I found the leprechaun outlets, I had shopped in the "your first bra" aisle. It's hard finding something without hearts and unicorns on it there.

My ancestors had immigrated to the good old U.S. of A. in the 1800s. Somehow through the generations, the women all managed to retain the distinct red hair and green eyes of our Irish homeland. My freckles, though, are hidden under a spell my dad bought me for my thirteenth birthday. He had the tiny amulet put into a pinky ring. I never leave home without it.

A sigh slipped from me as I tugged my bag back up onto my shoulder. The leather pants, red ankle boots, and the spaghetti strap halter weren't too far from what I usually wore on casual Fridays to tick off my boss, but put them on a street corner at night . . . "Crap," I muttered to Jenks. "I look like a hooker."

His only response was a snort. I forced myself not to react as I turned back to the bar. It was too rainy for the early crowd, and apart from my backup and the "ladies" down the way, the street was empty. I'd been standing out here nearly an hour with no sign of my mark. I might as well go in and wait. Besides, if I were inside, I might look like a solicitee rather than a solicitor.

Taking a resolute breath, I pulled a few strands of my shoulder-length curls from my topknot, took a moment to arrange it artfully to fall about my face, and finally spit out my gum. The click of my boots made a snappy counterpoint to the jangling of the handcuffs pinned to my hip as I strode across the wet street and into the bar. The steel rings looked like a tawdry prop, but they were real and very well-used. I winced. No wonder Mr. One Eyebrow had stopped. Used for *work*, thank you, and not the kind you're thinking of.

Still, I'd been sent to the Hollows in the rain to collar a leprechaun for tax evasion. How much lower, I wondered, could I sink? It must have been from tagging that Seeing

Eye dog last week. How was I supposed to know it wasn't a werewolf? It matched the description I'd been given.

As I stood in the narrow foyer shaking off the damp, I ran my gaze over the typical Irish bar crap: long-stemmed pipes stuck to the walls, green-beer signs, black vinyl seats, and a tiny stage where a wannabe-star was setting up his dulcimers and bagpipes amid a tower of amps. There was a whiff of contraband Brimstone. My predatory instincts stirred. It smelled three days old, not strong enough to track. If I could nail the supplier, I'd be off my boss's hit list. He might even give me something worth my talents.

"Hey," grunted a low voice. "You Tobby's replacement?"

Brimstone dismissed, I batted my eyes and turned, coming eye-to-chest with a bright green T-shirt. My eyes traveled up a huge bear of a man. Bouncer material. The name on the shirt said CLIFF. It fit. "Who?" I purred, blotting the rain from what I generously call my cleavage with the hem of his shirt. He was completely unaffected; it was depressing.

"Tobby. State-assigned hooker? She ever gonna show up again?"

From my earring came a tiny singsong voice. "I told you so."

My smile grew forced. "I don't know," I said through my teeth. "I'm not a hooker."

He grunted again, eyeing my outfit. I pawed through my bag and handed him my work ID. Anyone watching would assume he was carding me. With readily available age-disguising spells, it was mandatory—as was the spell-check amulet he had around his neck. It glowed a faint red in response to my pinky ring. He wouldn't do a full check on me for that, which was why all the charms in my bag were currently uninvoked. Not that I'd need them tonight.

"Inderland Security," I said as he took the card. "I'm on a run to find someone, not harass your regular clientele. That's why the—uh—disguise."

"Rachel Morgan," he read aloud, his thick fingers almost enveloping the laminated card. "Inderland Security runner.

You're an I.S. runner?" He looked from my card to me and back, his fat lips splitting in a grin. "What happened to your hair? Run into a blowtorch?"

My lips pressed together. The picture was three years old. It hadn't been a blowtorch, it had been a practical joke, an informal initiation into my full runner status. Real funny.

The pixy darted from my earring, setting it swinging with his momentum. "I'd watch your mouth," he said, tilting his head as he looked at my ID. "The last lunker who laughed at her picture spent the night in the emergency room with a drink umbrella jammed up his nose."

I warmed. "You know about that?" I said, snatching my card and shoving it away.

"Everybody in appropriations knows about that." The pixy laughed merrily. "And trying to tag that Were with an itch spell and losing him in the john."

"You try bringing in a Were that close to a full moon without getting bit," I said defensively. "It's not as easy as it sounds. I had to use a potion. Those things are expensive."

"And then Nairing an entire bus of people?" His dragonfly wings turned red as he laughed and his circulation increased. Dressed in black silk with a red bandanna, he looked like a miniature Peter Pan posing as an inner city gang member. Four inches of blond bothersome annoyance and quick temper.

"That wasn't my fault," I said. "The driver hit a bump." I frowned. Someone had switched my spells, too. I had been trying to tangle his feet, and ended up removing the hair from the driver and everyone in the first three rows. At least I had gotten my mark, though I wasted an entire paycheck on cabs the next three weeks, until the bus would pick me up again.

"And the frog?" Jenks darted away and back as the bouncer flicked a finger at him. "I'm the only one who'd go out with you tonight. I'm getting hazard pay." The pixy rose several inches, in what had to be pride.

Cliff seemed unimpressed. I was appalled. "Look," I said.

"All I want is to sit over there and have a drink, nice and quietlike." I nodded to the stage where the postadolescent was tangling the lines from his amps. "When does that start?"

The bouncer shrugged. "He's new. Looks like about an hour." There was a crash followed by cheers as an amp fell off the stage. "Maybe two."

"Thanks." Ignoring Jenks's chiming laughter, I wove my way through the empty tables to a bank of darker booths. I chose the one under a moose head, sinking three inches more than I should have in the flaccid cushion. Soon as I found the little perp, I was out of there. This was insulting. I had been with the I.S. for three years—seven if you counted my four years of clinicals—and here I was, doing intern work.

It was the interns that did the nitty-gritty day-to-day policing of Cincinnati and its largest suburb across the river, affectionately known as the Hollows. We picked up the supernatural stuff that the human-run FIB—short for the Federal Inderland Bureau—couldn't handle. Minor spell disturbances and rescuing familiars out of trees were in the realm of an I.S. intern. But I was a full runner, damn it. I was better than this. I *had done* better than this.

It had been I who single-handedly tracked down and apprehended the circle of dark witches who were circumventing the Cincinnati Zoo's security spells to steal the monkeys, selling them to an underground biolab. But did I get any recognition for that? No.

It had been I who realized that the loon digging up bodies in one of the churchyards was linked to the spate of deaths in the organ replacement wing in one of the human-run hospitals. Everyone assumed he was gathering materials to make illegal spells, not charming the organs into temporary health, then selling them on the black market.

And the ATM thefts that plagued the city last Christmas? It had taken me six simultaneous charms to look like a man, but I nailed the witch. She had been using a love charm/forget spell combo to rob naive humans. That had been an especially satisfying tag. I'd chased her for three streets, and there had been no time for spell casting when she turned to hit me with what could have been a lethal charm, so I was completely justified in knocking her out cold with a roundhouse kick. Even better, the FIB had been after her for three months, and tagging her took me two days. I made them look like fools, but did I get a "Good job, Rachel?" Did I even get a ride back to the I.S. tower with my swollen foot? No.

And lately I was getting even less: sorority kids using charms to steal cable, familiar theft, prank spells, and I couldn't forget my favorite—chasing trolls out from under bridges and culverts before they ate all the mortar. A sigh shifted me as I glanced over the bar. Pathetic.

Jenks dodged my apathetic attempts to swat him as he resettled himself on my earring. That they had to pay him triple to go out with me did not bode well.

A green-clad waitress bounced over, frighteningly perky for this early. "Hi!" she said, showing teeth and dimples. "My name is Dottie. I'll be your server tonight." All smiles, she set three drinks before me: a Bloody Mary, an old-fashioned, and a Shirley Temple. How sweet.

"Thanks, hon," I said with a jaded sigh. "Who they from?"

She rolled her eyes toward the bar, trying to portray bored sophistication but coming off like a high schooler at the big dance. Peering around her thin, apron-tied waist, I glanced over the three stiffs, lust in their eyes, horses in their pockets. It was an old tradition. Accepting a drink meant I accepted the invitation behind it. One more thing for Ms. Rachel to take care of. They looked like norms, but one never knew.

Sensing no more conversation forthcoming, Dottie skipped away to do barmaid things. "Check them out, Jenks," I whispered, and the pixy flitted away, his wings pale pink in his excitement. No one saw him go. Pixy surveillance at its finest.

The pub was quiet, but as there were two tenders behind

the bar, an old man and a young woman, I guessed it would pick up soon. The Blood and Brew was a known hot spot where norms went to mix with Inderlanders before driving back across the river with their doors locked and the windows up tight, titillated and thinking they were hot stuff. And though a lone human sticks out among Inderlanders like a zit on a prom queen's face, an Inderlander can easily blend into humanity. It's a survival trait honed since before Pasteur. That's why the pixy. Fairies and pixies can literally sniff an Inderlander out quicker than I can say "Spit."

I halfheartedly scanned the nearly empty bar, my sour mood evaporating into a smile when I found a familiar face from the office. Ivy.

Ivy was a vamp, the star of the I.S. runner lineup. We had met several years ago during my last year of internship, paired up for a year of semi-independent runs. She had just hired on as a full runner, having taken six years of university credit instead of opting for the two years of college and four years of internship that I had. I think assigning us to each other had been someone's idea of a joke.

Working with a vampire—living or not—had scared the peas out of me until I found out she wasn't a practicing vamp and had sworn off blood. We were as unalike as two people could be, but her strengths were my weakness. I wish I could say her weaknesses were my strengths, but Ivy didn't have any weaknesses—other than the tendency to plan the joy out of everything.

We hadn't worked together for years, and despite my grudgingly given promotion, Ivy still outranked me. She knew all the right things to say to all the right people at all the right times. It helped that she belonged to the Tamwood family, a name as old as Cincinnati itself. She was its last living member, in possession of a soul and as alive as me, having been infected with the vamp virus through her then still-living mother. The virus had molded Ivy even as she grew in her mother's womb, giving Ivy a little of both worlds, the living and the dead.

At my nod, she sauntered over. The men at the bar jostled elbows, all three turning to watch her in appreciation. She flicked them a dismissing glance, and I swear I heard one sigh. "How's it going, Ivy?" I said as she eased onto the bench opposite me.

Vinyl seat squeaking, she reclined in the booth with her back against the wall, the heels of her tall boots on the long bench, and her knees showing over the edge of the table. She stood half a head over me, but where I just looked tall, she pulled off a svelte elegance. Her slightly Oriental cast gave her an enigmatic look, upholding my belief that most models had to be vamps. She dressed like a model, too: modest leather skirt and silk blouse, top-of-the-line, all-vamp construction; black, of course. Her hair was a smooth dark wave, accenting her pale skin and oval-shaped face. No matter what she did with her hair, it made her look exotic. I could spend hours with mine and it always came out red and frizzy. Mr. One Eyebrow wouldn't have stopped for her; she was too classy.

"Hey, Rachel," Ivy said. "Whatcha doing down in the Hollows?" Her voice was melodious and low, flowing with all the subtleties of gray silk. "I thought you'd be catching some skin cancer on the coast this week," she added. "Is Denon still ticked about the dog?"

I shrugged sheepishly. "Nah." Actually, the boss nearly blew a vein. I had been a step away from being promoted to office broom pusher.

"It was an honest mistake." Ivy let her head fall back in a languorous motion to expose the long length of her neck. There wasn't a scar on it. "Anyone could have made it."

Anyone but you, I thought sourly. "Yeah?" I said aloud, pushing the Bloody Mary toward her. "Well, let me know if you spot my take." I jingled the charms on my cuffs, touching the clover carved from olive wood.

Her thin fingers curved around the glass as if they were caressing it. Those same fingers could break my wrist if she put some effort into it. She'd have to wait until she was dead before she had enough strength to snap it without a thought, but she was still stronger than me. Half the red drink disappeared down her throat. "Since when is the I.S. interested in leprechauns?" she asked, eyeing the rest of the charms.

"Since the boss's last rainy day."

She shrugged, pulling her crucifix out from behind her shirt to run the metal loop through her teeth provocatively. Her canines were sharp, like a cat's, but no bigger than mine. She'd get the extended versions after she died. I forced my eyes from them, watching the metal cross instead. It was as long as my hand and made of a beautifully tooled silver. She had begun wearing it lately to irritate her mother. They weren't on the best of terms.

I fingered the tiny cross on my cuffs, thinking it must be difficult having your mother be undead. I had met only a handful of dead vampires. The really old ones kept to themselves, and the new ones tended to get staked unless they learned to keep to themselves.

Dead vamps were utterly without conscience, ruthless instinct incarnate. The only reason they followed society's rules was because it was a game to them. And dead vampires knew about rules. Their continued existence depended upon rules which, if challenged, meant death or pain, the biggest rule of course being no sun. They needed blood daily to keep sane. Anyone's would do, and taking it from the living was the only joy they found. And they were powerful, having incredible strength and endurance, and the ability to heal with an unearthly quickness. It was hard to destroy them except for the traditional beheading and staking through the heart.

In exchange for their soul, they had the chance for immortality. It came with a loss of conscience. The oldest vampires claimed that was the best part: the ability to fulfill every carnal need without guilt when someone died to give you pleasure and keep you sane one more day.

Ivy possessed both the vamp virus and a soul, caught in

the middle ground until she died and became a true undead. Though not as powerful or dangerous as a dead vamp, the ability to walk under the sun and worship without pain made her envied by her dead brethren.

The metal rings of Ivy's necklace clicked rhythmically against her pearly whites, and I ignored her sensuality with a practiced restraint. I liked her better when the sun was up and she had more control over her mien of sexual predator.

My pixy returned to land on the fake flowers in their vase full of cigarette butts. "Good God," Ivy said, dropping her cross. "A pixy? Denon must be pissed."

Jenks's wings froze for an instant before returning to a blur of motion. "Go Turn yourself, Tamwood!" he said shrilly. "You think fairies are the only ones who have a nose?"

I winced as Jenks landed heavily upon my earring. "Nothing but the best for Ms. Rachel," I said dryly. Ivy laughed, and the hair on the back of my neck prickled. I missed the prestige of working with Ivy, but she still set me on edge. "I can come back if you think I'll mess up your take," I added.

"No," she said. "You're stat. I've got a pair of needles cornered in the bathroom. I caught them soliciting out-of-season game." Drink in hand, she slid to the end of the bench and stood with a sensual stretch, an almost unheard moan slipping from her. "They look too cheap to have a shift spell," she said when she finished. "But I've got my big owl outside just in case. If they try to bat their way out a broken window, they're bird chow. I'm just waiting them out." She took a sip, her brown eyes watching me over the rim of her glass. "If you make your tag early enough, maybe we can share a cab uptown?"

The soft hint of danger in her voice made me nod noncommittally as she left. Fingers nervously playing with a drooping curl of my red hair, I decided I'd see what she looked like before getting in a cab with her this late at night. Ivy might not need blood to survive, but it was obvious she still craved it, her public vow to abstain aside.

Condolences were made at the bar as only two drinks remained at my elbow. Jenks was still fussing in a high-pitched tantrum. "Relax, Jenks," I said, trying to keep him from ripping my earring out. "I like having a pixy backup. Fairies don't do squat unless their union clears it."

"You've noticed?" he all but snarled, tickling my ear with the wind from his fitfully moving wings. "Just because of some maggoty-jack, pre-Turn poem written by a drunk lard-butt, they think they're better than us. Publicity, Rachel. That's all it is. Good old-fashioned greasy palms. Did you know fairies get paid more than pixies for the same work?"

"Jenks?" I interrupted, fluffing my hair from my shoulder. "What's going on at the bar?"

"And that picture!" he continued, my earring quivering. "You've seen it? The one of that human brat crashing the frat party? Those fairies were so drunk, they didn't even know they were dancing with a human. And they're still getting the royalties."

"Hose yourself off, Jenks," I said tightly. "What's up at the bar?"

There was a tiny huff, and my earring twisted. "Contestant number one is a personal athletic trainer," he grumbled. "Contestant number two fixes air conditioners, and contestant number three is a newspaper reporter. Day-trippers. All of them."

"What about the guy on stage?" I whispered, making sure I didn't look that way. "The I.S. gave me only a sketch description, since our take is probably under a disguise spell."

"*Our* take?" Jenks said. The wind from his wings ceased, and his voice lost its anger.

I fastened on that. Maybe all he needed was to be included. "Why not check him out?" I asked instead of demanding. "He doesn't seem to know which end of his bagpipes to blow into."

Jenks made a short bark of laughter and buzzed off in a better mood. Fraternization between runner and backup was discouraged, but what the heck. Jenks felt better, and perhaps my ear would still be in one piece when the sun came up.

The bar jocks jostled elbows as I ran an index finger around the rim of the old-fashioned to make it sing while I waited. I was bored, and a little flirtation was good for the soul.

A group came in, their loud chatter telling me the rain had picked up. They clustered at the far end of the bar, all talking at once, their arms stretching for their drinks as they demanded attention. I looked them over, a faint tightening of my gut telling me that at least one in their party was a dead vamp. It was hard to tell whom under the goth paraphernalia.

My guess was the quiet young man in the back. He was the most normal looking in the tattooed, body-pierced group, wearing jeans and a button shirt instead of rain-spotted leather. He must have been doing well to have such a bevy of humans with him, their necks scarred and their bodies thin and anemic. But they seemed happy enough, content in their close-knit, almost familylike group. They were being especially nice to a pretty blonde, supporting her and working together to coax her to eat some peanuts. She looked tired as she smiled. Must have been his breakfast.

As if pulled by my thoughts, the attractive man turned. He shifted his sunglasses down, and my face went slack as he met my eyes over them. I took a breath, seeing from across the room the rain on his eyelashes. A sudden need to brush them free filled me. I could almost feel the dampness of the rain on my fingers, how soft it would feel. His lips moved as he whispered, and it seemed I could hear but not understand his words swirling behind me to push me forward.

Heart pounding, I gave him a knowing look and shook my head. A faint, charming smile tugged the corners of his mouth, and he looked away.

My held breath slipped from me as I forced my eyes away. Yeah. He was a dead vamp. A living vamp couldn't have bespelled me even that little bit. If he had been really trying, I wouldn't have had a chance. But that's what the laws were for, right? Dead vamps were only supposed to take willing initiates, and only after release papers were signed, but who was to say if the papers were signed before or after? Witches, Weres, and other Inderlanders were immune to turning vampire. Small comfort if the vamp lost control and you died from having your throat torn out. 'Course, there were laws against that, too.

Still uneasy, I looked up to find the musician making a beeline for me, his eyes alight with a fevered itch. Stupid pixy. He had gotten himself caught.

"Come to hear me play, beautiful?" the kid said as he stopped at my table, clearly struggling to make his voice low.

"My name is Sue, not Beautiful," I lied, staring past him toward Ivy. She was laughing at me. Swell. This was going to look just fantastic in our office newsletter.

"You sent your fairy friend to *check—me—out*," he said, half singing the words.

"He's a pixy not a fairy," I said. The guy was either a stupid norm or a smart Inderlander pretending to be a stupid norm. I was betting on the former.

He opened his fist and Jenks flew a wobbly trail to my earring. One of his wings was bent, and pixy dust sifted from him to make brief sunbeams on the table and my shoulder. My eyes closed in a strength-gathering blink. I was going to get blamed for this. I knew it.

Jenks's irate snarling filled my ear, and I frowned in thought. I didn't think any of his suggestions were anatomically possible—but at least I knew the kid was a norm.

"Come and see my big pipe in the van," the kid said. "Bet you could make it sing-g-g-g."

I looked up at him, the dead vamp's proposition making me jittery. "Go away."

"I'm gonna make it big, Suzy-Q," he boasted, taking my hostile stare as an invitation to sit. "I'm going to the coast, soon as I get enough money. Got a friend in the music biz.

He knows this guy who knows this guy who cleans Janice Joplin's pool."

"Go away," I repeated, but he only leaned back and screwed his face up, singing "Sue-sue-sussudio" in a high falsetto, pounding on the table in a broken rhythm.

This was embarrassing. Surely I would be forgiven for nacking him? But no, I was a good little soldier in the fight for crimes against norms, even if no one but I thought so. Smiling, I leaned forward until my cleavage showed. That always gets their attention, even if there isn't much of it. Reaching across the table, I grabbed the short hairs on his chest and twisted. That gets their attention, too, and it's far more satisfying.

The yelp as his singing cut off was like icing, it was so sweet. "Leave," I whispered. I pushed the old-fashioned into his hand and curled his slack fingers around it. "And get rid of this for me." His eyes grew wider as I gave a little tug. My fingers reluctantly loosened, and he beat a tactful retreat, sloshing half the drink as he went.

There was a cheer from the bar. I looked to see the old bartender grinning. He touched the side of his nose, and I inclined my head. "Dumb kid," I muttered. He had no business being in the Hollows. Someone ought to sling his butt back across the river before he got hurt.

One glass remained before me, and bets were probably being made as to whether I would drink or not. "You all right, Jenks?" I asked, already guessing the answer.

"The sawed-off lunker nearly pulps me, and you ask if I'm *all right*?" he snarled. His tiny voice was hilarious, and my eyebrows rose. "Nearly cracked my ribs. Slime stink all over me. *Great God almighty*, I reek of it. And look what he did to *my clothes*. Do you know how hard it is to get stink out of silk! My wife is gonna make me sleep in the flower boxes if I come home smelling like this. You can shove the triple pay, Rache. You aren't worth it!"

Jenks never noticed when I quit listening. He hadn't said a thing about his wing, so I knew he'd be okay. I slumped into the back of the booth and stewed, dead in the water with Jenks leaking dust as he was. I was royally Turned. If I came in empty-handed, I'd get nothing but full moon disturbances and bad charm complaints until next spring. It wasn't my fault.

With Jenks unable to fly unnoticed, I knew I might as well go home. If I bought him some Maitake mushrooms, he might not tell the guy in appropriations how his wing got bent. *What the heck,* I thought. *Why not make a party of it?* Sort of a last fling before the boss nailed my broom to a tree, so to speak. I could stop at the mall for some bubble bath and a new disc of slow jazz. My career was taking a nose-dive, but there was no reason I couldn't enjoy the ride.

With a perverse glow of anticipation, I took my bag and the Shirley Temple, rising to make my way to the bar. Not my style to leave things hanging. Contestant number three stood with a grin and a shake of his leg to adjust himself. God, help me. Men can be so disgusting. I was tired, ticked-off, and grossly unappreciated. Knowing he would take anything I said as playing hard to get and follow me out, I tipped the ginger pop down his front and kept walking.

I smirked at his cry of outrage, then frowned at his heavy hand on my shoulder. Turning into a crouch, I sent my leg in a stiff half spin to trip him onto the floor. He hit the wood planking with a loud thump. The bar went silent after a momentary gasp. I was sitting on him, straddling his chest, before he even realized he had gone down.

My bloodred manicure stood out sharply as I gripped his neck, flicking the bristles under his chin. His eyes were wide. Cliff stood at the door with his arms crossed, content to watch.

"Damn, Rache," Jenks said, swinging wildly from my earring. "Who taught you that?"

"My dad," I answered, then leaned until I was in his face. "So sorry," I breathed in a thick Hollows accent. "You want to play, cookie?" His eyes went frightened as he realized I was an Inderlander and not a bit of fluff out looking for a wild night of pretend. He was a cookie, all right. A little treat to be enjoyed and forgotten. I wouldn't hurt him, but he didn't know that.

"Sweet mother of Tinker Bell!" Jenks exclaimed, jerking my attention from the sniveling human. "Smell that? Clover."

My fingers loosened, and the man scrabbled out from under me. He awkwardly gained his feet, dragging his two cohorts to the shadows with a whispered muttering of face-saving insults. "One of the bartenders?" I breathed as I rose.

"It's the woman," he said, sending a wash of excitement through me.

My eyes rose, taking her in. She filled out her tight, high-contrast uniform of black and green admirably, giving the impression of bored competence as she moved confidently behind the counter. "You flaking out, Jenks?" I murmured as I tried to surreptitiously pull my leather pants out from where they had ridden up. "It can't be her."

"Right!" he snapped. "Like *you* could tell. *Ignore* the pixy. I could be home right now in front of my TV. But no-o-o-o-o. I'm stuck spending the night with some beanpole of backward feminine intuition who thinks she can do my job better than me. I'm cold, hungry, and my wing is bent nearly in two. If that main vein snaps, I'll have to regrow the entire wing. Do you have any idea how long that takes?"

I glanced over the bar, relieved to see that everyone had returned to their conversations. Ivy was gone and had probably missed the entire thing. Just as well. "Shut up, Jenks," I muttered. "Pretend you're a decoration."

I sidled to the old man. He grinned a gap-toothed smile as I leaned forward. Wrinkles creased his leathered face in appreciation as his eyes rove everywhere but my face. "Gimme something," I breathed. "Something sweet. Something that will make me feel good. Something rich and creamy and oh-so-bad for me."

"I'll be needing to see yer ID, lassie," the old man said in a thick Irish accent. "Ye dunna look old enough to be out from under yer mum's shadow."

His accent was faked, but my smile at his compliment wasn't. "Why, sure thing, hon." I dug in my bag for my driver's license, willing to play the game, since we both obviously enjoyed it. "Oops!" I giggled as the card slipped to fall behind the counter. "Silly little me!"

With the help of the bar stool, I leaned halfway across the counter to get a good peek behind it. Having my rear in the air not only distracted the menfolk admirably but afforded me an excellent look. Yes, it was degrading if you thought about it too long, but it worked. I looked up to find the old man grinning, thinking I was checking him out, but it was the woman I was interested in now. She was standing on a box.

She was nearly the right height, in the right place, and Jenks had marked her. She looked younger than I would have expected, but if you're a hundred fifty years old, you're bound to pick up a few beauty secrets. Jenks snorted in my ear, sounding like a smug mosquito. "Told you."

I settled back on the stool, and the bartender handed me my license along with a dead man's float and a spoon: a dollop of ice cream in a short glass of Bailey's. Yum. Tucking the card away, I gave him a saucy wink. I left the glass where it was, turning as if scoping out the patrons that had just come in. My pulse increased and my fingertips tingled. Time to go to work.

A quick look around to make sure no one was watching, and I tipped my glass. I gasped as it spilled, and my distress wasn't entirely faked as I lurched to catch it, trying to save at least the ice cream.

The kick of adrenaline shook me as the woman bartender met my apologetic smile with her patronizing one. The jolt was worth more to me than the check I found shoved into my desk every week. But I knew the feeling would wane as fast as it had come. My talents were being wasted. I didn't even need a spell for this one.

If this was all the I.S. would give me, I thought, *maybe I should blow off the steady pay and go out on my own.* Not many left the I.S., but there was precedence. Leon Bairn was a living legend before he went independent—then promptly got wasted by a misaligned spell. Rumor had it the I.S. had been the one to put the price on his head for breaking his thirty-year contract. But that was over a decade ago. Runners went missing all the time, taken out by prey more clever or luckier than them. Blaming it on the I.S.'s own assassin corps was just spiteful. No one left the I.S. because the money was good and the hours were easy, that's all.

Yeah, I thought, ignoring the whisper of warning that took me. Leon Bairn's death was exaggerated. Nothing was ever proven. And the only reason I still had a job was because they couldn't legally fire me. Maybe I should go out on my own. It couldn't be any worse than what I was doing now. They would be glad to see me leave. *Sure,* I thought, smiling. Rachel Morgan, private runner for hire. All rights earnestly upheld. All wrongs sincerely avenged.

I knew my smile was misty as the woman obligingly swiped her towel between my elbows to mop up the spill. My breath came in a quick sound. Left hand dropping, I snatched the cloth, tangling her in it. My right swung back, then forward with my cuffs, clicking them about her wrists. In an instant it was done. She blinked, shocked. Damn, I'm good.

The woman's eyes widened as she realized what had happened. "Blazes and condemnation!" she cried, sounding elegant with her Irish accent. Hers wasn't faked. "What the 'ell do you think you're doin'?"

The jolt flared to ash, and a sigh slipped from me as I eyed the lone scoop of ice cream that was left of my drink. "Inderland Security," I said, slapping my I.S. identification down. The rush was gone already. "You stand accused of fabricating a rainbow for the purpose of misrepresenting the income generated from said rainbow, failure to file the appropriate requisition forms for said rainbow, failure to notify Rainbow Authority of said rainbow's end—"

"It's a lie!" the woman shouted, contorting in the cuffs. Her eyes darted wildly about the bar as all attention focused on her. "All a lie! I found that pot legally."

"You retain the right to keep your mouth shut," I ad-libbed, digging out a spoonful of ice cream. It was cold in my mouth, and the hint of alcohol was a poor replacement for the waning warmth of adrenaline. "If you forego your right to keep your mouth shut, I will shut it for you."

The bartender slammed the flat of his hand on the counter. "Cliff!" he bellowed, his Irish accent gone. "Put the Help Wanted sign in the window. Then get back here and help me."

"Yeah, boss," came Cliff's distant, I-couldn't-care-less shout.

Setting my spoon aside, I reached across the bar and yanked the leprechaun over the counter and onto the floor before she got much smaller. She was shrinking as the charms on my cuffs slowly overpowered her weaker size spell. "You have a right to a lawyer," I said, tucking my ID away. "If you can't afford one, you're toast."

"You canna catch me!" the leprechaun threatened, struggling as the crowd's shouts became enthusiastic. "Rings of steel alone canna hold me. I've escaped from kings, and sultans, and nasty little children with nets!"

I tried to finger-curl my rain-damp hair as she fought and wrestled, slowly coming to grips that she was caught. The cuffs shrank with her, keeping her confined. "I'll be out of this—in—just a moment," she panted, slowing enough to look at her wrists. "Aw, for the love of St. Pete." She slumped, sending her eyes over the yellow moon, green clover, pink heart, and orange star that decorated my cuffs. "May the devil's own dog hump your leg. Who squealed about the charms?" Then she looked closer. "You caught me with four? *Four?* I didn't think the old ones still worked."

"Call me old-fashioned," I said to my glass, "but when something works, I stick with it."

Ivy walked past, her two black-cloaked vamps before her,

elegant in their dark misery. One had a bruise developing under his eye; the other was limping. Ivy wasn't gentle with vamps preying on the underage. Remembering the pull from the dead vamp at the end of the bar, I understood why. A sixteen-year-old couldn't fight that. Wouldn't *want* to fight that.

"Hey, Rachel," Ivy said brightly, looking almost human now that she wasn't actively working. "I'm heading uptown. Want to split the fare?"

My thoughts went back to the I.S. as I weighed the risk of being a starving entrepreneur to a lifetime of running for shoplifters and illegal-charm sellers. It wasn't as if the I.S. would put a price on my head. No, Denon would be thrilled to tear up my contract. I couldn't afford an office in Cincinnati, but maybe in the Hollows. Ivy spent a lot of time down here. She'd know where I could find something cheap. "Yeah," I said, noting her eyes were a nice, steady brown. "I want to ask you something."

She nodded and pushed her two takes forward. The crowd pressed back, the sea of black clothing seeming to soak up the light. The dead vamp at the outskirts gave me a respectful nod, as if to say "Good tag," and with a pulse of emotion giving me a false high, I nodded back.

"Way to go, Rachel," Jenks chimed up, and I smiled. It had been a long time since I'd heard that.

"Thanks," I said, catching sight of him on my earring in the bar's mirror. Pushing my glass aside, I reached for my bag, my smile widening when the bartender gestured it was on the house. Feeling warm from more than the alcohol, I slipped from my stool and pulled the leprechaun stumbling to her feet. Thoughts of a door with my name painted on it in gold letters swirled through me. It was freedom.

"No! Wait!" the leprechaun shouted as I grabbed my bag and hauled her butt to the door. "Wishes! Three wishes. Right? You let me go, and you get three wishes."

I pushed her into the warm rain ahead of me. Ivy had a cab already, her catch stashed in the trunk so there would be more room for the rest of us. Accepting wishes from a felon was a sure way to find yourself on the wrong end of a broomstick, but only if you got caught.

"Wishes?" I said, helping the leprechaun into the backseat. "Let's talk."

Two

"What did you say?" I asked as I half turned in the front seat to see Ivy. She gestured helplessly from the back. The rhythm of bad wipers and good music fought to outdo each other in a bizarre mix of whining guitars and hiccuping plastic against glass. "Rebel Yell" screamed from the speakers. I couldn't compete. Jenks's credible imitation of Billy Idol gyrating with the Hawaiian dancer stuck to the dash didn't help. "Can I turn it down?" I asked the cabbie.

"No touch! No touch!" he cried in an odd accent. The forests of Europe, maybe? His faint musky scent put him as a Were. I reached for the volume knob, and he took his fur-backed hand from the wheel and slapped at me.

The cab swerved into the next lane. His charms, all gone bad by the look of them, slid across the dash to spill onto my lap and the floor. The chain of garlic swinging from the rearview mirror hit me square in the eye. I gagged as the stench fought with the odor of the tree-shaped cardboard, also swinging from the mirror.

"Bad girl," he accused, veering back into his lane and throwing me into him.

"If I good girl," I snarled as I slid back into my seat, "you let me turn music down?"

The driver grinned. He was missing a tooth. He would be missing another one if I had my way. "Yah," he said.

"They talking now." The music fell to nothing, replaced by a fast-talking announcer shouting louder than the music had been.

"Good Lord," I muttered, turning the radio down. My lips curled at the smear of grease on the knob. I stared at my fingers, then wiped them off on the amulets still in my lap. They weren't good for anything else. The salt from the driver's too-frequent handlings had ruined them. Giving him a pained look, I dumped the charms into the chipped cup holder.

I turned to Ivy, sprawled in the back. One hand was up to keep her owl from falling out of the rear window as we bounced along, the other was propped behind her neck. Passing cars and the occasional functioning streetlight briefly illuminated her black silhouette. Dark and unblinking, her eyes met mine, then returned to the window and the night. My skin prickled at the air of ancient tragedy about her. She wasn't pulling an aura—she was just Ivy—but it gave me the willies. Didn't the woman ever smile?

My take had pressed herself into the other corner, as far from Ivy as she could get. The leprechaun's green boots just reached the end of the seat, and she looked like one of those dolls they sell on TV. *Three easy payments of $49.95 for this highly detailed rendition of Becky the Barmaid. Similar dolls have tripled, even quadrupled, in value!* This doll, though, had a sneaky glint in her eye. I gave her a sly nod, and Ivy's gaze flicked suspiciously to mine.

The owl gave a pained hoot as we hit a nasty bump, opening its wings to keep its balance. But it was the last. We had crossed the river and were back in Ohio. The ride now was smooth as glass, and the cabbie's pace slowed as he seemed to remember what traffic signs were for.

Ivy removed her hand from her owl and ran her fingers through her long hair. "I said, 'You never took me up on a ride before.' What's up?"

"Oh, yeah." I draped an arm over the seat. "Do you know where I can rent a cheap flat? In the Hollows, maybe?"

Ivy faced me squarely, the perfect oval of her face looking pale in the streetlights. There were lights now at every corner, making it nearly bright as day. Paranoid norms. Not that I blamed them. "You moving into the Hollows?" she asked, her expression quizzical.

I couldn't help my smile at that. "No. I'm quitting the I.S."

That got her attention. I could tell by the way she blinked. Jenks stopped trying to dance with the tiny figure on the dash and stared at me. "You can't break your I.S. contract," Ivy said. She glanced at the leprechaun, who beamed at her. "You're not thinking of . . ."

"Me? Break the law?" I said lightly. "I'm too good to have to break the law. I can't help it if she's the wrong leprechaun, though," I added, not feeling a bit guilty. The I.S. had made it abundantly clear they didn't want my services anymore. What was I supposed to do? Roll on my back with my belly in the air and lick someone's, er, muzzle?

"Paperwork," the cabbie interjected, his accent abruptly as smooth as the road as he switched to the voice and manners needed to get and keep fares on this side of the river. "Lose the paperwork. Happens all the time. I think I've Rynn Cormel's confession in here somewhere from when my father shuttled lawyers from quarantine to the courts during the Turn."

"Yeah." I gave him a nod and smile. "Wrong name on the wrong paper. Q.E.D."

Ivy's eyes were unblinking. "Leon Bairn didn't just spontaneously explode, Rachel."

My breath puffed out. I wouldn't believe the stories. They were just that, stories to keep the I.S.'s flock of runners from wanting to break their contracts once they learned all the I.S. had to teach them. "That was over ten years ago," I said. "And the I.S. had nothing to do with it. They aren't going to kill me for breaking my contract; they want me to leave." I frowned. "Besides, being turned inside out would be more fun than what I'm doing now."

Ivy leaned forward, and I refused to back away. "They say it took three days to find enough of him to fit in a shoe box," she said. "Scraped the last off the ceiling of his porch."

"What am I supposed to do?" I said, pulling my arm back. "I haven't had a decent run in months. Look at this." I gestured to my take. "A tax-evading leprechaun. It's an insult."

The little woman stiffened. "Well, excu-u-u-use me."

Jenks abandoned his new girlfriend to sit on the back rim of the cabbie's hat. "Yeah," he said. "Rachel's gonna be pushing a broom if I have to take time off for workman's comp."

He fitfully moved his damaged wing, and I gave him a pained smile. "Maitake?" I said.

"Quarter pound," he countered, and I mentally upped it to a half. He was okay, for a pixy.

Ivy frowned, fingering her crucifix chain. "There's a reason no one breaks their contract. The last person to try was sucked through a turbine."

Jaw clenched, I turned to look out the front window. I remembered. It was almost a year ago. It would have killed him if he hadn't been dead already. The vamp was due back in the office any day now. "I'm not asking for your permission," I said. "I'm asking you if you know anyone with a cheap place to rent." Ivy was silent, and I shifted to see her. "I have a little something tucked away. I can put up a shingle, help people that need it—"

"Oh, for the love of blood," Ivy interrupted. "Leaving to open up a charm shop, maybe. But your own agency?" She shook her head, her black hair swinging. "I'm not your mother, but if you do this, you're dead. Jenks? Tell her she's dead."

Jenks nodded solemnly, and I flopped around to stare out the window. I felt stupid for having asked for her help. The cabbie was nodding. "Dead," he said. "Dead, dead, dead."

This was better and better. Between Jenks and the cab driver, the entire city would know I quit before I gave notice. "Never mind. I don't want to talk about it anymore," I muttered.

Ivy draped an arm over the seat. "Did it occur to you someone may be setting you up? Everyone knows leprechauns try to buy their way out. If you get caught, your butt is buttered."

"Yeah," I said. "I thought of that." I hadn't, but I wasn't going to tell her. "My first wish will be to not get caught."

"Always is," the leprechaun said slyly. "That your first wish?" In a flash of anger, I nodded, and the leprechaun grinned, dimples showing. She was halfway home.

"Look," I said to Ivy. "I don't need your help. Thanks for nothing." I shuffled in my bag for my wallet. "Drop me here," I said to the cabbie. "I want a coffee. Jenks? Ivy will get you back to the I.S. Can you do that for me, Ivy? For old times' sake?"

"Rachel," she protested, "you're not listening to me."

The cabbie carefully signaled, then pulled over. "Watch your back, Hot Stuff."

I got out, yanked open the rear door, and grabbed my leprechaun by her uniform. My cuffs had completely masked her size spell. She was about the size of a chunky two-year-old. "Here," I said, tossing a twenty onto the seat. "That should cover my share."

"It's still raining!" the leprechaun wailed.

"Shut up." Drops pattered against me, ruining my topknot and sticking the trailing strands to my neck. I slammed the door as Ivy leaned to say something. I had nothing left to lose. My life was a pile of magic manure, and I couldn't even make compost out of it.

"But I'm getting wet," the leprechaun complained.

"You want back in the car?" I asked. My voice was calm, but inside I was seething. "We can forget the whole thing if you want. I'm sure Ivy will take care of your paperwork. Two jobs in one night. She'll get a bonus."

"No," came her meek, tiny voice.

Ticked, I looked across the street to the Starbucks catering to uptown snits who needed sixty different ways to brew a bean in order to not be happy with any of them. Being on this side of the river, the coffeehouse would likely be empty at this hour. It was the perfect place to sulk and regroup. I half dragged the leprechaun to the door, trying to guess the cost of a cup of coffee by the number of pre-Turn doodads in the front window.

"Rachel, wait." Ivy had rolled down her window, and I could hear the cabbie's music cranked again. Sting's "A Thousand Years." I could almost get back in the car.

I yanked the door of the café open, sneering at the chimes' merry jingle. "Coffee. Black. And a booster seat," I shouted to the kid behind the counter as I strode to the darkest corner, my leprechaun in tow. Tear it all. The kid was a vision of upright character in his red-and-white-striped apron and perfect hair. Probably a university student. I could have gone to the university instead of the community college. At least for a semester or two. I'd been accepted and everything.

The booth, though, was cushy and soft. There was a real tablecloth. And my feet didn't stick to the floor, a definite plus. The kid was eyeing me with a superior look, so I pulled off my boots and sat cross-legged to harass him. I was still dressed like a hooker. I think he was trying to decide whether he should call the I.S. or its human counterpart, the FIB. That'd be a laugh.

My ticket out of the I.S. stood on the seat across from me and fidgeted. "Can I have a latte?" she whined.

"No."

The door chimed, and I looked to see Ivy stride in with her owl on her arm, its talons pinching the thick armband she had. Jenks was perched on her shoulder, as far from the owl as he could get. I stiffened, turning to the picture above the table of babies dressed up as a fruit salad. I think it was supposed to be cute, but it only made me hungry.

"Rachel. I have to talk to you."

This was apparently too much for Junior. "Excuse me, ma'am," he said in his perfect voice. "No pets allowed. The owl must remain outside."

Ma'am? I thought, trying to keep the hysterical laughter from bubbling up.

He went pale as Ivy glanced at him. Staggering, he almost fell as he sightlessly backed up. She was pulling an aura on him. Not good.

Ivy turned her gaze to me. My air whooshed out as I hit the back of the booth. Black, predator eyes nailed me to the vinyl seat. Raw hunger clutched at my stomach. My fingers convulsed.

Her bound tension was intoxicating. I couldn't look away. It was nothing like the gentle question the dead vamp had poised to me in The Blood and Brew. This was anger, domination. Thank God she wasn't angry with me, but at Junior behind the counter.

Sure enough, as soon as she saw the look on my face, the anger in her eyes flickered and went out. Her pupils contracted, setting her eyes back to their usual brown. In a clock-tick the shroud of power had slipped from her, easing back into the depths of hell that it came from. It had to be hell. Such raw domination couldn't come from an enchantment. My anger flowed back. If I was angry, I couldn't be afraid, right?

It had been years since Ivy pulled an aura on me. The last time, we had been arguing over how to tag a low-blood vamp under suspicion of enticing underage girls with some asinine, role-playing card game. I had dropped her with a sleep charm, then painted the word "idiot" on her fingernails in red nail polish before tying her in a chair and waking her up. She had been the model friend since then, if a bit cool at times. I think she appreciated that I hadn't told anyone.

Junior cleared his throat. "You—ah—can't stay unless you order something, ma'am?" he offered weakly.

Gutsy, I thought. *Must be an Inderlander.*

"Orange juice," Ivy said loudly, standing before me. "No pulp."

Surprise made me look up. "Orange juice?" Then I frowned. "Look," I said, unclenching my hands and roughly pulling my bag of charms onto my lap. "I don't care if Leon Bairn did end up as a film on the sidewalk. I'm quitting. And nothing you say is going to change my mind."

Ivy shifted from foot to foot. It was her disquiet that cooled the last of my anger. Ivy was worried? I'd never seen that.

"I want to go with you," she finally said.

For a moment, I could only stare. "What?" I finally managed.

She sat down across from me with an affected air of non-chalance, putting her owl to watch the leprechaun. The tearing sound as she undid the fasteners of her armband sounded loud, and she set it on the bench beside her. Jenks half hopped to the table, his eyes wide and his mouth shut for a change. Junior showed up with the booster chair and our drinks. We silently waited as he placed everything with shaking hands and went to hide in the back room.

My mug was chipped and only half full. I toyed with the idea of coming back to stick a charm under the table that would sour any cream that got within four feet of it, but decided I had more important things to contend with. Like why Ivy was going to flush her illustrious career down the proverbial toilet.

"Why?" I asked, floored. "The boss loves you. You get to pick your assignments. You got a paid vacation last year."

Ivy was studying the picture, avoiding me. "So?"

"It was for four weeks! You went to Alaska for the midnight sun!"

Her thin black eyebrows bunched, and she reached to arrange her owl's feathers. "Half the rent, half the utilities, half of everything is my responsibility, half is yours. I bring in and do my business, you bring in and handle yours. If need be, we work together. Like before."

I settled back, my huff not as obvious as I wanted it to be, since there was only the cushy upholstery to fall into. "Why?" I asked again.

Her fingers dropped from her owl. "I'm very good at what I do," she said, not answering me. A hint of vulnerability had crept into her voice. "I won't drag you down, Rachel. No vamp will dare move against me. I can extend that to you. I'll keep the vamp assassins off of you until you come up with the money to pay off your contract. With my connections and your spells, we can stay alive long enough to get the I.S. to drop the price on our heads. But I want a wish."

"There's no price on our heads," I said quickly.

"Rachel . . ." she cajoled. Her brown eyes were soft in worry, alarming me. "Rachel, there will be." She leaned forward until I fought not to retreat. I took a shallow breath to look for the smell of blood on her, smelling only the tang of juice. She was wrong. The I.S. wouldn't put a price on my head. They wanted me to leave. She was the one who should be worried.

"Me, too," Jenks said suddenly. He vaulted to the rim of my mug. Iridescent dust sifted from his bent wing to make an oily film on my coffee. "I want in. I want a wish. I'll ditch the I.S. and be both your backups. You're gonna need one. Rache, you get the four hours before midnight, Ivy the four after, or whatever schedule you want. I get every fourth day off, seven paid holidays, and a wish. You let me and my family live in the office, real quietlike in the walls. Pay me what I'm making now, biweekly."

Ivy nodded and took a sip of her juice. "Sounds good to me. What do you think?"

My jaw dropped. I couldn't believe what I was hearing. "I can't give you my wishes."

The leprechaun bobbed her head. "Yes, you can."

"No," I said impatiently. "I mean, I need them." A pang of worry had settled into my gut at the thought that maybe Ivy was right. "I already used one to not get caught letting her go," I said. "I have to wish to get out of my contract, for starters."

"Uh," the leprechaun stammered. "I can't do anything about that if it's in writing."

Jenks gave a snort of derision. "Not that good, eh?"

"Shut your mouth—bug!" she snapped, color showing on her cheeks.

"Shut your own, moss wipe!" he snarled back.

This can't be happening, I thought. All I wanted was out, not to lead a revolt. "You're not serious," I said. "Ivy, tell me this is your twisted sense of humor finally showing itself."

She met my gaze squarely. I never could tell what was going on behind a vamp's eyes. "For the first time in my career," she said, "I'm going back empty-handed. I let my take go." She waved a hand in the air. "Opened the trunk and let them run. I broke regulations." A closed-lipped smile flickered over her and was gone. "Is that serious enough for you?"

"Go find your own leprechaun," I said, catching myself as I reached for my cup. Jenks was still sitting on the handle.

She laughed. It was cold, and this time I did shiver. "I pick my runs," she said. "What do you think would happen if I went after a leprechaun, muffed it, then tried to leave the I.S.?"

Across from me, the leprechaun sighed. "No amount of wishing could make that look good," she piped up. "It's going to be hard enough making this look like a coincidence."

"And you, Jenks?" I said, my voice cracking.

Jenks shrugged. "I want a wish. It can give me something the I.S. can't. I want sterility so my wife won't leave me." He flew a ragged path to the leprechaun. "Or is that too hard for you, greenie weenie?" he mocked, standing with his feet spread wide and his hands on his hips.

"Bug," she muttered, my charms jingling as she threatened to squish him. Jenks's wings went red in anger, and I wondered if the dust sifting from him could catch fire.

"Sterility?" I questioned, struggling to keep to the topic at hand.

He flipped the leprechaun off and strutted across the table to me. "Yeah. You know how many brats I've got?"

Even Ivy looked surprised. "You'd risk your life over that?" she asked.

Jenks made a tinkling laugh. "Who said I'm risking my life? The I.S. couldn't care less if I leave. Pixies don't sign contracts. They go through us too fast. I'm a free agent. I always have been." He grinned, looking far too sly for so small a person. "I always will be. I figure my life span will be marginally longer with only you two lunkers to watch out for."

I turned to Ivy. "I know you signed a contract. They love you. If anyone should be worried about a death threat, it's you, not me. Why would you risk that for—for—" I hesitated. "For nothing? What wish could be worth that?"

Ivy's face went still. A hint of black shadow drifted over her. "I don't have to tell you."

"I'm not stupid," I said, trying to hide my disquiet. "How do I know you aren't going to start practicing again?"

Clearly insulted, Ivy stared at me until I dropped my gaze, chilled to the bone. *This,* I thought, *is definitely not a good idea.* "I'm not a practicing vamp," she finally said. "Not anymore. Not ever again."

I forced my hand down, realizing I was playing with my damp hair. Her words were only slightly reassuring. Her glass was half empty, and I only remembered her taking the one sip.

"Partners?" Ivy said, extending her hand across the table.

Partners with Ivy? With Jenks? Ivy was the best runner the I.S. had. It was more than a little flattering that she wanted to work with me on a permanent basis, if also a bit worrisome. But it wasn't as if I had to live with her. Slowly I stretched my hand to meet hers. My perfectly shaped red nails looked garish next to her unpolished ones. All my wishes—gone. But I would've probably wasted them anyway. "Partners," I said, shivering at the coldness of Ivy's hand as I took it.

"All right!" Jenks crowed, flitting to land on top of our handshake. The dust sifting from him seemed to warm Ivy's touch. "Partners!"

Three

"**D**ear God," I moaned under my breath. "Don't let me be sick. Not here." I shut my eyes in a long blink, hoping the light wouldn't hurt so much when I opened them. I was in my cubicle, twenty-fifth floor of the I.S. tower. The afternoon sun slanted in, but it would never reach me, my desk being toward the middle of the maze. Someone had brought in doughnuts, and the smell of the frosting made my stomach roil. All I wanted was to go back home and sleep.

Tugging open my top drawer, I fumbled for a pain amulet, groaning when I found I'd used them all. My forehead hit the edge of the metal desk, and I stared past my frizzy length of hair to my ankle boots peeping past the hem of my jeans. I had worn something conservative in deference to my quitting: a tuck-in red linen shirt and pants. No more tight leather for a while.

Last night had been a mistake. It had taken far too many drinks for me to get stupid enough to officially give my remaining wishes to Ivy and Jenks. I had really been counting on the last two. Anyone who knows anything about wishes knows you can't wish for more. The same goes for wishing for wealth. Money doesn't just appear. It has to come from somewhere, and unless you wish not to get caught, they always get you for theft.

Wishes are tricky things, which was why most Inderlanders had lobbied to get a minimum of three-per-go. In hindsight, I hadn't done too badly. Having wished to not get caught letting the leprechaun go would at least allow me to leave the I.S. with a clear record. If Ivy was right and they were going to nack me for breaking my contract, they would have to make it look like an accident. But why would they bother? Death threats were expensive, and they wanted me gone.

Ivy had gotten a marker to call her wish in later. It looked like an old coin with a hole in it, and she had laced it on a purple cord and hung it about her neck. Jenks, though, spent his wish right in the bar, buzzing off to give the news to his wife. I should have left when Jenks had, but Ivy didn't seem to want to leave. It had been a long time since I'd had a girls' night out, and I thought I might find the courage at the bottom of a glass to tell the boss I was leaving. I hadn't.

Five seconds into my rehearsed speech, Denon flipped open an manila envelope, pulled out my contract, and tore it up, telling me to be out of the building in half an hour. My badge and I.S.-issue cuffs were in his desk; the charms that had decorated them were in my pocket.

My seven years with the I.S. had left me with an accumulated clutter of knickknacks and outdated memos. Fingers trembling, I reached for a cheap, thick-walled vase that hadn't seen a flower for months. It went into the trash, just like the cretin who had given it to me. My dissolution bowl went into the box at my feet. The salt-encrusted blue ceramic grated harshly on the cardboard. It had gone dry last week, and the rime of salt left from evaporation was dusty.

A wooden dowel of redwood clattered in next to it. It was too thick to make a wand out of, but I wasn't good enough to make a wand anyway. I had bought the dowel to make a set of lie-detecting amulets and never got around to it. It was easier to buy them. Stretching, I grabbed my phone list of past contacts. A quick look to be sure no one was watching, and I shoved it out of sight next to my dissolution bowl, sliding my disc player and headphones to cover it.

I had a few reference books to go back to Joyce across the aisle, but the container of salt propping them up had been my dad's. I set it in the box, wondering what Dad would think of me leaving. "He would be pleased as punch," I whispered, gritting my teeth against my hangover.

I glanced up, sending my gaze over the ugly yellow partitions. My eyes narrowed as my coworkers looked the other way. They were standing in huddled groups as they gossiped, pretending to be busy. Their hushed whispers grated on me. Taking a slow breath, I reached for my black-and-white picture of Watson, Crick, and the woman behind it all, Rosalind Franklin. They were standing before their model of DNA, and Rosalind's smile had the same hidden humor of Mona Lisa. One might think she knew what was going to happen. I wondered if she had been an Inderlander. Lots of people did. I kept the picture to remind myself how the world turns on details others miss.

It had been almost forty years since a quarter of humanity died from a mutated virus, the T4 Angel. And despite the frequent TV evangelists' claim otherwise, it wasn't our fault. It started and ended with good old-fashioned human paranoia.

Back in the fifties, Watson, Crick, and Franklin had put their heads together and solved the DNA riddle in six months. Things might have stopped there, but the then-Soviets grabbed the technology. Spurred by a fear of war, money flowed into the developing science. By the early sixties we had bacteria-produced insulin. A wealth of bioengineered drugs followed, flooding the market with offshoots of the U.S.'s darker search for bioengineered weapons. We never made it to the moon, turning science inward instead of outward to kill ourselves.

And then, toward the end of the decade, someone made a mistake. The debate as to whether it was the U.S. or the Soviets is moot. Somewhere up in the cold Arctic labs, a lethal chain of DNA escaped. It left a modest trail of death to Rio that was identified and dealt with, the majority of the public unaware and ignorant. But even as the scientists wrote their conclusionary notes in their lab books and shelved them, the virus mutated.

It attached itself to a bioengineered tomato through a weak spot in its modified DNA that the researchers thought too minuscule to worry about. The tomato was officially known as the T4 Angel tomato—its lab identification—and from there came the virus's name, Angel.

Unaware that the virus was using the Angel tomato as an intermediate host, it was transported by the airlines. Sixteen hours later it was too late. The third world countries were decimated in a frightening three weeks, and the U.S. shut down in four. Borders were militarized, and a governmental policy of "Sorry, we can't help you" was instituted. The U.S. suffered and people died, but compared to the charnel pit the rest of the world became, it was a cakewalk.

But the largest reason civilization remained intact was that most Inderland species were resistant to the Angel virus. Witches, the undead, and the smaller species like trolls, pixies, and fairies were completely unaffected. Weres, living vamps, and leprechauns got the flu. The elves, though, died out completely. It was believed their practice of hybridizing with humans to bolster their numbers backfired, making them susceptible to the Angel virus.

When the dust settled and the Angel virus was eradicated, the combined numbers of our various species had neared that of humanity. It was a chance we quickly seized. The Turn, as it came to be called, began at noon with a single pixy. It ended at midnight with humanity huddling under the table, trying to come to grips with the fact that they'd been living beside witches, vampires, and Weres since before the pyramids.

Humanity's first gut reaction to wipe us off the face of the earth petered out pretty fast when it was shoved under their noses that we had kept the structure of civilization up and running while the world fell apart. If not for us, the death rate would have been far higher.

Even so, the first years after the Turn were a madhouse.

Afraid to strike out at us, humanity outlawed medical research as the demon behind their woes. Biolabs were leveled, and the bioengineers who escaped the plague stood trial and died in little more than legalized murder. There was a second, subtler wave of death when the source of the new medicines were inadvertently destroyed along with the biotechnology.

It was only a matter of time before humanity insisted on a purely human institution to monitor Inderlander activities. The Federal Inderland Bureau arose, dissolving and replacing local law enforcement throughout the U.S. The out-of-work Inderlander police and federal agents formed their own police force, the I.S. Rivalry between the two remains high even today, serving to keep a tight lid on the more aggressive Inderlanders.

Four floors of Cincinnati's main FIB building are devoted to finding the remaining illegal biolabs where, for a price, one can still get clean insulin and something to stave off leukemia. The human-run FIB is as obsessed in finding banned technology as the I.S. is with getting the mind-altering drug Brimstone off the streets.

And it all started when Rosalind Franklin noticed her pencil had been moved, and someone was where they ought not be, I thought, rubbing my fingertips into my aching head. Small clues. Little hints. That's what makes the world turn. That's what made me such a good runner. Smiling back at Rosalind, I wiped the fingerprints off the frame and put it in my keep box.

There was a burst of nervous laughter behind me, and I yanked open the next drawer, shuffling through the dirty self-stick notes and paper clips. My brush was right where I always left it, and a knot of worry loosened as I tossed it into the box. Hair could be used to make spells target specific. If Denon was going to slap a death threat on me, he would have taken it.

My fingers found the heavy smoothness of my dad's pocket watch. Nothing else was mine, and I slammed the drawer shut, stiffening as my head seemed to nearly explode. The watch's hands were frozen at seven to midnight. He used to tease me that it had stopped the night I was conceived. Slouching in my chair, I wedged it into my front pocket. I could almost see him standing in the doorframe of the kitchen, looking from his watch to the clock over the sink, a smile curving over his long face as he pondered where the missing moments had gone.

I set Mr. Fish—the Beta-in-bowl I had gotten at last year's office Christmas party—into my dissolution basin, trusting chance would keep both the water and the fish from sloshing out. I tossed the canister of fish flakes after him. A muffled thump from the far end of the room pulled my attention beyond the partitions and to Denon's closed door.

"You won't get three feet out that door, Tamwood," came his muffled shout, silencing the buzz of conversations. Apparently, Ivy had just resigned. "I've got a contract. You work for me, not the other way around! You leave and—" There was a clatter behind the closed door. "Holy shit . . ." he continued softly. "How much is that?"

"Enough to pay off my contract," Ivy said, her voice cold. "Enough for you and the stiffs in the basement. Do we have an understanding?"

"Yeah," he said in what sounded like greedy awe. "Yeah. You're fired."

My head felt as if it was stuffed with tissue, and I rested it in my cupped hands. Ivy had money? Why hadn't she said anything last night?

"Go Turn yourself, Denon," Ivy said, clear in the absolute hush. "I quit. You didn't fire me. You may have my money, but you can't buy into high-blood. You're second-rate, and no amount of money can change that. If I have to live in the gutters off rats, I'll still be better than you, and it's killing you I won't have to take your orders anymore."

"Don't think this makes you safe," the boss raved. I could almost see that vein popping on his neck. "Accidents happen around her. Get too close, and you might wake up dead."

Denon's door swung open and Ivy stormed out, slamming his door so hard the lights flickered. Her face was tight, and I don't think she even saw me as she whipped past my cubicle. Somewhere between having left me and now, she had donned a calf-length silk duster. I was secure enough in my own gender preference to admit she made it look very good. The hem billowed as she crossed the floor with murderous strides. Spots of anger showed on her pale face. Tension flowed from her, almost visible it was so strong.

She wasn't going vampy; she was just mad as all get-out. Even so, she left a cold wake behind her that the sunlight streaming in couldn't touch. An empty canvas bag hung over her shoulder, and her wish was still about her neck. *Smart girl,* I thought. *Save it for a rainy day.* Ivy took the stairs, and I closed my eyes in misery as the metal fire door slammed into the wall.

Jenks zipped into my cubicle, buzzing about my head like a deranged moth as he showed off the patch job on his wing. "Hi, Rache," he said, obnoxiously cheerful. "What's cooking?"

"Not so loud," I whispered. I would have given anything for a cup of coffee but wasn't sure it was worth the twenty steps to the coffeepot. Jenks was dressed in his civvies, the colors loud and clashing. Purple doesn't go well with yellow. It never has; it never will. God help me, his wing tape was purple, too. "Don't you get hung over?" I breathed.

He grinned, settling himself on my pencil cup. "Nope. Pixy metabolisms are too high. The alcohol turns to sugar too fast. Ain't that fine!"

"Swell." I carefully wrapped a picture of Mom and me up in a wad of tissue and set it next to Rosalind. I briefly entertained the idea of telling my mom I didn't have a job, deciding not to for obvious reasons. I'd wait until I found a new one. "Is Ivy okay?" I asked.

"Yeah. She'll be all right." Jenks flitted to the top of my pot of laurel. "She's just ticked it took everything she had to buy her way out of her contract and cover her butt."

I nodded, glad they wanted me gone. Things would be a lot easier if neither of us had a price on our head. "Did you know she had money?"

Jenks dusted off a leaf and sat down. He adopted a superior look, which is hard to manage when you're only four inches tall and dressed like a rabid butterfly. "Well, duh . . . She's the last living blood-member of her house. I'd give her some space for a few days. She's as mad as a wet wasp. Lost her house in the country, the land, stocks, everything. All that's left is the city manor on the river, and her mother has that."

I eased back into my chair, unwrapped my last piece of cinnamon gum, and stuck it in my mouth. There was a clatter as Jenks landed in my cardboard box and began poking about. "Oh, yeah," he muttered. "Ivy said she has a spot rented already. I've got the address."

"Get out of my stuff." I flicked a finger at him, and he flew back to the laurel, standing atop the highest branch to watch everyone gossip. My temple pounded as I bent to clean out my bottom drawer. *Why had Ivy given Denon everything she had? Why not use her wish?*

"Heads up," Jenks said, slithering down the plant to hide in the leaves. "Here he comes."

I straightened to find Denon halfway to my desk. Francis, the bootlicking, butt-kissing office snitch, pulled away from a cluster of people, following. My ex-boss's eyes fastened on me over the walls of my cubicle. Choking, I accidentally swallowed my gum.

Put simply, the boss looked like a pro wrestler with a doctorate in suave: big man, hard muscles, perfect mahogany skin. I think he was a boulder in a previous life. Like Ivy, Denon was a living vamp. Unlike Ivy, he had been born human and turned. It made him low-blood, a distant second-class in the vamp world.

Even so, Denon was a force to reckon with, having worked hard to overcome his ignoble start. His overabundance of muscles were more than just pretty; they kept him alive while with his stronger, adopted kin. He possessed that ageless look of someone who fed regularly on a true undead. Only the undead could turn humans into a vampire, and by his healthy appearance, Denon was a clearly a favorite. Half the floor wanted to be his sex toy. The other half he scared the crap out of. I was proud to be a card-carrying member of the latter.

My hands shook as I took up my coffee cup from the day before and pretended to take a sip. His arms swung like pistons as he moved, his yellow polo shirt contrasting with his black pants. They were neatly creased, showing off his muscular legs and trim waist. People were getting out of his way. A few left the floor. God help me if I'd muffed my only wish and was going to get caught.

There was a creak of plastic as he leaned against the top of my four-foot walls. I didn't look, concentrating instead upon the holes my thumbtacks had made in the burlap-textured partitions. The skin on my arms tingled as if Denon were touching me. His presence seemed to swirl and eddy around me, backwashing against the partitions of my cubicle and rising until it seemed he was behind me, too. My pulse quickened, and I focused on Francis.

The snot had settled himself on Joyce's desk and was unfastening the button on his blue polyester jacket. He was grinning to show his perfect, clearly capped teeth. As I watched, he pushed the sleeves of his jacket back up to show his skinny arms. His triangular face was framed by ear-length hair, which he was constantly flipping out of his eyes. He thought it made him look boyishly charming. I thought it made him look like he had just woken up.

Though it was only three in the afternoon, a thick stubble shadowed his face. The collar of his Hawaiian shirt was intentionally flipped up around his neck. The joke around the office was he was trying to look like Sonny Crockett, but his narrow eyes squinted and his nose was too long and thin to pull it off. Pathetic.

"I know what's going on, Morgan," Denon said, jerking

my attention to him. He had that throaty low voice only black men and vampires were allowed to have. It's a rule somewhere. Low and sweet. Coaxing. The promise in it pulled my skin tight, and fear washed through me.

"Beg pardon?" I said, pleased my voice didn't crack. Emboldened, I met his eyes. My breath came quick, and I tensed. He was trying to pull an aura at three in the afternoon. *Damn.*

Denon leaned over the partition to rest his arms on the top. His biceps bunched, making the veins swell. The hair on the back of my neck prickled, and I fought the urge to look behind me. "Everyone thinks you're leaving because of the piss-poor assignments I've been giving you," he said, his soothing voice caressing the words as they passed his lips. "They'd be right."

He straightened, and I jerked as the plastic creaked. The brown of his eyes had entirely vanished behind his widening pupils. *Double damn.*

"I've been trying to get rid of you for the last two years," he said. "You don't have bad luck." He smiled, showing me his human teeth. "You have me. Shoddy backup, garbled messages, leaks to your takes. But when I finally get you to leave, you take my best runner with you." His eyes grew intense. I forced my hands to unclench, and his attention flicked to them. "Not good, Morgan."

It hadn't been me, I thought, my alarm hesitating in the sudden realization. It wasn't me. All those mistakes *weren't* me. But then Denon moved to the gap in the walls that was my door.

In a sliding rattle of metal and plastic, I found myself on my feet and pressed up against my desk. Papers scrunched and the mouse fell off the desk, swinging. Denon's eyes were pupil-black. My pulse hammered.

"I don't like you, Morgan," he said, his breath washing over me with a clammy feel. "I never have. Your methods are loose and sloppy, just like your father's. Unable to tag that leprechaun is beyond belief." His gaze went distant, and

I found I was holding my breath as they glazed over and understanding seemed to dance just out of reach.

Please work, I thought desperately. *Could my wish please work?* Denon leaned close, and I stabbed my nails into my palm to keep from shirking. I forced myself to breathe. "Beyond belief," he said again, as if trying to figure it out. But then he shook his head in mock dismay.

My breath slipped out as he drew back. He broke eye contact, putting his gaze on my neck, where I knew my pulse hammered. My hand crept up to cover it, and he smiled like a lover to his one and only. He had only one scar on his beautiful neck. I wondered where the rest were. "When you hit the street," he whispered, "you're fair game."

Shock mixed with my alarm in a nauseating mix. He was going to put a price on my head. "You can't . . ." I stammered. "You wanted me to leave."

He never moved, but just his stillness made my fear tighten. My eyes went wide at his slow intake of breath and his lips going full and red. "Someone's going to die for this, Rachel," he whispered, the way he said my name making my face go cold. "I can't kill Tamwood. So you're going to be her whipping girl." He eyed me from under his brow. "Congratulations."

My hand dropped from my neck as he eased out of my office. He wasn't as smooth as Ivy. It was the difference between high- and low-blood; those born a vamp and those born human and turned. Once in the aisle, the heavy threat in his eyes dissipated. Denon pulled an envelope from his back pocket and tossed it to my desk. "Enjoy your last paycheck, Morgan," he said loudly, more to everyone else than me. He turned and walked away.

"But you wanted me to quit. . . ." I whispered as he disappeared into the elevator. The doors closed; the little red arrow pointing down turned bright. He had his own boss to tell. Denon had to be joking. He wouldn't put a price on my head for something as stupid as Ivy leaving with me. Would he?

"Good going, Rachel."

My head jerked up at the nasal voice. I had forgotten Francis. He slid from Joyce's desk and leaned up against my wall. After seeing Denon do the same thing, the effect was laughable. Slowly, I slipped back into my swivel chair.

"I've been waiting six months for you to get steamed up enough to leave," Francis said. "I should've known all you needed was to get drunk."

A surge of anger burned away the last of my fear, and I returned to my packing. My fingers were cold, and I tried to rub some warmth back into them. Jenks came out of hiding and silently flitted to the top of my plant.

Francis pushed the sleeves of his jacket back to his elbows. Nudging my check out of the way with a single finger, he sat on my desk with one foot on the floor. "It took a lot longer than I thought," he mocked. "Either you're really stubborn or really stupid. Either way, you're really dead." He sniffed, making a rasping noise through his thin nose.

I slammed a desk drawer shut, nearly catching his fingers. "Is there a point you're trying to make, *Francis*?"

"It's Frank," he said, trying to look superior but coming off as if he had a cold. "Don't bother dumping your computer files. There're mine, along with your desk."

I glanced at my monitor with its screen saver of a big, bug-eyed frog. Every so often it ate a fly with Francis's face on it. "Since when are the stiffs downstairs letting a *warlock* run a case?" I asked, hammering at his classification. Francis wasn't good enough to rank witch. He could invoke a spell, but didn't have the know-how to stir one. I did, though I usually bought my amulets. It was easier, and probably safer for me and my mark. It wasn't my fault thousands of years of stereotyping had put females as witches and males as warlocks.

Apparently it was just what he wanted me to ask. "You're not the only one who can cook, Rachel-me-gal. I got my license last week." Leaning, he picked a pen out of my box and set it back in the pencil cup. "I'd have made witch a long time ago. I just didn't want to dirty my hands learning how to stir a spell. I shouldn't have waited so long. It's too easy."

I plucked the pen back out and tucked it in my back pocket. "Well, goody for you." *Francis made the jump to witch?* I thought. *They must have lowered the standards.*

"Yup," Francis said, cleaning under his fingernails with one of my silver daggers. "Got your desk, your caseload, even your company car."

Snatching my knife out of his hand, I tossed it in the box. "I don't have a company car."

"I do." He flicked the collar of his shirt covered with palm trees as if very pleased with himself. I made a vow to keep my mouth shut lest I give him another chance to brag. "Yeah," he said with an overdone sigh. "I'll be needing it. Denon has me going out to interview Councilman Trenton Kalamack on Monday." Francis snickered. "While you were out flubbing your measly snag and drag, I led the run that landed two kilos of Brimstone."

"Big freaking deal," I said, ready to strangle him.

"It's not the amount." He tossed his hair out of his eyes. "It was who was carrying it."

That got my interest. Trent's name in connection with Brimstone? "Who?" I said.

Francis slid off my desk. He stumbled over my fuzzy pink office slippers, nearly falling. Catching himself, he sighted down his finger as if it were a pistol. "Watch your back, Morgan."

That was my limit. Face twisting, I lashed my foot out, tucking it neatly under his. He went down with a gratifying yelp. I had my knee on the back of his nasty polyester coat as he hit the floor. My hand slapped my hip for my missing cuffs. Jenks cheered, flitting overhead. The office went quiet after a gasp of alarm. No one would interfere. They wouldn't even look at me.

"I've got nothing to lose, cookie," I snarled, leaning down until I could smell his sweat. "Like you said, I'm already dead, so the only thing keeping me from ripping your eyelids off right now is simple curiosity. I'm going to ask you again. Who did you tag with Brimstone?"

"Rachel," he cried, able to knock me on my butt but afraid to try. "You're in deep—Ow! Ow!" he exclaimed as my nails dug into the top of his right eyelid. "Yolin. Yolin Bates!"

"Trent Kalamack's secretary?" Jenks said, hovering over my shoulder.

"Yeah," Francis said, his face scraping the carpeting as he turned his head to see me. "Or rather, his late secretary. Damn it, Rachel. Get off me!"

"He's dead?" I dusted off my jeans as I got to my feet.

Francis was sullen as he stood, but he was getting some joy out of telling me this or he would have already walked. "She, not he," he said as he adjusted his collar to stand upright. "They found her stone-dead in I.S. lockup yesterday. Literally. She was a warlock."

He said the last with a condescending tone, and I gave him a sour smile. How easy it is to find contempt for something you were only a week ago. *Trent,* I thought, feeling my gaze go distant. If I could prove Trent dealt in Brimstone and give him to the I.S. on a silver platter, Denon would be forced to get off my back. The I.S. had been after him for years as the Brimstone web continued to grow. No one even knew if he was human or Inderlander.

"Jeez, Rachel," Francis whined, dabbing at his face. "You gave me a bloody nose."

My thoughts cleared, and I turned a mocking eye on him. "You're a witch. Go stir a spell." I knew he couldn't be that good yet. He would have to borrow one like the warlock he used to be, and I could tell it irritated him. I beamed as he opened his mouth to say something. Thinking better of it, he pinched his nose shut and spun away.

There was a tug as Jenks landed on my earring. Francis was making his hurried way down the aisle, his head tilted at an awkward angle. The hem of his sport coat swayed with his stilted gate, and I couldn't help my snicker as Jenks hummed the theme for *Miami Vice*.

"What a moss wipe," the pixy said as I turned back to my desk.

My frown returned as I wedged my pot of laurel into my box of stuff. My head hurt, and I wanted to go home and take a nap. A last look at my desk, and I scooped up my slippers, dropping them in the box. Joyce's books went on her chair with a note saying I'd call her later. *Take my computer, eh?* I thought, pausing to open a file. Three clicks and I made it all but impossible to change the screen saver without trashing the entire system.

"I'm going home, Jenks," I whispered, glancing at the wall clock. It was three-thirty. I'd been at work only half an hour. It felt like ages. A last look about the floor showed only downward-turned heads and backs. It was as if I didn't exist. "Who needs them," I muttered, snatching up my jacket from the back of my chair and reaching for my check.

"Hey!" I yelped as Jenks pinched my ear. "Cripes, Jenks. Knock it off!"

"It's the check," he exclaimed. "Damn it, woman. He's cursed the check!"

I froze. Dropping my jacket into the box, I leaned over the innocent-seeming envelope. Eyes closed, I breathed deeply, looking for the scent of redwood. Then I tasted against the back of my throat for the scent of sulfur that lingered over black magic. "I can't smell anything."

Jenks gave a short bark of laughter. "I can. It's got to be the check. It's the only thing Denon gave you. And watch it, Rachel. It's black."

A sick feeling drifted through me. Denon couldn't be serious. He couldn't.

I glanced over the room, finding no help. Worried, I pulled my vase out of the trash. Some of Mr. Fish's water went into it. I leveled a portion of salt into the vase, dipped my finger to taste it, then added a bit more. Satisfied the salinity was equal to that of the ocean, I upended the mix over the check. If it had been spelled, the salt would break it.

A whisper of yellow smoke hovered over the envelope. "Aw shhhhoot," I whispered, suddenly frightened. "Watch your nose, Jenks," I said, ducking below my desk.

With an abrupt fizz, the black spell dissolutioned. Yellow, sulfuric smoke billowed up to be sucked into the vents. Cries of dismay and disgust rose with it. There was a small stampede as everyone surged for the doors. Even prepared, the stench of rotten eggs stung at my eyes. The spell had been a nasty one, tailored to me since both Denon and Francis had touched the envelope. It hadn't come cheap.

Shaken, I came out from under my desk and glanced over the deserted floor. "Is it okay now?" I said around a cough. My earring shifted as Jenks nodded. "Thanks, Jenks."

Stomach churning, I tossed my dripping check into the box and stalked past the empty cubicles. It looked like Denon was serious about his death threat. Absolutely swell.

Four

"**R**a-a-a-achel-l-l-l," sang a tiny, irritating voice. It cut clearly through the shifting gears and choking gurgle of the bus's diesel engine. Jenks's voice grated on my inner ear worse than chalk on a blackboard, and my hand trembled in the effort to not make a grab for him. I'd never touch him. The little twit was too fast.

"I'm not asleep," I said before he could do it again. "I'm resting my eyes."

"You're going to rest your eyes right past your stop—*Hot Stuff*." He nailed the nickname last night's cabbie had given me hard, and I slit an eyelid.

"Don't call me that." The bus went around a corner, and my grip tightened on the box balanced on my lap. "I've got two more blocks," I said through gritted teeth. I'd kicked the nausea, but the headache lingered. And I knew it was two blocks because of the sound of Little League practice in the park just down from my apartment. There'd be another after the sun went down for the nightwalkers.

There was a thrum of wings as Jenks dropped from my earring and into the box. "Sweet mother of Tink! Is that all they pay you?" he exclaimed.

My eyes flashed open. "Get out of my stuff!" I snatched my damp check and crammed it into a jacket pocket. Jenks made a mocking face, and I rubbed my thumb and finger together as if squishing something. He got the idea and moved his purple and yellow silk pantaloons out of my reach, settling on the top of the seat in front of me. "Don't you have somewhere to be?" I asked. "Like helping your family move?"

Jenks gave a yelp of laughter. "Help them move? No freaking way." His wings quivered. "Besides, I should sniff around your place and make sure everything is okay before you blow yourself up when you try to use the john." He laughed hysterically, and several people looked at me. I shrugged as if to say, "Pixies."

"Thanks," I said sourly. A pixy bodyguard. Denon would laugh himself to death. I was indebted to Jenks for finding the spell on my check, but the I.S. hadn't time to rig anything else. I figured I had a few days if he was really serious about this. More likely it was a "don't let the spell kill you on the way out" kind of a thing.

I stood as the bus came to a halt. Struggling down the steps, I landed in the late afternoon sun. Jenks made more annoying circles around me. He was worse than a mosquito. "Nice place," he said sarcastically as I waited for traffic to clear before crossing the street to my apartment house. I silently agreed. I lived uptown in Cincinnati in what was a good neighborhood twenty years ago. The building was a four-story brick, originally built for university upperclassmen. It had seen its last finals party years ago and was now reduced to this.

The black letterboxes attached to the porch were dented and ugly, some having obviously been broken into. I got my mail from the landlady. I had a suspicion she was the one who broke the boxes so she could sort through her tenants' mail at her leisure. There was a thin strip of lawn and two bedraggled shrubs to either side of the wide steps. Last year, I had planted the yarrow seeds I had gotten in a *Spell Weekly* mail promotion, but Mr. Dinky, the landlady's Chihuahua, had dug them up—along with most of the yard. Little divots were everywhere, making it look like a fairy battlefield.

"And I thought my place was bad," Jenks whispered as I skipped the step with dry rot.

My keys jingled as I balanced the box and unlocked the door at the same time. A little voice in my head had been saying the same thing for years. The odor of fried food assaulted me as I entered the foyer, and my nose wrinkled. Green indoor/outdoor carpet ran up the stairs, threadbare and fraying. Mrs. Baker had unscrewed the lightbulb in the stairway again, but the sun spilling in the landing window to fall on the rosebud wallpaper was enough to find my way.

"Hey," Jenks said as I went upstairs. "That stain on the ceiling is in the shape of a pizza."

I glanced up. He was right. Funny, I never noticed it before.

"And that dent in the wall?" he said as we reached the first floor. "It's just the right size for someone's head. Man . . . if these walls could talk . . ."

I found I could still smile. Wait until he got to my apartment. There was a dip in the living room floor where someone had burned out a hearth.

My smile faded as I rounded the second landing. All my things were in the hall.

"What the devil?" I whispered. Shocked, I set my box on the floor and looked down the hall to Mrs. Talbu's door. "I paid my rent!"

"Hey, Rache?" Jenks said from the ceiling. "Where's your cat?"

Anger growing, I stared at my furniture. It seemed to take up a lot more space when it was jammed into a hallway on her lousy plastic carpeting. "Where does she get off—"

"Rachel!" Jenks shouted. "Where's your cat?"

"I don't have a cat," I all but snarled. It was a sore spot with me.

"I thought all witches had a cat."

Lips pursed, I strode down the hall. "Cats make Mr. Dinky sneeze."

Jenks flew alongside my ear. "Who is Mr. Dinky?"

"Him," I said, pointing to the framed, oversized picture of a white Chihuahua hanging across from my landlady's door. The butt-ugly, bug-eyed dog wore one of those bows parents put on a baby so you know it's a girl. I pounded on the door. "Mrs. Talbu? Mrs. Talbu!"

There were the muffled yaps of Mr. Dinky and the sound of nails on the backside of the door, shortly followed by my landlady screeching to try and get the thing to shut up. Mr. Dinky redoubled his noise, scrabbling at the floor to dig his way to me.

"Mrs. Talbu!" I shouted. "Why is my stuff in the hall?"

"Word's out on you, Hot Stuff," Jenks said from the ceiling. "You're damaged goods."

"I told you not to call me *that!*" I shouted, hitting her door with my last word.

I heard the slamming of a door from inside, and Mr. Dinky's barking grew muffled and more frenzied. "Go away," came a thin, reedy voice. "You can't live here anymore."

The flat of my hand hurt, and I massaged it. "You think I can't pay my rent?" I said, not caring that the entire floor could hear me. "I've got money, Mrs. Talbu. You can't kick me out. I've got next month's rent right here." I pulled out my soggy check and waved it at the door.

"I changed your lock," Mrs. Talbu quavered. "Go away before you get killed."

I stared at the door in disbelief. She had found out about the I.S.'s threat? And the old lady act was a sham. She shouted clear enough through my wall when she thought I played my music too loud. "You can't evict me!" I said desperately. "I've got rights."

"Dead witches have no rights," Jenks said from the light fixture.

"Damn it, Mrs. Talbu!" I shouted at the door. "I'm not dead yet!"

There was no answer. I stood there, thinking. I didn't have much recourse, and she knew it. I supposed I could stay at my new office until I found something. Moving back in with my mother was not an option, and I hadn't talked to my brother since I joined the I.S.

"What about my security deposit?" I asked, and the door remained silent. My temper shifted to a slow, steady burn, one that could last for days. "Mrs. Talbu," I said quietly. "If you don't give me the balance of this month's rent and my security deposit, I'm going to sit right in front of your door." I paused, listening. "I'm going to sit here until they spell me. I'll probably explode right here. Make a big bloody stain on your carpet that won't come out. And you're going to have to look at that big bloody stain everyday. Hear me, Mrs. Talbu?" I quietly threatened. "Pieces of me will be on your hall ceiling."

There was a gasp. "Oh my, Dinky," Mrs. Talbu quavered. "Where's my checkbook?"

I looked at Jenks and smiled bitterly. He gave me a thumbs-up.

There was a rustle, followed by a moment of silence and the distinctive sound of paper tearing. I wondered why she bothered with the old lady act. Everyone knew she was tougher than petrified dinosaur dung and would probably outlive us all. Even Death didn't want her.

"I'm putting the word out on you, hussy," Mrs. Talbu shouted through the door. "You won't find a place to rent in the entire city."

Jenks darted down as a slip of white was shoved under the door. After hovering over it for a moment, he nodded it was okay. I picked it up and read the amount. "What about my security deposit?" I asked. "You want to come with me to my apartment and look it over? Make sure there're no nail holes in the walls or runes under the carpet?"

There was a muffled curse, shortly followed by more scratching, and another white slip appeared. "Get out of my building," Mrs. Talbu yelled, "before I set Mr. Dinky on you!"

"I love you, too, old bat." I took my key from my key ring and dropped it. Angry but satisfied, I snatched up the second check.

I went back to my things, slowing at the telltale scent of sulfur emanating from them. My shoulders tightened in worry as I stared at my life heaped against the walls. Everything was spelled. I could touch nothing. God help me. I was under an I.S. death threat.

"I can't douse everything in salt," I said as there was a click of a closing door.

"I know this guy who has storage." Jenks sounded unusually sympathetic, and I looked up as I gripped my elbows. "If I ask him, he'll come get it, put everything away for you. You can dissolution the spells later." He hesitated, looking over my music discs carelessly dumped into my largest copper spell bowl.

I nodded, slumping against the wall and sliding down until my rear hit the floor. My clothes, my shoes, my music, my books . . . *my life*?

"Oh no," Jenks said softly. "They spelled your disc of *The Best of Takata*."

"It's autographed," I whispered, and the hum from his wings dropped in pitch. The plastic would survive a dip in saltwater, but the paper folder would be ruined. I wondered if I wrote to Takata if he would send me another. He might remember me. We did spend a wild night chasing shadows over the ruins of Cincinnati's old biolabs. I think he made a song about it. "New moon rising, sight unseen, / Shadows of faith make a risky vaccine." It hit the top twenty for sixteen weeks straight. My brow furrowed. "Is there anything they didn't spell?" I asked.

Jenks landed on the phone book and shrugged. It had been left open to coroners.

"Swell." Stomach knotting, I got to my feet. My thoughts swung to what Ivy had said last night about Leon Bairn. Little bits of witch splattered all over his porch. I swallowed hard. I couldn't go home. *How the hell was I going to pay Denon off?*

My head started hurting again. Jenks alighted on my earring, keeping his big mouth shut as I picked up my cardboard box and went downstairs. First things first. "What's the name of that guy you know?" I asked when I reached the foyer. "The one with storage? If I give him something extra, will he dissolution my things?"

"If you tell him how. He's not a witch."

I thought, struggling to regroup. My cell phone was in my bag, but the battery was dead. The charger was somewhere in my spelled stuff. "I can call him from the office," I said.

"He doesn't have a phone." Jenks slipped off my earring, flying backward at eye level. His wing tape had frayed, and I wondered if I should offer to fix it. "He lives in the Hollows," Jenks added. "I'll ask him for you. He's shy."

I reached for the doorknob, then hesitated. Putting my back to the wall, I pushed aside the sun-faded, yellow curtain to peek out the window. The tatty yard lay quiet in the afternoon sun, empty and still. The drone of a lawn mower and the whoosh from passing cars was muffled through the glass. Lips pressed tight, I decided I'd wait there until I heard the bus coming.

"He likes cash," Jenks said, dropping down to stand on the sill. "I'll bring him by the office after he's locked up your stuff."

"You mean everything that hasn't walked off by itself in the meantime," I said, but knew everything was reasonably safe. Spells, especially black ones, were supposed to be target specific, but you never know. No one would risk extinction for my cheap stuff. "Thanks, Jenks." That was twice now he had saved my butt. It made me uneasy. And a little bit guilty.

"Hey, that's what partners do," he said, not helping at all.

Smiling thinly at his enthusiasm, I set my box down to wait.

Five

The bus was quiet, as most traffic was coming out of the Hollows this time of day. Jenks had left via the window shortly after we crossed the river into Kentucky. It was his opinion the I.S. wouldn't tag me on a bus with witnesses. I wasn't ready to believe it, but I wasn't going to ask him to stay with me, either.

I had told the driver the address, and he agreed to tell me when we were there. The human was skinny, his faded blue uniform hanging loose on him despite the vanilla wafers he was cramming into his mouth like jelly beans.

Most of Cincinnati's mass-transit drivers were comfortable with Inderlanders, but not all. Humanity's reactions to us varied widely. Some were afraid, some weren't. Some wanted to be us, some wanted to kill us. A few took advantage of the lower tax rate and lived in the Hollows, but most didn't.

Shortly after the Turn, an unexpected migration occurred when almost every human who could afford it moved deep into the cities. The psychologists of the day had called it a "nesting syndrome," and in hindsight the countrywide phenomenon was understandable. Inderlanders were more than eager to snap up the properties on the outskirts, lured by the prospect of a little more earth to call their own, not to mention the drastically falling home prices.

The population demographics have only recently started

to even out, as well-to-do Inderlanders move back into the city and the less fortunate, more informed humans decide they would rather live in a nice Inderland neighborhood than a trashy human one. Generally, though, apart from a small section around the university, humans lived in Cincinnati and Inderlanders lived across the river in the Hollows. We don't care that most humans shun our neighborhoods like pre-Turn ghettoes.

The Hollows have become a bastion of Inderland life, comfortable and casual on the surface, with its potential problems carefully hidden. Most humans are surprised at how normal the Hollows appear, which, when you stop to think about it, makes sense. Our history is that of humanity's. We didn't just drop out of the sky in '66; we emigrated in through Ellis Island. We fought in the Civil War, World War One, and World War Two—some of us in all three. We suffered in the Depression, and we waited like everyone else to find out who shot JR.

But dangerous differences exist, and any Inderlander over the age of fifty spent the earliest part of his or her life disguising them, a tradition that holds true even to this day.

The homes are modest, painted white, yellow, and occasionally pink. There are no haunted houses except for Loveland Castle in October, when they turn it into the baddest haunted house on either side of the river. There are swing sets, aboveground pools, bikes on the lawns, and cars parked on the curb. It takes a sharp eye to notice that the flowers are arranged in antiblack magic hexes and the basement windows are often cemented over. The savage, dangerous reality blooms only in the depths of the city, where people gather and emotions run rampant: amusement parks, dance clubs, bars, churches. *Never* our homes.

And it's quiet—even at night when all its denizens are up. It was always the stillness that a human noticed first, setting them on edge and sending their instincts into full swing.

I found my tension easing as I stared out the window and counted the black, light-proof blinds. The quiet of the neighborhood seemed to soak into the bus. Even the few people riding had grown still. There was just something about the Hollows that said "Home."

My hair swung forward as the bus stopped. On edge, I jerked when the guy behind me bumped my shoulder as he got up. Boots clattering, he hastened down the steps and into the sun. The driver told me my stop was next, and I stood as the nice man trundled down a side street to give me curb service. I stepped down into the patchy shade, standing with my arms wrapped around the box and trying not to breathe the fumes as the bus drove away. It disappeared around a corner, taking its noise and the last vestiges of humanity with it.

Slowly it grew quiet. The sound of birds drifted into existence. Somewhere close there were kids calling—no, kids screaming—and the barking of a dog. Multicolored chalk runes decorated the cracked sidewalk, and a forgotten doll with fangs painted on it smiled blankly at me. There was a small stone church across the street, its steeple rising far above the trees.

I turned on a heel, eyeing what Ivy had rented for us: a one-story house that could easily be converted to an office. The roof looked new, but the chimney mortar was crumbling. There was grass out front, looking like it should have been cut last week. It even had a garage, the door gaping open to show a rusting mower.

It will do, I thought as I opened the gate to the chain-link fence enclosing the yard. An old black man sat on the porch, rocking the afternoon away. *Landlord?* I mused, smiling. I wondered if he was a vamp, since he wore dark glasses against the late afternoon sun. He was scruffy looking despite being clean-shaven, his tightly curled hair going gray around the temples. There was mud on his shoes and a hint of it on the knees of his blue jeans. He looked worn-out and tired—put away like an unwanted plow horse who was still eager for one more season.

He set a tall glass on the porch railing as I came up the

walk. "Don't want it," he said as he took off his glasses and tucked them in a shirt pocket. His voice was raspy.

Hesitating, I peered up at him from the bottom of the stairs. "Beg pardon?"

He coughed, clearing his throat. "Whatever you're selling out of that box. Don't want it. I've got enough curse candles, candy, and magazines. And I don't have the money for new siding, water purifier, or a sunroom."

"I'm not selling anything," I said. "I'm your new tenant."

He sat up straighter, somehow making himself look even more unkempt. "Tenant? Oh, you mean across the street."

Confused, I shifted my box to my other hip. "This isn't 1597 Oakstaff, is it?"

He chuckled. "That's across the street."

"Sorry to have bothered you." I turned to leave, hoisting the box higher.

"Yep," the man said, and I paused, not wanting to be rude. "The numbers are backward on this street. Odd numbers on the wrong side of the road." He smiled, creasing the wrinkles around his eyes. "But they didn't ask me when they put the numbers up." He extended his hand. "I'm Keasley," he said, waiting for me to climb the stairs and take his hand.

Neighbors, I thought, rolling my eyes as I went up the stairs. *Best to be nice.* "Rachel Morgan," I said, pumping his arm once. He beamed, patting my shoulder in a fatherly fashion. The strength of his grip was surprising, as was the scent of redwood coming from him. He was a witch, or at the very least a warlock. Not comfortable with his show of familiarity, I took a step back as he released me. It was cooler on his porch, and I felt tall under the low ceiling.

"Are you friends with the vamp?" he said, gesturing across the street with his chin.

"Ivy? Yeah."

He nodded slowly, as if it were important. "Both of you quit together?"

I blinked. "News travels fast."

He laughed. "Yup. It does at that."

"Aren't you afraid I'm going to get spelled on your front porch and take you with me?"

"No." He leaned back in his rocker and picked up his glass. "I took that one off you." He held up a tiny self-stick amulet between his finger and thumb. As my lips parted, he dropped it into his glass. What I thought had been lemonade foamed as the spell dissolutioned. Yellow smoke billowed, and he waved his hand dramatically. "Oooh doggies, that's a nasty one."

Saltwater? He grinned at my obvious shock. "That guy on the bus . . ." I stammered as I backed off the porch. The yellow sulfur eddied down the stairs as if trying to find me.

"Nice meeting you, Ms. Morgan," the man said I stumbled onto the walk and into the sun. "A vamp and pixy might keep you alive a few days, but not if you aren't more careful."

My eyes turned to look down the street at the long gone bus. "The guy on the bus . . ."

Keasley nodded. "You're right in that they won't try anything when there's a witness, leastwise, not at first, but you have to watch for the amulets that won't trigger till you're alone."

I had forgotten about delayed spells. And were was Denon getting the money? My face scrunched up as I figured it out; Ivy's bribe money was paying for my death threat. Swell.

"I'm home all day," Keasley was saying. "Come on over if you want to talk. I don't get out much anymore. Arthritis." He slapped his knee.

"Thanks," I said. "For—finding that charm."

"My pleasure," he said, his gaze on the ceiling of the porch and the lazily spinning fan.

My stomach was knotting as I made my way back to the sidewalk. Was the entire city aware I had quit? Maybe Ivy had talked to him.

I felt vulnerable in the empty street. Edgy, I crossed the road looking for house numbers. "Fifteen ninety-three," I muttered, glancing at the small yellow house with two bikes tangled on the lawn. "Sixteen hundred and one," I said, looking the other way to the well-kept brick home. My lips pursed. The only thing between them was that stone church. I froze. A church?

A harsh buzzing zipped past my ears, and I instinctively ducked.

"Hi, Rache!" Jenks came to a hovering halt just out of my reach.

"Damn it, Jenks!" I shouted, warming as I heard the old man laugh. "Don't do that!"

"Got your stuff set," Jenks said. "I made him put everything up on blocks."

"It's a church," I said.

"No shit, Sherlock. Wait until you see the garden."

I stood unmoving. "It's a *church*."

Jenks hovered, waiting for me. "There's a huge yard in back. Great for parties."

"Jenks," I said through gritted teeth. "It's a church. The backyard is a *graveyard*."

"Not all of it." He began weaving impatiently. "And it's not a church anymore. It's been a day care for the last two years. No one's been buried there since the Turn."

I stood, staring at him. "Did they move the bodies out?"

His darting ceased and he hung motionless. "'Course they moved the bodies out. You think I'm *stupid*? You think I'd live where there were dead *humans*? God help me. The bugs coming off 'em, diseases, viruses, and crap soaking into the soil and getting into everything!"

I adjusted my grip on my stuff, striding across the shady street and up the wide steps of the church. Jenks didn't have a clue as to whether the bodies had been moved out. The gray stone steps were bowed in the middle from decades of use, and they were slippery. There were twin doors taller than I, made of a reddish wood and bound with metal. One had a plaque screwed into it. "Donna's Daycare," I muttered, reading the inscription. I tugged a door open, surprised at the strength needed to shift it. There wasn't even a lock on it, just a sliding bolt on the inside.

"Of course they moved the bodies out," Jenks said, then flitted over the church. I'd put a hundred on it that he was going out to the backyard to investigate.

"Ivy?" I shouted, trying to slam the door behind me. "Ivy, are you here?" The echo of my voice came back from the yet unseen sanctuary, a thick, stained-glassed quiet hush of sound. The closest I'd been to a church since my dad died was reading the cutesy catch phrases off those backlit signs they all put on their front lawns. The foyer was dark, having no windows and black wooden panels. It was warm and still, thick with the presence of past liturgy. I set the box on the wooden floor and listened to the green and amber hush slipping in from the sanctuary.

"Be right down!" came Ivy's distant shout. She sounded almost cheerful, but where on earth was she? Her voice was coming from everywhere and nowhere at all.

There was the soft click of a latch, and Ivy slipped from behind a panel. A narrow spiral stairway went up behind her. "I've got my owls up in the belfry," she said. Her brown eyes were more alive than I'd ever seen them. "It's perfect for storage. Lots of shelves and drying racks. Someone left their stuff up there, though. Want to go through it with me later?"

"It's a church, Ivy."

Ivy stopped. Her arms crossed and she looked at me, her face abruptly empty.

"There are dead people in the backyard," I added, and she levered herself up and went into the sanctuary. "You can see the tombstones from the road," I continued as I followed her in.

The pews were gone, as was the altar, leaving only an empty room and a slightly raised stage. That same black wood made a wainscot that ran below the tall stained-glassed windows that wouldn't open. A faded shadow on the wall remained where an enormous cross once hung over the altar. The ceiling was three stories up, and I sent my gaze to the open woodwork, thinking it would be hard to keep this room warm in winter. It was nothing but a stripped down open space . . . but the stark emptiness seemed to add to the feeling of peace.

"How much is this going to cost?" I asked, remembering I was supposed to be angry.

"Seven hundred a month, utilities—ah—included," Ivy said quietly.

"Seven hundred?" I hesitated, surprised. That would be three fifty for my share. I was paying four fifty uptown for my one-room castle. That wasn't bad. Not bad at all. Especially if it had a yard. *No,* I thought, my bad mood returning. *It was a graveyard.*

"Where are you going?" I said as Ivy walked away. "I'm talking to you."

"To get a cup of coffee. You want one?" She disappeared through the door at the back of the raised stage.

"Okay, so the rent is cheap," I said. "That's what I said I wanted, but it's a church! You can't run a business from a church!" Fuming, I followed her past the opposing his-and-her bathrooms. Farther down was a door on the right. I peeked past it to find a nice-sized empty room, the floor and smooth walls giving back an echo of my breathing. A stained-glass window of saints was propped open with a stick to air the place out, and I could hear the sparrows arguing outside. The room looked as if it had once been an office, having since been modified for toddlers' nap cots. The floor was dusty, but the wood was sound under the light scratches.

Satisfied, I peeked around the door across the hall. There was a made-up bed and open boxes. Before I could see more, Ivy reached in front of me and pulled the door shut.

"That's your stuff," I said, staring at her.

Ivy's face was empty, chilling me more than if she had been pulling an aura. "I'm going to have to stay here until I can rent a room somewhere." She hesitated, tucking her black hair behind an ear. "Got a problem with that?"

"No," I said softly, closing my eyes in a long blink. For the love of St. Philomena. I was going to have to live at the office until I got myself set. My eyes opened, and I was startled by the odd look Ivy had, a mix of fear and—anticipation?

"I'm going to have to crash here, too," I said, not liking this at all but seeing no other option. "My landlady evicted me. The box by the front door is all I've got until I can get my stuff despelled. The I.S. black-charmed everything in my apartment, almost nailed me on the bus. And thanks to my landlady, no one within the city limits will rent to me. Denon put a contract out on me, just like you said." I tried to keep the whine out of my voice, but it was there.

That odd light was still in Ivy's eyes, and I wondered if she had told me the truth about being a nonpracticing vamp. "You can have the empty room," she said, her voice carefully flat.

I gave her a terse nod. *Okay,* I thought, taking a deep breath. I was living in a church—with bodies in the backyard—an I.S. death threat on me—and a vamp across the hall. I wondered if she would notice if I put a lock on the inside of my door. I wondered if it would matter.

"The kitchen's back here," she said, and I followed her and the smell of coffee. My mouth fell open as I rounded the open archway, and I forgot to be angry again.

The kitchen was half the size of the sanctuary, as fully equipped and modern as the sanctuary was barren and medieval. There was gleaming metal, shiny chrome, and bright, fluorescent lights. The refrigerator was enormous. A gas stove and oven sat at one end of the room; an electric range and stovetop took up the other. Centered in the middle of it all was a stainless steel island with empty shelves beneath. The rack above it was festooned with metal utensils, pans, and bowls. It was a witch's dream kitchen; I wouldn't have to stir my spells and dinner on the same stove.

Apart from the beat-up wooden table and chairs in the corner, the kitchen looked like one you might see on a cooking show. One end of the table was set up like a computer desk, the wide-screen monitor blinking furiously to itself as it cycled through the open lines to find and claim the best continuous link to the net. It was an expensive program, and my eyebrows rose.

Ivy cleared her throat as she opened a cupboard beside the sink. There were three mismatched mugs on the bottom shelf; other than that, it was empty. "They put in the new kitchen five years ago for the health department," she said, jerking my attention back to her. "The congregation wasn't very big, so when all was said and done, they couldn't afford it. That's why they're renting it out. To try and pay off the bank."

The sound of coffee being poured filled the room as I ran my finger over the unblemished metal on the island counter. It had never seen a single apple pie or Sunday school cookie.

"They want their church back," Ivy said, looking thin as she leaned against the counter with her mug cradled in her pale hands. "But they're dying. The church, I mean," she added as I met her eyes. "No new members. It's sad, really. The living room is back here."

I didn't know what to say, so I kept my mouth shut and followed her into the hallway and through a narrow doorway at the end of the hall. The living room was cozy, and furnished so tastefully that I had no doubt these were all Ivy's things. It was the first softness and warmth I had seen in the entire place—even if everything was in shades of gray—and the windows were just plain glass. Heavenly. I felt my tension loosen. Ivy snatched up a remote, and midnight jazz drifted into existence. Maybe this wouldn't be so bad.

"You almost got tagged?" Ivy tossed the remote onto the coffee table and settled herself in one of the voluptuous gray suede chairs beside the empty fireplace. "Are you all right?"

"Yeah," I admitted sourly, seeming to sink nearly to my ankles in the expansive throw rug. "Is all this your stuff? A guy bumped into me, slipped me a charm that wouldn't invoke until there were no witnesses or causalities—other than me. I can't believe Denon is serious about this. You were right." I worked hard to keep my voice casual so Ivy wouldn't know how shaken I was. Hell, I didn't want to know how shaken I was. I'd get the money to pay off my contract somehow. "It was lucky as toast the old guy across the street took it off me." I picked up a picture of Ivy and a golden retriever. She was smiling to show her teeth; I stifled a shiver.

"What old guy?" Ivy said quickly.

"Across the street. He's been watching you." I set the metal frame down and adjusted the pillow in the chair opposite hers before I sat. Matching furniture; how nice. An old mantel clock ticked, soft and soothing. There was a wide-screen TV with a built-in CD player in one corner. The disc player under it had all the right buttons. Ivy knew her electronics.

"I'll bring my things over once I get them dissolutioned," I said, then winced, thinking how cheap my stuff would look next to hers. "What will survive the dip," I added.

Survive the dip? I thought suddenly, closing my eyes and scrubbing my forehead. "Oh no," I said softly. "I can't dissolution my charms."

Ivy balanced her mug on a knee as she leafed through a magazine. "Hmm?"

"Charms," I half moaned. "The I.S. overlaid black spells on my stash of charms. Dunking them in saltwater to break the spell will ruin them. And I can't buy more." I grimaced at her blank look. "If the I.S. got my apartment, I'm sure they've been to the store, too. I should have brought a bunch yesterday before I quit, but I didn't think they'd care if I left." I listlessly adjusted the shade of the table lamp. They hadn't cared until Ivy had left with me. Depressed, I tossed my head back and looked at the ceiling.

"I thought you already knew how to make spells," Ivy said warily.

"I do, but it's a pain in the butt. And where am I going to get the raw materials?" I closed my eyes in misery. I was going to have to *make* all my charms.

There was a rustle of paper, and I lifted my head to see Ivy perusing her magazine. There was an apple and Snow White on the cover. Snow White's leather corset was cut to show her belly button. A drop of blood glittered like a jewel at the corner of her mouth. It put a whole new twist on the enchanted sleep thing. Mr. Disney would be appalled. Unless, of course, he had been an Inderlander. That would explain a lot.

"You can't just buy what you need?" Ivy asked.

I stiffened at the touch of sarcasm in her voice. "Yeah, but everything will have to be dunked in saltwater to make sure it hasn't been tampered with. It'll be nearly impossible to get rid of all the salt, and that will make the mix wrong."

Jenks buzzed out of the fireplace with a cloud of soot and an irritating whine. I wondered how long he had been listening in the flue. He landed on a box of tissue and cleaned a spot off his wing, looking like a cross between a dragonfly and a miniature cat. "My, aren't we obsessed," he said, answering my question as to whether he had been eavesdropping.

"You have the I.S. trying to nack you with black magic and see if you aren't a little paranoid." Anxious, I thwacked the box he was sitting on until he took to the air.

He hovered between me and Ivy. "Haven't seen the garden yet, have you, Sherlock?"

I threw the pillow at him, which he easily dodged. It knocked the lamp beside Ivy, and she casually reached out and caught it before it hit the floor. She never looked up from her magazine, never spilled a drop of her coffee perched on her knee. The hair on my neck prickled. "Don't call me that, either," I said to cover my unease. He looked positively smug as he hovered before me. "What?" I said snidely. "The garden has more than weeds and dead people?"

"Maybe."

"Really?" This would be the first good thing to happen to me today, and I got up to look out the back door. "Coming?" I asked Ivy as I reached for the handle.

Her head was bent over a page of leather curtains. "No," she said, clearly uninterested.

So it was Jenks who accompanied me out the back door and into the garden. The lowering sun was heady and strong, making the scents clear as it pulled moisture from the damp ground. There was a rowan somewhere. I sniffed deeply. And a birch and oak. What had to be Jenks's kids were darting noisily about, chasing a yellow butterfly over the rising mounds of vegetation. Banks of plants lined the walls of the church and surrounding stone fence. The man-high wall went completely around the property, to tactfully isolate the church from the neighbors.

Another wall low enough to step over separated the garden from the small graveyard. I squinted, seeing a few plants out among the tall grass and headstones, but only those that became more potent growing among the dead. The closer I looked, the more awestruck I became. The garden was complete. Even the rarities were there.

"It's perfect," I whispered, running my fingers through a patch of lemongrass. "Everything I could ever need. How did it all get here?"

Ivy's voice came from right behind me. "According to the old lady—"

"Ivy!" I said, spinning around to see her standing still and quiet on the path in a shaft of late amber sun. "Don't do that!" *Creepy vamp,* I thought. *I ought to put a bell on her.*

She squinted from under her hand, raised against the fading light. "She said their last minister was a witch. He put in the garden. I can get fifty taken off the rent if one of us keeps it up the way it is."

I looked over the treasure trove. "I'll do it."

Jenks flew up from a patch of violets. His purple trousers had pollen stains on them matching his yellow shirt. "Manual labor?" he questioned. "With those nails of yours?"

I glanced at the perfect red ovals my nails made. "This isn't work, this is—therapy."

"Whatever." His attention went to his kids, and he zoomed across the garden to rescue the butterfly they were fighting over.

"Do you think everything you need is here?" Ivy asked as she turned to go inside.

"Just about. You can't spell salt, so my stash is probably okay, but I'll need my good spell pot and all my books."

Ivy paused on the path. "I thought you had to know how to stir a brew by heart to get your witch license."

Now I was embarrassed, and I bent to tug a weed free from beside a rosemary plant. Nobody made their own charms if they could afford to buy them. "Yeah," I said as I dropped the weed, flicking the dirt from under my nails. "But I'm out of practice." I sighed. This was going to be harder than it looked.

Ivy shrugged. "Can you get them off the net? The recipes, I mean."

I looked askance at her. "Trust anything off the net? Oh, there's a good idea."

"There're some books in the attic."

"Sure," I said sarcastically. "One hundred spells for the beginner. Every church has a copy of that."

Ivy stiffened. "Don't get snotty," she said, the brown of her eyes disappearing behind her dilating pupils. "I just thought if one of the clergy was a witch, and the right plants were here, he might have left his books. The old lady said he ran off with one of the younger parishioners. That's probably his stuff in the attic in case he had the guts to come back."

The last thing I wanted was an angry vamp sleeping across the hall. "Sorry," I apologized. "I'll go look. And if I'm lucky, when I go out to the shed to find a saw to cut my amulets, there'll be a bag of salt for when the front steps get icy."

Ivy gave a little start, turning to look at the closet-sized shed. I passed her, pausing on the sill. "Coming? I said, determined not to let her think popping in and out of vamp mode was shaking me. "Or will your owls leave me alone?"

"No, I mean yes." Ivy bit her lip. It was decidedly a human gesture, and my eyebrows rose. "They'll let you up there, just don't go making a lot of noise. I'll—I'll be right there."

"Whatever . . ." I muttered, turning to find my way up to the belfry.

As Ivy had promised, the owls left me alone. It turned out the attic had a copy of everything I had lost in my apartment, and then some. Several of the books were so old they were falling apart. The kitchen had a nest of copper pots, probably used, Ivy had claimed, for chili cook-offs. They were perfect for spell casting, since they hadn't been sealed to reduce tarnish. Finding everything I needed was eerie, so much so that when I went out to look for a saw in the shed, I was relieved to not find any salt. No, that was on the floor of the pantry.

Everything was going too well. Something had to be wrong.

Six

Ankles crossed, I sat atop Ivy's antique kitchen table and swung my feet in their fuzzy pink slippers. The sliced vegetables were cooked to perfection, still crisp and crunchy, and I pushed them around in the little white cardboard box with my chopsticks, looking for more chicken. "This is fantastic," I mumbled around my full mouth. Red tangy spice burned my tongue. My eyes watered. Grabbing the waiting glass of milk, I downed a third of it. "Hot," I said as Ivy glanced up from the box cradled in her long hands. "Cripes, it's really hot."

Ivy arched her thin black eyebrows. "Glad you approve." She was sitting at the table at the spot she had cleared before her computer. Looking into her own take-out box, her wave of black hair fell to make a curtain over her face. She tucked it behind an ear, and I watched the line of her jaw slowly move as she ate.

I had just enough experience with chopsticks to not look like an idiot, but Ivy moved the twin sticks with a slow precision, placing bits of food into her mouth with a rhythmic, somehow erotic, pace. I looked away, suddenly uncomfortable.

"What's it called?" I asked, digging into my paper box.

"Chicken in red curry."

"That's it?" I questioned, and she nodded. I made a small

noise. I could remember that. I found another piece of meat. Curry exploded in my mouth, and I washed it down with a gulp of milk. "Where did you get it?"

"Piscary's."

My eyes widened. Piscary's was a combination pizza den and vamp hangout. Very good food in a rather unique atmosphere. "This came from Piscary's?" I said as I crunched through a bamboo shoot. "I didn't know they delivered anything but pizza."

"They don't—generally."

The throaty pitch of her voice pulled my attention up, to find that she was absorbed in her food. She raised her head at my lack of movement and blinked her almond-shaped eyes at me. "My mother gave him the recipe," she said. "Piscary makes it special for me. It's no big deal."

She went back to eating. A feeling of unease drifted through me, and I listened to the crickets over the twin soft scraping of our sticks. Mr. Fish swam in his bowl on the windowsill. The soft, muted noise of the Hollows at night was almost unheard over the rhythmic thumps of my clothes in the dryer.

I couldn't bear the thought of wearing the same clothes again tomorrow, but Jenks told me it wouldn't be until Sunday that his friend could have my clothes despelled. The best I could do was wash what I had and hope I didn't run into anyone I knew. Right now I was in the nightgown and robe Ivy had lent me. They were black, obviously, but Ivy said the color suited me fine. The faint scent of wood ash on them wasn't unpleasant, but it seemed to cling to me.

My gaze went to the empty spot above the sink where a clock should be. "What time do you think it is?"

"A little after three," Ivy said, not glancing at her watch.

I dug around, sighing when I realized I had eaten all the pineapple. "I wish my clothes would get done. I am so tired."

Ivy crossed her legs and leaned over her dinner. "Go ahead. I'll get them out for you. I'll be up until five or so."

"No, I'll stay up." I yawned, covering my mouth with the back of my hand. "It isn't like I have to get up and go to work tomorrow," I finished sourly. A small noise of agreement came from Ivy, and my digging about in my dinner slowed. "Ivy, you can tell me to back off if it's none of my business, but why did you join the I.S. if you didn't want to work for them?"

She seemed surprised as she looked up. In a flat voice that spoke volumes, she said, "I did it to tick my mother off." A flicker of what looked like pain flashed over her, vanishing before I could be sure it existed. "My dad isn't pleased I quit," she added. "He told me I should have either stuck it out or killed Denon."

Dinner forgotten, I stared, not knowing if I was more surprised at learning her father was still alive or at his rather creative advice on how to get ahead at the office. "Uh, Jenks said you were the last living member of your house," I finally said.

Ivy's head moved in a slow, controlled nod. Brown eyes watching me, she moved her chopsticks between the box and her lips in a slow dance. The subtle display of sensuality took me aback, and I shifted uneasily on my perch on the table. She had never been this bad when we had worked together. Of course, we usually quit work before midnight.

"My dad married into the family," she said between dips into the box, and I wondered if she knew how provocative she looked. "I'm the last living blood member of my house. Because of the prenuptial, my mother's money is all mine, or it was. She is as mad as all hell I quit. She wants me to find a nice, living, high-blood vamp, settle down, and pop out as many kids as I can to be sure her living bloodline doesn't die out. She'll kill me if I croak before having a kid."

I nodded as if I understood, but I didn't. "I joined because of my dad," I admitted. Embarrassed, I put my attention into my dinner. "He worked for the I.S. in the arcane division.

He'd come home every morning with these wild stories of people he had helped or tagged. He made it sound so exciting." I snickered. "He never mentioned the paperwork. When he died, I thought it would be a way to get close to him, sort of remember him by. Stupid, isn't it?"

"No."

I looked up, crunching through a carrot. "I had to do something. I spent a year watching my mother fall off her rocker. She isn't crazy, but it's like she doesn't want to believe he's gone. You can't talk to her without her saying something like, 'I made banana pudding today; it was your father's favorite.' She knows he's dead, but she can't let him go."

Ivy was staring out the black kitchen window and into a memory. "My dad's like that. He spends all his time keeping my mother going. I hate it."

My chewing slowed. Not many vamps could afford to remain alive after death. The elaborate sunlight precautions and liability insurance alone was enough to put most families on the street. Not to mention the continuous supply of fresh blood.

"I hardly ever see him," she added, her voice a whisper. "I don't understand it, Rachel. He has his entire life left, but he won't let her get the blood she needs from anyone else. If he's not with her, he's passed out on the floor from blood loss. Keeping her from dying completely is killing him. One person alone can't support a dead vampire. They both know that."

The conversation had taken an uncomfortable turn, but I couldn't just leave. "Maybe he's doing it because he loves her?" I offered slowly.

Ivy frowned. "What kind of love is that?" She stood, her long legs unfolding in a slow graceful movement. Cardboard box in hand, she vanished into the hall.

The sudden silence hammered on my ears. I stared at her empty chair in surprise. She walked out. How could she just walk out? We were talking. The conversation was too interesting to drop, so I slid from the table and followed her into the living room with my dinner.

She had collapsed into one of the gray suede chairs, sprawled out in a look of total unconcern, with her head on one of the thick arms and her feet dangling over the other. I hesitated in the doorway, taken aback at the picture she made. Like a lioness in her den, satiated from the kill. *Well,* I thought, *she is a vampire.* What did I expect her to look like?

Reminding myself that she wasn't a practicing vamp and that I had nothing to worry about, I cautiously settled in the chair across from her, the coffee table between us. Only one of the table lamps was on, and the edges of the room were indistinct and lost in shadow. The lights from her electronic equipment glowed. "So, joining the I.S. was your dad's idea?" I prompted.

Ivy had set her little white cardboard box atop her stomach. Not meeting my gaze, she lay on her back and indolently ate a bamboo shoot, looking at the ceiling as she chewed. "It was my mother's idea, originally. She wanted me to be in management." Ivy took another bite. "I was supposed to stay nice and safe. She thought it would be good for me to work on my people skills." She shrugged. "I wanted to be a runner."

I kicked off my slippers and tucked my feet under me. Curled up around my take-out box, I flicked a glance at Ivy as she slowly pulled her chopsticks out from between her lips. Most of the upper management in the I.S. were undead. I always thought it was because the job was easier if you didn't have a soul.

"It wasn't as if she could stop me," Ivy continued, talking to the ceiling. "So to punish me for doing what I wanted instead of what she wanted, she made sure Denon was my boss." A snicker escaped her. "She thought I'd get so ticked that I'd jump to a management position as soon as one opened up. She never considered I'd trade my inheritance to get out of my contract. I guess I showed her," she said sarcastically.

I shuffled past a tiny corncob to get to a chunk of tomato. "You threw away all your money because you didn't like your boss? I don't like him, either, but—"

Ivy stiffened. The force of her gaze struck me cold. My words froze in my throat at the hatred in her expression. "Denon is a ghoul," Ivy said, her words drawing the warmth from the room. "If I had to take his flack for one more day, I was going to rip his throat out."

I hesitated. "A ghoul?" I said, confused. "I thought he was a vamp."

"He is." When I said nothing, she swung herself upright to put her boots on the floor. "Look," she said, sounding bothered. "You must have noticed Denon doesn't look like a vamp. His teeth are human, right? He can't maintain an aura at noon? And he moves so loud you can hear him coming a mile away?"

"I'm not blind, Ivy."

She cradled her white paperboard box and stared at me. The night air coming in through the window was chilly for late spring, and I drew her robe tighter about my shoulders.

"Denon was bitten by an undead, so he has the vampire virus in him," Ivy continued. "That lets him do a few tricks and makes him real pretty, and I imagine he's as scary as all hell if you let him bully you, but he's someone's lackey, Rachel. He's a toy and always will be."

There was a small scrape as she put her white box on the coffee table between us and edged forward to the end of her chair so she could reach it. "Even if he dies and someone bothers to turn him into an undead, he'll be second-class," she said. "Look at his eyes next time you see him. He's afraid. Every time he lets a vamp feed on him, he has to trust that they'll bring him back as an undead if they lose control and accidentally kill him." She took a slow breath. "He should be afraid."

The red curry went tasteless. Heart pounding, I searched

her gaze, praying it would just be Ivy staring back at me. Her eyes were still brown, but something was in them. Something old that I didn't understand. My stomach clenched, and I was suddenly unsure of myself. "Don't be afraid of ghouls like Denon," she whispered. I thought her words were meant to be soothing, but they tightened my skin until it tingled. "There are a lot more dangerous things to be afraid of."

Like you? I thought, but didn't say it. Her sudden air of repressed predator set off alarm bells in my head. I thought I should get up and leave. Get my scrawny witch butt back in the kitchen where it belonged. But she had eased herself back into her chair with her dinner, and I didn't want her to know she was scaring the crap out of me. It wasn't as if I hadn't seen Ivy go vampy before. Just not after midnight. In her living room. Alone.

"Things like your mother?" I said, hoping I hadn't gone too far.

"Things like my mother," she breathed. "That's why I'm living in a church."

My thoughts went to my tiny cross on my new bracelet with the rest of my charms. It never failed to impress me that something so small could stop so powerful a force. It wouldn't slow a living vamp down at all—only the undead—but I'd take whatever protection I could get.

Ivy put her boot heels on the edge of the coffee table. "My mother has been a true undead for the last ten years or so," she said, startling me from my dark thoughts. "I hate it."

Surprised, I couldn't help but ask, "Why?"

She pushed her dinner away in what was obviously a gesture of unease. There was a frightening emptiness in her face, and she wouldn't meet my gaze. "I was eighteen when my mother died," she whispered. Her voice was distant, as if she wasn't aware she was even talking.

"She lost something, Rachel. When you can't walk under the sun, you lose something so nebulous, you can't even say for sure what it is. But it's gone. It's as if she's stuck following a pattern of behavior but can't remember why. She still loves me, but she doesn't remember why she loves me. The only thing that brings any life to her is the taking of blood, and she's so damned savage about it. When she's sated, I can almost see my mother in what's left of her. But it doesn't last. It's never enough."

Ivy looked up from under her lowered brow. "You do have a crucifix, don't you?"

"Right here," I said with forced brightness. I wouldn't let her know she was putting me on edge; I wouldn't. Holding up my hand, I gave it a little shake so the robe's sleeve fell to my elbow to show my new charm bracelet.

Ivy put her boots on the floor. I relaxed at the less provocative position until she leaned halfway over the coffee table. Her hand went out with an unreal quickness, gripping my wrist before I knew she had moved. I froze, very aware of the warmth of her fingers. She studied the wood-inlaid metal charm intently as I fought the urge to pull away. "Is it blessed?" she asked.

Face cold, I nodded, and she released me, easing back with an eerie slowness. It seemed I could still feel her grip on me, an imprisoning firmness that wouldn't tighten unless I pulled away. "Mine, too," she said, drawing her cross out from behind her shirt.

Impressed anew with her crucifix, I set aside my dinner and scooted forward. I couldn't help but reach out for it. The tooled silver begged to be touched, and she leaned across the table so I could bring it closer. Ancient runes were etched into it, along with the more traditional blessings. It was beautiful, and I wondered how old it was.

Suddenly, I realized Ivy's warm breath was on my cheek.

I sat back, her cross still in my hand. Her eyes were dark and her face blank. There was nothing there. Frightened, I flicked my gaze from her to the cross. I couldn't just drop it. It would smack her right in the chest. But I couldn't set it gently down against her, either.

"Here," I said, terribly uncomfortable at her blank stare. "Take it."

Ivy reached out, her fingers grazing mine as she grasped the old metal. Swallowing hard, I scooted back into my chair and adjusted Ivy's robe to cover my legs.

Moving with a provocative slowness, Ivy took her cross off. The silver chain caught against the black sheen of her hair. She pulled her hair free, and it fell back in a cascading shimmer. She set the cross on the table between us. The click of the metal meeting the wood was loud. Eyes unblinking, she curled up in her chair opposite mine with her feet tucked under her and stared at me.

Holy crap, I thought in a sudden wash of understanding and panic. She was coming on to me. That's what was going on. How blind could I be?

My jaw clenched as my mind raced to find a way out of this. I was straight. Never a thought contrary to that. I liked my men taller than me and not so strong that I couldn't pin them to the floor in a surge of passion if I wanted. "Um, Ivy . . ." I started.

"I was born a vampire," Ivy stated softly.

Her gray voice ran down my spine, shutting off my throat. Breath held, I met the black of her eyes. I didn't say anything, afraid it might trigger her into movement, and I desperately didn't want her to move. Something had shifted, and I wasn't sure what was going on anymore.

"Both of my parents are vampires," she said, and though she didn't move, I felt the tension in the room swell until I couldn't hear the crickets. "I was conceived and born before my mother became a true undead. Do you know what that means—Rachel?" Her words were slow and precise, falling from her lips with the soft permanence of whispered psalms.

"No," I said, hardly breathing.

Ivy tilted her head so her hair made an obsidian wave that glistened in the low light. She watched me from around it. "The virus didn't have to wait until I was dead before shaping me," she said. "It molded me as I grew in my mother's womb, giving me a little of both worlds, the living and the dead."

Her lips parted, and I shuddered at the sight of her sharp teeth. I hadn't meant to. Sweat broke out on the small of my back, and as if in response, Ivy took a breath and held it. "It's easy for me to pull an aura," she said as she exhaled. "Actually, the trick is to keep it suppressed."

She uncurled from her chair, and my breath hissed in through my nose. Ivy jerked at the sound. Slow and methodical, she put her boots on the floor. "And although my reflexes and strength aren't as good as a true undead, they're better than yours," she said.

I knew all of this, and the question of why she was telling me increased my fear tenfold. Struggling not to show my alarm, I refused to shrink backward as she put her palms flat on the table to either side of her cross and leaned forward.

"What's more, I'm guaranteed to become an undead, even if I die alone in a field with every last drop of blood inside me. No worries, Rachel. I'm eternal already. Death will only make me stronger."

My heart pounded. I couldn't look away from her eyes. Damn. This was more than I wanted to know.

"And you know the best part?" she asked.

I shook my head, afraid my voice would crack. I was walking a knife edge, wanting to know what kind of a world she lived in but fighting to keep from entering it.

Her eyes grew fervent. Torso unmoving, she levered one of her knees up onto the coffee table, and then the other. God help me. She was coming at me.

"Living vamps can bespell people—if they want to be," she whispered. The softness of her voice rubbed against my skin until it tingled. Double damn.

"What good is it if it only works on those who let you?" I asked, my voice harsh next to the liquid essence of hers.

Ivy's lips parted to show the tips of her teeth. I couldn't look away. "It makes for great sex—Rachel."

"Oh." The faint utterance was all I could manage. Her eyes were lost in lust.

"And I've got my mother's taste for blood," she said, kneeling on the table between us. "It's like some people's craving for sugar. It's not a good comparison but it's the best I can do unless you . . . try it."

Ivy exhaled, moving her entire body. Her breath sent a shock reverberating through me. My eyes went wide in surprise and bewilderment as I recognized it as desire. What the hell was going on? I was straight. Why did I suddenly want to know how soft her hair was?

All I'd have to do was reach out. She was inches from me. Poised. Waiting. In the silence, I could hear my heart pound. The sound of it echoed in my ears. I watched in horror as Ivy broke her gaze from mine, running it down my throat to where I knew my pulse throbbed.

"No!" I cried, panicking.

I kicked out, gasping in fear as I found her weight on me, pinning me to the chair.

"Ivy, no!" I shrieked. I had to get her off. I struggled to move. I took a lungful of air, hearing it explode from me in a cry of helplessness. How could I have been so stupid! She was a vampire!

"Rachel—stop."

Her voice was calm and smooth. Her one hand gripped my hair, pinning my head back to expose my neck. It hurt, and I heard myself whimper.

"You're making things worse," she said, and I wiggled, gasping as her grip on my wrist tightened until it hurt.

"Let me go. . . ." I panted, breathless, as if I had been running. "God, help me, Ivy. Let me go. Please. I don't want this." I was pleading. I couldn't help it. I was terrified. I'd seen the pictures. It hurt. God, it was going to hurt.

"Stop," she said again. Her voice was strained. "Rachel. I'm trying to let go of you, but you have to stop. You're making things worse. You have to believe me."

I took a gasping breath and held it. I flicked my gaze at what I could see of her. Her mouth was inches from my ear. Her eyes were black, the hunger in them a frightening contrast to the calm sound of her voice. Her gaze was fixed to my neck. A drop of saliva dropped warm onto my skin. "God, no," I whispered, shuddering.

Ivy quivered, her body trembling where it touched mine. "Rachel. Stop," she said again, and terror swept me at the new edge of panic in it. My breath came in a ragged pant. She really was trying to get off me. And by the sound of it, she was losing the battle.

"What do I do?" I whispered.

"Close your eyes," she said. "I need your help. I didn't know it was going to be this hard."

My mouth went dry at the little-lost-girl sound of her voice. It took all my will to close my eyes.

"Don't move."

Her voice was gray silk. Tension slammed through me. Nausea gripped my stomach. I could feel my pulse pushing against my skin. For what felt like a full minute I lay under her, all my instincts crying out to flee. The crickets chirped, and I felt tears slip from under my fluttering eyelids as her breath came and went on my exposed neck.

I cried out when her grip on my hair loosened. My breath came in a ragged gasp as her weight lifted from me. I couldn't smell her anymore. I froze, unmoving. "Can I open my eyes?" I whispered.

There was no answer.

I sat up to find myself alone. There was the faintest sound of the sanctuary door closing and the fast cadence of her boots on the sidewalk, then nothing. Numb and shaken, I reached up to first wipe my eyes and then my neck, smearing her saliva into a cold spot. My eyes rove over the room, finding no warmth in the soft gray. She was gone.

Drained, I stood up, not knowing what to do. I clutched my arms about myself so tight it hurt. My thoughts went back to the terror, and before that, the flash of desire that had washed through me, potent and heady. She had said she could only bespell the willing. Had she lied to me, or had I really wanted her to pin me to the chair and rip open my throat?

Seven

The sun was no longer slanting into the kitchen, but it was still warm. Not warm enough to reach the core of my soul, but nice. I was alive. I had all my body parts and fluids intact. It was a good afternoon.

I was sitting at the uncluttered end of Ivy's table, studying the most battered book I had found in the attic. It looked old enough to have been printed before the Civil War. Some of the spells I'd never heard of. It made for fascinating reading, and I would admit the chance to try one or two of them filled me with a dangerous titillation. None even hinted at the dark arts, which pleased me to no end. Harming someone with magic was foul and wrong. It went against everything I believed in—and it wasn't worth the risk.

All magic required a price paid by death in various shades of severity. I was strictly an earth witch. My source of power came gently from the earth through plants and was quickened by heat, wisdom, and witch blood. As I dealt only in white magic, the cost was paid by ending the life of plants. I could live with that. I wasn't going to delve into the morality of killing plants, otherwise I'd go insane every time I cut my mom's lawn. That wasn't to say that there weren't black earth witches—there were—but black earth magic had nasty ingredients like body parts and sacrifices. Just gathering the materials needed to stir a black spell was enough to keep most earth witches white.

Ley line witches, however, were another story. They drew their power right from the source, raw and unfiltered through living things. They, too, required death, but it was a subtler death—the slow death of the soul, and it wasn't necessarily theirs. The soul-death needed by white ley line witches wasn't as severe as that required by black witches, going back to the cutting the grass analogy vs. slaughtering goats in your basement. But creating a powerful spell designed to harm or kill left a definite wound on one's being.

Black ley line witches got around that by fostering that payment onto someone else, usually attaching it right on the charm to give the receiver a double whammy of back luck. But if the person was insanely "pure of spirit" or more powerful, the cost, though not the charm, came right back to the maker. It was said that enough black on one's soul made it easy for a demon to pull you involuntarily into the ever-after.

Just as my dad had been, I thought as I rubbed my thumb against the page before me. I knew with all my being that he had been a white witch to the end. He would have had to be able to find his way back into reality, even though he didn't last to see the next sunrise.

A small sound jerked my attention up. I stiffened upon finding Ivy in a black silk robe, slumped against the doorframe. The memory of last night washed through me, knotting my stomach. I couldn't stop my hand from creeping up to my neck, and I changed the motion to adjusting my earring as I pretended to study the book before me. "'Morning," I said cautiously.

"What time is it?" Ivy asked in a ragged whisper.

I flicked a glance at her. Her usually smooth hair was rumpled, waves from her pillow creasing it. Her eyes had dark circles under them, and her oval face was slack. Early afternoon lassitude had completely overwhelmed her air of stalking predator. She held a slim leather-bound book in her hand, and I wondered if her night had been as sleepless as mine.

"It's almost two," I said warily as I used a foot to push out a chair across the table from me so she wouldn't sit beside me. She seemed all right, but I didn't know how to treat her anymore. I was wearing my crucifix—not that it would stop her—and my silver ankle knife—which wasn't much better. A sleep amulet would drop her, but they were in my bag, sitting out of easy reach on a chair. It would take a good five seconds to invoke one. In all honesty, though, she didn't look like much of a threat right now.

"I made muffins," I said. "They were your groceries. I hope you don't mind."

"Uh," she said, shuffling across the shiny floor to the coffeepot in her black slippers. She poured herself a cup of lukewarm brew, leaning back against the counter to sip it. Her wish was gone from around her neck. I wondered what she had wished for. I wondered if it had anything to do with last night. "You're dressed," she whispered as she slumped into the chair I had kicked out for her in front of her computer. "How long have you been up?"

"Noon." *Liar*, I thought. I'd been up all night pretending to sleep on Ivy's couch. I decided to officially start my day when I put my clothes back on. Ignoring her, I turned a yellowing page. "Spent your wish, I see," I murmured cautiously. "What was it?"

"None of your business," she said, the warning obvious.

My breath left me in a slow exhalation, and I kept my eyes lowered. An uncomfortable silence descended and I let it grow, refusing to break it. I had almost left last night. But the certain death waiting for me outside Ivy's protection outweighed the possible death at Ivy's hands. Maybe. Maybe I wanted to know what it felt like for her teeth to sink into me.

This was *not* where I wanted my thoughts to go. Ivy had scared the crap out of me, but seeing her in the bright light of post noon, she looked human. Harmless. Dare I say, a grump?

"I have something I want you to read," she said, and I looked up as the thin book she had been holding hit the table between us. There was nothing written on the cover, the embossing almost completely worn away.

"What is it?" I said flatly, not reaching for it.

Eyes dropping, she licked her lips. "I'm sorry about last night," she said, and my gut tightened. "You probably won't believe me, but it scared me, too."

"Not as much as you scared me." Working with her for a year hadn't prepared me for last night. I'd only seen her professional side. I hadn't considered she was different away from the office. I flicked my eyes up at her and away. She looked entirely human. Neat trick, that.

"I haven't been a practicing vamp for three years," she said softly. "I wasn't prepared for . . . I didn't realize—" She looked up, her brown eyes pleading. "You have to believe me, Rachel. I didn't want that to happen. It's just that you were sending me all wrong signals. And then you got frightened, and then you panicked, and then it got worse."

"Worse?" I said, deciding anger was better than fear. "You nearly ripped out my throat!"

"I know," she implored. "I'm sorry. But I didn't."

I fought to keep from shuddering as I remembered the warmth of her saliva on my neck.

She nudged the book closer. "I know we can avoid a repeat of last night. I want this to work. There's no reason it can't. I owe you something for taking one of your wishes. If you leave, I can't protect you against the vamp assassins. You don't want to die at their hands."

My jaw clenched. No. I didn't want to die at the hands of a vampire. Especially one who would say she was sorry while killing me.

I met her gaze across the cluttered table. She sat in her black robe and kick-off slippers, looking as dangerous as a sponge. Her need for me to accept her apology was so raw and obvious, it was painful. I couldn't do it. Not yet. I reached a finger out to pull the book closer. "What is it?"

"A—uh—dating guide?" she said hesitantly.

I took a quick breath and drew my hand back as if stung. "Ivy. No."

"Wait," she said. "That's not what I mean. You're giving

me mixed signals. My head knows you don't mean it, but my instincts . . ." Her brow furrowed. "It's embarrassing, but vampires, whether living or dead, are driven by instincts triggered mostly by . . . smell?" she finished apologetically. "Just read up on the turn-ons, okay? And don't do them."

I settled back into my chair. Slowly, I pulled the book closer, seeing how old it was by the binding. She had said instincts, but I thought hunger was more accurate. It was only the realization of how hard it had been for her to admit that she could be manipulated by something as stupid as smell that kept me from throwing the book back in her face. Ivy prided herself on her control, and to have confessed such a weakness to me told me more than a hundred apologies that she was really sorry. "All right," I said flatly, and she gave me a relieved, closed-lipped smile.

She took a muffin and pulled the evening edition of the *Cincinnati Enquirer* that I had found against the front door to her. The air was still tense, but it was a start. I didn't want to leave the security of the church, but Ivy's protection was a double-edged sword. She had bottled up her blood lust for three years. If she broke, I might be just as dead.

" 'Councilman Trenton Kalamack blames I.S. negligence in secretary's death,' " she read, clearly trying to change the subject.

"Yeah," I said cautiously. I put her book in the pile with my spell books to read later. My fingers felt dirty, and I wiped them on my jeans. "Ain't money grand? There's another story of him being cleared of all suspicion of dealing in Brimstone."

She said nothing, turning pages between bites of muffin until she found the article. "Listen to this," she said softly. "He says, 'I was shocked to learn of Mrs. Bates's second life. She seemed the model employee. I will, of course, pay for her surviving son's education.' " Ivy gave a short snort of mirthless laughter. "Typical." She turned to the comics. "So will you be spell crafting today?"

I shook my head. "I'm going to the records vault before

they close for the weekend. This," I flicked a finger at the paper, "is useless. I want to see what really happened."

Ivy set down her muffin, thin eyebrows high in question.

"If I can prove Trent is dealing in Brimstone and give him to the I.S.," I said, "they'll forget about my contract. They have a standing warrant for him." *And then I can get the hell out of this church,* I added silently.

"Prove Trent runs Brimstone?" Ivy scoffed. "They can't even prove if he's human or Inderlander. His money makes him slipperier than frog spit in a rainstorm. Money can't buy innocence, but it can buy silence." She picked at her muffin. Dressed in her robe and with her sloppy hair, she could have been any of my sporadic roommates over the past years. It was unnerving. Everything changed when the sun was up.

"These are good," Ivy said as she held up a muffin. "Tell you what. I'll buy groceries if you make dinner. Breakfast and lunch I can get on my own, but I don't like cooking."

I made a face in understanding and agreement—I didn't appreciate the finer arts of culinary expertise, either—but then I thought about it. It would take up my time, but not having to go to the store sounded great. Even if Ivy only offered so I wouldn't have to put my life on the line for a can of beans, it sounded fair. I'd be cooking either way, and cooking for two was easier than cooking for one. "Sure," I said slowly. "We can try it for a while."

She made a soft noise. "It's a deal."

I glanced at my watch. It was one-forty. My chair squeaked across the linoleum as I stood up and grabbed a muffin. "Well, I'm out of here. I've got to get a car or something. This bus thing is awful."

Ivy laid out the comics atop the clutter surrounding her computer. "The I.S. isn't going to let you just walk in."

"They have to. Public record. And no one's going to tag me with a bunch of witnesses they will have to pay off. Cuts into their profits," I finished bitterly.

The arch to Ivy's eyebrows said more clearly than words she wasn't convinced.

"Look," I said as I pulled my bag from atop a chair and sorted through it. "I was going to use a disguise spell, all right? And I'll leave at the first sign of trouble."

The amulet I waved in the air seemed to satisfy her, but as she went back to her comics, she muttered, "Take Jenks with you?"

It really wasn't a question, and I grimaced. "Yeah. Sure." I knew he was a babysitter, but as I poked my head out the back door and yelled for him, I decided it would be nice having the company, even if it was a pixy.

Eight

I scrunched deeper into the corner of the bus seat, trying to make sure no one could look over my shoulder. The bus was crowded, and I didn't want anyone to know what I was reading.

"If your vampire lover is sated and won't be stirred," I read, "try wearing something of his or hers. It needn't be much, perhaps as little as a handkerchief or tie. The smell of your sweat mingling is something even the most restrained vampire can't resist."

Okay. Don't wear Ivy's robe or nightgown anymore.

"Often the mere washing of your clothes together leaves enough of a scent to let your lover know you care."

Fine. Separate loads.

"If your vampire lover moves to a more private location in the middle of a conversation, be assured that he or she isn't spurning you. It's an invitation. Go all out. Take some food or drink with you to get the jaws loosened up and the saliva moving. Don't be a flirt. Red wine is passé. Try an apple or something equally crunchy."

Damn.

"Not all vampires are alike. Find out if your lover likes pillow talk. Foreplay can take many forms. A conversation about past ties and bloodlines is sure to strike a chord and stir pride unless your lover is from a secondary house."

Double damn. I was a harlot. I was a freaking vampire hussy.

Eyes closed, I let my head fall against the back of the seat. A warm breath tickled my neck. I jerked upright, spinning. The heel of my hand was already in motion. It smacked into the palm of an attractive man. He laughed at the resounding pop, raising his hands in placation. But it was the soft, speculative amusement in his eyes that stopped me.

"Have you tried page forty-nine?" he asked, leaning forward to rest his crossed arms on the back of my seat.

I stared blankly at him, and his smile grew seductive. He was almost too pretty, his smooth features holding a child-like eagerness. His gaze slipped to the book in my hand. "Forty-nine," he repeated, his words dropping in pitch. "You'll never be the same."

On edge, I flipped to the right page. Oh—my—God. Ivy's book was illustrated. But then I hesitated, squinting as I became confused. Was there a third person in there? And what the hell was that bolted to the wall?

"This way," the man said, reaching over the seat and turning the book sideways in my grip. His cologne was woodsy and clean. It was as nice as his easy voice and soft hand intentionally brushing mine. He was the classic vampire flunky: nice build, dressed in black, and a frightening need to be liked. Not to mention his lack of understanding personal space.

I tore my gaze from his when he tapped the book. "Oh," I said, as it suddenly made sense. "Oh!" I exclaimed, warming as I slammed the book shut. There were two people. Three if you count the one with the . . . whatever it was.

My eyes rose to his. "You survived that?" I asked, not sure if I should be appalled, horrified, or impressed.

His gaze went almost reverent. "Yeah. I couldn't move my legs for two weeks, but it was worth it."

Heart pounding, I shoved the book into my bag. He rose with a charming smile and ambled forward to get off. I couldn't help but notice that he limped. I was surprised he could walk. He watched me as he descended the stairs, his deep eyes never leaving mine.

Swallowing hard, I forced myself to look away. Curiosity got the better of me, and even before the last of the people had gotten off the bus, I had pulled Ivy's book back out. My fingers were cold as I thumbed it open. I ignored the picture, reading the small print under the cheerful "How to" instructions. My face went cold and my stomach knotted.

It was a warning to not allow your vampire lover to coerce you into it until you had been bit at least three times. Otherwise, there might not be enough vamp saliva in your system to overwhelm the pain receptors, fooling your brain into thinking pain was pleasure. There were even instructions on how to keep from passing out if you indeed didn't have enough vamp saliva and you found yourself in agonizing pain. Apparently if the blood pressure dropped, so did the enjoyment of your vampire lover. Nothing on how to get him or her to stop, though.

Eyes closing, I let my head thump against the window. The chatter of the oncoming passengers pulled my eyes open, and I blinked as my gaze went to the sidewalk. The man was standing there, watching me. I clasped an arm about myself, chilled. He was smiling as if his groin hadn't been delicately incised and his blood pulled from him and consumed as if in communion. He had enjoyed it, or at least he thought he had.

He held up three fingers in the Boy Scout's salute, touched the tips of them to his lips, and blew me a kiss. The bus jerked into motion, and he walked away, the hem of his duster swinging.

Staring out the window, I felt nausated. Had Ivy ever been a part of something like that? Maybe she had accidentally killed someone. Maybe that's why she wasn't practicing anymore. Maybe I should ask her. Maybe I should keep my mouth shut so I could sleep at night.

Closing the book, I pushed it to the bottom of my bag, starting as I found a slip of paper slid between the pages with a phone number on it. Crumpling it, I shoved it and the book in my bag. I looked up to see Jenks flitting back from where he had been talking with the driver.

He landed on the back of the seat in front of me. Apart from a gaudy red belt, he was wearing head-to-toe black: his work clothes. "No spells aimed at you on the new riders," he said cheerfully. "What did that guy want?"

"Nothing." I pushed the memory of that picture out of my mind. Where was Jenks last night when Ivy had pinned me? That's what I wanted to know. I would have asked him but was afraid he might tell me last night had been my fault.

"No, really," Jenks insisted. "What did he want?"

I stared at him. "No, really. Nothing. Now, drop it," I said, thankful I was already under my disguise spell. I did *not* want Mr. Page Forty-nine recognizing me on the street at some future date.

"All right, all right," he said, darting to land on my earring. He was humming "Strangers in the Night," and I sighed, knowing the song would be running in my head for the rest of the day. I pulled out my hand mirror and pretended to primp my hair, careful to whack the earring Jenks was sitting on at least twice.

I was a brunette now, with a big nose. A rubber band held my now brown hair back in a ponytail. It was still long and frizzy. Some things are harder to spell than others. My jeans jacket was turned inside out to show a flowered paisley. I had a leather Harley-Davidson cap on. I'd be giving it back to Ivy with many apologies as soon as I saw her, and would never wear it again. With all the no-no's I'd pulled last night, it was no wonder Ivy had lost it.

The bus entered the shadow of tall buildings. My stop was next, and I gathered my things and stood. "I've got to get some transportation," I said to Jenks as my boots hit the sidewalk and I scanned the street. "Maybe a bike," I grumbled, timing it so I didn't have to touch the glass-paneled door to enter the lobby of the I.S. records building.

From my earring came a snort. "I wouldn't," he advised.

"It's too easy to tamper with a motorbike. Stick with public transport."

"I could park it inside," I protested, nervously eyeing the few people in the small foyer.

"Then you couldn't ride it, Sherlock," he said sarcastically. "Your boot is untied."

I looked down. It wasn't. "Very funny, Jenks."

The pixy muttered something I couldn't hear. "No," he said impatiently. "I meant, pretend to tie your boot while I see if you're passably safe."

"Oh." I obediently went to a corner chair and retied my boot. I could hardly track Jenks as he hovered over the few runners that were about, sniffing for spells aimed at me. My timing had been precise. It was Saturday. The vault was open only as a courtesy, and only for a few hours. Still, a few people were about: dropping off information, updating files, copying stuff, trying to make a good impression by working on the weekend.

"Smells okay," Jinks said as he returned. "I don't think they expected you to come here."

"Good." Feeling more confident than I had any right to, I strode to the front desk. I was in luck. Megan was working. I gave her a smile and her eyes widened. She quickly reached to adjust her glasses. The wood-framed spectacles were spelled to see through almost everything. Standard issue for I.S. receptionists. There was a blur of motion before me, and I jerked to a halt.

"Heads up, woman!" Jenks shouted, but it was too late. Someone brushed against me. Instinct alone kept me standing as a foot slipped between my feet to trip me up. Panicked, I spun around into a crouch. My face went cold as I landed, ready for anything.

It was Francis. *What the Turn was he doing here?* I thought, rising to a stand as he held a hand to his stomach and laughed at me. I should have ditched my bag. But I hadn't expected to see anyone who knew me under my disguise charm.

"Nice hat, Rachel," Francis all but whined as he flicked the collar of his loud shirt back up. His tone was a disgusting mix of bravado and fading fright at me having nearly attacked him. "Hey, I bought six squares in the office pool yesterday. Is there any way you could die tomorrow between seven and midnight?"

"Why don't you tag me yourself?" I said with a sneer. Either the man had no pride or he didn't realize how ridiculous he looked, standing with one of his boat shoes untied and his stringy hair falling out of the spell-enhanced wave. And how could he have a stubble that thick this early in the day? He must have spray-painted it on.

"If I tagged you myself, I'd lose." Francis adopted his more usual air of superiority, a look entirely wasted on me. "I don't have time to talk with a dead witch," he said. "I have an appointment with Councilman Trenton Kalamack and need to do some research. You know, research? Ever done any of that?" He sniffed through his thin nose. "Not that I've heard."

"Go stuff a tomato, *Francis*," I said softly.

He glanced down the hall that led to the vault. "Ooooh," he drawled. "I'm scared. You'd better leave now if you want any chance of getting back to your church alive. If Meg didn't trip the alarm that you're here, I will."

"Quit screaming into my jazz," I said. "You're really starting to tick me off."

"See you later, Rachel-me-gal. Like in the obituaries." His laugh was too high-pitched.

I gave him a withering look, and he signed the log-in book before Megan with a flourish. He turned and mouthed, "Run, witch. Run." Pulling out his cell phone, he punched a few buttons and strutted past the VIP's dark offices to the vault. Megan winced apologetically as she buzzed him through the gate.

My eyes closed in a long blink. When I opened them, I gave Megan a wave to say, "Just a minute," and sat in one of the lobby's chairs to dig in my bag as if looking for something. Jenks landed on my earring. "Let's go," he said, sounding worried. "We'll come back tonight."

"Yeah," I agreed. Denon spelling my apartment had been simple harassment. Sending an assassin team would be too expensive. I wasn't worth it. But why take chances?

"Jenks," I whispered. "Can you get in the vault without the cameras seeing you?"

"'Course I can, woman. Sneaking around is what pixies do best. 'Can I get past the cameras?' she asks. Who do you think does the maintenance on them? I'll tell you. Pixies. And do we ever get an ounce of credit? No-o-o-o-o. It's the lunker of a repairman who sits on his lard-butt at the bottom of the ladder, who drives the truck, who opens the toolbox, who scarfs down the doughnuts. But does he ever *do* anything? No-o-o-o-o—"

"That's great, Jenks. Shut up and listen." I glanced at Megan. "Go see what records Francis looks at. I'll wait for you as long as I can, but if there's any sign of a threat, I'm leaving. You can get home from here all right, can't you?"

Jenks's wings made a breeze, shifting a strand of hair to tickle my neck. "Yeah, I can do that. You want I should pix him for you while I'm in there?"

My eyebrows rose. "Pix him? You can do that? I thought it was a—uh—fairy tale."

He hovered before me, his small features smug. "I'll give him the itch. It's what pixies do second best." He hesitated, grinning roguishly. "No, make that third."

"Why not?" I said with a sigh, and he silently rose on his dragonfly wings, studying the cameras. He hung for a moment to time their sweep. Shooting straight up to the ceiling, he arched down the long hallway, past the offices and to the vault's door. If I hadn't been watching, I'd never have seen him go.

I pulled a pen out of my bag, tugged the tie closed, and strode to Megan. The massive mahogany desk completely separated the lobby from the unseen grunt offices behind it. It was the final bastion between the public and the nitty-gritty workforce that kept the records straight. The sound of a female voice raised in laughter filtered out through the open archway behind Megan. No one did much work on Saturday. "Hi, Meg," I said as I drew closer.

"Good afternoon, Ms. Morgan," she said overly loudly as she adjusted her glasses.

Her attention was fixed over my shoulder, and I fought the urge to turn around. *Ms. Morgan?* I thought. *Since when was I Ms. Morgan?* "What gives, Meg?" I said, glancing behind me to the empty lobby.

She held herself stiffly. "Thank God you're still alive," she whispered from between her teeth, her lips still curled in a smile. "What are you doing here? You should be hiding in a basement." Before I could answer, she cocked her head like a spaniel, smiling like the blonde she wished she was. "What can I do for you today—Ms. Morgan?"

I made a quizzical face, and Megan sent her eyes meaningfully over my shoulder. A strained look came over her. "The camera, idiot," she muttered. "The camera."

My breath slipped from me in understanding. I was more worried about Francis's phone call than the camera. No one looked at the tapes unless something happened. By then it would be too late.

"We're all pulling for you," Megan whispered. "The odds are running two hundred to one you make it through the week. Personally, I give you a hundred to one."

I felt ill. Her gaze jumped behind me, and she stiffened. "Someone's behind me, aren't they?" I said, and she winced. I sighed, swinging my bag to rest against my back and out of the way before I turned on a slow heel.

He was in a tidy black suit, starched white shirt, and thin black tie. His arms were confidently laced behind his back. He didn't take his sunglasses off. I caught the faint scent of musk, and by the soft reddish beard, I guessed he was a werefox.

Another man joined him, standing between me and the front door. He didn't take his shades off, either. I eyed them, sizing them up. There would be a third somewhere, probably behind me. Assassins always worked in threes. *No more. No less. Always three,* I thought dryly, feeling my stomach tighten. Three against one wasn't fair. I looked down at the hall to the vault. "See you at home, Jenks," I whispered, knowing he couldn't hear me.

The two shades stood straighter. One unbuttoned his jacket coat to show a holster. My brow rose. They wouldn't gun me down in cold blood in front of a witness. Denon might be ticked, but he wasn't stupid. They were waiting for me to run.

I stood with my hands on my hips and my feet spread for balance. Attitude is everything. "Don't suppose we could talk about this boys?" I said tartly, my heart hammering.

The one who had unbuttoned his coat grinned. His teeth were small and sharp. A mat of fine red hair covered the back of his hand. Yup. A werefox. Great. I had my knife, but the point was to stay far enough away that I wouldn't have to use it.

From behind me came Megan's irate shout, "Not in my lobby. Take it outside."

My pulse leapt. Meg would help? *Maybe,* I thought as I vaulted over her counter in a smooth move, *she just didn't want a stain on her carpet.*

"That way." Megan pointed behind her to the archway to the back offices.

There was no time for thanks. I darted through the doorway, finding myself in an open office area. Behind me were muffled thumps and shouted curses. The warehouse-sized room was divided with corporate's favorite four-foot walls, a maze of biblical proportions.

I smiled and waved at the startled faces of the few people working, my bag whacking into the partitions as I ran. I shoved the water cooler over in passing, shouting an insincere "Sorry" as it tipped. It didn't shatter but did come apart. The heavy glugging of water was soon overpowered by the cries of dismay and calls for a mop.

I glanced behind me. One of the shades was entangled with three office workers struggling to gain control of the heavy bottle. His weapon was hidden. So far, so good. The back door beckoned. I ran to the far wall, flinging open the fire door, relishing the colder air.

Someone was waiting. She was pointing a wide-mouth weapon at me.

"Crap!" I exclaimed, backpedaling to slam the door shut. Before it closed, a wet splat hit the partition behind me, leaving a gelatinous stain. The back of my neck burned. I reached up, crying out when I found a blister the size of silver dollar. My fingers touching it burned.

"Swell," I whispered as I wiped the clear goo off on the hem of my jacket. "I don't have time for this." Kicking the emergency lock into place, I darted back into the maze. They weren't using delayed spells anymore. These were primed and loaded into splat balls. Just freaking great. My guess was it had been a spontaneous combustion spell. Had I gotten more than a back splash, I'd be dead. Nice little pile of ash on the Berber carpet. There was no way Jenks could have smelled this coming, even if he had been with me.

Personally, I'd rather be killed by a bullet. That, at least, was romantic. But it was harder to track down the maker of a lethal spell than it was to identify the manufacturer of a bullet or conventional gun. Not to mention that a good charm left no evidence. Or in the case of spontaneous combustion spells, not much of a body. No body. No crime. No need to do time.

"There!" someone shouted. I dove under a desk. Pain jolted my elbow as I landed on it. My neck felt like it was on fire. I had to get some salt on it, neutralize the spell before it spread.

My heart pounded as I shimmied out of my jacket. Splatters of goo decorated it. If I hadn't been wearing it, I'd probably be dead. I jammed it into someone's trashcan.

The calls for a mop were loud as I dug a vial of saltwater out of my bag. My fingers were burning and my neck was in agony. Hands shaking, I bit off the tube's plastic top. Breath held, I dumped the vial across my fingers and then my bowed neck. My breath hissed out at the sudden sting and whiff of sulfur as the black spell broke. Saltwater dripped from me to the floor. I spent one glorious moment relishing the cessation of pain.

Shaking, I dabbed at my neck with the hem of my sleeve. The blister under my careful fingers hurt, but the throb from the saltwater was soothing compared to the burn. I stayed where I was, feeling like an idiot as I tried to figure out how I was going to get out of there. I was a good witch. All my charms were defensive, not offensive. Slap 'em up and keep them off their feet until you subdue them was the name of the game. I'd always been the hunter, never the hunted. My brow furrowed as I realized I had nothing for this.

Megan's overloud fussing told me exactly where everyone was. I felt my blister again. It wasn't spreading. I was lucky. My breath caught at the soft pacing a few cubicles over. I wished I wasn't sweating so much. Weres have excellent noses, but one-track minds. It was probably only the lingering scent of sulfur that had kept him from finding me already. I couldn't stay here. A faint pounding on the back door told me it was time to go.

Tension throbbed in my head as I cautiously peeked over the walls to see shade number one padding through the cubicles to let shade number three in. Taking a soft breath, I moved the opposite way in a crouched run. I was betting my life that the assassins had kept one of their number at the front door and that I wouldn't bump into him halfway there.

Thanks to Megan's nonstop harangue about the water on the floor, I made it to the archway to the lobby with no one the wiser. Face cold, I looked around the doorframe to find the reception desk deserted. Papers littered the floor. Pens rolled under my feet. Megan's keyboard hung from its cord, still swaying. Hardly breathing, I skulked my way to the opening in the counter where it flipped up. Still at ground level, I shot a quick glance past the front desk.

My heart gave a quick pound. There was a shade fidgeting by the door, looking surly at having been left behind. But getting past one was better odds than getting past two.

Francis's whiny voice came faint from the vault. "Here? Denon set them on her here? He must be pissed. Nah, I'll be right back. I gotta see this. It ought to be worth a laugh."

His voice was getting closer. *Maybe Francis would like to go for a stroll with me,* I thought, hope bringing my muscles tight. One thing you could count on with Francis was that he was curious *and* stupid, a dangerous combination in our profession. I waited, adrenaline singing through me, until he lifted the counter panel and came behind the desk.

"What a mess," he said, more interested in the clutter on the floor than me rising behind him. He never saw me coming, too busy scratching. Like clockwork, I slipped an arm about his neck, wrenching one of his arms back behind him, nearly lifting him off his feet.

"Ow! Damn it, Rachel!" he shouted, too cowed to know how easy it would be to elbow me in the gut and get away. "Lemme go! This isn't funny."

Swallowing, I sent my frightened eyes to the shade by the door, his weapon pulled and aimed. "No it isn't, cookie," I breathed in Francis's ear, painfully aware how close to death we were. Francis didn't have a clue, and the thought he might do something stupid scared me more than the gun. My heart pounded and I felt my knees go loose. "Hold still," I told him. "If he thinks he can get a shot off on me, he might take it."

"Why should I care?" he snarled back.

"You see anyone else out here but you, me, and the gun?" I said softly. "Wouldn't be hard to get rid of one witness, now would it?"

Francis stiffened. I heard a small gasp as Megan appeared in the doorway to the back offices. More people peered over and around her, whispering loudly. I sent my gaze darting over them, feeling the pinch of panic. There were too many people. Too many opportunities for something to go wrong.

I felt better when the shade eased from his crouch and tucked his pistol away. He put his arms to his side, palms out in an insincere gesture of acquiescence. Tagging me before so many witnesses would be too costly. Stalemate.

I kept Francis before me as an unwilling shield. There was a whisper of sound as the other two shades ghosted out of the office area. They held themselves against the back wall of Megan's office. One had a drawn weapon. He took in the situation and holstered it.

"Okay, Francis," I said. "It's time for your afternoon constitutional. Nice and slow."

"Shove it, Rachel," he said, his voice shaking and sweat beading his forehead.

We edged out from behind the desk, me struggling to keep Francis upright as he slipped on the rolling pens. The Were by the door obligingly stepped aside. His attitude was clear enough. They were in no hurry. They had time. Under their watchful eyes, Francis and I backed out the door and into the sun.

"Lemme go," Francis said, beginning to struggle. Pedestrians gave us a wide birth, and the passing cars slowed to watch. I hate rubberneckers, but maybe it would work for me. "Go on, run," Francis said. "That's what you do best, Rachel."

I tightened my grip until he grunted. "You got that right. I'm a better runner than you'll ever be." The surrounding people were starting to scatter, realizing this was more than a lover's quarrel. "You might want to start running, too," I said, hoping to add to the confusion.

"What the hell are you talking about?" His sweat stank over his cologne.

I dragged Francis across the street, weaving between the slowed cars. The three shades had come out to watch. They stood with taut alertness by the door in their dark glasses and black suits. "I imagine they think you're helping me. I mean really," I taunted, "a big, strong witch like you not able to get away from a frail wisp of a girl like me?" I heard his quick intake of breath in understanding. "Good boy," I said. "Now run."

With the traffic between me and the shades, I dropped Francis and ran, losing myself in the pedestrian traffic. Francis took off the other way. I knew if I got enough distance between us, they wouldn't follow me home. Weres were superstitious and wouldn't violate the sanctuary of holy ground. I'd be safe—until Denon sent something else after me.

Nine

"**S**omething else," I mused as I turned a brittle yellow page that smelled of gardenias and ether. A spell of inconspicuousness would be great, but it called for fern seed. Not only didn't I have time to gather enough, but also it wasn't the right season. Findlay Market would have it, but I didn't have the time. "Get real, Rachel," I breathed, shutting the book and straightening my back painfully. "You can't stir anything that difficult."

Ivy was lounging across from me at the kitchen table, filling out the change of address forms she had picked up and crunching through the last of her celery and dip. It was all the supper I had time to make. She didn't seem to care. Maybe she was going out later and pick up a snack. Tomorrow, if I lived to see it, I'd make a real supper. Maybe pizza. The kitchen was not conducive to food preparation tonight.

I was spelling; I'd made a mess. Half-chopped plants, dirt, green-stained bowls with strained gratings left to cool, and dirty copper pots overflowed the sink. It looked like Yoda's kitchen meets the *Galloping Gourmet*. But I had my detection amulets, sleep inducers, even some new disguise charms to make me look old instead of younger. I couldn't help a wash of satisfaction for having made them myself. As soon as I found a strong enough spell to break into the I.S. records vault, Jenks and I were out of here.

Jenks had come in that afternoon with a slow, shaggy Were of a man trailing after him, his friend who had my stuff. I bought the musty-smelling cot he had with him, thanking him for bringing over the few articles of clothing that hadn't been spelled: my winter coat and a pair of pink sweats that were stuck in a box in the back of my closet. I had told the man not to bother with anything else right now but my clothes, music, and kitchen stuff, and he shuffled away with a hundred clutched in his grip, promising to at least have my clothes by tomorrow.

Sighing, I looked up from my book, past Mr. Fish on the windowsill and into the black garden. My hand cupped over the blister on my neck, and I pushed the book away to make room for the next. Denon must have been seriously ticked to set the Weres after me in broad daylight, when they were at a severe disadvantage. If it had been night, I'd probably be dead—new moon or not. That he was wasting money told me he must have been taken apart for letting Ivy go.

After eluding the Weres, I had splurged for a cab home. I justified it by saying it was to avoid the possible hit men on the bus, but the reality was, I didn't want anyone to see me with the shakes. They started three blocks after I got in the cab and didn't quit until I was in the shower long enough to have drained all the hot water from the water heater. I had never been on the hunted end of the game. I didn't like it. But what scared me almost as much was the thought that I might have to make and use a black spell to keep myself alive.

Much of my job had entailed bringing in "gray spell" crafters—witches who took a perfectly good spell like a love charm and turned it to a bad use. But the serious black magic users were out there, and I'd brought them in, too: the ones specializing in the darker forms of entrapment, the people who could make you go missing—and for a few dollars more, spell your relatives into not remembering you even existed—the handful of Inderlanders driving Cincinnati's underground power struggles. Sometimes the best I had been able to do was to cover up the ugly reality so that humanity never knew how difficult it was to rein in the Inderlanders who thought of humans as free-range cattle. But never had I had anyone come at me like that before. I wasn't sure how to keep myself safe and my karma clean at the same time.

The last of my daylight hours had been spent in the garden. Messing about in the dirt with pixy children getting in the way is a great way to ground oneself, and I found I owed Jenks a very large thank-you—in more ways than one. It wasn't until I went inside with my spell-crafting materials and a sunburnt nose that I found out what their cheerful shouts and calls had been about. They hadn't been playing hide and seek; they were intercepting splat balls.

The small pyramid of splat balls neatly stacked by the back door had shocked the peas out of me. Each one held my death. I hadn't known. Not a freaking clue. Seeing them there ticked me off, making me angry instead of afraid. Next time the hunters found me, I vowed, I'd be ready.

After my whirlwind of spell crafting, my bag was full of my usual charms. The dowel of redwood from work had been a lifesaver. Any wood can store spells, but redwood lasts the longest. The amulets not in my bag hung from the cup hooks in the otherwise empty cupboard. They were all great spells, but I needed something stronger. Sighing, I opened the next book.

"Transmutation?" Ivy said, setting the forms aside and pulling her keyboard closer. "You're that good?"

I ran a thumbnail under a fingernail to get the dirt out from under it. "Necessity is the mother of courage," I mumbled. Not meeting her eyes, I scanned the index. I needed something small, preferably that could defend itself.

Ivy returned to her surfing with a loud crunch of celery. I had been watching her closely since sundown. She was the model roommate, clearly making an effort to keep her nor-

mal vampy reactions to a minimum. It probably helped that
I had rewashed my clothes. The moment she started looking
seductive, I was asking her to leave.

"Here's one," I said softly. "A cat. I need an ounce of rosemary, half a cup of mint, one teaspoon of milkweed extract
gathered after the first frost . . . Well, that's out. I don't have
any extract, and I'm not about to go to the store now."

Ivy seemed to swallow back a chuckle, and I flipped to the
index. Not a bat; I didn't have an ash tree in the garden, and
I'd probably need some of the inner bark. Besides, I wasn't
going to spend the rest of the night learning to fly by echolo-
cation. The same went for birds. Most of those listed didn't
fly at night. A fish was just silly. But maybe . . .

"A mouse," I said, turning to the proper page and looking
over the list of ingredients. Nothing was exotic. Almost
everything I needed was already in the kitchen. There was a
handwritten note at the bottom, and I squinted to read a
faded, masculine-looking script: *Can be safely adapted for
any rodent.* I glanced at the clock. This would do.

"A mouse?" Ivy said. "You're going to spell yourself into
a mouse?"

I stood, went to the stainless steel island in the center of
the kitchen, and propped the book up. "Sure. I've got everything but the mouse hair." My eyebrows rose. "Do you think
I could have one of your owl's pellets? I need to strain the
milk past some fur."

Ivy tossed her wave of black hair over her shoulder, her
thin eyebrows high. "Sure. I'll get you one." Shaking her
head, she closed the site she was looking at and rose with a
stretch tall enough to show her bare midriff. I blinked at the
red jewel piercing her belly button, then looked away. "I
need to let them out anyway," she said as she collapsed in on
herself.

"Thanks." I turned back to my recipe, going over exactly
what I needed and gathering it on the kitchen island. By the
time Ivy padded down from the belfry, everything was measured and waiting. All that was left was the stirring.

"It's all yours," she said, setting a pellet on the counter and going to wash her hands.

"Thank you," I whispered. I took a fork and teased the felt mass apart, pulling three hairs from among the tiny bones. I made a face, reminding myself that it hadn't gone all the way through the owl, just been regurgitated.

Grabbing a fistful of salt, I turned to her. "I'm going to make a salt circle. Don't try to cross it, okay?" She stared, and I added, "It's a potentially dangerous spell. I don't want anything to get into the pot by accident. You can stay in the kitchen, just don't cross the circle."

Looking unsure, she nodded. "Okay."

I kind of liked seeing her off balance, and I made the circle bigger than usual, enclosing the entirety of the center island with all my paraphernalia. Ivy levered herself up to sit on a corner of the counter. Her eyes were wide with curiosity. If I was going to do this a lot, I might want to blow off the security deposit and etch a groove in the linoleum. What good is a security deposit if you're dead from a misaligned spell?

My heart beat fast. It had been a while since I'd closed a circle, and Ivy watching made me nervous. "All right, then . . ." I murmured. I took a slow breath, willing my mind to empty and my eyes to close. Slowly, my second sight wavered into focus.

I didn't do this often, as it was confusing as all get-out. A wind that wasn't from this side of reality lifted the lighter strands of my hair. My nose wrinkled at the smell of burnt amber. Immediately I felt like I was outside as the surrounding walls vanished to silvery hints. Ivy, even more transitory than the church, was gone. Only the landscape and plants remained, their outlines quavering with the same reddish glow that thickened the air. It was as if I stood in the same spot before mankind found it. My skin crawled when I realized the gravestones existed in both worlds, as white and solid looking as the moon would be if it were up.

Eyes still closed, I reached out with my second sight, searching for the nearest ley line. "Holy crap," I murmured in surprise, finding a reddish smear of power running right through the graveyard. "Did you know there's a ley line running through the cemetery?"

"Yes," Ivy said softly, her voice coming from nowhere.

I stretched out my will and touched it. My nostrils flared as force surged into me, backwashing at my theoretical extremities until the power equalized. The university was built on a ley line so big that it could be drawn upon almost anywhere in Cincinnati. Most cities are built on at least one. Manhattan has three of considerable size. The largest ley line on the East Coast runs through a farm outside of Woodstock. Coincidence? I think not.

The ley line in my backyard was tiny, but it was so close and underused that it gave me more strength than the university's ever had. Though no real breeze touched me, my skin prickled from the wind blowing in the ever-after.

Tapping into a ley line was a rush, albeit a dangerous one. I didn't like it. Its power ran through me like water, seeming to leave an ever-growing residue. I couldn't keep my eyes closed any longer, and they flew open.

The surreal red vision of the ever-after was replaced by my humdrum kitchen. I stared at Ivy perched on the counter, seeing her with the earth's wisdom. Sometimes a person looks totally different. I was relieved to see Ivy looked the same. Her aura—her real aura, not her vamp aura—was streaked with sparkles. How very odd. She was looking for something.

"Why didn't you tell me there was a ley line so close?" I asked.

Ivy's eyes flicked over me. Shrugging, she crossed her legs and kicked off her shoes to land them under the table. "Would it have made any difference?"

No. It didn't make any difference. I shut my eyes to strengthen my fading second sight while I closed the circle. The heady flood of latent power made me uncomfortable. With my will, I moved the narrow band of salt from this dimension into the ever-after. It was replaced with an equal ring of ever-after reality.

The circle snapped shut with a skin-tingling jolt, and I jumped. "Cripes," I whispered. "Maybe I used too much salt." Most of the force I had pulled from the ever-after now flowed through my circle. What little remained eddying through me still made my skin crawl. The residue would continue to grow until I broke the circle and disconnected from the ley line.

I could feel the barrier of ever-after reality surrounding me as a faint pressure. Nothing could cross the quickly shifting bands of alternate realities. With my second sight, I could see the shimmering wave of smudged red rising up from the floor to arch to a close just over my head. The half sphere went the same distance beneath me. I would do a closer inspection later to be sure I wasn't bisecting any pipes or electrical lines, making the circle vulnerable to breakage should anything actively try to get through that way.

Ivy was watching me when I opened my eyes. I gave her a mirthless smile and turned away. Slowly my second sight diminished to nothing, overwhelmed by my usual vision. "Locked down tight," I said as her aura seemed to vanish. "Don't try to cross it. It'll hurt."

She nodded, her placid face solemn. "You're—witchier," she said slowly.

I smiled, pleased. Why not let the vamp see the witch had teeth, too? Taking the smallest copper mixing bowl, about the size of my cupped hands, I set it over the lit campfire-in-a-can that Ivy had bought for me earlier. I had used the stove for crafting my lesser spells, but again, a working gas line would have left an opening in the circle. "Water . . ." I murmured, filling my graduated cylinder with spring water and squinting to make sure I read it properly. The vat sizzled as I added it, and I raised the bowl up from the flame. "Mouse, mouse, mouse," I mused, trying not to show how nervous I was. This was the hardest spell I had tried outside of class.

Ivy slipped from the counter, and I stiffened. The hair on the back of my neck rose as she came to stand behind my

shoulder but still out of the circle. I stopped what I was doing and gave her a look. Her smile went sheepish and she
moved to the table.

"I didn't know you tapped into the ever-after," she said,
settling before her monitor.

I looked up from the recipe. "As an earth witch, I don't
very often. But this spell will physically change me, not just
give the illusion I'm a mouse. If something gets in the pot by
accident, I might not be able to break it, or end up only
halfway changed . . . or something."

She made a noncommittal noise, and I set the mouse hair
into a sieve to pour milk over. There is an entire branch of
witchcraft that uses ley lines instead of potions, and I had
spent two semesters cleaning up after one of my professor's
labs so I wouldn't have to take more than the basic course. I
had told everyone it was because I didn't have a familiar
yet—which was a safety requirement—but the truth of it
was, I simply didn't like them. I'd lost a good friend when
he decided to major in ley lines and drifted into a bad crowd.
Not to mention my dad's death had been linked to them.
And it didn't help that the ley lines were gateways to the
ever-after.

It's claimed the ever-after used to be a paradise where the
elves had dwelt, popping into our reality long enough to
steal human children. But when demons took over and
trashed the place, the elves were forced to bide here for
good. Of course, that was even before Grimm was writing
his fairy tales. It's all there in the older, more savage
stories/histories. Almost every one of them ends with, "And
they lived happy in the ever-after." Well . . . that's the way
it's supposed to go. Grimm lost the "in the" part somewhere.
That some witches use ley lines probably accounted for the
longstanding misinterpretation that witches aligned themselves with demons. I shudder to think how many lives that
mistake had ended.

I was strictly an earth witch, dealing solely with amulets,
potions, and charms. Gestures and incantations were in the

realm of ley line magic. Witches specializing in this branch of craft tapped directly into ley lines for their strength. It was a harsher magic, and I thought less structured and beautiful, since it lacked much of the discipline earth enchantment had. The only benefit I could see in ley line magic was that it could be invoked instantly with the right word. The drawback was that one had to carry around a slice of ever-after in their chi. I didn't care that there were ways to isolate it from your chakras. I was convinced that the demonic taint from the ever-after left some sort of accumulated smut on your soul. I'd seen too many friends lose their ability to clearly see what side of the fence their magic was on.

Ley line magic was where the greatest potential for black magic lay. If a charm was hard to trace back to its maker, finding out who cursed your car with ley line magic was nigh impossible. That's not to say all ley line witches were bad—their skills were in high demand in the entertainment, weather control, and security industries—but with such a close association with the ever-after and the greater power at one's disposal, it was easy to lose one's morals.

My lack of advancement with the I.S. might be placed at the feet of my refusal to use ley line magic to apprehend the big bad uglies. But what was the difference if I tagged them with a charm instead of an incantation? I had gotten very good fighting ley line magic with earth, though one wouldn't be able to tell that looking at my tag/run ratio.

The memory of that pyramid of splat balls outside my back door twinged through me, and I poured the milk over the mouse hair and into the pot. The mixture was boiling, and I raised the bowl even higher on its tripod, stirring it with a wooden spoon. Using wood while spelling wasn't a good idea, but all my ceramic spoons were still cursed, and to use metal other than copper would be inviting disaster. Wood spoons tended to act like amulets, absorbing spell and leading to embarrassing mistakes, but if I soaked it in my vat of saltwater when done, I'd be fine.

Hands on my hips, I read over the spell again and set the

timer. The simmering mix was starting to smell musky. I hoped that was all right.

"So," Ivy said as she clicked and clacked at her keyboard. "You're going to sneak into the records vault as a mouse. You won't be able to open the file cabinet."

"Jenks says he has a copy of everything already. We just have to go look at it."

Ivy's chair creaked as she leaned back and crossed her legs, her doubt that we two midgets would be able to handle a keyboard obvious in how she had her head cocked. "Why don't you just change back to a witch once you're there?"

I shook my head as I double-checked the recipe. "Transformations invoked by a potion last until you get a solid soaking in saltwater. If I wanted, I could transform using an amulet, break into the vault, take it off, find what I need as a human, and then put the amulet back on to get out. But I'm not going to."

"Why not?"

She was just full of questions, and I looked up from adding the fuzz of a pussytoes plant. "Haven't you ever used a transformation spell?" I questioned. "I thought vamps used them all the time to turn into bats and stuff."

Ivy dropped her eyes. "Some do," she said softly.

Obviously Ivy had never transformed. I wondered why. She certainly had the money for it. "It's not a good idea to use an amulet for transforming," I said. "I'd have to tie the amulet to me or wear it around my neck, and all my amulets are bigger than a mouse. Kind of awkward. And what if I was in a wall and dropped it? Witches have died from despelling back to normal and solidifying with extra parts—like a wall or cage." I shuddered, giving the brew a quick clockwise stir. "Besides," I added softly, "I won't have any clothes on when I turn back."

"Ha!" Ivy barked, and I jerked. "Now we hear the real reason. Rachel, you're shy!"

What could I say to that? Mildly embarrassed, I closed my spell book and shelved it under the island with the rest of my new library. The timer dinged, and I blew out the flame. There wasn't much liquid left. It wouldn't take long to reach room temperature.

Wiping my hands off on my jeans, I reached across the clutter for a finger stick. Many a witch before the Turn had feigned a mild case of diabetes in order to get these little gems for free. I hated them, but it was better than using a knife to open a vein, as they had in less enlightened times. Poised to jab myself, I suddenly hesitated. Ivy couldn't cross the circle, but last night was still very real in my thoughts. I'd sleep in a salt circle if I could, but the continuous connection to the ever-after would make me insane if I didn't have a familiar to absorb the mental toxins the lines put out. "I—uh—need three drops of my blood to quicken it," I said.

"Really?" Her look entirely lacked that intent expression that generally proceeded a vamp's hunting aura. Still, I didn't trust her.

I nodded. "Maybe you should leave."

Ivy laughed. "Three drops drawn from a finger stick isn't going to do anything."

Still I hesitated. My stomach clenched. How could I be sure she knew her limits? Her eyes narrowed and red spots appeared on her pale cheeks. If I insisted she leave, she would take offense, I could tell. And I wasn't about to show I was afraid of her. I was absolutely safe within my circle. It could stop a demon; stopping a vamp was nothing.

I took a breath and stuck my finger. There was a flicker of black in her eyes and a chill through me, then nothing. My shoulders eased. Emboldened, I massaged three drops into the brew. The brown, milky liquid looked the same, but my nose could tell the difference. I closed my eyes, bringing the smell of grass and grain deep into my lungs. I would need three more drops of my blood to prime each dose before use.

"It smells different."

"What?" I jumped, cursing my reaction. I had forgotten she was there.

"Your blood smells different," Ivy said. "It smells woody. Spicy. Like dirt, but dirt that's alive. Human blood doesn't smell like that, or vampire."

"Um," I muttered, quite sure I didn't like that she could smell three drops of my blood from halfway across the room through a barrier of ever-after. But it was reassuring to know she had never bled a witch.

"Would my blood work?" she asked intently.

I shook my head as I gave the brew a nervous stir. "No. It has to be from a witch or warlock. It's not the blood but the enzymes that are in it. They act as a catalyst."

She nodded, clicking her computer into sleep mode and sitting back to watch me.

I rubbed the tip of my finger to smear the slick of blood to nothing. Like most, this recipe made seven spells. The ones I didn't use tonight, I'd store as potions. If I cared to put them in amulets, they would last a year. But I wouldn't transform with an amulet for anything.

Ivy's eyes were heavy on me as I carefully divided the brew into the thumb-sized vials and capped them tightly. Done. All that was left was to break the circle and my connection to the ley line. The former was easy, the second was a tad more difficult.

Giving Ivy a quick smile, I reached out with my fuzzy pink slipper and pushed a gap into the salt. The background thrum of ever-after power swelled. My breath hissed in through my nose as all the strength that had been flowing through the circle now flowed through me.

"What's the matter?" Ivy asked from her chair, sounding alert and concerned.

I made a conscious effort to breathe, thinking I might hyperventilate. I felt like an overinflated balloon. Eyes on the floor, I waved her away. "Circle's broken. Stay back. Not done yet," I said, feeling both giddy and unreal.

Taking a breath, I started to divorce myself from the line. It was a battle between the baser desire for power and the knowledge that it would eventually drive me insane. I had to force it from me, pushing it out from my head to my toes until the power returned back to the earth.

My shoulders slumped as it left me, and I staggered, reaching out for the counter.

"Are you okay?" Ivy asked, close and intent.

Gasping, I looked up. She was holding my elbow to keep me upright. I hadn't seen her move. My face went cold. Her fingers were warm through my shirt. "I used too much salt. The connection was too strong. I—I'm all right. Let go of me."

The concern in her face vanished. Clearly affronted, she let me go. The sound of the salt crunching under her feet was loud as she went back to her corner and sat in her chair, looking hurt. I wasn't going to appologize. I hadn't done anything wrong.

Heavy and uncomfortable, the silence weighed on me as I put all but one vial away in the cabinet with my extra amulets. As I gazed at them, I couldn't help but feel a twinge of pride. I had made them. And even if the insurance I'd need to sell them was more than I made in a year at the I.S., I could use them.

"Do you want some help tonight?" Ivy asked. "I don't mind covering your back."

"No," I blurted. It was a little too quick, and her features folded into a frown. I shook my head, smiling to soften my refusal, wishing I could bring myself to say, "Yes, please." But I still couldn't quite trust her. I didn't like putting myself in a situation where I had to trust anyone. My dad had died because he trusted someone to get his back. "Work alone, Rachel," he had told me as I sat beside his hospital bed and gripped his shaking hand as his blood lost its ability to carry oxygen. "Always work alone."

My throat tightened as I met Ivy's eyes. "If I can't lose a couple of shades, I deserve to be tagged," I said, avoiding the real issue. I put my collapsible bowl and a bottle of salt-water into my bag, adding one of my new disguise amulets that no one from the I.S. had seen.

"You aren't going to try one first?" Ivy asked when it became obvious I was leaving.

I nervously brushed a curling strand of hair back. "It's getting late. I'm sure it's fine."

Ivy didn't seem very happy. "If you aren't back by morning, I'm coming after you."

"Fair enough." If I wasn't back by morning, I'd be dead. I snagged my long winter coat from a chair and shrugged into it. I gave Ivy a quick, uneasy smile before I slipped out the back door. I'd go through the graveyard and pick up the bus on the next street over.

The spring night air was cold, and I shivered as I eased the screen door shut. The pile of splat balls at my feet was a reminder I didn't appreciate. Feeling vulnerable, I slipped into the shadow of the oak tree to wait for my eyes to adjust to a night with no moon. It was just past new and wouldn't be up until nearly dawn. *Thank you, God, for small favors.*

"Hey, Ms. Rachel!" came a tiny buzz, and I turned, thinking for an instant it was Jenks. But it was Jax, Jenks's oldest son. The preadolescent pixy had kept me company all afternoon, nearly getting snipped more times than I would care to recall as his curiosity and attention to "duty" brought him perilously close to my scissors while his father slept.

"Hi, Jax. Is your dad awake?" I asked, offering him a hand to alight upon.

"Ms. Rachel?" he said, his breath fast as he landed. "They're waiting for you."

My heart gave a thump. "How many? Where?"

"Three." He was glowing pale green in excitement. "Up front. Big guys. Your size. Stink like foxes. I saw them when old man Keasley chased them off his sidewalk. I would've told you sooner," he said urgently, "but they didn't cross the street, and we already stole the rest of their splat balls. Papa said not to bother you unless someone came over the wall."

"It's okay. You did good." Jax took flight as I eased into motion. "I was going to cut across the backyard and pick up the bus on the other side of the block anyway." I squinted in the faint light, giving Jenks's stump a soft tap. "Jenks," I said softly, grinning at the almost subliminal roar of irritation that flowed from the old ash stump. "Let's go to work."

Ten

The pretty woman sitting across from me on the bus stood to get off. She paused, standing too close to me for comfort, and I looked up from Ivy's book. "Table 6.1," she said as I met her gaze. "It's *all* you need to know." Her eyes closed, and she shuddered as if in pleasure.

Embarrassed, I thumbed to the back. "Jiminy Cricket," I whispered. It was a table of accessories and suggested uses. My face warmed. I wasn't a prude, but some of it . . . and with a vampire? Maybe with a witch. If he was drop-dead gorgeous. Without the blood. *Maybe.*

I jerked as she crouched in the aisle. Leaning far too close, she dropped a black business card into the open book. "In case you want a second," she whispered, smiling with a quick kinship I didn't understand. "Newbies shine like stars, bringing out the best in them. I don't mind playing second fiddle to your first night. And I could help you . . . afterward. Sometimes they forget." A flash of fear crossed her, quick but very real.

Jaw hanging, I could say nothing as she stood and walked away and down the stairs.

Jenks flitted close, and I snapped the book shut. "Rache," he said as he landed on my earring. "Whatcha reading? You've had your nose in it since we got on the bus."

"Nothing," I said, feeling my pulse hammer. "That woman. She was human, right?"

"The one talking to you? Yeah. By the smell of it, she's a vamp flunky. Why?"

"No reason," I said as I shoved the book to the bottom of my bag. I was never reading this thing in public again. Fortunately, my stop was next. Ignoring Jenks's nonstop inquisition, I strode into the mall's food court. My long coat flapped about my ankles as I immersed myself in the hustle of predawn Sunday shopping. I invoked my old lady disguise in the bathroom, hoping to throw off anyone who might have recognized me. Still, I thought it prudent to lose myself in a crowd before I headed to the I.S.: kill some time, gather my courage, pick up a hat to replace the one of Ivy's I'd lost today—buy some soap to cover any lingering smell of her on me.

I strode past an amulet outlet without my usual, wistful hesitation. I could make anything I wanted, and if someone was looking for me, that's where they would watch. *But no one would expect me to buy a pair of boots,* I thought, my steps slowing as I passed a window. The leather curtains and dim lights said more clearly than the name of the shop that it catered to vamps.

What the heck? I thought. *I live with a vamp.* The sales associate couldn't be any worse than Ivy. I was savvy enough to buy something without leaving any blood behind. So, ignoring Jenks's complaints, I went in. My thoughts flicked from Table 6.1 to the flirtatious, handsome clerk who had warned the other salesmen off after taking a peek at me through a pair of wood-rimmed glasses. His name tag said VALENTINE, and I ate up his attention with a spoon as he helped me choose a good pair of boots, ooohing over my silk stockings and caressing my feet with his strong, cool fingers. Jenks waited in the hall in a potted plant, sullen and bad-tempered.

God help me, but Valentine was pretty. It had to be in the vamp job description, like wearing black and knowing how to flirt without triggering any of my proximity alarms. It didn't hurt to look, right? I could look and still not join the club, yes?

But as I walked out in my new, too expensive boots, I wondered at my sudden curiosity. Ivy had as much as admitted to me that she was driven by smell. Perhaps they all put out pheromones to subliminally soothe and lure the unsuspecting. It would make it far easier to seduce their prey. I had thoroughly enjoyed myself with Valentine, as relaxed as if he had been an old friend, letting him take teasing liberties with his hands and words that I normally wouldn't. Shaking the uncomfortable thought away, I continued my shopping.

I had to stop at the Big Cherry for some pizza sauce. Humans would boycott any store that sold tomatoes—even though the T-4 Angel variety was long extinct—so the only place you could get them was a specialty shop where it wouldn't matter if half the world's population refused to cross your threshold.

It was nerves that made me stop at the sweet shop. Everyone knows chocolate soothes the jitters; I think they did a study on it. And for five glorious minutes, Jenks stopped talking while he ate the caramel I bought him.

Stopping at The Bath and Body was a must—I wouldn't use Ivy's shampoo and soap anymore. And that led me to a scent shop. With Jenks's grudging help, I picked out a new perfume that helped hide Ivy's lingering scent. Lavender was the only thing that came close. Jenks said I stank like an explosion in a flower factory. I didn't especially like it, either, but if it kept me from triggering Ivy's instincts, I'd drink it, much less simply bathe in it.

Two hours before sunup I was back on the street and headed for the records vault. My new boots were deliciously quiet, seeming to float me above the pavement. Valentine had been right. I turned onto the deserted street with no hesitation. My old lady spell was still working—which might account for the odd looks in the leather shop—but if no one saw me, all the better.

The I.S. chose their buildings carefully. Nearly all of the offices on this street kept to a human clock and had been closed since Friday night. Traffic hummed two streets away, but here it was quiet. I glanced behind me as I slipped into the alley between the records building and the adjacent insurance tower. My heart pounded as I passed the fire door where I had nearly been tagged. I wouldn't bother trying to get in that way. "See a drainpipe, Jenks?" I asked.

"I'll check around," he said, flitting ahead to do a little reconnaissance.

I followed at a slower pace, angling for the faint tapping of metal that I heard now. Thoroughly enjoying the rush of adrenaline, I slid between a truck-sized trashcan and a pallet of cardboard. A smile edged over me as I spotted Jenks sitting on the curve of a downspout, tapping it with his boot heels. "Thanks, Jenks," I said, taking off my bag and setting it on the dew-damp cement.

"No problem." He flitted up to sit on the edge of a Dumpster. "For the love of Tink," he moaned, holding his nose. "You know what's in here?" I flicked a glance at him. Encouraged, he said, "Three-day-old lasagna, five varieties of yogurt cups, burnt popcorn . . ." He hesitated, his eyes closing as he sniffed. ". . . south of the border style, a million candy wrappers, and someone has an almost unholy need for superchunk burritos."

"Jenks? Shut up." The soft hiss of wheels on pavement warned me into immobility, but even the best night vision would have a difficult time spotting me back there. The alley stunk so bad, I didn't have to worry about Weres. Even so, I waited until the street was quiet before I dug in my bag for a detection spell and finger stick. The sharp jab of it made me jump. I squeezed the required three drops onto the amulet. They soaked in immediately, and the wooden disk glowed a faint green. I let out a breath I hadn't known I had been holding. No sentient creature but Jenks was within a hundred feet of me—and I had my doubts about Jenks. It was safe enough to spell myself into a mouse.

"Here, watch this and tell me if it turns red," I told Jenks as I balanced the disk beside him on the rim of the Dumpster.

"Why?"

"Just do it!" I whispered. Sitting on a bundle of card-board, I unlaced my new boots, took off my socks, and set a bare foot on the cement. It was cold and damp from last night's rain, and a small sound of disgust slipped from me. I shot a quick glance to the end of the alley, then arranged my boots out of sight behind a bin of shredded paper with my winter coat. Feeling like a Brimstone addict, I crouched in the gutter and pulled out my vial of brew. "Way to go, Rache," I whispered as I remembered I hadn't set up my dis-solution bowl yet.

I was confident Ivy would know what to do if I showed up as a mouse, but she'd never let me live it down. The saltwa-ter glugged nosily into the bowl, and I tucked the empty jug away. The screw top to the vial went plinking into the Dumpster, and I winced as I massaged another three drops of blood out of my throbbing finger. But my discomfort paled as my blood hit the liquid and the warm meadow fra-grance arose.

My stomach clenched as I mixed the vial by hitting the side with a series of gentle thwacks. Nervous, I wiped a hand on my jeans and glanced at Jenks. Making a spell is easy. It's trusting you did it right that's hard. When it came down to it, courage was the only thing separating a witch from a warlock. *I am a witch,* I told myself, my feet going cold. *I did this right. I will be a mouse, and I will be able to turn back with a dip in saltwater.*

"Promise you won't tell Ivy if this doesn't work?" I asked Jenks, and he grinned, roguishly tugging his cap lower over his eyes.

"Whatcha going to give me?"

"I won't lace your stump with ant killer."

He sighed. "Just do it," he encouraged. "I'd like to get home before the sun goes nova. Pixies sleep at night, you know."

I licked my lips, too anxious to come up with a retort. I had never transformed before. I'd taken the classes, but tu-ition didn't cover the cost to buy a professional-grade transformation spell, and liability insurance hadn't allowed us students to sample our own brew. Liability insurance. You gotta love it.

My fingers tightened on the vial and my pulse hammered. This was going to really hurt.

In a sudden rush, I closed my eyes and downed it. It was bitter, and I swallowed it in one gulp, trying not to think of the three mouse hairs. Yuck.

My stomach cramped and I bent double. I gasped as I lost my balance. The cold cement rushed up, and I put a hand out to stop my fall. It was black and furry. *It's working!* I thought in both delight and fright. This wasn't so bad.

Then a sharp pain ripped through my spine. Like blue flame it ran from my skull to my backbone. I cried out, panicking as a guttural shriek tore my ears. Hot ice ran through my veins.

I convulsed, agony taking my breath from me. Terror struck me as my vision went black. Blind, I reached out, hearing a terrifying scrabbling. "No!" I shrieked. The pain swelled, driving everything from me, swallowing me up.

Eleven

"**R**ache? Rachel, wake up. Are you all right?"

A warm, low, unfamiliar voice was a black thread pulling me back to consciousness. I stretched, feeling different muscles work. My eyes flashed open to see shades of gray. Jenks stood in front of me with his hands on his hips and his feet spread wide. He looked six feet tall. "Crap!" I swore, hearing it come out as a harsh squeak. I was a mouse. I was a freaking mouse!

Panic raced through me as I remembered the pain of transforming. I was going to have to go through it all again to turn back. No wonder transforming was a dying art. It hurt like hell.

My fear slowed, and I wiggled out from under my clothes. My heart was pounding terribly fast. That awful lavender perfume was thick on my clothes, choking me. I wrinkled my nose and tried not to gag as I realized I could smell the alcohol used to carry the flowery scent. Under it was that incenselike ash smell I identified with Ivy, and I wondered if a vamp's nose was as sensitive as a mouse's.

Wobbling on four legs, I sank down to a crouch and looked at the world through my new eyes. The alley was the size of a warehouse, the black sky above threatening. Everything was shades of gray and white; I was color-blind. The sound of the distant traffic was loud, and the reek of the alley was an assault. Jenks was right. Someone really liked burritos.

Now that I was facedown in it, the night seemed colder. Turning to my pile of clothes, I tried to hide my jewelry. Next time I'd leave everything at home but my ankle knife.

I turned back to Jenks, jerking in surprise. *Whoa, baby!* Jenks was hell on wings. He had strong, clearly defined shoulders to support his ability to fly. He had a thin waist and a muscular physique. His shock of fair hair fell artfully over his brow to give him a devil-may-care attitude. A spiderweb of glitters laced his wings. Seeing him from his size-perspective, I could see why Jenks had more kids than three pairs of rabbits.

And his clothes . . . Even in black and white his clothes were stunning! The hem and collar of his shirt was embroidered with the likeness of foxgloves and ferns. His black bandanna, which had once looked red, was inlaid with tiny shimmers in an eye-riveting pattern.

"Hey, Hot Stuff," he said cheerfully, his voice surprisingly low and rich to my rodent ears. "It worked. Where did you find a spell for a mink?"

"Mink?" I questioned, hearing only a squeak. Tearing my gaze from him, I looked at my hands. My thumbs were small, but my fingers were so dexterous it didn't seem to matter. Tiny savage nails tipped them. I reached up to feel a short triangular muzzle, and I turned to see my long, luxuriant, flowing tail. My entire body was one sleek line. I'd never been this skinny. I lifted a foot, to find that my feet were white with little white pads. It was hard to judge sizes, but I was a great deal bigger than a mouse, more like a large squirrel.

A mink? I thought, sitting up and running my front paws over my dark fur. How cool was that? I opened my mouth to feel my teeth. Nasty sharp teeth. I wouldn't have to worry about cats—I was almost as big as one. Ivy's owls were better hunters than I thought. My teeth clicked shut and I looked up at the open sky. Owls. I still had to worry about owls. And dogs. And anything else bigger than me. What had a mink been doing in the city?

"You look good, Rache," Jenks said.

My eyes jerked to him. *So do you, little man.* I idly wondered if there was a spell to turn people pixy size. If Jenks was any indication, it might be nice to take a vacation as a pixy and troll Cincinnati's better gardens. Color me Thumbelina and I'd be a happy girl.

"I'll see you up on the roof, okay?" he added, grinning as he noticed my ogling. Again I nodded, watching him flit upward. *Maybe I could find a spell to make pixies bigger?*

My wistful sigh came out as a rather odd squeak, and I scampered to the drainpipe. There was a puddle from last night's rain at the bottom, and my whiskers brushed the sides as I easily crawled up. My nails, I was pleased to note, were sharp and could find purchase in what seemed smooth metal. They were as good a potential weapon as my teeth.

I was panting by the time I reached the flat roof. I practically flowed out of the drainpipe, gracefully loping to the dark shadow of the building's air conditioner and Jenks's loud hail. My hearing was better, otherwise I would never have heard him.

"Over here, Rache," he called. "Someone's bent the intake screen."

My silky tail was twitching in excitement as I joined him at the air conditioner. One corner of the screen was missing a screw. Even more helpful, the screen was bent. It wasn't hard to squeeze in with Jenks levering it open for me. Once through, I crouched in the more certain dark and waited for my eyes to adapt as Jenks flitted about. Slowly another mesh screen came into focus. My rodent eyebrows rose as Jenks pulled aside a triangular cut in the wire. Clearly we had found the I.S. vault's unadvertised back door.

Full of a new confidence, Jenks and I explored our way into the building's air ducts. Jenks never shut up, his unending commentary about how easy it would be to become lost and die of starvation no help at all. It became clear that the maze of ductworks was used frequently. The drops and steeper inclines actually had quarter-inch rope tied to the top of them, and the old smell of other animals was strong. There was only one way to go—down—and after a few false turns, we found ourselves looking out into the familiar expanse of the record vault.

The vent we peered from was directly over the terminals. Nothing moved in the soft glow from the copiers. Sterile rectangular tables and plastic chairs were scattered across the ugly red carpet. Built into the walls were the files themselves. These were only the active records, a measly fraction of the dirt the I.S. had on the Inderland and human populations, both living and dead. Most were stored electronically, but if a file was pulled, a paper copy stayed in the cabinets for ten years, fifty for a vampire.

"Ready, Jenks?" I said, forgetting it would come out as a squeak. I could smell burnt coffee and sugar from the table by the door, and my stomach growled. Lying down, I stretched an arm through the vent's slats, scraping my elbow to awkwardly reach the opening lever. It gave way with an unexpected suddenness, swinging with a loud squeak to hang by its hinges. Crouched in the shadows, I waited until my pulse slowed before poking my nose out.

Jenks stopped me as I went to push a waiting coil of rope out of the duct. "Hold on," he whispered. "Let me trip the cameras." He hesitated, his wings going dark. "You, ah, won't tell anyone about this, right? It's kind of a—uh—pixy thing. It helps us get around unnoticed." He gave me a chagrined look, and I shook my head.

"Thanks," he said, and he dropped into space. I waited a breathless moment before he zipped back up and settled himself on the edge of the opening and dangled his feet. "All set," he said. "They will record a fifteen-minute loop. Come on down. I'll show you what Francis looked at."

I pushed the rope out of the ductwork and started to the floor. My nails made it easy.

"He made an extra copy of everything he wanted," Jenks was saying, waiting by the copier's recycle bin. He grinned as I tipped the can over and began rifling through the papers. "I kept tripping the copier from inside. He couldn't figure out why it was giving him two of everything. The intern thought he was an idiot."

I looked up, just about dying to say, "Francis is an idiot."

"I knew you would be all right," Jenks said as he began arranging the papers in a long line on the floor. "But it was really hard to sit here and do nothing when I heard you run. Don't ask me to do that again, all right?"

His jaw was clenched. I didn't know what to say, so I nodded. Jenks was more of a help than I had thought to give him credit for. Feeling bad for having discounted him, I tugged the scattered pages into order. There wasn't much, and the more I read, the more discouraged I became.

"According to this," Jenks said, standing on the first page with his hands on his hips, "Trent is the last of his family. His parents died under circumstances reeking of magic. Almost the entire house staff was under suspicion. It took three years before the FIB and the I.S. gave up and decided to officially look the other way."

I skimmed the statement of the I.S. investigator. My whiskers twitched when I recognized his name: Leon Bairn, the same who ended up as a thin smear on the sidewalk. Interesting.

"His parents refused to claim kinship to human or Inderland," Jenks said, "as does Trent. And there wasn't enough left of them to do an autopsy. Just like his parents, Trent employs Inderlanders as well as humans. Everyone but pixies and fairies."

It wasn't surprising. Why risk a discrimination lawsuit?

"I know what you're thinking," Jenks said. "But he doesn't seem to lean either way. His personal secretaries are always warlocks. His nanny was a human of some repute, and he roomed at Princeton with a pack of Weres." Jenks scratched his head in thought. "Didn't join the fraternity, though. You won't find it in the records, but the word is he's not a Were, or a vamp, or anything." Seeing my shrug, he continued. "Trent doesn't smell right. I've talked to a pixy who got a whiff of him while backing up a runner out at Trent's stables. She says it's not that Trent doesn't smell human, but that something subtle about him screams Inderlander."

I thought of the spell I had used to disguise my looks tonight. Opening my mouth to ask Jenks about that, I shut it with a snap. I couldn't do anything but squeak. Jenks grinned, and pulled a broken pencil lead from a pocket. "You're going to have to spell it," he said, writing down the alphabet on the bottom of one of the pages.

I bared all my teeth, which only made him laugh. But I had little choice. Skittering across the page like it was a Ouija board, I pointed out, "Charm?"

Jenks shrugged. "Maybe. But a pixy could smell through it, just as I can smell witch under the mink stink. But if it's a disguise, it would explain the warlock secretary. The more you use magic, the stronger you smell." I looked at him quizzically, and he added, "All witches smell alike, but those who work the most magic smell stronger, more unearthly. You, for example, reek from your recent spelling. You pulled on the ever-after tonight, didn't you?"

It wasn't a question, and I sat back on my haunches, surprised. He could tell from my smell?

"Trent might have another witch invoke his spells for him," Jenks said. "That way, he could be able to cover his smell with a charm. The same goes for a Were or vamp."

Struck by a sudden idea, I spelled out, "Ivy's smell?"

Jenks flitted uneasily into the air before I had even finished. "Uh, yeah," he stammered. "Ivy stinks. Either she's a dabbler that quit sipping blood last week or an intense practitioner that quit last year. I can't tell. She's probably somewhere in between—probably."

I frowned—as much as a mink can frown. She'd said it had been three years. She must have been very, very intense. Swell.

I glanced to the vault clock. We were running out of time. Impatient, I turned to Trent's skimpy record. According to the I.S., he lived and worked in a huge estate outside the city. He raised racehorses on the property, but most of his income came from farming: orange and pecan groves in the south, strawberries on the coast, wheat in the Midwest. He even had an island off the Eastern seaboard that grew tea. I already knew this. It was standard newspaper fodder.

Trent grew up as an only child, losing his mother when he was ten and his father when he was a freshman at college. His parents had two other children that didn't survive infancy. The doctor wouldn't give up the records without being subpoenaed, and shortly after the request, the office had burnt to the ground. Tragically, the doctor had been working late and hadn't made it out. *The Kalamacks,* I thought dryly, *played for keeps.*

I sat up from the records and snapped my teeth. There was nothing here I could use. I had a feeling the FIB records, if I could by some miracle see them, would be even less helpful. Someone had gone to a lot of trouble to ensure that very little was known about the Kalamacks.

"Sorry," Jenks said. "I know you were really counting on the records."

I shrugged, pushing and tugging the papers back into the bin. I wouldn't be able to put the basket upright, but at least it would look like it fell over and hadn't been rifled through.

"You want to go with Francis on his interview concerning his secretary's death?" Jenks asked. "It's this coming Monday at noon."

Noon, I thought. What a safe hour. It wasn't ridiculously early in the day for most Inderlanders, and a perfectly reasonable time for humans. Maybe I could tag along with Francis and help. I felt my rodent lips pull back across my teeth in a smile. Francis wouldn't mind. It might be my only chance to dig something up on Trent. Nailing him as a distributor of Brimstone would be enough to pay off my contract.

Jenks flew up to stand on the rim of the basket, his wings moving fitfully to keep his balance. "Mind if I come with you to get a good sniff of Trent? I bet I could tell what he is."

My whiskers brushed the air as I thought about it. It'd be nice having a second pair of eyes. I could hitch a ride with Francis. Not as a mink, though. He would probably scream like a sissy and throw things if he found me hiding in the backseat. "Talk later," I spelled out. "Home."

Jenks's smile grew sly. "Before we go, do you want to see your record?"

I shook my head. I had seen my record lots of times. "No," I wrote. "I want to shred it."

Twelve

I've got to get a car," I whispered as I lurched off the bus steps. I snatched my coat out of the closing doors and held my breath as the diesel engine roared to life and the bus lumbered off. "Soon," I added, pulling my bag closer.

I hadn't slept well in days. Salt had dried all over me and I itched everywhere. It seemed I couldn't go five minutes without accidentally hitting the blister on my neck. Coming off the caramel-induced sugar high, Jenks was cranky. In short, we were very good company.

A false dawn had brightened the eastern sky, giving the thin blue a beautiful translucence. The birds were loud and the streets were hushed. The chill in the air made me glad for my coat. I would guess the sun was only an hour from rising. Four in the morning in June was a golden hour when all good vampires are tucked into bed and wise humans hadn't yet poked their noses out to find the early edition of the paper. "I am so ready for bed," I whispered.

"Evening, Ms. Morgan," came a gravely voice, and I spun, falling into a crouch.

Jenks made a snuff of sarcastic laughter from my earring. "It's the neighbor," he said dryly. "Jeez, Rache. Give me some credit."

Heart pounding, I slowly stood, feeling as old as I was supposed to be under my age spell. Why wasn't he in bed? "'Morning, rather," I said, stepping even with Keasley's gate. He was unmoving in his rocker, his face shadowed and unseen.

"Been shopping?" He wiggled his foot to tell me he noticed my boots were new.

Tired, I leaned on the top of the chain-link fence. "Would you like a chocolate?" I asked, and he motioned for me to enter.

Jenks hummed in worry. "A splat ball's range is longer than my sense of smell, Rache."

"He's a lonely old man," I whispered as I unlatched the gate. "He wants a chocolate. Besides, I look like an old hag. Anyone watching will think I'm his date." I eased the lock down quietly, and I thought I saw Keasley hide a smile behind a yawn.

A tiny, dramatic sigh slipped from Jenks. I settled my bag on the porch and sat down on the uppermost stair. Twisting, I pulled a paper sack from my coat pocket and extended it.

"Ah . . ." he said, his gaze on the horse-and-rider trademark. "Some things are worth risking your life for." As I expected, he chose a dark piece. A dog barked in the distance. Jaw moving, he looked past me into the silent street. "You've been to the mall."

I shrugged. "Among other places."

Jenks's wings fanned my neck. "Rachel . . ."

"Cool your jets, Jenks," I said, peeved.

Keasley got to his feet with a pained slowness. "No. He's right. It's late."

Between Keasley's obtuse comments and Jenks's instincts, I became decidedly wary. The dog barked again, and I lurched to my feet. My thoughts returned to that pile of splat balls outside my door. Maybe I should have hiked in through the graveyard, disguised or not.

Keasley moved with a pained slowness to his door. "Watch your step, Ms. Morgan. Once they know you can slip past them, they'll change tactics." He opened the door and went inside. The screen shut without a sound. "Thank you for the chocolate."

"You're welcome," I whispered as I turned away, knowing he could hear me.

"Creepy old man," Jenks said, making my earring swing as I crossed the street and headed for the motorbike parked in front of the church. The false dawn glinted on its chrome, and I wondered if Ivy had gotten her bike back from the shop.

"Maybe she'll let me use it," I mused aloud, eyeing it appreciatively in passing. It was all shiny and black, with its gold trim and silky leather; a Nightwing. Yummy. I ran an envious hand across the seat, leaving a smear where I wiped the dew away.

"Rache!" Jenks shrilled. "Drop!"

I dropped. Heart pounding, my palms hit the pavement. There was the hiss of something overhead where I had stood. Adrenaline surged, making my head hurt. I shoved myself into a roll, putting the bike between me and the opposite street.

I held my breath. Nothing moved among the shrubs and overgrown bushes. I pushed my bag in front of my face, my hands searching inside.

"Stay down," Jinks hissed. His voice was tight, and a purple glow laced his wings.

The prick of the finger stick jolted me to my toes. My sleep charm was invoked in 4.5 seconds; my best time yet. Not that it would do me much good if whoever it was stayed in the bushes. Maybe I could throw it at him. If the I.S. was going to make a habit of this, I might want to invest in a splat gun. I was more of a confront-them-directly-and-knock-them-unconscious kind of a gal. Hiding in the bushes like a sniper was cheesy, but when in Rome . . .

I gripped the charm by the cord so it wouldn't affect me and waited.

"Save it," Jenks said, relaxing as we were abruptly surrounded by a host of darting pixy children. They swirled over us, talking so fast and high I couldn't keep up. "They're gone," Jenks added. "Sorry about that. I knew they were there, but—"

"You knew they were there?" I exclaimed, my neck hurting as I peered up at him. A dog barked, and I lowered my voice. "What the hell were you doing?"

He grinned. "I had to flush them out."

Peeved, I got to my feet. "Great. Thanks. Let me know next time I'm bait." I shook out my long coat, grimacing as I realized I'd squished my chocolates.

"Now, Rache," he cajoled, hovering by my ear. "If I had told you, your reactions would have been off and the fairies would have just waited until I wasn't watching."

My face went slack. "Fairies?" I said, chilled. Denon must be off his rocker. They were expe-e-e-e-ensive. Perhaps they gave him a discount because of the frog incident.

"There're gone," Jenks said, "but I wouldn't stay out here for long. The word is the Weres want another crack at you." He took off his red bandanna and handed it to his son. "Jax, you and your sisters can have their catapult."

"Thanks, Papa!" The small pixy rose up two feet in excitement. Wrapping the red scarf around his waist, he and about six other pixies broke from the group and zipped across the street.

"Be careful!" Jenks shouted after them. "It might be booby-trapped!"

Fairies, I thought as I clutched my arms about me and looked over the quiet street. Crap.

The remainder of Jenks's kids was clustered around him, all talking at once as they tried to drag him around back. "Ivy's with someone," Jenks said as he started to drift upward, "but he checks out okay. You mind if I call it a night?"

"Go ahead," I said, glancing at the bike. It wasn't Ivy's after all. "And, uh, thanks."

They rose like a swarm of fireflies. Close behind them were Jax and his sisters, working together to carry a catapult as small as they were. With a dry clattering of wings and shouts, they flew up and beyond the church, leaving a hard silence in the morning street.

I turned my back and shuffled up the stone stairs. Glancing across the road, I saw a curtain fall against the single lit window. *Show's over. Go to sleep, Keasley,* I thought, tugging open the heavy door and slipping inside. Easing it shut, I slid the oiled dead bolt in place behind me, feeling better despite knowing most of the I.S.'s assassins wouldn't use a door. *Fairies? Denon must be royally ticked.*

Blowing wearily, I leaned back against the thick timbers, to shut out the coming morning. All I wanted was to take a shower and go to bed. As I slowly crossed the empty sanctuary, the sound of soft jazz and Ivy's voice raised in anger filtered out from the living room.

"Damn it, Kist," I heard as I entered the dark kitchen. "If you don't get your butt out of that chair right now, I'm going to sling you halfway to the sun."

"Aw, lighten up, Tamwood. I'm not gonna do anything," came a new voice. It was masculine, deep but with a hint of a whine, as if whomever it came from was indulged in almost everything. I paused to dump my used amulets into the pot of saltwater beside the refrigerator. They were still good, but I knew better than to leave active amulets lying around.

The music snapped off with a jarring suddenness. "Out," Ivy said softly. "Now."

"Ivy?" I called loudly, curiosity getting the better of me. Jenks said whoever it was had the all clear. Leaving my bag on the kitchen counter, I headed for the living room. My exhaustion spilled into a tinge of anger. We had never discussed it, but I assumed that until the price was off my head, we would try to keep a low profile.

"Ooooh," the unseen Kist mocked. "She's back."

"Behave yourself," Ivy threatened him as I entered the room. "Or I'll have your hide."

"Promise?"

I took three steps into the living room and jerked to a halt. My anger vanished, washed away in a surge of primal instinct. A leather-clad vamp sprawled in Ivy's chair, looking like he belonged. His immaculate boots were on the coffee table, and Ivy shoved them off in disgust. She moved quicker than I'd ever seen before. She took two steps from him and fumed, her hip cocked and her arms crossed aggressively. The mantel clock ticked loudly.

Kist couldn't be a dead vamp—he was on holy ground and it was almost sunup—but burn my britches if he didn't come close. His feet hit the floor with an exaggerated slowness. The indolent look he gave me went right to my core, settling over me like a wet blanket to tighten my gut. And yeah, he was pretty. Dangerously so. My thoughts jerked back to Table 6.1, and I swallowed.

His face was lightly stubbled, giving him a rugged appearance. Straightening, he tossed his blond hair out of his eyes in a movement of artful grace that must have taken him years to perfect. His leather jacket was open to show a black cotton shirt pulled tight over an attractively muscled chest. Twin stud earrings glittered from one ear. The other had a single earring and a long-healed tear. Otherwise, he hadn't a visible scar anywhere. I wondered if I would be able to feel them if I ran my finger down his neck.

My heart pounded, and I dropped my gaze, promising myself I wouldn't look again. Ivy didn't scare me as much as this one did. He moved on feral instinct, governed by whim.

"Aw," Kist said, scooting himself up in the chair. "She's cute. You should have told me she was such a dar-r-r-rling." I felt him take a deep breath, as if tasting the night. "She reeks of you, Ivy love." His voice dropped in pitch. "Isn't that the sweetest?"

Cold, I clutched the collar of my coat closed and backed up until I was in the threshold.

"Rachel," Ivy said dryly. "This is Kisten. He's leaving. Aren't you, Kist."

It wasn't a question, and my breath caught as he got to his feet with a fluid, animal grace. Kist stretched, his hands reaching for the ceiling. His lean body moved like a cord to show every gorgeous curve of muscle on him. I couldn't look away. His arms fell and our eyes met. They were brown. His lips parted in a soft smile as he knew I had been watching him. His teeth were sharp like Ivy's. He wasn't a ghoul. He was a living vamp. I looked away even though living vamps couldn't bespell the wary. "You have a taste for vamps, little witch?" he whispered.

His voice was like wind over water, and my knees went loose at the compulsion he put in it. "You can't touch me," I said, unable to resist looking at him as he tried to bespell me. My voice sounded like it was coming from inside my head. "I haven't signed any papers."

"No?" he whispered. His eyebrows were raised in sultry confidence. He eased close, his steps soundless. Heart pounding, I looked at the floor. I felt behind me to touch the doorframe. He was stronger than me, and faster. But a knee in the groin would drop him like any man.

"The courts won't care," he breathed as he drifted to a stop. "You're already dead."

My eyes widened as he reached for me. His scent washed over me, the musty scent of black earth. My pulse pounded, and I stepped forward. His hand cupped my chin, warm. A shock went through me, buckling my knees. He gripped my elbow, supporting me against his chest. Anticipation of an unknown promise made my blood race. I leaned into him, waiting. His lips parted. A whisper of words I couldn't understand came from him, beautiful and dark.

"Kist!" Ivy shouted, startling both of us. A flash of ire filmed his eyes, then vanished.

My will flowed back with a painful swiftness. I tried to jerk away, finding myself held. I could smell blood. "Let go," I said, almost panicking when he didn't. "Let go!"

His hand dropped. He turned to Ivy, completely dismissing me. I fell back to the archway, shaking, but unable to voluntarily leave until I knew he was gone.

Kist stood before Ivy calm and collected, a study in opposites to Ivy's agitation. "Ivy, love," he persuaded. "Why do you torment yourself? Your scent covers her, but her blood still smells pure. How can you resist? She's asking for it.

She's screaming for it. She'll bitch and moan the first time, but she'll thank you for it in the end."

Expression going coy, he gently bit his lip. Crimson ran, wiped away with a slow, taunting, deliberate tongue. My breath sounded harsh even to me, and I held it.

Ivy went furious, her eyes going to black pits. The tension wouldn't let me breathe. The crickets outside chirped faster. With an exaggerated slowness, Kist cautiously leaned toward Ivy. "If you don't want to break her in," he said, his voice low with anticipation, "give her to me. I'll give her back to you." His lips parted to show his glistening canines. "Scout's honor."

Ivy's breath came in a quick pant. Her face was an unreal mix of lust and hatred. I could see her struggle to overcome her hunger, and I watched in a horrid fascination as it slowly vanished until only the hatred was left. "Get out," she said, her voice husky and wavering.

Kist took a slow breath. The tension flowed out of him as he exhaled. I found I could breathe again. I took quick, shallow breaths as my gaze darted between them. It was over. Ivy had won. I was—safe?

"It's stupid, Tamwood," Kist said as he adjusted his black leather jacket in a careful show of ease. "A waste of a good span of darkness for something that doesn't exist."

With swift, abrupt steps, Ivy went to the back door. Sweat trickled down the small of my back as the breeze from her passage touched me. Cold morning air spilled in, displacing the blackness that seemed to have filled the room. "She's mine," Ivy said as if I wasn't there. "She's under my protection. What I do or don't do with her is my business. You tell Piscary if I see one of his shadows at my church again, I'll assume he's making a bid of contention to what I hold. Ask him if he wants a war with me, Kist. You ask him that."

Kist passed between Ivy and me, hesitating on the sill. "You can't hide your hunger from her forever," Kist said, and Ivy's lips pressed together. "Once she sees, she'll run, and she'll be fair prey." In a clock-tick he slumped, a bad-boy look softening his features. "Come back," he cajoled with a sultry innocence. "I'm to tell you that you can have your old place again with only a minor concession. She's just a witch. You don't even know if she—"

"Out," Ivy said, pointing at the morning.

Kist stepped through the door. "An offer shunned makes dire enemies."

"An offer that really isn't one shames the one who makes it."

Shrugging, he pulled a leather cap from his back pocket and put it on. He glanced at me, his gaze going hungry. "Good-bye, love," he whispered, and I shuddered as if he had run a slow hand across my cheek. I couldn't tell if it was revulsion or desire. And he was gone.

Ivy slammed the door behind him. Moving with that same eerie grace, she crossed the living room and dropped into a chair. Her face was dark with anger, and I stared at her. *Holy crap. I was living with a vampire.* Nonpracticing or not, she was a vamp. What had Kist said? That Ivy was wasting her time? That I'd run when I saw her hunger? That I was hers? *Shit.*

Moving slowly, I edged backward out of the room. Ivy glanced up, and I froze. The anger drained from her face, replaced with what looked like alarm when she saw my fear.

Slowly, I blinked. My throat closed and I turned my back on her, going into the hallway.

"Rachel, wait," she called after me, her voice cajoling. "I'm sorry about Kist. I didn't invite him. He just showed up."

I strode into the hall, tensed to explode if she put a hand on me. Was this why Ivy had quit with me? She couldn't legally hunt me, but as Kist had said, the courts wouldn't care.

"Rachel . . ."

She was right behind me, and I spun. My stomach tightened. Ivy took three steps back. They were so quick it was hard to tell she had moved. Her hands were raised in placation. Her brow was pinched in worry. My pulse hammered, giving me a headache. "What do you want?" I asked, half hoping she would lie and tell me it was a mistake. From outside came the noise of Kist's bike. I stared at her as the sound of his departure faded.

"Nothing," she said, her brown eyes earnestly fixed to mine. "Don't listen to Kist. He's just jerking you around. He flirts with what he can't have."

"That's right!" I shouted so I wouldn't start shaking. "I'm yours. That's what you said, that I'm yours! I'm not anyone's, Ivy! Stay the hell away from me!"

Her lips parted in surprise. "You heard that?"

"Of course I heard that!" I yelled. Anger overpowered my fear, and I took a step forward. "Is that what you're really like?" I shouted, pointing to the unseen living room. "Like that—that animal? Is it? Are you hunting me, Ivy? Is this all about filling your gut with my blood? Does it taste better when you betray them? Does it?"

"No!" she exclaimed in distress. "Rachel, I—"

"You lied to me!" I shouted. "He bespelled me. You said a living vamp couldn't do that unless I wanted him to. And I sure as hell didn't!"

She said nothing, her tall shadow framed by the hallway. I could hear her breath and smell the sweet-sour tang of wet ash and redwood: our scents dangerously mingling. Her stance was tense, her very stillness sending a shock through me. Mouth dry, I backed up as I realized I was screaming at a vampire. The adrenaline spent itself. I felt nauseous and cold. "You lied to me," I whispered, retreating into the kitchen. She had lied to me. Dad was right. Don't trust anyone. I was getting my things and leaving.

Ivy's steps were overly loud behind me. It was obvious she was making an effort to hit the floor hard enough to make a sound. I was too angry to care.

"What are you doing?" she asked as I opened a cupboard and pulled a handful of charms off a hook, to put them in my bag.

"Leaving."

"You can't! You heard Kist. They're waiting for you!"

"Better to die knowing my enemies then to die sleeping innocently beside them," I retorted, thinking it was the stupidest thing I'd ever said. It didn't even make sense.

I jerked to a halt as she slipped in front of me and shut the cupboard. "Get out of my way," I threatened, my voice low so she wouldn't hear it shake.

Dismay pinched her eyes and furrowed her brow. She looked utterly human, and it scared the crap out of me. Just when I thought I understood her, she did something like this.

With my charms and finger sticks out of reach, I was helpless. She could throw me across the room and crack my head open on the oven. She could break my legs so I couldn't run. She could tie me to a chair and bleed me. But what she did was stand before me with a pained, frustrated look on her pale, perfect, oval face. "I can explain," she said, her voice low.

I fought off the shakes as I met her gaze. "What do you want with me?" I whispered.

"I didn't lie to you," she said, not answering my question. "Kist is Piscary's chosen scion. Most of the time Kist is just Kist, but Piscary can—" She hesitated. I stared at her, every muscle in my body screaming to run. But if I moved, she would move. "Piscary is older than dirt," she said flatly. "He's powerful enough to use Kist to go places he can't anymore."

"He's a servant," I spat. "He's a freaking lackey for a dead vamp. Does his daylight shopping for him, brings Papa Piscary humans to snack on."

Ivy winced. The tension was easing from her, and she took a more relaxed stance—still between me and my charms. "It's a great honor to be asked to be a scion for a vampire like Piscary. And it's not all one-sided. Because of it, Kist has more power than a living vamp should have. That's how he was able to bespell you. But Rachel," she rushed as I made a helpless noise, "I wouldn't have let him."

And I should be happy for that? That you don't want to

share? My pulse had slowed, and I sank down into a chair. I didn't think my knees would support me anymore. I wondered how much of my weakness was from the spent adrenaline and how much was Ivy pumping the air full of soothing pheromones. *Damn, damn, damn!* I was in way over my head. Especially if Piscary was involved.

Piscary was said to be one of the oldest vampires in Cincinnati. He didn't cause trouble and kept his few people in line. He worked the system for all it was worth, doing all the paperwork and making sure every take his people made was legal. He was far more than the simple restaurant owner he pretended to be. The I.S. had a "Don't ask, don't tell" policy on the master vampire. He was one of the aforementioned people who moved in Cincinnati's unseen power struggles, but as long as he paid his taxes and kept his liquor license current, there was nothing anyone could—or wanted to—do. But if a vampire looked harmless, it only meant they were smarter than most.

My eyes flicked to Ivy, standing with her arms clasped about herself as if she were upset. *Oh, God. What was I doing here?*

"What's Piscary to you?" I asked, hearing my voice tremble.

"Nothing," she said, and I made a scoffing noise. "Really," she insisted. "He's a friend of the family."

"Uncle Piscary, huh?" I said bitterly.

"Actually," she said slowly, "that's more accurate than you might think. Piscary started my mother's living-vamp bloodline in 1700s."

"And has been bleeding you slowly ever since," I said bitterly.

"It's not like that," she said, sounding hurt. "Piscary's never touched me. He's like a second father."

"Maybe he's letting the blood age in the bottle."

Ivy ran her hand over her hair in an unusual show of worry. "It's not like that. Really."

"Swell." I slumped to put my elbows on the table. Now I

had to worry about chosen scions invading my church with the strength of a master? Why didn't she tell me this before? I didn't want to play the damn game if the rules kept changing.

"What do you want with me?" I asked again, afraid she might tell me and I'd have to leave.

"Nothing."

"Liar," I said, but when I looked up from the table, she was gone.

My breath came in a quick sound. Heart pounding, I stood, my arms clasped about myself as I stared at the empty counters and silent walls. I hated it when she did that. Mr. Fish on the windowsill wiggled and squirmed, not liking it, either.

Slow and reluctant, I put my charms away. My thoughts swirled back to the fairy attack on my front steps, the Were splat balls stacked on my back porch, and then to Kist's words that the vamps were just waiting for me to leave Ivy's protection. I was trapped, and Ivy knew it.

Thirteen

I tapped on the outside of the passenger window of Francis's car to get Jenks's attention. "What time is it?" I said softly, since even whispers echoed down in the parking deck. Cameras were recording me, but no one watched the films unless someone complained of a break-in.

Jenks dropped from the visor and wedged the button for the power window down. "Eleven-fifteen," he said as the glass lowered. "Do you think they rescheduled Kalamack's interview?"

I shook my head and glanced over the tops of the cars to the elevator doors. "No. But if he makes me late, I'm going to be ticked." I tugged at the hem of my skirt. Much to my relief, Jenks's friend had come through with my clothes and jewelry yesterday. All my clothes were hanging in neat rows or resting in tidy piles in my closet. It felt good seeing them there. The Were had done a nice job washing, drying, and folding everything, and I wondered how much he'd charge to do my laundry every week.

Finding something to wear that was both conservative and provocative had been harder than I thought. I had finally settled on a short red skirt, plain tights, and a white blouse whose buttons could be undone or fastened according to need. My hoop earrings were too small for Jenks to perch on, which the pixy had spent the first half hour complaining about. With my hair piled atop my head and a snappy pair of red heels, I looked like a perky coed. The disguise spell helped; I was a big-nosed brunette again, reeking of that lavender perfume. Francis would know who I was, but then, I wanted him to.

I nervously picked at the dirt under my nails, making a mental note to repolish them. The red enamel had vanished when I turned into a mink. "Do I look okay?" I asked Jenks as I fussed with my collar.

"Yeah, fine."

"You didn't even look," I complained as the elevator chimed. "That might be him," I said. "Are you set with that potion?"

"I only have to nudge the top and it will be all over him." Jenks rolled the window up and darted into hiding. I had a vial of "sleepy-time" potion balanced between the ceiling of the car and the visor. Francis, though, would be led to believe it was something more sinister. It was incentive for him to agree to let me take his place at the Kalamack interview. Hijacking a full-grown man, wuss or not, was tricky. It wasn't quite as if I could knock him out and lug him into the trunk. And leaving him unconscious where anyone could find him would get me caught.

Jenks and I had been in the parking deck for an hour now, making small but telling modifications to Francis's sports car. It had taken Jenks only a few moments to short out the alarm and rig the driver's door and window locks. And while I had to wait outside the car for Francis, my bag was already tucked under the passenger seat.

Francis had earned himself a real cherry of a car: a red convertible with leather seats. There were dual climate controls. The windows could go opaque—I knew, because I had tried them. There was even a built-in cell phone whose batteries were now in my bag. The vanity plate read, BUSTED. The hateful thing had so many gadgets, all it needed was clearance to take off. And it still smelled new. A bribe, I wondered with a stab of jealousy, or hush money?

The light over the elevators went out. I ducked behind the pylon, hoping it was Francis. The last thing I wanted was to be late. My pulse settled into a fast, familiar pace, and a smile eased over me as I recognized Francis's quick foot-steps. He was alone. There was a jangle of keys and a sur-prised "Huh" when the car didn't make the expected welcoming chirp as he disengaged the alarm. My fingertips tingled in anticipation. This was going to be fun.

His car door squeaked open, and I sprang around the py-lon. As one, Francis and I slid into either side of the vehicle, our doors slamming shut simultaneously.

"What the hell?" Francis exclaimed, only now realizing he had company. His narrow eyes squinted and he flicked his limp hair out of his eyes. "Rachel!" he said, nearly oozing misplaced confidence. "You are so dead."

He went for the door. I reached across him to grip his wrist, pointing up to Jenks. The pixy grinned. His wings were a blur of anticipation as he patted the vial of brew. Francis went white. "Tag," I whispered, letting go of him and locking the doors from my side. "You're it."

"Wh-What do you think you're doing?" Francis stuttered, pale under his nasty stubble.

I smiled. "I'm taking your run to interview Kalamack. You just volunteered to drive."

He stiffened, a hint of backbone showing. "You can just Turn yourself," he said, his eyes on Jenks and the potion. "Like you'd dip into black magic and make something fatal. I'm tagging you right now."

Jenks made a disgusted sound and tilted the vial. "Not yet, Jenks!" I shouted, lunging across the seat. Nearly in Francis's lap, I snaked my right arm around the scrawny man's windpipe, gripping the headrest to pin him to the seat in a headlock. His fingers clutched at my arm but he couldn't do anything in the close confines. His sudden sweat mixed with the scrape of his polyester jacket against my arm, and I thought it more vile than my perfume. "Idiot!" I hissed into Francis's ear, glancing up at Jenks. "Do you know what that is, dangling above your crotch? You want to chance that it might be irreversible?"

Red-faced, he shook his head, and I eased myself closer despite the gearshift jabbing my hip. "You wouldn't make anything fatal," he said, his voice higher than usual.

From the visor, Jenks complained, "Aw, Rache. Let me spell him. I can coach you on how to drive a stick."

The fingers digging into my arm jerked. I tensed, using the pain as impetus to pin him to the seat all the tighter. "Bug!" Francis exclaimed. "You're a—" His words choked off with a rasp as I jerked my arm.

"Bug?" Jenks shouted, incensed. "You sack of sweat stink. I've got farts that smell sweeter than you. Think you're better than me? Poop ice cream cones, do you? Call me a *bug*! Rachel, let me do him now!"

"No," I said softly, my dislike for Francis dipping into real aversion. "I'm sure Francis and I can come to an understanding. All I want is a ride out to Trent's estate and that interview. Francis won't get into trouble. He's a victim, right?" I smiled grimly at Jenks, wondering if I could keep him from dosing Francis after such an insult. "And you aren't going to nack him afterward. Hear me, Jenks? You don't kill the donkey after he plows the field. You might need him next spring." I leaned into Francis, breathing into his ear. "Right, cookie?"

He nodded as much as he could, and I slowly let him go. His eyes were on Jenks.

"You squish my associate," I said, "and that vial will spill on you. You drive too fast, the vial will spill. If you attract attention—"

"I'll dump it all over you," Jenks interrupted, the light playfulness in his voice replaced with a hot anger. "You tick me off again, I'll spell you good." He laughed, sounding like evil wind chimes. "Got it, *Francine*?"

Francis's eyes squinted. He resettled himself in his seat, touching the collar of his white shirt before he pushed the sleeves of his jacket to his elbows and took the wheel. I thanked God that Francis had left his Hawaiian shirts at home in deference to his interview with Trent Kalamack.

Face tight, he jammed the keys in the ignition and started the car. Music blared, and I jumped. The sullen way Francis cranked the wheel and threw the car into gear made it obvious he hadn't given up; he was playing along until he could find a way out. I didn't care. All I needed was to get him away from the city. Once clear, it would be nappies for Francis.

"You're not going to get away with this," he said, sounding like a bad movie. He waved his parking pass at the automated gate, and we eased into the bright light and late morning traffic with Don Henley's "Boys of Summer" blasting. If I hadn't been wound so tight, I might have enjoyed it.

"Think you could put more of that perfume on, Rachel?" Francis said, a sneer twisting his narrow face. "Or are you wearing it to cover your pet bug's stench?"

"Shut him up!" Jenks shouted. "Or I will."

My shoulder tensed. This was so stupid. "Pix him if you want, Jenks," I said as I turned down the music. "Just don't let any of that brew hit him."

Jenks grinned and flipped Francis off. Pixy dust fanned over him, unseen by Francis but clearly visible from my angle, since it reflected the sun. Francis reached up to scratch behind an ear.

"How long does it take?" I asked Jenks.

"'Bout twenty minutes."

Jenks was right. By the time we had gotten out from under the shadow of buildings, through the burbs, and into the country, Francis put two and two together. He couldn't sit still. His comments got nastier and nastier, and his scratching more and more intense, until I pulled the duct tape out of my purse and threatened to tape his mouth shut. Red welts had appeared where his clothes met his skin. They oozed a clear liquid, looking like a bad case of poison ivy. When we hit deep country, he was scratching so much it seemed a struggle to keep the car on the road. I had been watching him intently. Driving a stick didn't look hard.

"You *bug*," he said with a snarl. "You did this to me Saturday, too, didn't you!"

"I'm gonna spell him!" Jenks said, the high pitch of his voice making my eyes ache.

Tired of it all, I turned to Francis. "All right, cookie. Pull it over."

Francis blinked. "What?"

Idiot, I thought. "How long do you think I can keep Jenks from tagging you if you keep insulting him? Pull over." Francis glanced nervously between the road and me. We hadn't seen a car in the last five miles. "I said, *pull over!*" I shouted, and he swerved to the dusty shoulder in a rattling of pebbles. I turned the car off and yanked the keys from the ignition. We lurched to a stop, my head smacking against the rearview mirror. "Out," I said, unlocking the doors.

"What? Here?" Francis was a city boy. He thought I was going to make him walk back. The idea was tempting, but I couldn't run the risk of him being picked up or finding his way to a phone. He got out with a surprising eagerness. I realized why when he started scratching.

I popped the trunk, and Francis's thin face went blank. "No way," he said, his skinny arms raised. "I'm not getting in there."

I felt the new bump on my forehead, waiting. "Get into the trunk or I'm going to teach you how I spell mink and make a pair of earmuffs out of you." I watched him think that over, wondering if he would make a run for it. I almost wished he would. It'd feel good to tackle him again. It had nearly been two whole days. I'd get him into the trunk somehow.

"Run," Jenks said, circling above his head with the vial. "Go on. Dare you, stink bag."

Francis seemed to deflate. "Oh, you'd like that, eh, bug?" he said with a sneer. But he wedged himself into the tiny space. He even gave me no trouble when I duct-taped his hands in front of him. We both knew he could get out of the wraps given enough time. But his superior look faltered as I held my hand up and Jenks landed on it with the vial.

"You said you wouldn't," he stammered. "You said it would turn me into a mink!"

"I lied. Both times."

The look Francis gave me was murderous. "I won't forget this," he said, his jaw clenching to make him look even more ridiculous than his boat shoes and wide-cuffed slacks. "I'm coming after you myself."

"I hope you do." I smiled, dumping the vial over his head. "Nighty night."

He opened his mouth to say more, but his expression slackened as soon as the fragrant liquid hit him. I watched, fascinated, as he fell asleep amid the scent of bay leaf and lilac. Satisfied, I slammed the trunk shut and called it good.

Settling uneasily behind the wheel, I adjusted the seat and mirrors. I hadn't ever driven a stick before, but if Francis could do it, I sure as heck could.

"Put it in first," Jenks said, sitting on the rearview mirror and mimicking what I should do. "Then give it more gas than you think you need while you let up on the clutch."

I gingerly pushed the stick back and started the car.

"Well?" Jenks said from the mirror. "We're waiting. . . ."

I pushed the gas pedal and let up on the clutch. The car lurched backward, slamming into a tree. Panicking, I pulled my feet from the pedals, and the car stalled. I stared wide-eyed at Jenks as he laughed. "It's in reverse, witch," he said, darting out the window.

Through the rearview mirror, I watched him zip to the back and assess the damage. "How bad is it?" I asked as he came back.

"It's okay," he said, and I felt a wash of relief. "Give it a few months, and you won't be able to see where it was hit," he added. "The car's busted, though. You broke a taillight."

"Oh," I said, realizing he'd been talking about the tree, not the car. My nerves were jittery as I jammed the stick forward, double-checked it, and started the car again. Another deep breath, and we lurched forward on our way.

Fourteen

Jenks turned out to be a passable instructor, enthusiastically shouting advice through the window as I practiced starting from a dead stop until I got the hang of it. My new-found confidence evaporated as I turned onto Kalamack's drive, slowing at the gatehouse. It was low and formidable looking, the size of a small jail. Tasteful plantings and low walls hid the security system that prevented anyone from driving around it.

"And how did you plan to get past that?" Jenks said as he flitted to hide atop the visor.

"No problem," I said, my mind whirling. Visions of Francis in the trunk assailed me, and smiling my prettiest at the guard, I brought the car to a halt before the white stick across the road. The amulet beside the guard's watch stayed a nice green. It was a spell checker, much cheaper than the wood-framed glasses that could see through charms. I had been very careful to keep the amount of magic used in my disguise spell below the level of most vanity charms. As long as his amulet stayed green, he would assume I was under a standard makeup spell, not a disguise.

"I'm Francine," I said on the spur of the moment. I pitched my voice high, smiling brainlessly, as if I had been planting Brimstone all night. "I have an appointment with Mr. Kalamack?" Trying to look like a nitwit, I twirled a stray strand of hair. I was a brunette today, but it probably still worked. "Am I late?" I asked, tugging my finger free of the knot I had accidentally put in my hair. "I didn't think it would take me this long. He lives a long way out!"

The gateman was unaffected. Maybe I was losing my touch. Maybe I should have undone another button on my blouse. Maybe he liked men. He looked at his clipboard, then me.

"I'm from the I.S.," I said, putting my tone somewhere between petulance and spoiled annoyance. "Do you want to see my ID?" I rummaged in my bag for my nonexistent badge.

"Your name isn't on the list, ma'am," the stone-faced guard said.

I flopped back with a huff. "Did that guy in dispatch put me down as Francis again? Darn him!" I exclaimed, hitting the wheel with an ineffective fist. "He's always doing that, ever since I refused to go on a date with him. I mean, really. He didn't even have a car! He wanted to take me to the movies on a bus. Ple-e-e-e-ease," I moaned. "Can you see me on a *bus*?"

"Just a moment, ma'am." He picked up a phone and began speaking. I waited, trying to keep my ditzy smile in place, praying. The gateman's head bobbed in an unconscious expression of agreement. Still, his face was seriously empty when he turned back.

"Up the drive," he said, and I struggled to keep my breath even. "Third building on the right. You can park in the visitor lot directly off the front steps."

"Thank you," I sang merrily, sending the car lurching forward when the white bar rose. Through the rearview mirror I watched the guard go back inside. "Easy as pie," I muttered.

"Getting out might be harder," Jenks said dryly.

Up the drive was three miles through an eerie wood. My mood went subdued as the road wound between the close, silent sentinels. Despite the overpowering impression of age, I began to get the feeling that everything had been planned out, even to the surprises, like the waterfall I found around a bend in the road. Disappointed somehow, I continued on as the artificial woods thinned and turned into rolling pasture. A second road joined mine, well-traveled and busy. Apparently I had come in the back way. I followed the traffic, taking an offshoot labeled VISITORS PARKING. Rounding a turn in the road, I saw the Kalamack estate.

The huge fortress of a building was a curious mix of modern institution and traditional elegance, with glass doors and carved angels on the downspouts. Its gray rock was softened by old trees and bright flower beds. There were several low buildings attached to it, but the main one rose three stories up. I brought the car to a halt in one of the visitor parking spots. The sleek vehicle next to mine made Francis's car look like a toy from the bottom of a cereal box.

Dropping Francis's wad of keys into my bag, I eyed the gardener tending the bushes surrounding the lot. "Still want to split up?" I breathed as I primped in the rearview mirror, carefully picking out that knot I'd put in my hair. "I don't like what happened at the front gate."

Jenks flitted down onto the stick shift and stood with his hands on his hips in his Peter Pan pose. "Your interview runs the usual forty minutes?" he said. "I'll be done in twenty. If I'm not here when you're done, wait about a mile down from the gatehouse. I'll catch up."

"Sure," I said as I tightened the string on my bag. The gardener was wearing shoes, not boots, and they were clean. What gardener has clean shoes? "Just be careful," I said, nodding to the small man. "Something smells off."

Jenks snickered. "The day I can't elude a gardener is the day I become a baker."

"Well, wish me luck." I cracked the window for Jenks and got out. My heels clacked smartly as I went to take a peek at the back of Francis's car. As Jenks had said, one of the taillights was broken. There was a nasty dent, too. I turned away with a flash of guilt. Taking a steadying breath, I strode up the shallow steps to the twin, double doors.

A man stepped from a recessed nook as I approached, and

I jerked to a halt, startled. He was tall enough to need two looks to see all of him. And thin. He reminded me of a starving post-Turn refugee from Europe: prim, proper, and stuck-up. The man even had a hawklike nose and permanent frown cemented to his lightly wrinkled face. Gray brushed his temples, marring his otherwise coal black hair. His inconspicuous gray slacks and white business shirt fitted him perfectly, and I tugged my collar straight. "Ms. Francine Percy?" he said, his smile empty and his voice slightly sarcastic.

"Yes, hello," I said, purposely giving the man a limp-wristed handshake. I could almost see him stiffen in aversion. "I have a noon meeting with Mr. Kalamack."

"I'm Mr. Kalamack's publicity adviser, Jonathan," the man said. Apart from taking great care in his pronunciation, he had no accent. "If you would accompany me? Mr. Kalamack will meet with you in his back office." He blinked, his eyes watering. I imagined it was from my perfume. Maybe I had overdone it, but I wasn't going to risk triggering Ivy's instincts.

Jonathan opened the door for me, motioning me to go before him. I stepped through, surprised to find the building brighter inside than out. I had expected a private residence, and this wasn't it. The entryway looked like the headquarters of any Fortune-twenty business, with the familiar glass and marble motif. White pillars held up the distant ceiling. An impressive mahogany desk stretched before the twin staircases that rose to the second and third floors. Light streamed in. Either it was piped in from the roof or Trent was spending a fortune on natural-light bulbs. A soft, mottled green carpet muffled any echo. There was a buzz of muted conversations and a steady but sedate flow of people going about their business.

"This way, Ms. Percy," my escort said softly.

I dragged my eyes from the man-sized pots of citrus trees and followed Jonathan's measured pace past the front desk and through a series of hallways. The farther we went, the lower the ceilings, the darker the lighting, and the more comforting the colors and textures became. Almost unnoticed, the soothing sound of running water drifted into existence. We hadn't met anyone since leaving the front entryway, and I felt a touch uneasy.

Clearly we had left the public face behind and entered the more private areas. What, I wondered, was going on? Adrenaline shook me as Jonathan paused and put a fingertip to his ear.

"Excuse me," he murmured, stepping a few feet away. His wrist, I noticed as he raised his hand to his ear, had a microphone on his watchband. Alarmed, I strained to catch his words as he had turned to prevent me from reading his lips.

"Yes, Sa'han," he whispered, his tone respectful.

I waited, holding my breath so I could hear.

"With me," he said. "I was informed you had an interest, so I have taken the liberty of escorting her to your back porch." Jonathan shifted uncomfortably. He gave me a long, sideways look of disbelief. "Her?"

I wasn't sure to take that as a compliment or insult, and I pretended to be busy rearranging the back of my stockings and pulling another strand of hair from my topknot to dangle beside my earring. I wondered if someone had investigated the trunk. My pulse quickened as I realized how quickly this could come tumbling down about me.

His eyes widened. "Sa'han," he said urgently, "accept my apologies. The gatehouse said—" His words cut off and I could see him stiffen under what must be a rebuke. "Yes, Sa'han," he said, tilting his head in an unconscious show of deference. "Your front office."

The tall man seemed to gather himself as he turned back to me. I shot him a dazzling smile. There was no expression in his blue eyes as he stared at me as if I was a puppy present on the new rug. "If you would return that way?" he said flatly, pointing.

Feeling more like a prisoner than a guest, I took Jonathan's subtle directions and retraced our path to the front. I led the way. He kept himself behind me. I didn't like this at all. It didn't help that I felt short next to him or that my footsteps were the only ones I could hear. Slowly, the soft colors and textures returned to corporate walls and bustling efficiency.

Keeping those same three steps behind me, Jonathan directed me down a small hallway just off the lobby. Frosted-glass doors were set on either side. Most were propped open and had people working inside, but Jonathan indicated the end office. Its door was wood, and he almost seemed to hesitate before he reached in front of me to open it. "If you would wait here," he said, a hint of a threat in his precise voice. "Mr. Kalamack will be with you shortly. I'll be at his secretary's desk if you need anything."

He pointed to a conspicuously empty desk tucked in a recessed nook. I thought of Ms. Yolin Bates, clay-cold dead in the I.S. lockup three days ago. My smile grew forced. "Thank you, Jon," I said brightly. "You've been a dear."

"It's Jonathan." He shut the door firmly behind me. There was no click of a lock.

I turned, glancing over Kalamack's front office. It looked normal enough—in a disgustingly wealthy executive sort of way. There was a bank of electronic equipment inlaid in the wall next to his desk that held so many buttons and switches it would put a recording studio to shame. The opposite wall had a huge window, the sun spilling in to set the soft carpet glowing. I knew I was too far into the building for the window and its accompanying sunbeam to be real, but it was good enough to warrant a severe going-over.

I set my bag beside the chair opposite the desk and went to the "window." Hands on my hips, I eyed the shot of yearlings arguing over fallen apples. My eyebrows rose. The engineers were off. It was noon, and the sun wasn't low enough to be casting beams that long.

Finding satisfaction in their error, I turned my attention to the freestanding fish tank against the back wall behind the desk. Starfish, blue damsels, yellow tangs, and even sea horses coexisted peacefully, seemingly unaware the ocean was five hundred miles east. My thoughts turned to my Mr. Fish, swimming contentedly in his little glass bowl. I frowned, not jealous, but annoyed at the fickleness of the luck of the world.

Trent's desk had the usual stuff on top, complete with a small fountain of black rock for the water to chatter over. His computer's screen saver was a scrolling line of three numbers: twenty, five, one. A rather enigmatic message. Stuck in the corner where the walls met the ceiling was a conspicuous camera, its red light winking at me. I was under surveillance.

My thoughts went back to Jonathan's conversation with his mysterious Sa'han. Clearly my story of Francine had been breached. But if they wanted me arrested, they would have done it by now. It seemed I had something Mr. Kalamack wanted. *My silence?* I ought to find out.

Grinning, I waved at the camera and settled myself behind Trent's desk. I imagined the stir I was causing as I began rummaging about. The datebook was first, laid invitingly open on the desktop. Francis's appointment had a line through his name and a question mark penciled beside it. Wincing, I leafed back to the day where Trent's secretary had been tagged with Brimstone. There was nothing out of the ordinary. The phrase "Huntingtons to Urlich" caught my eye. Was he smuggling people out of the country? Big whoop.

The top drawer held nothing unusual: pencils, pens, sticky notepads, and a gray touchstone. I wondered what Trent could possibly be concerned about to warrant that. The side drawers contained color-coded files concerning his off-estate interests. As I waited for someone to stop me, I browsed, learning his pecan groves had suffered from a late frost this year but that his strawberries on the coast made up the loss. I slammed the drawer shut, surprised no one had come in yet. Perhaps they were curious as to what I was looking for? I knew I was.

Trent had a thing for maple candy and pre-Turn whiskey,

if the stash I found in a lower drawer meant anything. I was tempted to crack the near forty-year-old bottle and sample it but decided that would bring my watchers out faster than anything else would.

The next drawer was full of neatly arranged discs. *Bingo!* I thought, opening it farther.

"Alzheimer's," I whispered, running a finger across a hand-made label. "Cystic fibrosis, cancer, cancer . . ." In all, there were eight labeled cancer. Depression, diabetes . . . I continued until I found Huntington. My gaze went to the datebook and I shut the drawer. *Ahhhh . . .*

Settling back into Trent's plush chair, I pulled his appointment book onto my lap. I started at January, turning pages slowly. Every fifth day or so a shipment went out. My breath quickened as I noticed a pattern. Huntington went out the same day every month. I flipped back and forth. They all went out on the same day of the month, within a few days of each other. Taking a slow breath, I glanced at the drawer of discs. Sure I was on to something, I popped one into the computer and jiggled the mouse. Damn. Password protected.

There was a small click of a latch. Jumping to my feet, I jabbed the eject button.

"Good afternoon, Ms. Morgan."

It was Trent Kalamack, and I tried not to flush as I slipped the small disc into a pocket. "Beg pardon?" I said, turning the ditzy charm on full. They knew who I was. Big surprise.

Trent adjusted the lowest button on his gray linen jacket as he shut the door behind him. A disarming smile curved over his clean-shaven features, giving him the air of someone my age.

His hair had a transparent whiteness to it that some children have, and he was comfortably tan, looking as if it wouldn't take much to get him poolside. He looked far too pleasant to be as wealthy as he was rumored to be. It wasn't fair to have money and good looks both.

"You'd rather be Francine Percy?" Trent said, eyeing me over his wire-rimmed glasses.

I tucked an escaped curl behind an ear, striving for an air of nonchalance. "Actually—no," I admitted. I must still have a few cards to play or he wouldn't be bothering with me.

Trent moved to the back of his desk with a preoccupied poise, forcing me to retreat to the other side. He held his dark blue tie to himself as he sat. Glancing up, he looked charmingly surprised as he noticed I was still standing. "Please sit," he said, flashing me small, even teeth. He pointed a remote at the camera. The red light went out, and he tucked the remote away.

Still I stood. I didn't trust his casual acceptance. Warning bells were going off in my head, making my stomach clench. *Fortune* magazine had put him on its cover as last year's most eligible bachelor. It had been a head-to-knee shot, with him leaning casually against a door with his company name on it in gold letters. His smile had been a compelling mix of confidence and secrecy. Some women are drawn to a smile like that. Me, I get wary. He gave me the same smile now as he sat, his hand tucked under his chin as his elbow rested on the desktop.

I watched the short hair about his ears drift, and I thought his carefully styled hair had to be incredibly soft if just the draft from the vent could lift it like that.

Trent's lips tightened as he saw my attention on his hair, then returned to that smile. "Let me apologize for the mistake at the front gate, and then with Jon," he said. "I wasn't expecting you for at least another week."

I sat down as my knees went weak. *He was expecting me?* "I'm sure I don't understand," I said boldly, relieved my voice didn't crack.

The man reached for a pencil with a casual ease, but his eyes jerked to mine when I shifted my feet. If I'd known him better, I would have said he was wound tighter than I was. He meticulously erased the question mark by Francis's name and wrote mine in. Setting the pencil down, he ran a hand over his head to get his hair to lay flat.

"I'm a busy man, Ms. Morgan," he said, his voice rising

and falling pleasantly. "I have found it more cost-effective to lure key employees from other companies rather than raise them up from scratch. And where I would be loath to suggest I was in competition with the I.S., I've found their training methods and the skill sets they foster are commensurate with my needs. In all honesty, I would have preferred to see if you had the ingenuity to survive an I.S. death threat before I brought you in. Perhaps nearly finding your way to my back porch is enough."

I crossed my legs and arched my eyebrows. "Are you offering me a job, Mr. Kalamack? You want me for your new secretary? Type your letters? Fetch your coffee?"

"Heavens, no," he said, ignoring my sarcasm. "You smell too strongly of magic for a secretarial position, despite trying to cover it with that—mmm—perfume?"

I flushed, determined not to drop from his questioning gaze.

"No," Trent continued matter-of-factly. "You're too interesting to be a secretary, even one of mine. Not only have you quit the I.S., but you're baiting them. You went shopping. You broke into their records vault to shred your file. Locking a runner unconscious in his own car?" he said with a carefully cultivated laugh. "I like that. But even better is your quest to improve yourself. I applauded your drive to expand your horizons, learn new skills. The willingness to explore options most shun is a mind-set I strive to instill in my employees. Though reading that book on the bus shows a certain lack of . . . judgment." A sliver of dark humor showed behind his eyes. "Unless your interest in vampires has an earthier source, Ms. Morgan?"

My stomach tightened, and I wondered if I had enough charms to fight my way out of here. How had Trent found all that out when the I.S. couldn't even keep tabs on me? I forced myself to be calm as I realized how deep in the pixy dust I was. What had I been thinking, walking in here? The man's secretary was dead. He ran Brimstone, no matter how generous he was during charity fund-raisers or that he golfed with the mayor's husband. He was too smart to be content running a good third of Cincinnati's manufacturing. His hidden interests webbed the underworld, and I was pretty sure he wanted to keep it that way.

Trent leaned forward with an intent expression, and I knew he was done with the idle chitchat. "My question, Ms. Morgan," he said softly, "is what do you want with me?"

I said nothing. My confidence trickled away.

He gestured to his desk. "What were you looking for?"

"Gum?" I said, and he sighed.

"For the sake of eliminating a great deal of wasted time and effort, I suggest we be honest with each other." He took off his glasses and set them aside. "Inasmuch as we need to. Tell me why you risked death to visit me. You have my word the record of your actions today will be—misplaced? I simply want to know where I stand. What have I done to warrant your attention?"

"I walk free?" I said, and he leaned back in his seat, nodding. His eyes were a shade of green I had never seen before. There was no blue in them. Not even a whisper.

"Everyone wants something, Ms. Morgan," he said, each word precise but flowing into the next like water. "What is it you want?"

My heart pounded at his promise of freedom. I followed his gaze to my hands and the dirt under my nails. "You," I said, curling my fingertips under my palms to hide them. "I want the evidence that you killed your secretary. That you're dealing in Brimstone."

"Oh . . ." he said with a poignant sigh. "You want your freedom. I should have guessed. You, Ms. Morgan, are more complex than I gave you credit for." He nodded, his silk-lined suit making a soft whisper as he moved. "Giving me to the I.S. would certainly buy your independence. But you can understand I won't allow it." He straightened, becoming all business again. "I'm in the position of offering you something just as good as freedom. Perhaps better. I can arrange for your I.S. contract to be paid off. A loan, if you will. You can work it off over the course of your career with me. I can set you up in a decent establishment, perhaps a small staff."

My face went cold, then hot. He wanted to buy me. Not noticing my slow anger, he opened a file from his in-box. Pulling a pair of wood-rimmed glasses from an inner pocket, he balanced them on his small nose. I grimaced as he looked me over, clearly seeing past my disguise. He made a small sound before he bent his fair head to read what it contained. "Do you like the beach?" he asked lightly, and I wondered why he was even pretending he needed the glasses to read. "I have a macadamia plantation I have been looking to expand. It's in the South Seas. You could even pick out the colors for the main house."

"You can go Turn yourself, Trent," I said, and he looked up over his glasses, seemingly surprised. It made him look charming, and I forced the thought from me. "If I wanted someone tugging on my leash, I would have stayed with the I.S. Brimstone is grown on those islands. And I might as well be human that close to the sea. I couldn't even bring up a love charm there."

"Sun," he said persuasively as he tucked his glasses away. "Warm sand. Setting your own hours." He closed the file and put a hand upon it. "You can bring your new friend. Ivy, is it? A Tamwood vampire. Quite a catch." A wry smile flickered over him.

My temper burned. He thought he could buy me off. The trouble was, I was tempted, and that made me angry with myself. I glared, my hands stiff in my lap.

"Be honest," Trent said, his long fingers twirling a pencil with a mesmerizing dexterity. "You're resourceful, perhaps even skilled, but no one eludes the I.S. permanently without help."

"I have a better way," I said as I struggled to remain seated. I had nowhere to go until he let me. "I'm going to tie you to a post in the center of the city. I'm going to prove you were involved with your secretary's death and you're dealing in Brimstone. I quit my job, Mr. Kalamack, not my morals."

Ire flickered behind his green eyes, but his face remained calm as he set his pencil back in the cup with a sharp tap. "You can trust me to keep my word. I always keep my word, promises or threats." His voice seemed to pool on the floor, and I fought the idiotic urge to lift my feet from the carpet. "A businessman has to," he intoned, "or he won't be in business very long."

I swallowed, wondering what the hell he was. He had the grace, the voice, the quickness, and the confident power of a vampire. And as much as I disliked the man, the raw attraction was there, heightened by his personal strength rather than a teasing manner and sexual innuendos. But he wasn't a living vampire. Though warm and good-natured on the surface, he had a very large personal space that most vampires lacked. He kept people at arm's length, too far to seduce with a touch. No, he wasn't a vamp, but maybe . . . a human scion?

My eyebrows rose. Trent blinked, seeing the idea crossing me and not knowing what it was. "Yes, Ms. Morgan?" he murmured, seeming uncomfortable for the first time.

My heart pounded. "Your hair is floating again," I said, trying to jolt him. His lips parted, and he seemed at a loss for words.

I jumped as the door opened and Jonathan strode in. He was stiff and angry, with the attitude of a protector fettered by the very one he has been pledged to defend. In his hands was a head-sized glass ball. Jenks was inside it. Frightened, I stood, clutching my bag to myself.

"Jon," Trent said, smoothing his hair as he got to his feet. "Thank you. If you would please escort Ms. Morgan and her associate out?"

Jenks was so angry his wings were a black blur. I could see him mouthing something but couldn't hear him. His gestures, though, were unmistakable.

"My disc, Ms. Morgan?"

I spun, gasping as I realized Trent had come around his desk and was right behind me. I hadn't heard him move. "Your what?" I stammered.

His right hand was outstretched. It was smooth and un-worked but carried a taut strength. He had a single gold band on his ring finger. I couldn't help but notice that he was only a few inches taller than me. "My disc?" he prompted, and I swallowed.

Tensed to react, I dug it from my pocket with two fingers and handed it to him. Something swept over him. It was as subtle as a shade of blue, as indistinguishable as a snowflake among thousands, but it was there. In that instant I knew it wasn't Brimstone that Trent was afraid of. It was something on that disc.

My thoughts shot to his neatly arranged discs, and it was with an incredible resolve that I kept my eyes on his instead of following my suspicions to his desk drawer. God, help me. The man ran biodrugs along with Brimstone. The man was a freaking biodrug lord. My heart hammered and my mouth went dry. You were jailed for running Brimstone. But you were staked, burned, and scattered for running biodrugs. And he wanted me to work for him.

"You've shown an unexpected capacity to plan, Ms. Morgan," Trent said, interrupting my racing thoughts. "Vampire assassins won't attack you while under a Tamwood's protection. And arranging a pixy clan to protect you against fairies as well as living in a church to keep the Weres at bay are beautiful in their simplicity. Let me know when you change your mind about working for me. You would find satisfaction here—and recognition. Something the I.S. has been most remiss with."

I steeled my face, concentrating on keeping my voice from shaking. I hadn't planned anything. Ivy had, and I wasn't sure what her motives were. "With all due respect, Mr. Kalamack, you can go Turn yourself."

Jonathan stiffened, but Trent simply nodded and went back behind his desk.

A heavy hand hit my shoulder. I instinctively grabbed it, crouching to fling whoever had touched me over my shoulder and to the floor. Jonathan hit with a surprised grunt. I was kneeling on his neck before I realized I had moved. Frightened for what I had done, I rose and backed away. Trent glanced up in unconcern from replacing the disc in the drawer.

Three other people had entered at Jonathan's heavy thump. Two centered about me, one stood before Trent.

"Let her go," Trent said. "It was Jon's error." He sighed with mild disappointment. "Jon," he added tiredly, "she isn't the fluff she pretends to be."

The tall man had risen smoothly to his feet. He tugged his shirt straight and ran his hand to smooth his hair. He eyed me with hatred. Not only had I bested him before his employer, but he had also been rebuked in front of me. The angry man scooped Jenks up with bad grace and motioned to the door.

I walked free, back out into the sun, more afraid of what I had turned down than of having left the I.S.

Fifteen

I yanked at the pizza dough, taking my frustrations concerning my fabulous afternoon out on the helpless yeast and flour. A crackle of stiff paper came from Ivy's wooden table. My attention jerked to her. Head bowed and brow furrowed, she kept her attention on her map. I'd be a fool not to recognize that her reactions had quickened with sunset. She moved with that unnerving grace again, but she looked irate, not amorous. Still, I was aware of her every move.

Ivy had a real run, I thought sourly as I stood at the center island and made pizza. Ivy had a life. Ivy wasn't trying to prove the city's most prominent, beloved citizen was a bio-drug lord and play head cook at the same time.

Three days on her own, and Ivy had already got a run to find a missing human. I thought it odd a human would come to a vamp for help, but Ivy had her own charms, or scary competence, rather. Her nose had been buried in her map of the city all night, plotting the man's usual haunts with colored markers and drawing out the paths he would likely take while driving from home to work and such.

"I'm no expert," Ivy said to the table, "but is that how you're supposed to do that?"

"You want to make dinner?" I snapped, then looked at what I was doing. The circle was more of a lopsided oval, so thin in places it almost broke through. Embarrassed, I pushed the dough to fill in the thin spot and tugged it to fit the baking stone properly. As I fussed with the edges, I surreptitiously watched her. At her first sultry glance or overly quick move, I was going out the door to hide behind Jenks's stump. The jar of sauce opened with a loud pop. My eyes flicked to Ivy. Seeing no change, I dumped most of it onto the pizza and recapped the jar.

What else should go on it? I wondered. It would be a miracle if Ivy let me top it with everything I usually did. Deciding not to even attempt the cashews, I pulled out the mundane toppings. "Peppers," I muttered. "Mushrooms." I glanced at Ivy. She looked like a meat kind of a gal. "Bacon left from breakfast."

The marker squeaked as Ivy drew a purple line from the campus to the Hollow's more hazardous strip of nightclubs and bars by the riverfront. "So," she drawled. "Are you going to tell me what's bothering you, or am I going to have to order pizza in after you burn that one?"

I put the pepper in the sink and leaned against the counter. "Trent runs biodrugs," I said, hearing the ugliness anew as I said it. "If he knew I was going to try and tag him with that, he'd kill me quicker than the I.S."

"But he doesn't." Ivy drew another line. "All he knows is you think he runs Brimstone and had his secretary murdered. If he was worried, he wouldn't have offered you that job."

"Job?" I said, turning my back to her as I washed the pepper. "It's in the South Seas—running his Brimstone plantations, no doubt. He wants me out of the way, that's all."

"How about that," she said as she capped her pen by pounding it on the table. Startled, I spun, flinging drops of water everywhere. "He thinks you're a threat," she finished, making a show of brushing away the water I had accidentally hit her with.

I gave her a sheepish smile, hoping she couldn't tell she had me on edge. "I hadn't thought about it that way," I said.

Ivy went back to her map, frowning as she dabbed at the stains the water had made on her crisp lines. "Give me some time to check around," she said in a preoccupied voice. "If we can get ahold of his financial records and a few of his buyers, we can find a paper trail. But I still say it's just Brimstone."

I yanked open the fridge for the Parmesan and mozzarella. If Trent didn't run biodrugs, then I was a pixy princess. There was a clatter as Ivy tossed one of her markers into the cup beside her monitor. My back was to her, and the noise startled me.

"Just because he has a drawer full of discs labeled with diseases once helped by biodrugs doesn't mean he's a drug lord," Ivy said, throwing another. "Maybe they're client lists. The man is big into philanthropy. Keeps half a dozen country hospitals running alone with his donations."

"Maybe," I said, unconvinced. I knew about Trent's generous contributions. Last fall he had been auctioned off in Cincinnati's For the Children charity for more money than I used to make in a year. Personally, I thought his efforts were a publicity front. The man was dirt.

"Besides," Ivy said as she leaned back in her chair and tossed another one of her markers into the cup in an unreal show of hand-eye coordination. "Why would he be running biodrugs? The man is independently wealthy. He doesn't need any more money. People are motivated by three things, Rachel. Love . . ." A red marker clattered in with the rest. "Revenge . . ." A black one landed next to it. "And power," she finished, tossing in a green one. "Trent has enough money to buy all three."

"You forgot one," I said, wondering if I should just keep my mouth shut. "Family."

Ivy grabbed the pens out of the cup. Leaning back in her chair to balance on two legs, she started tossing them again. "Doesn't family come in with love?" she asked.

I watched her from the corner of my sight. *Not if they were dead,* I thought, my memories turning to my dad. *In that case, it might come under revenge.*

The kitchen went silent as I sprinkled a thin dusting of

Parmesan on the sauce. Only the clacks of Ivy's pens broke the stillness. Every single one went in, the sporadic rattles getting on my nerves. The pens stopped, and I froze in alarm. Her face was shadowed. I couldn't see if her eyes were going black. My heartbeat quickened, and I didn't move, waiting.

"Why don't you just stake me, Rachel?" she said in exasperation as she flipped her hair aside to show me irate brown eyes. "I'm not going to jump you. I said Friday was an accident."

Shoulders easing, I rummaged loudly in the drawer for a can opener for the mushrooms. "A pretty freaking scary accident," I muttered under my breath as I drained them.

"I heard that." She hesitated. A pen landed in the cup with a rattle. "You, ah, did read the book, right?" she asked.

"Most of it," I admitted, then went alarmed. "Why, am I doing something wrong?"

"You're ticking me off, that's what you're doing wrong," she said, her voice raised. "Stop watching me. I'm not an animal. I may be a vampire, but I still have a soul."

I bit my tongue so I wouldn't even mouth an answer to that. There was a clatter as she dropped her remaining markers in the pencil cup. The silence grew heavy as she pulled her maps to her. I turned my back on her to prove I trusted her. I didn't, though. Putting the pepper on the cutting board, I yanked open a drawer and banged noisily about until I found a huge knife. It was too big to cut peppers, but I was feeling vulnerable and that was the knife I was going to use.

"Uh . . ." Ivy hesitated. "You're not putting peppers on that, are you?"

My breath slipped from me and I set the knife down. We probably wouldn't have anything on our pizza but cheese. Silently, I put the pepper back in the refrigerator. "What's a pizza without peppers?" I whispered under my breath.

"Edible," was her prompt response, and I grimaced. She wasn't supposed to hear that.

My eyes traveled over the counter and my assembled goodies. "Mushrooms okay?"

"Can't have pizza without them."

I layered slices of slimy brown atop the Parmesan. Ivy rattled her map, and I snuck an unhelped glance at her.

"You never did tell me what you did with Francis," she said.

"I left him in his open trunk. Someone will douse him in saltwater. I think I broke his car. It doesn't accelerate anymore, no matter what gear I put it in and how loud I race it."

Ivy laughed and my skin crawled. As if daring me to object, she rose, coming to lean against the counter. My tension flowed back. It doubled when she eased herself up with a controlled slowness to sit on the counter beside me. "So," she said, opening the bag of pepperoni and provocatively placing a slice in her mouth. "What do you think he is?"

She was eating. Great.

"Francis?" I asked, surprised she had to ask. "He's an idiot."

"No, Trent."

I held my hand out for the pepperoni and she set the bag on my palm. "I don't know, but he isn't a vamp. He thought my perfume was to cover up my witch smell, not—uh—yours." I felt awkward with her that close, and I dealt the pepperoni like cards onto the pizza. "And his teeth aren't sharp enough." Finished, I put the bag in the refrigerator, out of Ivy's reach.

"They could be capped." Ivy stared at the refrigerator and the unseen pepperoni. "It would be harder to be a practicing vamp, but it's been done."

My thoughts went back to Table 6.1, with its too helpful diagrams, and I shuddered, disguising it in my reach for the tomato. Ivy bobbed her head in agreement as my hand hovered over it in question. "No," I said confidently, "he doesn't have that lack of understanding of personal space every living vamp I've met besides you seems to have."

As soon as I said it, I wished I could take it back. Ivy stiffened, and I wondered if the unnatural distance she put between herself and everyone had everything to do with her being a nonpracticing vamp. It must be frustrating, second-guessing your every move, wondering if your head prompted it or your hunger. No wonder Ivy had a tendency to fly off the handle. She was fighting a thousand year instinct with no one to help her find her way. I hesitated, then asked, "Is there a way to tell if Trent is a human scion?"

"Human scion?" she said, sounding surprised. "There's a thought."

I sent the knife through the tomato to make little red squares. "It sort of fits. He has the inner strength, grace, and personal power of a vampire but without the touchy feely. And I'd stake my life that he's not a witch or warlock. It's more than him lacking even the barest hint of a redwood smell. It's the way he moves, the light in the back of his eyes. . . ." I went still as I recalled his unreadable green eyes.

Ivy slipped off the counter, pilfering a pepperoni off the pizza. I casually moved it to the other side of the sink and away from her. She followed, taking another. There was a soft buzz as Jenks flew in through the window. He had a mushroom in his arms almost as large as himself, bringing the smell of dirt into the kitchen. I glanced at Ivy, and she shrugged.

"Hey, Jenks," Ivy said as she moved back to her chair in the corner of the kitchen. Apparently we'd passed the "I can stand right next to you and not bite you" test. "What do you think? Is Trent a Were?"

Jenks dropped the mushroom, his tiny face shifting with anger. His wings blurred to nothing. "How should I know if Trent is a Were?" he snapped. "I didn't get close enough. I got caught. Okay? Jenks got caught. Happy now?" He flew to the window. Standing beside Mr. Fish with his hands on his hips, he stared into the dark.

Ivy shook her head with a look of disgust. "So you got caught. Big freaking deal. They knew who Rachel was, and you don't see her whining over it."

Actually, I had thrown my tantrum on the way home, which might have accounted for the odd noise Francis's car was making when I left it in the mall parking lot in the shade of a tree.

Jenks darted to hover three inches before Ivy's nose. His wings were red in anger. "You have a *gardener* trap you in a glass ball and see if it doesn't give you a new outlook on life, Little Miss Merry Sunshine."

My bad mood slipped away as I watched a four-inch pixy confront a vamp. "Knock it off, Jenks," I said lightly. "I don't think he was a real gardener."

"Really?" he said sarcastically, flying to me. "You think?"

Behind him, Ivy pretended to squish Jenks between her finger and thumb. Rolling her eyes, she returned to her maps. A silence grew, not comfortable, but not awkward, either. Jenks flitted down to his mushroom and brought it to me, dirt and all. He was dressed in a loose, very casual outfit. The flowing silk was the color of wet moss, and the cut of it made him look like a desert sheik. His blond hair was slicked back and I thought I smelled soap. I'd never seen a pixy relaxing at home. It was kind of nice.

"Here," he said awkwardly, rolling the mushroom to a stop beside me. "I found it in the garden. I thought you might want it. For your pizza tonight."

"Thanks, Jenks," I said, brushing off the dirt.

"Look," he said as he backed away three steps. His wings were a confusing flash of motion and stillness. "I'm sorry, Rachel. I was supposed to back you up, not get caught."

How embarrassing, I thought. Having someone no bigger than a dragonfly apologizing for not protecting me. "Yeah, well, we both screwed up," I said sourly, wishing Ivy wasn't witnessing this. Ignoring her puff of noise, I rinsed off his mushroom and sliced it. Jenks seemed satisfied and went to make annoying circles around Ivy's head until she swatted at him.

Abandoning her, he came back to me. "I'm going to find out what Kalamack smells like if it kills me," Jenks said as I placed his contribution on the pizza. "It's personal now."

Well, I thought, *why not?* I took a deep breath. "I'm going back tomorrow night," I said, thinking about my death threat. Eventually I was going to make a mistake. And unlike Ivy, I couldn't come back from the dead. "Want to go with me, Jenks? Not as a backup, but as a partner."

Jenks rose up, his wings shifting to purple. "You can bet your mother's panties I will."

"Rachel!" Ivy exclaimed. "What do you think you're doing?"

I tore open the bag of mozzarella and dumped it over the pizza. "I'm making Jenks a full partner. Got a problem with that? He's been working too much overtime for anything less."

"No," she said, staring at me across the kitchen. "I mean going back to Kalamack's!"

Jenks hovered next to me to make a united front. "Shut your mouth, Tamwood. She needs a disc to prove Kalamack is a biodrug runner."

"I don't have a choice," I said, pushing the cheese so hard it spilled over the edge.

Ivy leaned back in her chair with an exaggerated slowness. "I know you want him, but think it through, Rachel. Trent can accuse you of everything from trespassing to impersonating I.S. personnel to looking at his horses cross-eyed. If you get caught, you're toast."

"If I accuse Trent without solid proof, he will slide through the courts on a technicality." I couldn't look at her. "It has to be fast and idiot proof. Something the media can get their teeth into and run with." My motions were jerky as I picked up the cheese I had spilled and put it back on the pizza. "I have to get one of those discs, and tomorrow I will."

A small noise of disbelief came from Ivy. "I can't believe you're rushing back, no plans, no preparations. Nothing. You already tried the no-thinking approach and you got caught."

My face burned. "Just because I don't plan out my trips to the bathroom, it doesn't mean I'm not a good runner," I said tightly.

Her jaw clenched. "I never said you weren't a good runner. I only meant a little planning might save you some embarrassing mistakes, like what happened today."

"Mistakes!" I exclaimed. "Look here, Ivy. I'm a damn fine runner."

She arched her thin eyebrows. "You haven't had a clean tag in the last six months."

"That wasn't me, that was Denon! He admitted it. And if you are so unimpressed with my abilities, why did you beg that I let you come with me?"

"I didn't," Ivy said. Her eyes narrowed and spots of anger appeared on her cheeks.

Not wanting to argue with her, I turned to put the pizza in the oven. The dry whoosh of air made my cheeks tighten and sent wisps of my hair floating into my eyes. "Yes, you did," I muttered, knowing she could hear me, then said louder, "I know exactly what I'm going to do."

"Really?" she said from right behind me. I stifled a gasp and whipped around. Jenks was standing on the windowsill next to Mr. Fish, white-faced. "So tell me," she said, her voice dripping with sarcasm. "What's your *perfect plan*?"

Not wanting her to know she had scared me, I brushed past her, deliberately showing her my back as I scraped the flour off the counter with that big knife. The hair on the back of my neck rose, and I turned to find her just where I had left her, even if her arms were crossed and a dark shadow was flitting behind her eyes. My pulse quickened. I knew I shouldn't have been arguing with her.

Jenks darted between Ivy and me. "How are we going to get in, Rachel?" he asked, alighting beside me on the counter.

I felt safer with him watching her, and I purposely turned my back on Ivy. "I'm going in as a mink." Ivy made a noise of disbelief and I stiffened. Brushing the loosened flour into my hand, I dumped it into the trash. "Even if I'm spotted, they won't know it's me. It will be a simple snatch and dash." Trent's words about my activities flitted through me, and I wondered.

"Burglarizing the office of a councilman is not a simple snatch and dash," Ivy said, the tension seeming to ooze from her. "It's grand theft."

"With Jenks, I'll be in and out of his office in two minutes. Out of the building in ten."

"And buried in the basement of the I.S. tower in an hour," Ivy said. "You're nuts. Both of you are bloody nuts. It's a fortress in the middle of the freaking woods! And that's not a plan—it's an idea. Plans are on paper."

Her voice had become scornful, pulling my shoulders tight. "If I used plans, I'd be dead three times over," I said. "I don't need a plan. You learn all you can, then you just do it. Plans can't take into account surprises!"

"If you used a plan, you wouldn't have any surprises."

Ivy stared at me, and I swallowed. More than a hint of black swirled in her eyes, and my stomach clenched.

"I have a more enjoyable path if you're looking for suicide," she breathed.

Jenks landed on my earring, jolting my eyes from Ivy. "It's the first smart thing she's done all week," he said. "So back off, Tamwood."

Ivy's eyes narrowed, and I took a quick step back as she was distracted. "You're as bad as her, pixy," she said, showing her teeth. Vamp teeth were like guns. You didn't pull them unless you were going to use them.

"Let her do her job!" Jenks shouted back.

Ivy went wire tight. A cold draft hit my neck as Jenks shifted his wings as if to fly. "Enough!" I cried, before he could leave me. I wanted him right were he was. "Ivy. If you have a better idea, tell me. If not—shut up."

Together Jenks and I looked at Ivy, stupidly thinking we were stronger together than alone. Her eyes flashed to black. My mouth went dry. They were unblinking, alive with a promise as yet only hinted at. A tickle in my belly swirled up to close my throat. I couldn't tell if it was fear or anticipation. She fixed upon my eyes, not breathing. *Don't look at my neck,* I thought, panicking. *Oh. God. Don't look at my neck.* "Rot and hell," Jenks whispered.

But she shuddered, turning away to lean over the sink. I was shaking, and could swear I heard a sigh of relief from Jenks. This, I realized, could have been really, really bad.

Ivy's voice sounded dead when she next spoke. "Fine," she said to the sink. "Go get yourself killed. Both of you." She jerked herself into motion and I jumped. Hunched and pained-looking, she stalked out of the kitchen. Too soon to be believed came the sound of the church's front door slamming, then nothing.

Someone, I thought, *was going to get hurt tonight.*

Jenks left my earring, alighting on the windowsill. "What's with her?" he asked belligerently into the sudden quiet. "You would almost think she cared."

Sixteen

I woke from a sound sleep, jolted by the distant sound of glass breaking. I could smell wood incense. My eyes flashed open.

Ivy was bending over me, her face inches from mine.

"No!" I shouted, punching out in a blind panic. My fist caught her in the gut. Ivy clutched her middle and fell to the floor, struggling to breathe. I scrambled to crouch on my bed. My eyes darted from the gray window to the door. My heart pounded, and I went cold in a painful rush of adrenaline. She was between me and my only way out.

"Wait," she gasped, her robe sleeve falling to her elbow as she reached to catch me.

"You backstabbing, bloodsucking vamp," I hissed.

My breath caught in surprise as Jenks—no, it was Jax—flitted from the windowsill to hover before me. "Ms. Rachel," he said, distracted and tense. "We're under attack. Fairies." He nearly spat the last word.

Fairies, I thought in a wash of cold fear as I glanced at my bag. I couldn't fight fairies with my charms. They were too fast. The best I could do would be to try and squish one. Oh God. I'd never killed anyone in my entire life. Not even by accident. I was a runner, damn it. The idea was to bring them in alive, not dead. But fairies . . .

My gaze shot to Ivy, and I flushed as I realized what she

was doing in my room. With as much grace as I could find, I got off my bed. "Sorry," I whispered, offering her a hand up.

Her head tilted so she could see me past the curtain of her hair. Pain barely hid her anger. A white hand darted out and yanked me down. I hit the floor with a yelp, panicking again as she covered my mouth with a firm hand. "Shut up," she wheezed, her breath on my cheek. "You want to get us killed? They're already inside."

Eyes wide, I whispered around her fingers, "They won't come inside. It's a church."

"Fairies don't recognize holy ground," she said. "They couldn't care less."

They were already inside. Seeing my alarm, Ivy took her hand from my mouth. My eyes went to the heating vent. Reaching out a slow hand, I closed it, wincing at the squeak.

Jax lit upon on my pajama-covered knee. "They invaded our garden," he said, the murderous cast on his childlike face looking terribly wrong. "They're going to pay. And here I am, stuck babysitting you two lunkers." He flitted to the window in disgust.

There was a bump from the kitchen, and Ivy yanked me down as I tried to rise. "Stay put," she said softly. "Jenks will take care of them."

"But—" I bit back my protest as Ivy turned to me, her eyes black in the dim light of the early morning. What could Jenks do against fairy assassins? He was trained in backup, not guerrilla warfare. "Look, I'm sorry," I whispered. "For hitting you, I mean."

Ivy didn't move. A seething mix of emotion had gathered behind her eyes, and I felt my breath catch. "If I wanted you, little witch," she said, "you couldn't stop me."

Chilled, I swallowed hard. It sounded like a promise.

"Something's changed," she said, her attention on my closed door. "I didn't expect this for another three days."

A sick feeling washed over me. The I.S. had changed its tactics. I had brought this on myself. "Francis," I said. "It's my fault. The I.S. knows I can slip past their watchers now."

I pressed my fingertips into my temples. Keasley, the old man across the street, had warned me.

There was a third crash, louder this time. Ivy and I stared at the door. I could hear my heartbeat. I wondered if Ivy could, too. After a long moment, there was a tiny knock at the door. Tension slammed into me, and I heard Ivy take a slow breath, gathering herself.

"Papa?" Jax said softly. There was a whine of noise from the hall, and Jax darted to the door. "Papa!" he shouted.

I lurched to my feet, shoulders slumping. I flicked on the light, squinting in the sudden glare at the clock Ivy had lent me. Five-thirty. I'd only been asleep an hour.

Ivy rose with startling quickness, opening the door and stalking out with the hem of her robe furling. I winced as she left. I hadn't meant to hurt her. No, that wasn't true. I had. But I thought she was making me into an early morning snack.

Jenks careened in, nearly crashing into the window as he tried to land.

"Jenks?" I said, deciding my apology to Ivy could wait. "Are you all right?"

"We-e-e-e-ell," he drawled, sounding as if he were drunk. "We won't have to worry about fairies for a while." My eyes widened at the length of steel in his hand. It had a wooden handle and was the size of one of those sticks they put olives on. Staggering, he sat down hard, accidentally bending his lower set of wings under him.

Jax pulled his father to his feet. "Papa?" he said, worried. Jenks was a mess. One of his upper wings was in tatters. He was bleeding from several scratches, one right under his eye. The other was swollen shut. He leaned heavily on Jax, who was struggling to keep his father upright.

"Here," I said, tucking my hand under and behind Jenks, forcing him to sit on my palm. "Let's get you to the kitchen. The light's better in there. Maybe we can tape your wing."

"No light there," Jenks slurred. "Broke 'em." He blinked, struggling to focus. "Sorry."

Worried, I cupped my hand over him, ignoring his muffled protests. "Jax," I said, "get your mom." He grabbed his father's sword and darted out just below the ceiling. "Ivy?" I called as I edged my way through the dark hall. "What do you know about pixies?"

"Apparently not enough," she said from right behind me, and I jumped.

I elbowed the light switch as I entered the kitchen. Nothing. The lights were busted.

"Wait," Ivy said. "There's glass all over the floor."

"How can you tell?" I said in disbelief, but I hesitated, not willing to chance my bare feet in the dark. Ivy brushed past me in a whisper of black, and I shuddered as the breeze of her passage chilled me. She was going vampy. There was the crunch of glass, and the fluorescent bulb over the oven flickered into life, illuminating the kitchen in an uncomfortable glow.

Thin, fluorescent lightbulb glass littered the floor. There was a pungent haze in the air. My eyebrows rose as I realized it was a cloud of fairy dust. It caught in my throat, and I put Jenks on the counter before I sneezed and accidentally dropped him.

Breath held, I picked my way to the window to open it farther. Mr. Fish was laying helpless in the sink, his bowl shattered. I gingerly plucked him from between the thick shards, filling a plastic cup and plunking him in. Mr. Fish wiggled, shuddered, and sank to the bottom. Slowly his gills moved back and forth. He was okay.

"Jenks?" I said, turning to find him standing where I had left him. "What happened?"

"We got 'em," he said, barely audible, listing to the side.

Ivy took the broom from the pantry and began sweeping the glass into a pile.

"They thought I didn't know they were there," Jenks continued as I rummaged for some tape, starting as I found a severed fairy wing. It looked like a Luna moth's wing rather than a dragonfly's. The scales rubbed off on my fingers, staining them green and purple. I carefully set the wing aside. There were several very complicated spells that called for fairy dust.

Jeez, I thought, turning away. I was going to be sick. Someone had died, and I was considering using part of him to spell.

"Little Jacey spotted them first," Jenks said, his voice falling into an eerie cadence. "On the far side of the human graves. Pink wings in the lowering moon as the earth slipped 'round her silver light. They reached our wall. Our lines were strung. We held our land. What's said is done."

Bewildered, I looked at Ivy standing silent with her unmoving broom. Her eyes were wide. This was weird. Jenks wasn't swearing; he sounded poetic. And he wasn't done.

"The first went down beneath the oak, stung by the taste of steel in his blood. The second on holy ground did fall, stained with the cries of his folly. The third in the dust and salt did fail, sent back to his master, a silent warning given." Jenks looked up, clearly not seeing me. "This ground is ours. So it is said with broken wing, poisoned blood, and our unburied dead."

Ivy and I stared at each other through the ugly light. "What the hell?" Ivy whispered, and Jenks's eyes cleared. He turned to us, touched his head in salute, and slowly collapsed.

"Jenks!" Ivy and I cried, jolted into motion. Ivy got there first. She cupped Jenks into her hands and turned to me with a panicked look. "What do I do?" she cried.

"How should I know?" I shouted back. "Is he breathing?"

There was a sound of jangling wind chimes, and Jenks's wife darted into the room, trailing a wake of at least a dozen pixy children. "Your living room is clean," she said brusquely, her silk fog-colored cloak billowing to a stop around her. "No charms. Take him there. Jhem, go turn the light on ahead of Ms. Ivy, then help Jinni fetch my kit here. Jax, take the rest of this lot through the church. Start in the belfry. Don't miss a crack. The walls, the pipes, the cable and phone lines. Watch the owls, and mind you check that priest hole. You even think you smell a spell or one of those fairies, you sing out. Clear? Now go."

The pixy children scattered. Ivy, too, obediently followed the tiny woman's order and hotfooted it into the living room. I would have thought it amusing but for Jenks unmoving on her palm. Limping, I followed them.

"No, love," the tiny woman directed as Ivy went to set Jenks on a cushion. "The end table, please. I need a hard surface to cut against."

Cut against? I thought, moving Ivy's magazines off the table and onto the floor to make room. I sat down on the closest chair and tilted the lamp shade. My adrenaline was fading, leaving me light-headed and cold in my flannel pajamas. What if Jenks was really hurt? I was shocked he had actually killed two fairies. *He had killed them.* I had put people in the hospital before, sure, but kill someone? I thought back to my fear as I huddled in the dark next to a tense vampire and wondered if I could do the same.

Ivy set Jenks down as if he were made of tissue paper, then backed to the door. Her tall stance hunched, making her look nervous and out of place. "I'll check outside," she said.

Mrs. Jenks smiled, showing an ageless warmth in her smooth, youthful features. "No, love," she said. "It's safe now. We have at least a full day before the I.S. can find another fairy clan willing to breach our lines. And there's not enough money to get pixies to invade other pixies' gardens. It just proves fairies are uncouth barbarians. But you go search if you like. The youngest bairn could dance among the flowers this morning."

Ivy opened her mouth as if to protest, then realizing the pixy was entirely serious, she dropped her eyes and slipped out the back door.

"Did Jenks say anything before he passed out?" Mrs. Jenks asked as she arranged him so his wings were awkwardly splayed. He looked like a pinned bug on display, and I felt ill.

"No," I said, wondering at her calm attitude. I was nearly

frantic. "He started in like he was reciting a sonnet or something." I pulled my pajama top tighter to my throat and hunched into myself. "Is he going to be all right?"

She sank to her knees beside him, her relief obvious as she ran a careful finger under her husband's swollen eye. "He's fine. If he was cursing or reciting poetry, he's fine. If you told me he was singing, I'd be worried." Her hands slowed their motion over him, and her eyes went distant. "The one time he came home singing, we nearly lost him." Her eyes cleared. Pressing her lips together in a mirthless smile, she opened the bag her children had brought.

I felt a flush of guilt. "I'm really sorry about this, Mrs. Jenks," I said. "If it hadn't been for me, this never would have happened. If Jenks wants to break his contract, I'll understand."

"Break his contract!" Mrs. Jenks fixed her eyes on me with a frightening intensity. "Heavens, child. Not over a little bit of a thing like this."

"But Jenks shouldn't have to fight them," I protested. "They could've killed him."

"There were only three," she said, spreading a white cloth next to Jenks like a surgical kit, laying bandages, salve, even what looked like artificial wing membrane on it. "And they knew better. They saw the warnings. Their deaths were legitimate." She smiled, and I could see why Jenks had used his wish to keep her. She looked like an angel, even with the knife she held.

"But they weren't after you," I insisted. "They were after me."

Her head shook to send the tips of her wispy hair waving. "Doesn't matter," she said in her lyrical voice. "They would have gotten the garden regardless. But I think they did it for the *money*." She nearly spat the word. "It took a lot of I.S. money to convince them to try my Jenks's strength." She sighed, cutting out portions of the thin membrane to match the holes in Jenks's wing with the coolness of someone mending a sock.

"Don't fret," she said. "They thought that because we had just taken possession, they could catch us off balance." She turned a smug eye to me. "They found out wrong, didn't they?"

I didn't know what to say. The pixy/fairy animosity went far deeper than I had imagined. Being of the mind-set that no one could own the earth, pixies and fairies shunned the idea of property titles, relying upon the simple adage might makes right. And because they weren't in competition with anyone but each other, the courts turned a blind eye to their affairs, allowing them to settle their own disagreements, up to and including killing each other, apparently. I wondered what had happened to whoever had the garden before Ivy rented the church.

"Jenks likes you," the small woman said, rolling up the wing membrane and packing it away. "Calls you his friend. I'll give you the same title out of respect for him."

"Thanks," I stammered.

"I don't trust you, though," she said, and I blinked. She was as direct as her husband, and just about as tactful. "Is it true you made him a partner? For real and not just a cruel prank?"

I nodded, more serious than I had been all week. "Yes, ma'am. He deserves it."

Mrs. Jenks took a pair of tiny scissors in hand. They looked more like an heirloom than a functional piece of equipment, their wooden handles carved into the shape of a bird. The beak was metal, and my eyes widened as she took the cold iron and knelt before Jenks. "Please stay asleep, love," I heard her whisper, and I watched in astonishment as she delicately trimmed the frayed edges of Jenks's wing. The smell of cauterized blood rose thick in the shut-up room.

Ivy appeared in the doorway as if having been summoned. "You're bleeding," she said.

I shook my head. "It's Jenks's wing."

"No. You're bleeding. Your foot."

I straightened, squashing a flash of angst. Breaking eye

contact, I swung my foot up to look at its underside. A red smear covered my heel. I had been too busy to notice.

"I'll clean it up," Ivy said, and I dropped my foot, shrinking back. "The *floor*," Ivy said in disgust. "You left bloody footprints all over the *floor*." My gaze went to where she pointed to the hallway, my footprints obvious in the growing light of the new day. "I wasn't going to touch your foot," Ivy muttered as she stomped out.

I flushed. Well . . . I had woken up with her breathing on my neck.

There was a thumping of cupboard doors and a rush of water from the kitchen. She was mad at me. Maybe I ought to apologize. But for what? I already said I was sorry for hitting her.

"You sure Jenks is going to be okay?" I asked, avoiding the problem.

The pixy woman sighed. "If I can get the patches in place before he wakes up." She sat back on her heels, closed her eyes, and said a short prayer. Wiping her hands on her skirt, she took up a dull blade with a wooden handle. She set a patch in place and ran the flat of the blade along the edges, melting it to Jenks's wing. He shuddered, though didn't wake. Her hands were shaking when she finished, and pixy dust sifted from her to make her glow. An angel indeed.

"Children?" she called, and they appeared from everywhere. "Bring your father along. Josie, if you would go and make sure the door is open?"

I watched as the children descended upon him, lifting him up and carrying him out through the flue. Mrs. Jenks wearily got to her feet as her eldest daughter packed everything away in the bag. "My Jenks," she said, "sometimes reaches for more than a pixy ought to dream for. Don't get my husband killed in his folly, Ms. Morgan."

"I'll try," I whispered as she and her daughter vanished up the chimney. I felt guilty, as if I were intentionally manipulating Jenks to protect myself. There was a sliding clatter of glass into the trashcan, and I rose, glancing out the window.

The sun was up, shining on the herbs in the garden. It was way past my bedtime, but I didn't think I could go back to sleep.

Feeling weary and out of control, I shuffled into the kitchen. Ivy was on her hands and knees in her black robe, swabbing up my footprints. "I'm sorry," I said, standing in the middle of the kitchen with my arms clasped around myself.

Ivy looked up with narrowed eyes, playing the part of the martyr well. "For what?" she said, clearly wanting to drag me through the entire apology process.

"For, er, hitting you. I wasn't awake yet," I lied. "I didn't know it was you."

"You already apologized for that," she said, going back to the floor.

"For you cleaning up my footprints?" I tried again.

"I offered to."

I bobbed my head. She had. I wasn't going to delve into the possible motives behind that, but just accept her offer as her being nice. But she was mad about something. I hadn't a clue what. "Um, help me out here, Ivy," I finally said.

She rose and went to the sink, methodically rinsing the rag out. The yellow cloth was carefully set over the faucet to dry. She turned, leaning back against the counter. "How about a little trust? I said I wasn't going to bite you, and I'm not."

My mouth dropped open. Trust? Ivy was upset about trust? "You want trust?" I exclaimed, finding I needed to be angry to talk to Ivy about this. "Then how about more control from you. I can't even contradict you without you going vampy on me!"

"I do not," she said, her eyes widening.

"You do, too," I said, gesturing. "It's just like that first week we worked together and we would argue over the best way to bring in a shoplifter at the mall. Just because I don't agree with you doesn't mean I'm wrong. At least listen to me before you decide that I am."

She took a breath, then slowly let it out. "Yes. You're right."

I jerked back at her words. She thought I was right? "And another thing," I added, slightly mollified. "Stop with the running away during an argument. You stormed out of here tonight like you were going to rip someone's head off, then I wake up with you bending over me? I'm sorry for punching you, but you have to admit, you kind of deserved it."

A faint smile crossed her, then disappeared. "Yeah. I suppose." She rearranged the rag over the spigot. Turning, she clasped her arms around herself, gripping her elbows. "Okay, I won't leave in the middle of an argument, but you're going to have to not get so excited during them. You're jerking me around until I don't know which floor to stand on."

I blinked. Did she mean excited as in scared, angry, or both? "Beg pardon?"

"And maybe get a stronger perfume?" she added apologetically.

"I—I just bought some," I said in surprise. "Jenks said it covered everything."

A sudden distress pinched Ivy's face as she met my gaze. "Rachel . . . I can still smell me thick on you. You're like a big chocolate-chip cookie sitting all alone on an empty table. And when you get all agitated, it's as if you just came out of the oven, all warm and gooey. I haven't had a cookie in three years. Could you just calm down so you don't smell so damn good?"

"Oh." Suddenly cold, I sank down in my chair at the table. I didn't like being compared to food. And I'd never be able to eat another chocolate-chip cookie again. "I rewashed my clothes," I said in a small voice. "I'm not using your sheets or soap anymore."

Ivy's eyes were on the floor when I turned around. "I know," she said. "I appreciate it. It helps. This isn't your fault. A vampire's scent lingers on anyone they live with. It's a survival trait that tends to lengthen the life of a vampire's companion by telling other vamps to back off. I didn't think I would notice it, seeing as we were sharing floor space, not blood."

A shudder went through me as I recalled from my basic Latin class that the word companion stemmed from the word for food. "I don't belong to you," I said.

"I know." She took a careful breath, not looking at me. "The lavender is helping. Maybe if you hung satchels of it in your closet it would be enough. And tried not to get so emotional, especially when we're—discussing alternative actions?"

"Okay," I said softly, realizing how complex this arrangement was going to be.

"Are you still going out to Kalamack's tomorrow?" Ivy asked.

I nodded, relieved at the change of topics. "I don't want to go without Jenks, but I don't think I can wait for him to be flightworthy."

Ivy was silent for a long moment. "I'll drive you out. As close as you want to risk it."

My mouth dropped open for a second time. "Why? I mean, really?" I quickly amended, and she shrugged.

"You're right. If you don't get this done quickly, you won't last another week."

Seventeen

"**Y**ou aren't going, *dear*," Mrs. Jenks said tightly.
I dumped my last swallow of coffee down the sink,
gazing uncomfortably into the garden, bright with the early
afternoon sun. I would rather be anywhere else right now.

"The devil I'm not," Jenks muttered.

I turned around, too tired from a morning with not enough
sleep to enjoy watching Jenks get henpecked. He was standing on the stainless steel island with his hands aggressively
on his hips. Beyond him, Ivy was hunched at her wooden
table as she planned three routes to the Kalamack estate.
Mrs. Jenks was beside her. Her stiff stance said it all. She
didn't want him to go. And looking the way she did, I wasn't
about to contradict her.

"I say you aren't going," she said, a cord of iron laced
through her voice.

"Mind your place, woman," he said. A hint of pleading ruined his tough-guy stance.

"I am." Her tone was severe. "You're still broken. What I
say goes. That's our law."

Jenks gestured plaintively. "I'm fine. I can fly. I can fight.
I'm going."

"You aren't. You can't. You're not. And until I say, you're
a gardener, not a runner."

"I can fly!" he exclaimed, his wings blurring into motion.

He lifted a mere fingerbreadth off the counter and back down. "You just don't want me to go."

She stiffened. "I'll not have it said you were killed because of my failings. Keeping you alive is my responsibility, and I say *you're broken!*"

I fed Mr. Fish a crushed flake. This was embarrassing. If it had been up to me, I'd let Jenks go, flightless or not. He was recovering faster than I would have believed possible. Still, it had been less than ten hours since he was spouting poetry. I looked at Mrs. Jenks with an inquiring arch to my eyebrows. The pretty pixy woman shook her head. That was it, then.

"Jenks," I said. "I'm sorry, but until you have the green, you're garden-bound."

He took three steps, stopping at the edge of the counter. His fists clenched.

Uncomfortable, I joined Ivy at the table. "So," I said awkwardly. "You said you have an idea of how I can get in?"

Ivy took the end of the pen out from between her teeth. "I did some research this morning on the net—"

"You mean after I went back to bed?" I interrupted.

She looked up at me with her unreadable brown eyes. "Yes." Turning away, she rifled through her maps, pulling out a colored brochure. "Here, I printed this out."

I sat down as I took it. She had not only printed it out, but had folded it into the usual brochure folds. The colorful pamphlet was an advertisement for guided tours of the Kalamack botanical gardens. " 'Come stroll among the spectacular private gardens of Councilman Trenton Kalamack,' " I read aloud. " 'Call ahead for ticket prices and availability. Closed on the full moon for maintenance.' " There was more, but I had my way in.

"I've got another one for the stables," Ivy said. "They run tours all year, except for spring, when the foals are born."

"How considerate." I ran a finger over the crayon-bright sketch of the grounds. I had no idea Trent was interested in gardening. Maybe he *was* a witch. There was a loud, very obvious whine as Jenks flew the short distance to the table. He could fly, but barely.

"This is fantastic," I said, ignoring the belligerent pixy as he walked over the paper and into my line of sight. "I was planning on you dropping me off somewhere in the woods so I could hike my way in, but this is great. Thanks."

Ivy gave me an honest, closed-lipped smile. "A little research can save a lot of time."

I stifled a sigh. If Ivy had her way, we would have a six-step plan posted over the john for what to do if it backed up. "I could fit in a big purse," I said, warming to the idea.

Jenks sniffed. "A really big-ass purse."

"I have someone who owes me a favor," Ivy said. "If she bought the ticket, my name wouldn't be on the roster. And I could wear a disguise." Ivy grinned to show a faint slip of teeth. I returned it weakly. She looked altogether human in the bright afternoon light.

"Hey," Jenks said, glancing at his wife. "I could fit in a purse, too."

Ivy tapped her pen on her teeth. "I'll take the tour, and misplace my purse somewhere."

Jenks stood on the brochure, his wings moving in abrupt fits of motion. "I'm going."

I jerked the pamphlet out from under him, and he stumbled back. "I'll meet you tomorrow past the front gate in the woods. You could pick me up just out of sight."

"I'm going," Jenks said louder, ignored.

Ivy leaned back in her chair with a satisfied air. "Now *that* sounds like a plan."

This was really odd. Last night Ivy had nearly bit my head off when I suggested nearly the same thing. All she needed was to have some input. Pleased for having figured this small bit of Ivy out, I rose and opened my charm cupboard. "Trent knows about you," I said as I looked my spells over. "Only heaven knows how. You definitely need a disguise. Let's see . . . I could make you look old."

"Is no one listening to me?" Jenks shouted, his wings an

angry red. "I'm going. Rachel, tell my wife I'm fit enough to go."

"Uh, hold up," Ivy said. "I don't want to be spelled. I've got my own disguise."

I turned, surprised. "You don't want one of mine? It doesn't hurt. It's just an illusion. It's not anything like a transformation charm."

She wouldn't meet my gaze. "I have something in mind already."

"I said," Jenks shouted, "I'm going!"

Ivy scrubbed a hand over her eyes.

"Jenks—" I began.

"Tell her," he said, darting a glance at his wife. "If you say it's okay, she'll let me go. I'll be able to fly by the time I need to."

"Look," I said. "There will be other times—"

"To break into Kalamack's estate?" he cried. "Don't freaking think so. Either I go now, or never. This is my only shot at finding out what Kalamack smells like. No pixy or fairy has been able to tell what he is. And not you, or anyone else, is going to take that chance from me." A wisp of desperation had crept into his voice. "Neither of you are big enough."

I looked past him to Mrs. Jenks, my eyes pleading. He was right. There would be no other time. It would be too chancy to risk even my life if it hadn't already been in the blender and waiting for someone to push the button. The pretty pixy's eyes closed, and she clasped her arms about herself. Looking pained, she nodded. "All right," I said, my attention back on Jenks. "You can come."

"What?" Ivy yelped, and I shrugged helplessly.

"She says it's okay," I said, nodding to Mrs. Jenks. "But only if he promises to bug out the second I say. I'm not going to risk him any more than he can fly."

Jenks's wings blurred to an excited purple. "I'll leave when I decide."

"Absolutely not." I stretched my arms out along the table,

putting my fists to either side of him and glaring. "We are going in under my discretion, and we will leave on the same terms. This is a witchocracy, not a democracy. Clear?"

Jenks tensed, his mouth open to protest, but then his eyes slid from mine to his wife's. Her tiny foot was tapping. "'Kay," he said meekly. "But only this time."

I nodded and pulled my arms back to myself. "Will that fit in with your *plan*, Ivy?"

"Whatever." Chair scraping, she got to her feet. "I'll call for the ticket. We have to leave in time to get to my friend's house and out to the main bus station by four. The tours run from there." Her pace was edging into vamp mode as she strode from the kitchen.

"Jenks, dear?" the small pixy woman said softly. "I'll be in the garden if you—" Her last words choked off, and she flew out through the window.

Jenks spun, a heartbeat too late. "Matalina, wait," he cried, his wings blurring to nothing. But he was nailed to the table, unable to keep up with her. "The Turn take it! It's my only chance," he shouted after her.

I heard Ivy's muffled voice in the living room as she argued with someone on the phone. "I don't care if it is two in the afternoon. You owe me." There was a short silence. "I could come down there and take it out of your hide, Carmen. I've nothing to do tonight." Jenks and I jumped at the thunk of something hitting the wall. I think it was the phone. It seemed everyone was having a fabulous afternoon.

"All set!" she shouted with what was obviously forced cheerfulness. "We can pick up the ticket in a half hour. That gives us just enough time to change."

"Great," I said with a sigh, rising to pluck a mink potion from the cupboard. I couldn't imagine mere clothes would make a good enough disguise for a vamp. "Hey, Jenks?" I said softly as I rummaged in the silverware drawer for a finger stick. "How does Ivy smell?"

"What?" he all but snarled, clearly still upset about his wife.

My eyes shot to the empty hall. "Ivy," I said, even more softly so she couldn't possibly hear. "Before the fairy attack, she stormed out of here like she was going to rip someone's heart out. I'm not going to put myself in her purse until I know if . . ." I hesitated, then whispered, "Has she started practicing again?"

Jenks turned serious. "No." He steeled himself and made the short flight to me. "I sent Jax to watch her. Just to make sure no one slipped her a charm aimed at you." Jenks puffed with parental pride. "He did well on his first run. No one saw him. Just like his old man."

I leaned closer. "So where did she go?"

"Some vamp bar on the river. She sat in the corner, snarling at anyone who got close, and drank orange juice all night." Jenks shook his head. "It's really weird, if you ask me."

There was a small sound in the doorway, and Jenks and I straightened with a guilty quickness. I looked up, blinking in surprise. "Ivy?" I stammered.

She smiled weakly, with a pleased embarrassment. "What do you think?"

"Uh, great!" I managed. "You look great. I never would have recognized you." And I might not have.

Ivy was wrapped in a skintight yellow sundress. The thin straps holding it up stood out sharp against her shockingly white skin. Her black hair was a wave of ebony. Bright red lipstick was the only color to her face, making her look more exotic than usual. She had sunglasses on, and a wide-brimmed yellow hat that matched her high heels. Over her shoulders was a purse big enough to carry a pony.

She spun in a slow circle, looking like a stoic model on the runway. Her heels made a sharp click-clack, and I couldn't help but watch. I made a mental note—no more chocolate for me. Coming to a stop, she took her sunglasses off. "Think this will do?"

I shook my head in disbelief. "Uh, yeah. You actually wear that?"

"I used to. And it won't set off any spell-check amulets, either."

Jenks made a face as he levered himself up on the sill. "Much as I enjoy this horrific outpouring of estrogen, I'm going to go say good-bye to my wife. Let me know when you're ready. I'll be in the garden—probably next to the stink weed." He wobbled into flight and out the window. I turned back to Ivy, still amazed.

"I'm surprised it still fits," Ivy said as she looked down at herself. "It used to be my mother's. I got it when she died." She eyed me with a severe frown. "And if she ever shows up on our doorstep, don't let on I have it."

"Sure," I offered weakly.

Ivy tossed her purse to the table and sat with her legs crossed at the knees. "She thinks my great aunt stole it. If she knew I had it, she'd make me give it back." Ivy harrumphed. "Like she could wear it anymore. A sundress after dark is so tacky."

She turned, a bright smile on her face. I stifled a shudder. She looked like a human. A wealthy, desirable human. This, I realized, was a hunting dress.

Ivy went still at my almost horrified look. Her eyes dilated, sending my pulse hammering. That awful black drifted over her as her instincts were jerked into play. The kitchen faded from my awareness. Though she was across the room, Ivy seemed right before me. I felt myself go hot, then cold. She was pulling an aura in the middle of the freaking afternoon.

"Rachel . . ." she breathed, her gray voice enticing a shudder from me. "Stop being afraid."

My breath came quick and shallow. Frightened, I forced myself to turn so my back was almost to her. *Damn, damn, damn!* This wasn't my fault. I hadn't done anything! She had been so normal . . . and then this? From the corner of my sight I watched Ivy hold herself still, scrambling for control. If she moved, I was going out the window.

But she didn't move. Slowly my breath came easier. My pulse slowed, and her tension decreased. I took a deep breath, and the black in her eyes diminished. I flipped my hair out of my face and pretended to wash my hands, and she slumped to her chair by the table. Fear was an aphrodisiac to her hunger, and I had been unwittingly feeding it to her.

"I shouldn't have put this on again," she said, her voice low and strained. "I'll wait in the garden while you invoke your spell." I nodded, and she drifted to the door, clearly making a conscious effort to move at a normal speed. I hadn't noticed her standing up, but there she was, moving into the hallway. "And Rachel," she said softly, standing in the threshold. "If I ever do start practicing again, you'll be the first to know."

Eighteen

"**I** don't think I'll ever get my nose clear of the stink in that sack." Jenks took a dramatic breath of the night air.

"Purse," I said, hearing the word come out as a bland squeak. It was all I could manage. I had recognized right off what Ivy's mother's purse smelled like, and the thought that I had spent a good portion of my day in it gave me the willies.

"You ever smell anything like that?" Jenks continued blithely.

"Jenks, shut up." Squeak, squeak, chirp. Guessing what a vamp carried when she went hunting wasn't high on my list. I tried really hard not to think about Table 6.1.

"No-o-o-o," he drawled. "It was more of a musky, metallic kind of—oh."

But the night air was pleasant enough. It was edging toward ten, and Trent's public garden had the lush smell of rising damp. The moon was a thin sliver lost behind the trees. Jenks and I were hidden in the shrubbery behind a stone bench. Ivy was long gone.

She had tucked her purse under the seat this afternoon, pretending to be faint. After blaming her weariness on low blood sugar, half the men on the tour had offered to run up to the pavilion to fetch her a cookie. I had nearly blown our cover laughing at Jenks's nonstop, overly dramatic parody what was going on outside her purse. Ivy had left in a swirl of manly concern. I hadn't known whether to be worried or amused at how easily she had swayed them.

"This feels as wrong as Uncle Vamp at a sweet-sixteen party," Jenks said as he edged out of the shadows and onto the path. "I haven't heard a bird all afternoon. No fairies or pixies, either." He peered up at the black canopy from under his hat.

"Let's go," I squeaked as I looked down the abandoned path. Everything was in shades of gray. I still wasn't used to it.

"I don't think there *are* any fairies or pixies," Jenks continued. "A garden this size could support four clans, easy. Who takes care of the plants?"

"Maybe that way," I said, needing to talk even though he couldn't understand me.

"You've got that right," he said, continuing his one-sided conversation. "Lunkers. Thick-fingered clumsy oafs who rip out an ailing plant instead of giving it a dose of potash. Uh, present company excepted, of course," he added.

"Jenks," I chittered, "you're a real piece of work."

"You're welcome."

I didn't trust Jenks's belief that there might be no fairies or pixies, and I half expected them to descend upon us at any moment. Having seen the aftermath of a pixy/fairy skirmish, I wasn't in any hurry to experience it. Especially not when I was the size of a squirrel.

Jenks craned his neck and studied the upper branches as he adjusted his hat. He had told me earlier that it was a flaming red, and that the conspicuous color was a pixy's only defense when entering another clan's garden. It was a promise of good intent and quick departure. His constant fussing with it since leaving Ivy's purse had nearly driven me crazy. Being stuck behind a bench all afternoon had done nothing for my nerves, either. Jenks had spent most of the day sleeping, stirring back to wakefulness when the sun neared the unseen horizon.

A flash of excitement raced through me and was gone. Pushing the feeling away, I chittered for Jenks's attention and started toward the smell of carpet. The time spent in Ivy's purse, and then under the bench, had done Jenks a lot of good. Still, though, he was lagging behind. Worried the slight noise of his labored flight might alert someone, I came to a rolling halt, motioning Jenks to get on my back.

"Whatsa matter, Rache," he said, tugging his hat back down, "got an itch?"

I gritted my teeth. Crouched on my haunches, I pointed to him, then my shoulders.

"No freaking way." He glanced at the trees. "I won't be carted about like a baby."

I don't have time for this, I thought. I pointed again, this time straight up. It was our agreed sign that he was to go home. Jenks's eyes narrowed, and I bared my teeth. Surprised, he took a step back.

"Okay, okay," he grumbled. "But if you tell Ivy, I'm going to pix you every night for a week. Got it?" His light weight hit my shoulders, and he gripped my fur. It was an odd sensation, and I didn't like it. "Not too fast," he muttered, clearly uncomfortable as well.

Apart from his death grip on my fur, I hardly noticed him. I went as fast as I dared. I didn't like that there might be unfriendly eyes holding fairy steel watching us, and I immediately struck out off the path. The sooner we were inside, the better. My ears and nose worked nonstop. I could smell everything, and it wasn't as cool as one might think.

The leaves would shiver at every gust, making me freeze or dart deeper into the foliage. Jenks was singing a bothersome song under his breath. Something about blood and daisies.

I wove my hesitant way through a barrier of loose stone and brambles and slowed. Something was different. "The plants have changed," Jenks said, and I bobbed my head.

The trees I wove between as I moved downhill were markedly more mature. I could smell mistletoe. Old, well-conditioned earth held firmly established plants. Scent, not visual beauty, seemed more important. The narrow path I found was hard-packed dirt instead of brick. Ferns crowded the trail until only one person could pass. Somewhere, water ran. More wary, we continued until a familiar smell brought me to an alarmed standstill. Earl Grey tea.

From under the shadow of a wood lily, I stood motionless and searched for the smell of people. It was silent but for the night insects. "Over there," Jenks breathed. "A cup on the bench." He slipped from me to melt back into the shadows.

I eased forward, whiskers twitching and ears straining. The grove was empty. With a smooth motion, I flowed up onto the bench. There was a swallow of tea left in the cup, its rim decorated with dew. Its silent presence was as telling as the change in plant life. Somehow we had left the public gardens behind. We were in Trent's backyard.

Jenks perched himself upon the handle, his hands on his hips, scowling. "Nothing," he complained. "I can't smell squat off a teacup. I have to get inside."

I leapt from the bench to make an easy landing. The stink of habitation was stronger to the left, and we followed the dirt path through the ferns. Soon the scent of furniture, carpet, and electronics grew pungent, and it was with no surprise that I found the open-air deck. I looked up, making out the silhouette of a latticework cover. A night-blooming vine trailed over it, its fragrance fighting to be recognized over the stink of people.

"Rachel, wait!" Jenks exclaimed, yanking my ear as I stretched to step onto the moss-covered planks. Something brushed my whiskers, and I drew back, running my paws over them. It was sticky. It caught in my paws, and I accidentally glued my ears flat to my eyes. Panicking, I sat back on my haunches. I was stuck!

"Don't rub it, Rache," Jenks said urgently. "Hold still."

But I couldn't see. My pulse raced. I tried to shout, but my mouth was glued shut. The smell of ether caught at my throat. Frantic, I lashed out, hearing an irate buzz. I could barely breathe! What the devil was this stuff?

"Turn it all, Morgan," Jenks all but hissed. "Stop fighting me. I'll get it off you."

I yanked my instincts back and sank into a crouch, my breath fast and shallow. One of my paws was stuck to my whiskers and it hurt. It was all I could do not to go rolling in the dirt.

"Okay." There was a breeze from Jenks's wings. "I'm going to touch your eye."

My paws twitched as he pulled the stuff off an eyelid. His fingers were gentle and deft, but from the amount of pain, he was ripping half my eyelid off. Then it was gone and I could see. I squinted through one eye as Jenks rub his palms together, a small ball between them. Pixy dust sifted from him to make him glow. "Better?" he said, glancing at me.

"Heck yeah," I squeaked. It came out more mangled than usual, seeing as my mouth was still glued shut.

Jenks tossed the ball away. It was that sticky stuff, caked with dust. "Hold still, and I'll have the rest off you faster than Ivy can pull an aura." He yanked at my fur, turning the sticky stuff into little balls. "Sorry," he said as I yelped when he jerked my ear. "I did warn you."

"What?" I chirped, and for once he seemed to understand.

"About the sticky silk." Grimacing, he gave a hard yank, pulling a tuft of my hair out. "That's how I got caught yesterday," he said angrily. "Trent has sticky silk lacing his lobby ceiling just above human height. It's expensive stuff. I'm surprised he uses it anywhere else." Jenks flitted to my other side. "It's a pixy/fairy deterrent. You can get it off, but it takes time. I bet the entire canopy is netted. That's why there's nothing here that flies."

I twitched my tail to show I understood. I had heard of sticky silk, but the thought that I might run into it never crossed my mind. To anyone larger than a child, it felt like spiderweb.

Finally he was done, and I felt my nose, wondering if it was the same shape. Jenks took off his hat and shoved it under a rock. "Wish I had brought my sword," he said. Such was the territorial drive between pixies and fairies that if Jenks had trashed the conspicuous hat, I could stake my life that the garden was pixy and fairy free.

The slightly submissive air he had affected all afternoon vanished. From his point of view, the entire garden was probably now his, since there was no one to say different. He stood beside me with his hands on his hips, severely eyeing the deck.

"Watch this," Jenks said as he shook a cloud of pixy dust from him. His wings blurred to nothing, blowing the glowing dust toward the deck. The faint haze seemed to catch in the air. As if by magic, the pixy dust fixed itself to the silk, outlining a patch of net. Jenks gave me a sideways, satisfied smirk. "Good thing I brought Matalina's scissors," he said, pulling from his pocket the wooden-handled pair of sheers. He confidently strode up to the shimmering net and cut a mink-sized hole. "After you." He gestured grandly, and I flowed up onto the deck.

My heart gave a thump of excitement before settling down to a slow, deliberate pace. It was just another run, I told myself. Emotion was an expense I couldn't afford. Ignore that my life was involved. My nose twitched, searching for human or Inderlander. Nothing.

"I think it's a back office," Jenks said. "See, there's a desk."

Office? I thought, feeling my furry eyebrows rise. It was a deck. Or was it? Jenks lurched excitedly about, like a rabid bat. I followed at a more sedate pace. After about fifteen feet the mossy planking turned into a mottled carpet enclosed by three walls. Well-maintained potted plants were everywhere. The small desk against the far wall didn't look like much work was done there. There was a long couch and chairs arranged beside a wet bar, making the room a very comfortable place to relax or do a bit of light work. The room was a slice of outdoors, a feeling heightened by opening onto the shaded deck and in turn the garden.

"Hey!" Jenks said in excitement. "Look what I found."

I turned from the orchids I had been jealously eyeing to see Jenks hovering over a bank of electronic equipment. "It was hidden in the wall," Jenks explained. "Watch this." He flew feet first into a button set into the wall. The player and its accompanying discs slid back into hiding. Delighted, Jenks hit it again, and the equipment reappeared. "Wonder what that button does," he said, and distracted by the promise of new toys, he darted across the room.

Trent, I decided, had more music discs than a sorority house: pop, classical, jazz, new age, even some head-banger stuff. No disco, though, and my respect for him went up a notch.

I longingly ran a paw over a copy of *Takata's Sea*. The disc sank out of sight and into the player, and I jerked back. Alarmed, I jumped up to hit the button with a scrabbling of nails to send everything back into the wall.

"There's nothing here, Rache. Let's go." Jenks looked pointedly at the door and alighted on the handle. But it wasn't until I jumped up to add my weight that it clicked open. I fell to the floor in an awkward thump. Jenks and I listened at the crack for a breathless moment.

Pulse racing, I nosed the door open enough for Jenks to slip out. In a moment he buzzed back. "It's a hallway," he said. "Come on out. I've already fixed the cameras."

He disappeared around the door again, and I followed, needing all my weight to pull the door shut. The click of the lock was loud, and I cowered, praying it went unheard. I could hear running water and the rustling of night creatures being piped in from unseen speakers. Immediately I recognized the hallway as the one I had been in yesterday. The sounds had probably been there before, but so soft they were subliminal to anything but a rodent's hearing. My head bobbed in understanding. Jenks and I had found Trent's back office where he entertained his "special" guests.

"Which way?" Jenks whispered, hovering beside me. Either his wing was fully functional or he didn't want to risk being spotted riding a mink. I confidently started up the corridor. At every juncture I took the path less appealing and more sterile. Jenks played vanguard, setting every camera for a fifteen-minute loop so we were unseen. Fortunately, Trent went by a human clock—at least publicly—and the building was deserted. Or so I thought.

"Crap," Jenks whispered the same instant I froze. Voices were coming from up the hall. My pulse raced. "Go!" Jenks said urgently. "No! To the right. That chair and the potted plant."

I loped forward. The smell of citrus and terra-cotta blossomed, and I tucked behind the earthen pot as soft footsteps moved along the floor. Jenks flitted up to hide in the plant's branches.

"As much as that?" Trent's voice came sharp to my sensitive ears as he and another turned the corner. "Find out what Hodgkin is doing to get such an increase in productivity. If it's something you think can be applied to other sites, I want a report."

I held my breath as Trent and Jonathan walked past.

"Yes, Sa'han." Jonathan scribbled on an electronic notepad. "I've finished screening the potential applicants for your new secretary. It would be relativity simple to clear your calendar tomorrow morning. How many would you like to see?"

"Oh, limit it to the three you think are best suited and one you don't. Anyone I know?"

"No. I had to go out of state this time."

"Wasn't today your day off, Jon?"

There was a pause. "I opted to work, seeing as you lacked your usual secretary."

"Ah," Trent said with a comfortable laugh as they turned a corner. "So there's the reason for your zeal in finishing the interviews."

Jonathan's soft denial was the merest hint as they walked out of sight.

"Jenks," I squeaked. There was no response. "Jenks!" I squeaked again, wondering if he had gone and done something stupid like following them.

"I'm still here," he grumbled, and I felt a wash of relief. The tree shuddered as he shimmied down the trunk. He sat on the edge of the pot and dangled his feet. "I got a good sniff of him," he said, and I sank back on my haunches in expectation.

"I don't know what he is." Jenks's wings shifted to a dismal shade of blue as his circulation slowed and his mood dulled. "He smells meadowy, but not like a witch. There's no hint of iron, so he's not a vamp." Jenks's eyes crinkled in confusion. "I could smell his body rhythms slowing down, which means he sleeps at night. That rules out Weres or any other nocturnal Inderlander. Turn it all, Rache. He doesn't smell like anything I recognize. And you know what's more odd? That guy with him? He smells just like Trent. It's got to be a spell."

My whiskers twitched. Odd wasn't the word. "Squeak," I said, meaning, "I'm sorry."

"Yeah, you're right." He rose on slow dragonfly wings, slipping out to the middle of the hallway. "We should finish the run and get out of here."

A jolt shook me. *Out of here,* I thought as I left the security of the citrus tree. I was willing to bet we couldn't get out the way we came in. But I'd worry about that after I burgled Trent's office. We had already done the impossible. Getting out would be a snap.

"This way," I chittered, turning down a familiar hallway just before the lobby. I could smell the salt from the fish tank in Trent's office. The frosted glass doors we passed were black and empty. No one was working late. Trent's wooden door was predictably shut.

Swift and silent, Jenks went to work. The lock was electronic, and after a few moments of tinkering behind the panel bolted to the doorframe, the lock clicked and the door cracked open. "Standard stuff," Jenks said. "Jax could have done it."

The soft gurgling of the desk fountain drifted into the hall. Jenks pushed his way in first, taking care of the camera before I followed him in.

"No, wait," I squeaked as he angled feet first at the light switch. The room was bathed in a painful glare. "Hey!" I squeaked, hiding my face behind my paws.

"Sorry." The light went out.

"Turn on the light over the fish tank," I chittered, trying to see with my light-shocked eyes. "The fish tank," I repeated uselessly, sitting back on my haunches and pointing.

"Rache. Don't be stupid. You don't have time to eat." Then he hesitated, dropping an inch. "Oh! The light. Hee hee. Good idea."

The light flickered on, illuminating Trent's office in a soft green glow. I scrambled onto his swivel chair and then the desk, awkwardly flipping his datebook back a few months and tearing out a page. My pulse raced as I sent it to the floor, following it down.

Whiskers twitching, I pried open the desk drawer and found the discs. I wouldn't have put it past Trent to move everything. *Maybe,* I thought with a stab of pride, *he didn't think I was* that *much of a threat.* Taking the disc marked ALZHEIMERS, I eased back to the carpet and threw my weight against the drawer to shut it. His desk was made of a scrumptious cherry wood, and I dismally thought of the coming embarrassment of my pressboard furniture among Ivy's.

Sitting back on my haunches, I gestured to Jenks for the string. Jenks had already folded the paper into a wad he could manage, and as soon as I had the disc tied to me, we'd be gone.

"String, right?" Jenks dug in a pocket.

The overhead light exploded into existence, and I froze, cowering. Breath held tight, I crouched to look under the desk toward the door. There were two pairs of shoes—a soft slipper and an uncomfortable leather—framed in the light spilling into the hall.

"Trent," Jinks mouthed as he landed next to me with the folded paper.

Jonathan's voice was angry. "They're gone, Sa'han. I'll alert the grounds."

There was a tight sigh. "Go. I'll see what they took."

My pulse pounded, and I scrunched under the desk. The leather shoes turned and went into the hall. My adrenaline rushed as I considered darting out, but I couldn't run with the disc in my front paws. And I wasn't going to leave it behind.

The door to Trent's office closed, and I cursed my hesitation. I edged to the back panel of the desk. Jenks and I exchanged glances. I gave him the sign to go home, and he nodded emphatically. We scrunched down as Trent came around and stood before his fish tank.

"Hello, Sophocles," Trent breathed. "Who was it? If you could only tell me."

He had lost his business jacket, making him look vastly more informal. I wasn't surprised at the firm definition in his shoulders as they bunched under his lightweight shirt at his slightest movement. Sighing, he sat in his chair. His hand went to the drawer with the discs, and I felt myself go weak. I swallowed hard as I realized he was humming the first track to *Takata's Sea. Double damn. I had given myself away.*

" 'Is it no wonder the newborn cry?' " Trent said, whispering the lyrics. " 'The choice was real. The chance is a lie.' "

He went still, his fingers on the discs. Slowly he pushed the drawer shut with a foot. Its small click made me jump. He tucked closer under the desk, and I heard the sound of the datebook scraping across the desktop. He was so close, I could smell the outside on him. "Oh," he said with a soft surprise. "Imagine that.

"Quen!" he said loudly.

I stared at Jenks in confusion until a masculine voice came echoing into the room from a hidden speaker. "Sa'han?"

"Loose the hounds," Trent said. His voice reverberated with power, and I shivered.

"But it isn't the full of the—"

"Loose the hounds, Quen," Trent repeated, his voice no louder but carrying a deep anger. Under the desk, his foot began to shift rhythmically.

"Yes, Sa'han."

Trent's foot stilled. "Wait." I heard him take a deep breath, as if tasting the air.

"Sir?" came the hidden voice.

Trent sniffed again. He slowly rolled his chair away from the desk. My heart pounded, and I held my breath. Jenks flitted up to hide behind the back of a drawer. I froze as Trent stood, backed from his desk, and crouched down. I had nowhere to go. Trent's eyes met mine, and he smiled. Fear paralyzed me. "Belay that," he said softly.

"Yes, Sa'han." The speaker went dead with a soft pop.

I stared at Trent, feeling as if I was going to burst.

"Ms. Morgan?" Trent said, inclining his head cordially, and I shivered. "I wish I could say it was a pleasure." Still he smiled, inching forward. I bared my teeth and chittered. His hand drew back and he frowned. "Come out of there. You have something that belongs to me."

I felt the presence of the disc beside me. Being caught, I went from successful thief to village idiot in a heartbeat. How could I have thought I could get away with it? Ivy was right.

"Come along, Ms. Morgan," he said, reaching under the desk.

I sprang into the empty spaces behind the drawers, trying to escape. Trent reached up after me. I squeaked as a tight grip fastened on my tail. My nails grated as he pulled. Terrified, I twisted, sinking my teeth into the fatty part of his hand.

"You canicula!" he shouted, pulling me out in a helpless scrabbling. The world spun as he rose to his feet. Violently shaking his hand, he smacked me into the desk. Stars exploded into existence, seeming to go with the dusky cinnamon taste of his blood. The pain in my head loosened my jaws, and I spun from my tail as he held me.

"Let her go!" I heard Jenks cry.

The world gyrated in quick swings. "You brought your bug," Trent said calmly, slamming the flat of his hand against a panel on his desk. A faint smell of ether tickled my nose.

"Get out, Jenks!" I squeaked, recognizing the smell of sticky web.

Jonathan flung open the door. He stood in the threshold, his eyes wide. "Sa'han!"

"Shut the door!" Trent shouted.

I twisted frantically to escape. Jenks darted out just as my teeth closed upon Trent's thumb again. "Damn you, witch!" Trent shouted, swinging me into the wall. Stars exploded anew, dying to black embers. The embers grew, and I watched, numb, as they slowly overtook my sight until there was nothing else. I was warm, and I couldn't move.

I was dying.

I had to be.

Nineteen

"So, Ms. Sara Jane, the split schedule isn't an issue for you?"

"No sir. I don't mind working until seven if I have the afternoon for errands and such."

"I appreciate your flexibility. Afternoons are for contemplation. My best work is done in the morning and evening. I keep only a small staff after five, and I find the lack of distractions helps me concentrate."

The sound of Trent's smooth, public persona slipped into my awareness, jarring me awake. I opened my eyes, not understanding why everything was glaringly white and gray. Then I remembered. I was a mink. But I was alive. Barely.

The alternating high and low voices of Trent and Sara Jane's interview continued as I shakily got to my feet to find I was in a cage. My stomach tightened at a wave of nausea. I sank down, struggling not to vomit. "I am so wasted," I whispered as Trent flicked glances at me over his wire-rim glasses as he talked with a trim young woman in a pale interview suit.

My head hurt. If I didn't have a concussion, it was close. My right shoulder where I had hit his desk was sore, and it hurt to breathe. I tucked my front paw close and tried not to move. Staring at Trent, I tried to figure things out. Jenks was nowhere. *That's right,* I remembered in relief. He had made it out. He would have gone home to Ivy. Not that they could do anything for me.

My cage held a bottle of water, a bowl of pellets, a ferret hut large enough to curl up in, and an exercise wheel. *Like I would ever use it,* I thought bitterly.

I was sitting on a table at the back of Trent's office. According to the fake sunlight from the window, it was only a few hours after sunrise. Too early for me. And though it stuck in my craw, I was going to slink into that hut and go to sleep. I didn't care what Trent thought.

Taking a deep breath, I stood. "Ow! Ow!" I squeaked, wincing.

"Oh, you have a pet ferret," Sara Jane exclaimed softly.

I shut my eyes in misery. I wasn't a pet ferret; I was a pet mink. *Get it straight, lady.*

I heard Trent rise from behind his desk and felt, more than saw, both of them come close. Apparently the interview was over. Time to ogle the pet mink. The light was eclipsed, and I opened my eyes. They stood above me, staring.

Sara Jane looked professional in her classy interview dress, her long, fair hair falling midway to her elbows in a simple, sparse cut. The petite woman was cute as a button, and I imagined most people didn't take her seriously with her upturned nose, her high little-girl voice, and her short stature. But I could tell from the intelligent look in her wide-set eyes that she was used to working in a man's world and knew how to get things done. I imagined that if someone misjudged her, she wasn't opposed to using it to her advantage.

The woman's perfume was strong, and I sneezed, clenching in pain.

"This is—Angel," Trent said. "She's a mink." His sarcasm was subtle but loud in my ears. His left hand massaged his right. It was bandaged. *Three cheers for the mink,* I thought.

"She looks ill." Sara Jane's carefully polished fingernails were worn to almost the quick, and her hands looked unusually strong, almost like a laborer's.

"You don't mind rodents, Sara Jane?"

She straightened, and I shut my eyes as the light fell upon them. "I despise them, Mr. Kalamack. I hale from a farm. Vermin are killed on sight. But I'm not about to lose a potential position because of an animal." She took a slow breath. "I need this job. My entire family scrimped to put me through school, to get me out of the fields. I have to pay them back. I have a younger sister. She's too smart to spend her life digging sugar beets. She wants to be a witch, to get her degree. I can't help her unless I get a good job. I *need* this job. Please, Mr. Kalamack. I know I don't have the experience, but I'm smart and I know how to work hard."

I cracked an eyelid. Trent's face was serious in thought. His fair hair and complexion stood out sharply against his dark business suit, and he and Sara Jane made a handsome couple, though she was rather short beside him. "Nicely said, Sara Jane," he said, smiling warmly. "I appreciate honesty above all in my employees. When can you start?"

"Immediately," she said, her voice quavering. I felt ill. Poor woman.

"Wonderful." His gray voice sounded genuinely pleased. "Jon has a few papers for you to sign. He will walk you through your responsibilities, shadow you for your first week. Go to him with any questions. He's been with me for years and knows me better than I know myself."

"Thank you, Mr. Kalamack," she said, her narrow shoulders raised in excitement.

"My pleasure." Trent took her elbow and walked her to the door. *He touched her,* I thought. *Why hadn't he touched me?* Scared I might figure out what he was, maybe?

"Do you have a place to stay yet?" he was asking. "Be sure to ask Jon about the off-site housing we have available for employees."

"Thank you, Mr. Kalamack. No, I don't have an apartment yet."

"Fine. Take what time you need to get settled. If you like,

we can arrange for a portion of your compensation to be put in a trust fund for your sister, pretax."

"Yes, please." The relief in Sara Jane's voice was obvious, even from the hall. She was caught. Trent was a god to her, a prince rescuing her and her family. He could do no wrong.

My stomach roiled. The room was empty, though, and I dragged myself into my hut. I circled once to get my tail in place, then collapsed with my nose poking out. The door to Trent's office clicked shut, and I jumped, all my hurts starting up again.

"Good morning, Ms. Morgan," Trent said as he breezed past my cage. He sat at his desk and began sorting through the strewn papers. "I was going to keep you here only until I got a second opinion on you. But I don't know. You are *such* the conversation starter."

"Go Turn yourself," I said, baring my teeth. Again, it was all chirps and chitters.

"Really." He sat back and twirled his pencil. "That couldn't have been complimentary."

A knock made me scrunch out of sight. It was Jonathan, and Trent became busy as he came in. "Yes, Jon?" he said, his attention firmly on his calendar.

"Sa'han." The unusually tall man stood at a respectful distance. "Ms. Sara Jane?"

"She has exactly the qualifications I need." Trent put down his pencil. Leaning back in his chair, he took off his glasses and chewed idly on the tip of the earpiece until he noticed Jonathan watching with a prim, unspoken disapproval. Trent tossed them to the desktop with a bothered look. "Sara Jane's younger sister wants off the farm to become a witch," he said. "We must help excellence along in any way we can."

"Ah." Jonathan's narrow shoulders relaxed. "I see."

"If you would, find the asking price on Sara Jane's home farm. I may like to dabble in the sugar industry. Get the taste of it, as it were? Keep the labor force. Move Hodgkin in as foreman for six months to train the present foreman in his methods. Instruct him to watch Sara Jane's sister. If she has a brain, have him move her to where she has some responsibilities."

I wedged my head out my door, worried. Jonathan looked down his narrow nose at me in disgust. "With us again, Morgan?" he mocked. "If it had been up to me, I would have stuffed you down the garbage disposal in the employees' break room and flicked the switch."

"Bastard," I chittered, then flipped him off to make sure he understood.

Jonathan's few wrinkles deepened as he frowned. Long arm swinging, he smacked my cage with the folder in his hand.

Ignoring my pain, I lunged at him, clinging to the bars with my teeth bared.

He fell back in obvious shock. Flushing, the gaunt man pulled his arm back again.

"Jon," Trent said softly. Though his voice was a whisper, Jonathan froze. I clung to the bars, heart pounding. "You forget your place. Leave Ms. Morgan alone. If you misjudge her and she fights back, it's not her fault but yours. You've made this mistake before. Repeatedly."

Seething, I dropped to the floor of the cage and growled. I hadn't known I could growl, but there it was. Slowly, Jonathan's clenched hand loosened. "It's my place to protect you."

Trent's eyebrows rose. "Ms. Morgan isn't in the position to harm anyone. Stop it."

Eyes going from one to the other, I watched the older man take Trent's rebuke with an acceptance I wouldn't have expected. The two had a very odd relationship. Trent was clearly in charge, but remembering the bother in Trent's face when Jonathan expressed his disapproval of Trent chewing his glasses, it seemed it hadn't always been so. I wondered if Jonathan had seen to Trent's upbringing, however briefly, when his mother, and then his father, had died.

"Accept my apologies, Sa'han," Jonathan said, actually inclining his head.

Trent said nothing, returning to his papers. Though clearly dismissed, Jonathan waited until Trent looked up. "Is there something else?" Trent asked.

"Your eight-thirty is early," he said. "Shall I accompany Mr. Percy back?"

"Percy!" I squeaked, and Trent glanced at me. *Not Francis Percy!*

"Yes," Trent said slowly. "Please do."

Swell, I thought as Jonathan ducked into the hallway and eased the door shut behind him. Francis's interrupted interview. I paced the perimeter of my cage, nervous. My muscles were loosening, and the movement felt painfully good. I stopped as I realized Trent hadn't taken his gaze off me. Under his questioning look, I slunk into my hut, ashamed somehow.

I found Trent was still watching me as I curled my tail about myself, draping it across my nose to keep it warm. "Don't be angry with Jon," he said softly. "He takes his station seriously—as he should. If you push him too far, he'll kill you. Let's hope you don't need to learn the same lesson he does."

I lifted my lip to show my teeth, not liking him giving me wise-old-man crap.

A whiny voice pulled both our attentions to the hallway. Francis. I had told him I could turn into a mink. If he made the right connection, I was as good as dead. Well, more dead than I was. I didn't want him to see me. Neither, apparently, did Trent.

"Mmmm, yes," he said, hastily getting up and shifting one of his floor plants to hide my cage. It was a peace lily, and I could see past its wide leaves and still stay hidden. There was a knock, and Trent called, "Come in."

"No, really," Francis was saying as Jonathan all but pushed him in.

From behind the plant, I watched Francis meet Trent's eyes and swallow hard. "Uh, hello, Mr. Kalamack," he stammered, coming to an awkward standstill. He looked more unkempt than usual, one of his laces peeping out from under his pants almost undone, and his stubble having grown from potentially attractive to ugly. His black hair lay flat, and his squinty eyes had faint, tired lines at the corners. It was likely Francis hadn't been to bed yet, coming out for his interview at Trent's convenience rather than the I.S.'s.

Trent said nothing. He went to sit, easing behind his desk with the relaxed tension of a predator settling in beside the water hole.

Francis glanced at Jonathan, his shoulders hunched. There was the sound of sliding polyester as he pushed up his jacket sleeves, then pulled them back down. Tossing his hair from his eyes, Francis edged to the chair and sat on the very end. Stress drew the features on his triangular face tight, especially when Jonathan closed the door and stood behind him with his arms crossed and his feet spread wide. My attention flicked between them. What was going on?

"Would you explain yesterday to me?" Trent said with a smooth casualness.

Confusion made me blink, then my mouth dropped open in understanding. Frances worked for Trent? It would explain his fast advancement, not to mention how a short-order cook such as himself made witch. A chill ran through me. This arrangement wasn't with the I.S.'s blessing. The I.S. had no idea. Francis was a mole. The cookie was a freaking mole!

I looked at Trent through the wide leaves. His shoulders shifted slightly, as if agreeing with my thoughts. My nausea came rolling back. Francis wasn't good enough for anything this slimy. He was going to get himself killed.

"Uh—I—" Frances stammered.

"My head of security found you spelled in your own trunk," Trent said calmly, the barest hint of a threat in his voice. "Ms. Morgan and I had an interesting conversation."

"She—She said she would turn me into an animal," Frances interrupted.

Trent took a deep breath. "Why," he said with a tired patience, "would she do that?"

"She doesn't like me."

Trent said nothing. Francis cringed as he probably realized how childish that sounded.

"Tell me about Rachel Morgan," Trent demanded.

"She's a pain in the—um—butt," he said, flicking a nervous look at Jonathan.

Trent took a pen in hand and twirled it. "I know that. Tell me something else."

"That you don't already know?" Francis blurted. His pinched eyes were riveted to the revolving pen. "You've probably had your finger on her longer than on me. Did you give her a loan for tuition?" he said, sounding almost jealous. "Whisper in her I.S. interviewer's ear?"

I stiffened. How dare he suggest it. I had *worked* for my schooling. I'd gotten my job on *my own*. I looked to Trent, hating them all. I didn't owe anyone anything.

"No. I didn't." Trent set his pen down. "Ms. Morgan was a surprise. But I did offer her a job," he said, and Francis seemed to sink in on himself. His mouth worked, but nothing came out. I could smell the fear on him, sour and sharp.

"Not your job," Trent said, his disgust obvious. "Tell me what she is afraid of. What makes her angry? What does she cherish most in the world?"

Francis's breath came in a relieved sound. He shifted, going to cross his legs but hesitating at the last, awkward moment. "I don't know. The mall? I try to stay away from her."

"Yes," Trent said in his liquid voice. "Let's talk about that for a moment. After reviewing your activities the past few days, one might question your loyalties—Mr. Percy."

Francis crossed his arms. His breathing increased and he began to fidget. Jonathan took a menacing step closer, and Francis tossed his hair from his eyes again.

Trent went frighteningly intense. "Do you know how much it cost me to quiet the rumors when you ran from the I.S. records vault?"

He licked his lips. "Rachel said they'd think I was helping her. That I should run."

"And so you ran."

"She said—"

"And yesterday?" Trent interrupted. "You drove her to me."

The tight anger in his voice pulled me out of my hut. Trent leaned forward, and I swear I heard Francis's blood freeze. The businessman aura fell from Trent. What was left was domination. Natural, unequivocal domination.

I stared at the change. Trent's mien was nothing like a vamp's aura of power. It was like unsweetened chocolate: strong and bitter and oily, leaving an uncomfortable after-taste. Vamps used fear to command respect. Trent simply demanded it. And from what I could see, the thought never crossed his mind that it would be denied.

"She used you to get to me," he whispered, his eyes unblinking. "That is inexcusable."

Francis cowered in his chair, his thin face drawn and his eyes wide. "I—I'm sorry," he stammered. "It won't happen again."

Trent's breath slipped into him in a slow gathering of will, and I watched in horrified fascination. The yellow fish in the tank splashed at the surface. The hair on my back pricked. My pulse raced. Something rose, as nebulous as a whiff of ozone. Trent's face went empty and ageless. A haze seemed to edge him, and I wondered in a sudden shock if he were pulling on the ever-after. He'd have to be a witch or human to do that. And I would've sworn he was neither.

I tore my eyes from Trent. Jonathan's thin lips were parted. He stood behind Francis, watching Trent with a slack mix of surprise and worry. This raw show of anger wasn't expected, even by him. His hand rose in protest, hesitant and fearful.

As if in response, Trent's eye twitched and his breath eased out. The fish hid behind the coral. My skin eerily rippled, settling my fur flat. Jonathan's fingers trembled, and he made fists of them. Still not looking from Francis, Trent intoned, "I know it won't."

His voice was dust upon cold iron, the sounds sliding

from one meaning to the next in a liquid grace that was mesmerizing. I felt out of breath. Shuddering, I crouched where I was. What the blazes had happened? Had almost happened?

"What do you plan on doing now?" Trent asked.

"Sir?" Francis said, his voice cracking as he blinked.

"That's what I thought." Trent's fingertips quivered with his repressed anger. "Nothing. The I.S. is watching you too closely. Your usefulness is beginning to fade."

Francis's mouth opened. "Mr. Kalamack! Wait! Like you said, the I.S. is watching me. I can draw their attention. Keep them from the customs docks. Another Brimstone take will put me in the clear and distract them at the same time." Francis shifted on the edge of his seat. "You can move your— things?" he finished weakly.

Things, I thought. Why didn't he just say biodrugs? My whiskers quivered. Francis distracted the I.S. with a token amount of Brimstone while Trent moved the real moneymaker. How long? I wondered. How long had Francis worked for him? Years?

"Mr. Kalamack?" Francis whispered.

Trent placed his fingertips together as if in careful thought. Behind him, Jonathan furrowed his thin eyebrows, the worry that had filled him almost gone.

"Tell me when?" Francis begged, edging closer on his chair.

Trent pushed Francis to the back of his chair with a three-second glance. "I don't give chances, Percy. I take opportunities." He pulled his datebook closer, paging a few days ahead. "I would like to schedule a shipment on Friday. Southwest. Last flight before midnight to L.A. You can find your usual take at the main bus station in a locker. Keep it anonymous. My name has been in the papers too often lately."

Francis jumped to his feet in relief. He stepped forward as if to shake Trent's hand, then glanced at Jonathan and backed up. "Thank you, Mr. Kalamack," he gushed. "You won't be sorry."

"I can't imagine I would." Trent looked at Jonathan, then the door. "Enjoy your afternoon," he said in dismissal.

"Yes sir. You, too."

I felt as if I was going to be sick as Francis bounced out of the room. Jonathan hesitated in the threshold, watching Francis make obnoxious noises at the ladies he passed in the hall.

"Mr. Percy has made himself more of a liability than an asset," Trent breathed tiredly.

"Yes, Sa'han," Jonathan agreed. "I strongly urge you to remove him from the payroll."

My stomach clenched. Francis didn't deserve to die just because he was stupid.

Trent rubbed his fingertips into his forehead. "No," he finally said. "I'd rather keep him until I arrange for a replacement. And I may have other plans for Mr. Percy."

"As you like, Sa'han," Jonathan said, and softly closed the door.

Twenty

"Here, Angel," Sara Jane coaxed. A carrot wiggled through the bars of my cage. I stretched to take it before she could let it drop. Aspen chips didn't season them at all.

"Thanks," I chittered, knowing she couldn't understand me, but needing to say something regardless. The woman smiled and cautiously extended her fingers through the cage. I grazed my whiskers across them because I knew she would like it.

"Sara Jane?" Trent questioned from his desk, and the petite woman turned with a guilty swiftness. "I employ you to manage my office affairs, not be a zookeeper."

"Sorry sir. I was taking the opportunity to try and rid myself of my irrational fear of vermin." She brushed at her knee-length cotton skirt. It wasn't as crisp or professional as her interview suit, but still new. Just what I'd expect a farm girl would wear on her first day on the job.

I chewed ravenously on the carrot left over from Sara Jane's lunch. I was starving, since I refused to eat those stale pellets. *What's the matter, Trent?* I thought between chews. *Jealous?*

Trent adjusted his glasses and returned his attention to his papers. "When you're through ridding yourself of your irrational fears, I'd like you to go down to the library."

"Yes sir."

"The librarian has collated some information for me. But I want you to screen it for me. Bring up what you think is most pertinent."

"Sir?"

Trent set down his pen. "Information regarding the sugar beet industry." He smiled with a genuine warmth. I wondered if he had a patent on it. "I may be branching out in that direction, and need to learn enough to make an informed decision."

Sara Jane beamed, tucking her fair hair behind an ear in pleased embarrassment. Obviously she guessed Trent might be buying the farm her family was serfed upon. *You're a smart woman,* I thought darkly. *Follow it down. Trent will own your family. You'd be his, body and soul.*

She turned back to my cage and dropped a last celery stick. Her smile faded. Worry creased her brow. It would have looked endearing on her childlike face, except the woman's family was in real danger. She took a breath to say something, then closed her mouth. "Yes sir," she said, her eyes distant. "I'll bring the information up right away."

Sara Jane closed the door as she left, her footsteps sounding slow in the hallway.

Trent gave his door a suspicious glance as he reached for his cup of tea: Earl Grey, no sugar or milk. If he followed yesterday's pattern, it would be phone conversations and paperwork from three until seven, when the few people he kept late went home. I imagined it was easier to run illegal drugs from your office when no one was around to see you.

Trent had returned that afternoon from his three-hour lunch break with his wispy hair freshly combed and smelling of the outdoors. He had been decidedly refreshed. If I hadn't known better, I would have assumed he spent his midday break napping in his back office.

Why not? I thought as I stretched out on the hammock my cell had come with. He was wealthy enough to set his own hours.

I yawned, my eyes slipping shut. It was the second day of

my captivity, and I was quite sure it wouldn't be my last. I had spent last night thoroughly investigating my cage, only to find that it was Rachel proof. It had been designed for ferrets, and the two-story wire cage was surprisingly secure. My hours spent prying at the seams left me bone tired. It was pleasant to do nothing. My hope that Jenks or Ivy might rescue me was thin. I was on my own. And it might be a while before I managed to convey to Sara Jane that I was a person and get out of there.

I cracked an eyelid as Trent rose from his desk and strode restlessly to his music discs arranged in a recessed shelf beside the player. He cut a nice figure as he stood before them, so intent on his choice that he didn't realize I was rating his backside: 9.5 out of 10. I took the .5 off for most of his physique being hidden behind a business suit that cost more than some cars.

I'd gotten another yummy look at him last night when he took off his jacket after everyone went home. The man had a very strong back. Why he kept it hidden behind that jacket was both a mystery and a crime. His tight stomach was even better. He had to work out, though I don't know where he found the time. I would have given anything to see him in a bathing suit—or less. His legs had to be just as muscular, being the expert rider he was reputed to be. And if it sounded like I was a sex-starved nympho . . . Well, I didn't have anything to do but watch him.

Trent had worked long after sunset yesterday, seemingly alone in the silent building. The only light had been from that fake window. It slowly paled as the sun went down, mirroring the natural light outside until he clicked on the desk lamp. I had caught myself drowsing several times, waking up when he turned a page or the printer hummed to life. He hadn't quit until Jonathan came by to remind him to eat. I guess he earned his money, same as I did. 'Course, he had two jobs, being a reputable businessman and drug lord both. Probably filled up one's day right nicely.

My hammock swayed as I watched Trent choose a disc. It

spun up, and the soft cadence of drums drifted into existence. Eyeing me, Trent adjusted his gray linen suit and smoothed his wispy hair as if daring me to say anything. I gave him a sleepy thumbs-up, and his frown deepened. It wasn't the stuff I liked, but it was okay. This was older, carrying a forgotten sound of bound intensity, of lost sorrow chained to stir the soul. It wasn't half bad.

I could get used to this, I mused as I carefully stretched my healing body. I hadn't slept this well since I quit the I.S. It was ironic that here, in a cage in a drug lord's office, I was safe from my I.S. death threat.

Trent settled himself back at his work, his pen occasionally accompanying the drums as he paused in thought. Obviously this was one of his favorites. I slipped in and out of sleep as the afternoon wore on, soothed by the rumble of drums and whisper of music. The occasional phone call sent Trent's mellow voice to rise and fall in a soothing sound, and I found myself eagerly waiting for the next interruption just so I could hear it.

It was a commotion in the hall that jerked me from sleep. "I know where his office is," boomed an overly confident voice, reminding me of one of my more arrogant professors.

There was a half-heard scolding from Sara Jane, and Trent met my inquiring gaze.

"Turn it all to hell," he muttered, the corners of his expressive eyes crinkling. "I told him to send one of his assistants." He dug about in a drawer with unusual haste, the clatter bringing me fully awake. I blinked the sleep from me as he pointed a remote at the player. The pipes and drums ceased. He tossed the remote back into the drawer with a resigned air. If I didn't know better, I would have thought that Trent liked having someone to share his day with, someone he didn't have to pretend to be anything but what he was—*whatever* he was. His anger at Francis had set my creepy meter off the scale.

Sara Jane knocked and came in. "Mr. Faris is here to see you, Mr. Kalamack?"

Trent took a slow breath. He didn't look happy. "Send him in."

"Yes sir." She left the door open and her heels clicked away. They soon returned as she escorted in a heavyset man wearing a dark gray lab coat. The man looked huge standing beside the small woman. Sara Jane left, her eyes pinched in a lingering worry.

"Can't say I like your new secretary," Faris grumbled as the door closed. "Sara, is it?"

Trent rose to his feet and extended his hand, his distaste hidden behind his sincere-looking smile. "Faris. Thanks for coming on such short notice. It's only a small matter. One of your assistants would have been fine. I trust I haven't interrupted your research too badly?"

"Not at all. I'm always glad to get up into the sun," he puffed as if winded.

Faris squeezed the bites I had given Trent yesterday, and Trent's smile froze. The heavy man wedged himself into the chair across from Trent's desk as if he owned it. He propped an ankle up on one knee, sending his lab coat to fall open to show dress slacks and shiny shoes. A dark stain spotted his lapel, and the smell of disinfectant flowed from him, almost hiding the scent of redwood. Old pocketmarked scars were scattered across his cheeks and the skin visible on his beefy hands.

Trent returned to behind his desk and leaned back, hiding his bandaged hand under the other one. There was a moment of silence.

"So, what do you want?" Faris demanded, his voice rumbling.

I thought I saw a flash of annoyance cross Trent. "Direct as usual," he said. "Tell me what you can about this?"

He had pointed to me, and my breath caught. Disregarding my lingering stiffness, I lurched into my hut. Faris levered himself to his feet with a groan, and the sharp scent of redwood crashed over me as he came close. "Well well," he said. "Aren't you the stupid one."

Annoyed, I looked up at his dark eyes, almost lost among the folds of skin. Trent had come around to the front of his desk, sitting against it. "Recognize her?" he asked.

"Personally? No." He gave the bars of my cage a soft thunk with a thick finger.

"Hey!" I shouted from my hut. "I'm really getting tired of that."

"Shut up, you," he said disdainfully. "She's a witch," Faris continued, dismissing me as if I were nothing. "Just keep her out of your fish tank, and she won't be able to change back. It's a powerful spell. She must have the backing of a large organization, as only they could afford it. And she's stupid."

The last was directed at me, and I fought the urge to throw pellets at him.

"How so?" Trent went to rummage in his lower drawer, the chiming of lead crystal ringing out before he poured two shots of that forty-year-old whiskey.

"Transformation is a difficult art. You have to use potions rather than amulets, which means you stir an entire brew for only one occasion. The rest gets thrown away. Very expensive. You could pay your assistant librarian's salary for what this stirring cost, and staff a small office for the liability insurance to sell it."

"Difficult, you say?" Trent handed Faris a glass. "Could you make such a spell?"

"If I had the recipe," he said, puffing up his substantial chest, his pride clearly affronted. "It's old. Preindustry, perhaps? I don't recognize who stirred this spell." He leaned close, breathing deeply. "Lucky for him, or I might have to relieve the witch of his library."

This, I thought, *is becoming a very interesting conversation.*

"So you don't think she made it herself?" Trent asked. He was again sitting back against his desk, looking incredibly trim and fit next to Faris.

The heavyset man shook his head and sat back down. The shot glass was completely unseen, enfolded by his thick hands. "I'd stake my life on it. You can't be smart enough to competently stir a spell like that and be dumb enough to be caught. Doesn't make sense."

"Maybe she was impatient," Trent said, and Faris exploded into laughter. I jumped, covering my ears with my paws.

"Oh, yes," Faris said between guffaws. "Yes. She was impatient. I like that."

I thought Trent's usual polish was starting to look thin as he returned behind his desk and set his untasted drink aside.

"So who is she?" Faris asked, leaning forward like a mock conspirator. "An eager reporter trying for the story of her life?"

"Is there a spell that will allow me to understand her?" Trent asked, ignoring Faris's question. "All she does is squeak."

Faris grunted as he leaned to set his emptied glass on the desk in an unspoken request for more. "No. Rodents don't have vocal cords. You plan on keeping her for any length of time?"

Trent spun his glass in his fingers. He was alarmingly silent.

Faris smiled wickedly. "What's cooking in that nasty little head of yours, Trent?"

The creak of Trent's chair as he leaned forward seemed very loud. "Faris, if I didn't need your talents so badly, I would have you whipped in your own lab."

The large man grinned, sending the folds in his face to fall into each other. "I know."

Trent put the bottle away. "I may enter her in Friday's tournament."

Faris blinked. "The city's tournaments?" he said softly. "I've seen one of those. The bouts don't end until one is dead."

"So I've heard."

Fear pulled me to the wire mesh. "Whoa, wait a moment," I chittered. "What do you mean, dead? Hey! Someone talk to the mink!"

I threw a pellet at Trent. It went about two feet before arching down to the carpet. I tried again, this time kicking it rather than throwing it. It hit the back of his desk with a plink. "The Turn take you, Trent!" I shouted. "Talk to me."

Trent met my gaze, his eyebrows raised. "The rat fights, of course."

My heart gave a thump. Chilled, I sank back on my haunches. The rat fights. Illegal. Backroom. Rumors. To the death. I was going to be in the ring—fighting a rat to the death.

I stood in confusion, my long, white-furred feet planted on the wire mesh of my cage. I felt betrayed, of all things. Faris looked ill. "You're not serious," he whispered, his fat cheeks turning white. "You're really going to play her? You can't!"

"Why ever not?"

Faris's jowls dropped as he struggled for words. "She's a person!" he exclaimed. "She won't last three minutes. They'll rip her to shreds."

Trent shrugged with an indifference I knew wasn't faked. "Surviving is her problem, not mine." He put on his wire glasses and bent his head over his papers. "Good afternoon, Faris."

"Kalamack, this is too far. Even you aren't above the law."

As soon as he said it, both Faris and I knew it was a mistake. Trent pulled his gaze up. Silent, he eyed Faris from over his lenses. He leaned forward, an elbow on his accumulated work. I waited breathlessly, the tension making my fur rise. "How is your youngest daughter, Faris?" Trent asked, his beautiful voice unable to hide the ugliness of his question.

The large man went ashen. "She's fine," he whispered. His rough confidence had vanished, leaving only a frightened, fat man.

"What is she? Fifteen?" Trent eased back in his chair, set his glasses beside his in/out-box, and laced his long fingers over his middle. "Wonderful age. She wants to be an oceanographer, yes? Talk to the dolphins?"

"Yes." It was hardly audible.

"I can't tell you how pleased I am that the treatment for her bone cancer worked."

I looked at the back of Trent's drawer where the incriminating discs lay. My gaze lifted to Faris, taking in his lab coat with a new understanding. Cold struck through me, and I stared at Trent. He wasn't just running biodrugs, he was making them. I wasn't sure if it horrified me more that Trent was actively flirting with the same technology that wiped out half the world's population, or that he was blackmailing people with it, threatening their loved ones. He was so pleasant, so charming, so damned likable with his confident personality. How could something so foul lay next to something so attractive?

Trent smiled. "She's been in remission for five years now. Good physicians willing to explore illegal techniques are hard to find. And expensive."

Faris swallowed. "Yes—sir."

Trent eyed him with a questioning arch to his eyebrows. "Good afternoon—Faris."

"Slime," I hissed, ignored. "You are a slime, Trent! Scrapings from under my boot."

Faris moved shakily to the door. I tensed when I smelled a sudden defiance. Trent had backed him into a corner. The large man had nothing to lose.

Trent must have sensed it, too. "You're going to run now, aren't you," he said as Faris opened the door. The sound of office chatter filtered in. "You know I can't let you."

Faris turned with a hopeless look. Astonished, I watched Trent unscrew his pen and stick a small tuft in the empty barrel. With a short puff of air, he shot it at Faris.

The large man's eyes widened. He took a step toward Trent, then put his hand to his throat. A soft rasp came from him. His face began to swell. I watched, too shocked to be afraid, as Faris dropped to his knees. The heavy man grasped at a shirt pocket. His fingers fumbled, and a syringe fell to the floor. Faris reached for it, collapsing, stretching for the syringe.

Trent rose. His face blank, he nudged the syringe out of Faris's grasp with a foot.

"What did you do to him?" I squeaked, watching as Trent put his pen back together. Faris was turning purple. A ragged gasp came from him, then nothing.

Trent slipped his pen in a pocket and stepped over Faris to reach the open door. "Sara Jane!" he called out. "Call the paramedics. Something's wrong with Mr. Faris."

"He's dying!" I squeaked. "That's what's wrong with him! You freaking killed him!"

The sound of worried chatter rose as everyone came out of his or her office. I recognized Jonathan's fast footsteps. He lurched to a stop in the threshold, grimacing at Faris's bulk on the floor, then frowning at Trent in disapproval.

Trent was crouched beside Faris, feeling for a pulse. He shrugged at Jonathan and injected the syringe's contents into Faris's thigh through his slacks. I could tell it was too late. Faris wasn't making noises anymore. Faris was dead. Trent knew it.

"The paramedics are coming," Sara Jane said from the hall, her footsteps coming closer. "Can I get—" She stopped behind Jonathan and put a hand to her mouth, staring down at Faris.

Trent stood, the syringe slipping from him to fall dramatically to the floor. "Oh, Sara Jane," he said softly as he drew her back into the hallway. "I'm so sorry. Don't look. It's too late. I think it was a bee sting. Faris is allergic to bees. I tried to give him his antitoxin, but it didn't act soon enough. He must have brought a bee in with him unaware. He slapped his leg just before he collapsed."

"But he . . ." she stammered, glancing back once as Trent moved her away.

Jonathan crouched to pluck a tuft of fuzz from Faris's right leg. The fluff went into a pocket. The tall man met my eyes, a wry, sarcastic look on his face.

"I'm so sorry," Trent said from the hall. "Jon?" he called, and Jonathan rose. "Please see that everyone leaves early. Clear the building."

"Yes sir."

"This is terrible, just awful," Trent said, seeming to really mean it. "Go on home, Sara Jane. Try not to think about it."

I heard her choke back a sob as her hesitant footsteps retreated.

It had only been moments since Faris had been standing. Shocked, I watched Trent step over Faris's arm. Cool as broccoli, he went to his desk and pushed the intercom. "Quen? I'm sorry to disturb you, but will you please come up to my front office? There is a paramedic team on their way into the grounds, and after that, probably someone from the I.S."

There was a slight hesitation, and Quen's voice crackled from the speaker. "Mr. Kalamack? Yes. I'll be right there."

I stared at Faris, swollen and prostrate on the floor. "You killed him," I accused. "God help me. You killed him. Right in your office. In front of everyone!"

"Jon," Trent said softly, rummaging in apparent unconcern in a drawer. "See that his family gets the upgraded benefits package. I want his youngest daughter to be able to go to the school of her choice. Keep it anonymous. Make it a scholarship."

"Yes, Sa'han." His voice was casual, as if dead bodies were an everyday occurrence.

"That's real generous of you, Trent," I chittered. "She'd rather have her father, though."

Trent looked at me. There was a bead of sweat at his hairline. "I want to meet with Faris's assistant before the day is out," he said lightly. "What was his name . . . Darby?"

"Darby Donnelley, Sa'han."

Trent nodded, rubbing his forehead as if bothered. When his hand dropped, the sweat was gone. "Yes. That's it. Donnelley. I don't want this to put me behind schedule."

"What do you want me to tell him?"

"The truth. Faris is allergic to bee stings. His entire staff knows it."

Jonathan nudged Faris with a toe and left. His steps were

loud now that there was no background noise. The floor had emptied shockingly fast. I wondered how often this happened.

"Like to reconsider my previous offer?" Trent said, addressing me. He had his untasted shot of whiskey in his fingers. I wasn't sure, but I thought they were trembling. He considered the drink for a moment, then tossed it back with a smooth motion. The glass was set gently down. "The island is out," he said. "Having you closer would be prudent. The way you infiltrated my compound was impressive. I think I could persuade Quen to take you on. He laughed himself breathless watching you duct-tape Mr. Percy in his trunk, then almost murdered you after I told him you had broken into my front office."

Shock blanked my mind. I couldn't say anything. Faris was *dead on the floor,* and Trent was asking me to work for him?

"But Faris was quite struck with your stirring," he continued. "Deciphering pre-Turn gene-splicing techniques can't be much harder than stirring a complex spell. If you don't want to explore your limits in the physical arena, you could go toward the mental. Such a mix of skills you have, Ms. Morgan. It makes you curiously valuable."

I sank back on my haunches, dumbfounded.

"You see, Ms. Morgan," he was saying. "I'm not a bad man. I offer all my employees a fair situation, a chance for advancement, the opportunity to reach their full potential."

"Opportunity? Chance for advancement?" I sputtered, not caring that he couldn't understand me. "Who do you think you are, Kalamack? God? You can go Turn yourself."

"I think I got the gist of that." He gave me a quick smile. "If nothing else, I've taught you to be honest." He shifted his chair closer to his desk. "I'm going to break you, Morgan, until you will do anything to get out of that cage. I do hope it takes a while. Jon took nearly fifteen years. Not as a rat, but a slave all the same. I imagine you will break a lot faster."

"Damn you, Trent," I said, seething.

"Don't be crass." Trent picked up his pen. "I'm sure your

moral fiber is as strong as if not stronger than Jon's. But he didn't have rats trying to rip him apart. I had the luxury of time with Jon. I went slowly, and I wasn't as good then." Trent's eyes went distant in thought. "Even so, he never knew I was breaking him. Most don't. He still doesn't. And if you suggested it, he would kill you."

Trent's distant gaze cleared. "I quite like having all the cards faceup on the table. It adds to the satisfaction, don't you think? Not having to be delicate about it. Both of us knowing what's going on. And if you don't survive, it's no great loss. I haven't invested that much in you. A wire cage? Food chips? Wood shavings?"

The feeling of being in a cage crashed over me. Trapped. "Let me out!" I shouted, pulling at the mesh of my cell. "Let me out, Trent!"

There was a knock on the doorframe and I spun. Jonathan entered, sidestepping Faris. "The medical team is parking their van. They can get rid of Faris. The I.S. wants a statement, nothing more." His eyes flicked disparagingly at me. "What's wrong with your witch?"

"Let me out, Trent," I chittered, growing frantic. "Let me out!" I ran to the bottom of my cage. Heart pounding, I ran back up to the second floor. I threw myself against the bars, trying to knock the cage over. I had to get out!

Trent smiled, his expression calm and collected. "Ms. Morgan just realized how persuasive I can be. Hit her cage."

Jonathan hesitated in confusion. "I thought you didn't want me to torment her."

"Actually, I said not to react in anger when you misjudge how a person will respond. I'm not acting out of anger. I'm teaching Ms. Morgan her new place in life. She's in a cage; I can do anything I want to her." His cold eyes were fixed to mine. "Hit—her—cage."

Jonathan grinned. Taking the folder he had in his hand, he swung it against the wire mesh. I cowered at the loud smack even though I knew it was coming. The cage shook, and I gripped the mesh floor with all four of my paws.

"Shut up, witch," Jonathan added, a pleased gloating in his eye. I slunk to hide in my hut. Trent had just given him permission to torment me all he wanted. If the rats didn't kill me, Jonathan would.

Twenty-one

"Come on, Morgan. Do something," Jonathan breathed. The stick poked me, almost shoving me over. I trembled as I tried not to react.

"I know you're mad," he said, shifting his crouch to jam the dowel into my flank.

The floor of my cage was littered with pencils—all chewed in half. Jonathan had been tormenting me on and off all morning. After several hours of hissing and lunging at him, I realized not only was my frenzy exhausting, but it also made the sadistic freak all the more enthusiastic. Ignoring him was nowhere near as satisfying as yanking pencils out of his grip and gnawing them in half, but I was hoping he would eventually tire and go away.

Trent had left for his lunch/nap about thirty minutes ago. The building was quiet, as everyone slacked off when Trent left the floor. Jonathan, though, showed no sign of leaving. He had been content to stay and harass me between forkfuls of pasta. Even moving to the center of my cage hadn't helped. He had simply gotten a longer stick. My hut was long gone.

"Damn witch. Do something." Jonathan shifted his stick to tap me on the head. It hit me once, twice, three times, right between my ears. My whiskers quivered. I could feel my pulse begin to pound and my head ache with the struggle to do nothing. On the fifth tap I broke, rearing back and snapping the stick in two with a frustrated bite.

"You're dead!" I squeaked, throwing myself at the wire mesh. "Hear me? When I get out of here, you're dead!"

He straightened, his fingers running through his hair. "I knew I could get you to move."

"Try that when I'm out of here," I whispered, quivering with rage.

The sound of high heels in the hallway grew loud, and I crouched in relief. I recognized the cadence. Apparently so did Jonathan, as he straightened and took a step back. Sara Jane strode into the office without her usual knock. "Oh!" she exclaimed softly, her hand going to the collar of the new business suit she had bought yesterday. Trent paid his employees in advance. "Jon. I'm sorry. I didn't think anyone would still be here." There was an awkward silence. "I was going to give Angel the leftovers from my lunch before I ran my errands."

Jonathan looked down his nose at her. "I'll do it for you."

Oh please, no, I thought. He'd probably dip them in ink first, if he did at all. The leftovers from Sara Jane's lunches were the only thing I'd eat, and I was half starved.

"Thank you, but no," she said, and I sank to a relieved crouch. "I'll lock up Mr. Kalamack's office if you want to go."

Yes, leave, I thought, my pulse racing. *Go so I can try to tell Sara Jane I'm a person.* I'd been trying all day, but the one time I attempted it when Trent had been watching, Jonathan "accidentally" knocked my cage so hard it fell over.

"I'm waiting for Mr. Kalamack," Jonathan said. "Are you sure you don't want me to give them to her?" A smug look crossed his usually stoic face as he moved behind Trent's desk and pretended to tidy it. My hope that he would leave vanished. He knew better.

Sara Jane crouched to bring her eyes level with mine. I thought they were blue, but I couldn't be sure. "No. It won't take long. Is Mr. Kalamack working through lunch?" she asked.

"No. He just asked me to wait."

I crept forward at the smell of carrots. "Here, Angel," the small woman said, her high voice soothing as she opened a fold of napkin. "It's just carrots today. They were out of celery."

I glanced at Jonathan suspiciously. He was checking the sharpness of the pencils in Trent's pencil cup, so I cautiously reached for the carrot. There was a sharp bang, and I jumped.

A smirk quirked the corners of Jonathan's thin lips. He had dropped a file on the desk. Sara Jane's look was wrathful enough to curdle milk. "Just stop it," she said indignantly. "You've been pestering her all day." Lips pursed, she pushed the carrots through the mesh. "Here you go, sweetie," she soothed. "Take your carrots. Don't you like your pellets?" She dropped the carrots and left her fingers poking through the mesh.

I sniffed them, allowing her cracked and work-worn nails to brush the top of my head. I trusted Sara Jane, and my trust didn't come easily. I think it was because we were both trapped, and we both realized it. That she knew about Trent's biodrug dealings seemed unlikely, but she was too smart to not be worried about how her predecessor died. Trent was going to use her as he had Yolin Bates, leaving her dead in an alley somewhere.

My chest tightened as if I was going to cry. A faint scent of redwood came from her, almost overwhelmed by her perfume. Miserable, I pulled the carrots farther in and downed them as fast as I could. They smelled sharply of vinegar, and I wondered at Sara Jane's choice of salad dressing. She had only given me three. I could've eaten twice that.

"I thought you farmers hated chicken killers," Jonathan said, pretending indifference as he watched me for any un-minklike behavior.

Sara Jane's cheeks colored, and she rose quickly from her crouch. Before she could say anything, she reached out an unsteady hand and braced herself against my cage. "Oooh," she said, her eyes going distant. "I got up too fast."

"Are you all right?" he asked, his flat tone sounding as if he didn't care.

She put a hand to her eyes. "Yes. Yes, I'm fine."

I paused my chewing, hearing soft pacing in the hall, and Trent walked in. He had taken his coat off, and it was only his clothes that made him look like a Fortune-twenty executive rather than a head lifeguard. "Sara Jane, aren't you on lunch?" he asked amiably.

"Just leaving now, Mr. Kalamack," she said. She glanced worriedly between Jonathan and me before she left. Her heels thumped dimly in the hallway and vanished. I felt a wash of relief. If Trent was here, Jonathan would probably leave me alone and I could eat.

The haughty man folded himself carefully into one of the chairs opposite Trent's desk. "How long?" he said, putting an ankle on his knee and glancing at me.

"Depends." Trent fed his fish something from a freezer-dried pouch. The Yellow Tang bumped against the surface, making soft sounds.

"It must be strong," Jonathan said. "I didn't think it would affect her at all."

I paused in my chewing. *Her? Sara Jane?*

"I thought it might," Trent said. "She'll be fine." He turned, his face creased in thought. "In the future, I may have to be more direct in my dealings with her. All the information she brought up concerning the sugar beet industry was slanted toward a bad business venture."

Jonathan cleared his throat, making it sound patronizing. Trent closed the pouch and tucked it away in the cabinet under the tank. He went to stand behind his desk, his fair head bowed as he arranged his papers.

"Why not a spell, Sa'han?" Jonathan unfolded his long legs and stood, tugging out the creases in his dress pants. "I would imagine it would be more certain."

"It's against the rules to spell animals in competition." He scribbled a note in his planner.

A dry smile crossed Jonathan's face. "But drugs are all right? That makes perverted sense."

My chewing slowed. They were talking about me. The bitter taste of vinegar was stronger on this last carrot. And my tongue was tingling. Dropping the carrot, I touched my gums. They were numb. *Damn. It was Friday.*

"You bastard!" I shouted, throwing the carrot at Trent, only to have it bounce back against the mesh. "You drugged me. You drugged Sara Jane to get me!" Furious, I flung myself at the door, wedging my arm out, trying to reach the latch. Nausea and dizziness rose.

The two men came close, peering down at me, Trent's expression of domination sending a chill through me. Terrified, I raced up the ramp to the second level, then downstairs. The light hurt my eyes. My mouth was numb. I staggered, losing my balance. *He'd drugged me!*

A realization clawed through my panic. The door was going to open. This might be my only chance. I froze in the center of my cage, panting. Slowly, I tipped over. *Please,* I thought desperately. *Please open the door before I really do pass out.* My lungs heaved and my heart raced. Whether it was from my efforts or the drugs, I couldn't tell.

The two men were silent. Jonathan poked me with a pencil. I allowed my leg to quiver as if I was unable to move it. "I think she's down," he said. Excitement tinged his voice.

"Give it some time." The light hit my eyes as Trent moved away, and I slit them.

Jonathan, though, was blessedly impatient. "I'll get the carrying case."

The cage trembled as he unlatched the door. My pulse raced as Jonathan's long fingers closed about my body. I wiggled to life, my teeth bearing down on his finger.

"You little canicula!" Jonathan swore, yanking his hand out and pulling me with him. I loosened my hold, hitting the floor with a bone-shaking thump. Nothing hurt. Everything was numb. I leapt for the door, sprawling as my legs wouldn't work.

"Jon!" Trent exclaimed. "Get the door!"

The floor trembled, quickly followed by the slamming of the door. I hesitated, unable to think. I had to run. Where the hell was the door?

The shadow of Jonathan came close. I bared my teeth, and he hesitated, cowed by my tiny incisors. The sharp stink of fear was on him. He was afraid, the bully. Darting forward, he grasped the scruff of my neck. I twisted, sinking my teeth in the fatty part of his thumb.

He grunted in pain and let go. I hit the floor. "Damn witch!" he shouted. I staggered, unable to run. Jonathan's blood was thick on my tongue, tasting of cinnamon and wine.

"Touch me again," I panted, "and I'll take off your entire thumb."

Jonathan drew back, afraid. It was Trent who scooped me up. Deep under the drug, I could do nothing. His fingers were blessedly cold as he cradled me in his hands. He set me gently into the carrier and latched the door. It clicked shut, shaking the entire cage.

My mouth was fuzzy and my stomach was twisting. The carrier was lifted, swinging in a smooth arc until it landed on the desk. "We have a few minutes until we have to leave. Let's see if Sara Jane has any antibiotic cream in her desk for those bites of yours."

Trent's mellow voice grew as fuzzy as my thoughts. The darkness became overwhelming, and I lost my grip on consciousness, cursing myself for my stupidity.

Twenty-two

Someone was talking. I understood that. Actually, there were two voices, and now that I was regaining the ability to think, I realized they'd been alternating with each other for some time. One was Trent, and his wonderfully liquid voice lured me back to consciousness. Beyond him was the high-pitched squeaking of rats.

"Aw, hell," I whispered, having it come out as a thin moan of a squeak. My eyes were open, and I forced them closed. They felt as dry as sandpaper. A few more painful blinks and the tears started to flow again. Slowly the gray wall of my carrier swam into focus.

"Mr. Kalamack!" called a welcoming voice, and the world spun as the carrier turned. "The upstairs told me you were here. I'm so pleased." The voice got closer. "And with an entry! Wait and see, wait and see," the man nearly gushed as he pumped Trent's offered hand up and down. "Having an entry makes the games vastly more entertaining."

"Good evening, Jim," Trent said warmly. "Sorry for just dropping in on you."

The mellow cadence of Trent's voice was a balm, soothing my headache away. I both loved and hated it. How could something so beautiful belong to someone so foul?

"You're always welcome here, Mr. Kalamack." The man smelled like wood chips, and I scrunched back, bracing myself in the corner. "Have you checked in, then? Do you have your placing for the first round?"

"There will be more than one fight?" Jonathan interrupted.

"Indeed sir," Jim said brightly as he gently turned the grate of the carrier to face him. "You play your rat until it's dead or you pull it. Oh!" he said as he saw me. "A mink. How very—continental of you. This will change your odds, but no worry. We've fought badgers and snakes before. We thrive on individuality, and everyone loves it when an entrant is eaten."

My pulse quickened. I had to get out of there.

"Are you sure your animal will fight?" Jim asked. "The rats here have been bred for aggression, though we have a street rat making a surprising showing the last three months."

"I had to sedate her to get her in the carrier," Trent said, his voice tight.

"Oooh, a feisty one. Here," Jim offered solicitously as he snagged a notebook from a passing official. "Let me change your first round to one of the later matches so she has a chance to fully shake her sedation. No one wants those slots anyway. There's not much time for your animal to recover before the next bout."

I inched to the front of the carrier in helplessness. Jim was a nice-looking man with round cheeks and an ample belly. It would only take a small charm to make him into the mall Santa Claus. What was he doing in Cincinnati's underground?

The jovial man's gaze went over Trent's unseen shoulder and he gave someone a merry wave. "Please keep your animal with you at all times," he said, his eyes on the new arrival. "You have five minutes to place your entrant in the pit after you're called or you forfeit."

Pit, I thought. *Swell.*

"All I need to know now," Jim said, "is what you call your animal."

"Angel." Trent said it with a mocking sincerity, but Jim wrote it down without a moment of hesitation.

"Angel," he repeated. "Owned and trained by Trent Kalamack."

"You don't own me!" I squeaked, and Jonathan thunked my carrier.

"Back upstairs, Jon," Trent said as Jim shook his hand and left. "The noise of these rats is going right through my head."

I dropped to all fours to steady myself as the carrier swung. "I'm not going to fight, Trent," I squeaked loudly. "You can just forget it."

"Oh, do be still, Ms. Morgan," Trent said softly as we rose. "It's not as if you haven't been trained for this. Every runner knows how to kill. Working for me, working for them . . . There's no difference. It's only a rat."

"I've never killed anyone in my life!" I shouted, rattling the gate. "And I'm not going to start for you." But I didn't think I had a choice. I couldn't reason with a rat, tell it there'd been a big mistake and why couldn't we all just get along?

The noise of the rats dulled under loud conversations as we found the top of the stairs. Trent paused, taking it in. "Look there," he murmured. "There's Randolph."

"Randolph Mirick? Jonathan said. "Haven't you been trying to arrange a meeting with him about increasing your water rights?"

"Yes." Trent almost seemed to breathe the word. "For the last seven weeks. He's apparently a very busy man. And look there. That woman holding that vile little dog? She's the CEO of the glass factory we're contracted with. I'd very much like to speak with her about the possibility of getting a volume discount. I had no idea this would be an opportunity to network."

We drifted into motion, moving through the crowd. Trent kept his conversation light and friendly, showing me off as if

I was a prize mule. I huddled in the back of my cage and tried to ignore the sounds the women made at me. My mouth felt like the inside of a hair dryer, and I could smell old blood and urine. And rats.

I could hear them, too, squeaking in voices higher than most people's hearing. The battles were beginning already, though anyone on two legs couldn't know it. Bars and plastic might separate the participants, but threats of violence were already being promised.

Trent found a seat next to the freaking mayor of the city, and after tucking me between his feet, he talked to the woman in a sideways fashion about the overall benefits of rezoning his property as industry rather than commercial, seeing as a good portion of his land was used for industrial gain in some way or other. She wasn't listening until Trent commented he might have to move his more sensitive industries to more friendly pastures.

It was a nightmarish hour. The ultrasonic squeaks and shrieks cut through the lower sounds, going unheard by the crowd. Jonathan kept up a colorful commentary for my benefit, embellishing the monstrosities taking place in the pit. None of the rounds took long—ten minutes at best. The sudden hush followed by the watchers' wild explosions was barbaric. Soon I could smell the blood Jonathan seemed to enjoy expounding upon, and I was jumping at every shift of Trent's feet.

The audience politely applauded the official results of the latest bout. It was an obvious win. Thanks to Jonathan, I knew the victorious rat had ripped open the belly of its opponent before the loser had given up and died, its teeth still clamped upon the winning rat's foot.

"Angel!" Jim called, his voice deeper, carrying more showmanship over the loudspeaker. "Owned and trained by Kalamack."

My legs trembled at the rush of adrenaline. *I can best a rat,* I thought as the crowd cheered my adversary, the Bloody Baron, to the floor. I would not be killed by a rat.

My gut tightened as Trent slipped onto the empty bench beside the pit. The smell was a hundred times worse here. I knew even Trent could smell it as his smooth face wrinkled in distaste. Jonathan shifted eagerly from foot to foot behind him. For a prim and proper snob who pressed his collars and starched his socks, the man had a taste for blood sports. The squeaks of the rats were almost nonexistent now that half were dead and half were licking their wounds.

There was a moment or two of pleasantries between the owners, followed by a dramatic buildup of excitement orchestrated by Jim. I wasn't listening to his ringmaster patter, more concerned with my first view of the pit.

The circle was about the size of a kiddie wading pool with three-foot walls. The floor was sawdust. Dark splotches decorated it, the scatter pattern telling me it was probably blood. The scent of urine and fear rose so strong, I was surprised I couldn't see it as a haze in the air. Someone's warped humor had put animal toys in the arena.

"Gentlemen?" Jim said dramatically, yanking my attention back. "Place your entrants."

Trent pulled the grate close to his face. "I've changed my mind, Morgan," he murmured. "I don't want you as a runner. You're more valuable to me killing rats than you could ever be killing my competition. The contacts I can make here are astounding."

"Go Turn yourself," I snarled.

At my harsh squeak, he unlatched the grate and dumped me out.

I hit the sawdust softly. A quick shadow of movement at the far side of the pit heralded the arrival of the Bloody Baron. The crowd oohed over me, and I made a liquid hop to hide behind a ball. I was a hindsight more attractive than a rat.

Face down in it, the arena was awful: blood, urine, death. All I wanted was out. My eyes fell upon Trent, and he smiled knowingly. He thought he could break me; I hated him.

The audience cheered, and I turned to see old Bloody

himself galloping toward me. He wasn't as long as I was, but was stockier. I guessed we weighed about the same. Squeaks came from him nonstop as he ran. I froze, not knowing what to do. At the last moment I jumped out of the way, kicking him as he went by. It was an attack I had used as a runner hundreds of times. It was instinctive, though as a mink it lacked effectiveness and grace. I finished the spin kick in a crouch, watching the rat skid to a halt.

Baron hesitated, nuzzling his side where I struck him. He had gone silent.

Again he rushed me, the crowd urging him on. This time I aimed with more precision, scoring on his long face as I jumped aside. I landed in a crouch, my forepaws automatically moving into a block as if I was fighting a person. The rat slid to a faster halt, squeaking and weaving his head as if trying to focus. A rat's eyesight must be minimal. I could use that.

Chittering like a mad thing, Baron rushed me a third time. I tensed, planning to jump straight up, land on his back, and choke him into unconsciousness. I was nauseous and sick at heart. I wouldn't kill for Trent. Not even a rat. If I sacrificed one principle, one ethic, he would have me body and soul. If I gave in on rats, tomorrow it would be people.

The noise of the crowd swelled as Baron ran. I jumped. "Crap!" I squeaked as he slid to a stop under me, twisting onto his back. I was going to fall right on top of him!

I hit with a soft thunk, squealing as his teeth latched onto my nose. Panicking, I tried to pull away. But he held on, exerting just enough pressure that I couldn't break free. Twisting off him, I pawed at his grip, pummeling his belly with my feet. Squeaking in time with my strikes, he took the abuse, slowly loosening his hold. He finally let go enough that I could wiggle away.

I backed up, rubbing my nose and wondering why he hadn't taken it clean off.

Baron flipped to his feet. He touched his side where I had first stuck him, then his face, and then his middle where my feet had hit him, cataloging the list of hurts I'd given him. His paw reached up to rub his nose, and with a start I realized he was mimicking me. Baron was a person!

"Holy crap!" I squeaked, and Baron bobbed his head once. My breath came fast and my gaze darted to the surrounding walls and the people pressed against them. Together we might get out where alone we couldn't. Baron made soft noises at me, and the crowd went quiet.

There was no way I was going to lose this chance. He twitched his whiskers and I lunged. We rolled about the floor in a harmless tussle. All I had to do was figure out how to get out of there and communicate it to Baron without Trent realizing it.

We knocked into an exercise wheel and broke apart. I found my feet and turned, looking for him. Nothing. "Baron!" I shouted. But he was gone! I spun, wondering if a descending hand had plucked him out. A rhythmic scratching came from a nearby tower of blocks. I fought the urge to turn. Relief flooded me. He was still here. And now I had an idea.

The only time the hands came down was when the game was over. One of us was going to have to pretend to die.

"Hey!" I shouted as Baron crashed down on me. Sharp teeth latched onto my ear, tearing it. Blood coursed into my eyes, half blinding me. Furious, I flung him over my shoulder. "What the hell is wrong with you?" I cried as he tumbled to a halt. The crowd cheered wildly, clearly dismissing our previous unrodentlike behavior.

Baron started in with a long series of squeaks, no doubt trying to explain his thinking. I lunged, latching on to his windpipe and shutting him up. His hind feet pummeled me as I cut off his air supply. Twisting, he reached my nose, gouging it with his nails. I eased my grip under the needles of his claws, allowing air to him.

He went limp in understanding. "You're not supposed to be dead yet," I said, my squeaks mangled from his fur in my mouth. I clamped down until he squealed and began to inefficiently struggle. The crowd surged into noise, presumably thinking Angel was going to score her first win. I glanced at Trent. My heart gave a thump at his suspicious look. This wasn't going to work. Baron might escape, but not me. I was going to have to die, not Baron.

"Fight me," I squeaked, knowing he wouldn't understand. I loosened my hold until my jaws were slipping. Not understanding, Baron went limp. I jabbed a hind foot into his crotch.

He yelped in pain, yanking from my loose grip. I rolled away. "Fight me. Kill me," I chittered. Baron's head wove as he tried to focus. I gave my head a toss toward the crowd. He blinked, seeming to get it, and attacked. His jaws clamped about my windpipe, cutting off my air. I flailed about, sending us crashing into the walls. I heard the shouts of the people over the sound of the blood pulsing in my head.

His grip was tight, too tight to breathe. *Any time now,* I thought desperately. *You can let me breathe any time.* I sent us thumping into a ball, and still he wouldn't let up. Fear stirred. He was a person, wasn't he? I hadn't just let a rat get a death grip on me, had I?

I started to struggle in earnest. His grip tightened. My head felt as if it was going to explode. My blood pounded. I twisted and squirmed, clawing at an eye until the tears ran, but still he wouldn't let up. Flipping wildly, I sent us crashing into the walls. I found his neck and clamped down. Immediately he loosened his grip. I took a grateful gulp of air.

Furious, I bit hard, tasting his blood on my teeth. He bit me back, and I squeaked in pain. I eased my grip. He did the same. The noise of the crowd pressed down, almost as strong as the heat from the lights. We lay on the floor in the sawdust, struggling to slow our breathing so as to look as though we were suffocating each other. I finally understood. His owner knew he was a person as well. We both had to die.

The crowd was shouting, wanting to know who won or if we were both dead. I looked through cracked eyelids to find Trent. He didn't look happy, and I knew our ruse was halfway to being successful. Baron lay very still. A tiny squeak slipped from him, and I carefully answered. A pulse of excitement raced through me and was gone.

"Ladies! Gentlemen!" Jim's professional voice layered over the noise. "It seems we have a draw. Will the owners please retrieve their animals?" The crowd hushed. "We will have a short break to determine if either contestant is alive."

My heart raced as the shadows of hands came closer. Baron made three short squeaks and exploded into motion. I belatedly followed, grasping the first hand I found.

"Look out!" someone shouted. I was flung into the air as a hand jerked away. I arched through the air, tail whipping in frantic circles. I glimpsed a surprised face and landed on a man's chest. He screamed like a girl and brushed me off. I hit the floor hard, stunned. I took three quick breaths, then lurched under his chair.

The noise was astounding. One would think a lion was loose, not two rodents. People scattered. The rush of feet past the chair was unreal. Someone smelling of wood chips reached down. I bared my teeth and he drew back.

"I've got the mink," an official shouted over the noise. "Get me a net." He glanced away, and I ran. Pulse so fast it was almost a hum, I dodged feet and chairs, nearly slamming head first into the far wall. The blood from my ear was dripping into my eye, blurring my vision. How was I going to get out of there?

"Everyone remain calm!" came Jim's voice over the loudspeaker. "Please return to the lobby for refreshments while a search is made. We ask that you keep the outer doors closed until we have regained the contestants." There was a pause. "And somebody get that dog out of here," he finished loudly.

Doors? I thought as I peered into the madhouse. I didn't need a door. I needed Jenks.

"Rachel!" came a call from above me. I squeaked as Jenks landed on my shoulders with a light thump. "You look like crap," he shouted into my torn ear. "I thought that rat nacked you. When you jumped up and grabbed Jonathan's hand, I nearly pissed my pants!"

"Where's the door?" I tried to ask. How he found me would have to wait.

"Don't have a hissy," he said defensively. "I left like you said. I just came back. When Trent left with that cat box, I knew you were in it. I hitched a ride under the bumper. Betcha didn't know that's how pixies get around the city, did you? You'd better get your furry ass moving before someone sees you."

"Where!" I squeaked. "Where do I go!"

"There's a back way out. I did a survey during the first fight. Man, those rats are vicious. Did you see that one bite the other's foot right off? If you follow this wall for about twenty feet, then down three stairs, you'll come to a hallway."

I started moving. Jenks gripped my fur tighter.

"Ugh. Your ear is a mess," he said as I flowed down the three stairs. "Okay. Go down the hallway to the right. There's an opening—No! Don't take it," he shouted as I did just that. "It's the kitchen."

I turned, freezing at the sound of feet on the stairs. My pulse raced. I wouldn't be caught. I wouldn't.

"The sink," Jenks whispered. "The cupboard door isn't closed. Hurry!"

Spotting it, I scurried across the tile floor, my claws scraping softly. I wedged myself inside. Jenks flitted to peek around the door. Backing away to hide behind a bucket, I listened.

"They aren't in the kitchen," a voice shouted, sounding muffled. I felt a knot of worry loosen. He had said "they." Baron was still free.

Jenks turned, his wings an unseen blur as he stood in the cupboard. "Damn, it's good to see you. Ivy's done nothing but stare at a map of Trent's compound she dug up," he whispered. "All night muttering and scribbling on paper. Every sheet ends up crumpled in the corner. My kids are having a blast playing hide-and-seek in the pile she's made.

I don't think she knows I'm gone. She just sits at that map of hers, drinking orange juice."

I smelled dirt. As Jenks babbled like a Brimstone addict needing his fix, I explored the smelly cupboard to find that the pipe from the sink went under the house through a wood floor. The crack between the iron and the floor was just wide enough for my shoulder. I started chewing.

"I said, get that dog out of here," a muffled voice shouted. "No. Wait. You have a lead for him? He can find them."

Jenks came close. "Hey, the floor. That's a good idea! Let me help." Jenks alighted next to me, getting in my way.

"Get Baron," I tried to squeak.

"I can so help." Jenks pried a toothpick-sized stick of wood from around the hole.

"The rat," I chittered. "He can't see." Frustrated, I knocked over a canister of sink cleaner. The powder spilled out, and the smell of pine became overwhelming. Snatching Jenks's toothpick, I wrote out, "Get rat."

Jenks took to the air, a hand over his nose. "Why?"

"Man," I scrawled. "Can't see."

Jenks grinned. "You found a friend! Wait till I tell Ivy."

I bared my teeth, pointing at the door with my stick. Still he hesitated. "You'll stay here? Keep making that hole bigger?"

Frustrated, I threw the stick at him. Jenks hovered backward. "All right, all right! Don't lose your panties. No, wait. You don't have any, do you?"

His laughter chimed out, sounding like freedom itself, as he slipped past the crack in door. I went back to chewing the floor. It tasted awful, a putrid mix of soap, grease, and mold. I just knew I was going to get sick. Tension strung through me. The sudden thumps and crashes from up front jerked me. I was waiting for the triumphant cry of capture. Fortunately it seemed the dog didn't know what was expected of it. It wanted to play, and tempers were getting short.

My jaws ached, and I stifled a cry of frustration. Soap had gotten into the cut on my ear, and it was a flaming misery. I tried to stick my head through the hole and into the crawl space. If my head could make it, my body probably could, too. But it wasn't big enough yet.

"Look!" someone shouted. "He's working now. He's got their scent."

Frantic, I yanked my head out of the hole. My ear scraped and started bleeding again. There was a sudden scratching in the hallway, and I redoubled my efforts. Jenks's voice came faintly over the sounds of my gnawing. "It's the kitchen. Rachel is under the sink. No. The next cupboard. Hurry! I think they saw you."

There was a sudden rush of light and air, and I sat up, spitting pulpy wood from me.

"Hi! We're back! I found your rat, Rache."

Baron glanced at me. His eyes were bright. Immediately he bounded over. His head dipped into the hold and he started gnawing. There wasn't enough room for his wider shoulders. I continued to widen the hole at the top. The yapping of the dog came from the hall. We froze for a heartbeat, then chewed. My stomach clenched.

"Is it big enough?" Jenks shouted. "Go! Hurry!"

Pushing my head into the hole next to Baron's, I gnawed furiously. There was a scratching at the cupboard door. Shafts of light flickered as the door bumped against the frame. "Here!" a loud voice shouted. "He's got one in here."

Hope dying, I pulled my head up. My jaws ached. The pine soap had matted my fur and was burning my eyes. I turned to face the scrabbling of paws. I didn't think the opening was big enough yet. A sharp squeak drew my attention. Baron was crouched beside it, pointing down.

"It's not big enough for you," I said.

Baron lunged at me, yanking me to the hole and stuffing me down. The sound of the dog grew suddenly louder, and I dropped into space.

Arm and legs outstretched, I tried to snag the pipe. A front paw reached a welded seam. I jerked to a stop. Above me the dog barked wildly. There was a scrabble of claws on the wood floor, then a yelp. I started losing my hold. I dropped to the dry earth. I lay there, listening for Baron's death scream.

I should have stayed, I thought desperately. *I never should have let him shove me down that hole.* I knew it hadn't been big enough for him.

There was a quick scratching and a thump in the dirt beside me.

"You made it!" I squeaked, seeing Baron sprawled in the dirt.

Jenks flitted down, glowing in the dim light. There was a dog whisker in his hand. "You should have seen him, Rache," he said excitedly. "He bit that dog right on the nose. He-yah! Pow! Slam-bam, thank you, ma'am!"

The pixy continued his circles around us, too hyper to sit still. Baron, however, seemed to have the shakes. Curled into a huddled ball of fur, he looked like he was going to be sick. I crept forward, wanting to say thanks. I touched him on his shoulder, and he jumped, staring at me with wide black eyes.

"Get that dog out of here!" came an angry voice through the floor, and we looked up at the faint spot of light. The yapping grew faint, and my pulse eased. "Yup," Jim said. "Those are fresh chewings. One got out this way."

"How do we get down there?" It was Trent, and I cowered, pressing myself into the dirt.

"There's a trapdoor in the hallway, but the crawl space is open to the street through any of the vents." Their voices grew distant as they moved away. "I'm sorry, Mr. Kalamack," Jim was saying. "We've never had an escapee before. I'll get someone to go down there right away."

"No. She's gone." His voice held a controlled, soft frustration, and I felt a stir of victory. Jonathan wasn't going to have a very pleasant drive back. I straightened from my crouch and heaved a sigh. My ear and eyes were burning. I wanted to go home.

Baron squeaked for my attention, pointing to the ground. I looked to find he had written in careful letters, "Thanks."

I couldn't help my smile. Crouched beside him, I wrote, "You're welcome." My letters looked sloppy next to his.

"You two are *so sweet,*" Jenks mocked. "Can we get out of here now?"

Baron leapt to the screen across the vent, latching on with all four feet. Choosing carefully, he began to pull at the seams with his teeth.

Twenty-three

My spoon scraped the bottom of the cottage cheese container. Hunching over it, I pushed what remained into a pile. My knee was cold, and I tugged my midnight-blue, terry-cloth robe back over it. I was stuffing my face while Baron changed back into a person and showered in the second bathroom Ivy and I had independently determined was mine. I could hardly wait to see what he really looked like. Ivy and I agreed that if he had survived the rat fights for who knew how long, he had to be a hunk. God knew he was brave, chivalrous, and not fazed by vampires—the last one being the most intriguing, seeing as Jenks had said he was human.

Jenks had called Ivy collect from the first phone we found. The sound of her motorcycle—just out of the shop from her having slid it under a truck last week—had been like a choir singing. I almost cried at her concern when she swung from the seat wearing head-to-toe biker leather. Someone cared if I lived or died. It didn't matter if it was a vampire whose motives I still didn't understand.

Neither Baron or I would get into the box she had brought, and after a five-minute discussion consisting of her protests and our squeaks, she finally threw the box into the back of the alley with a grunt of frustration and let us ride up front. She hadn't been in the best of moods when she tooled on out of the alley, a mink and a rat standing on her gas tank with our forepaws on the tiny dash. By the time we cleared the worst of Friday rush-hour traffic and were able to pick up speed, I knew why dogs hung their heads out the window.

Riding a bike was always a thrill, but as a rodent, it was a scent-ual rush. Eyes squinting and my whiskers bent back by the wind, I rode home in style. I didn't care that Ivy was getting odd looks and people kept blowing their horns at us. I was sure I was going to have a brain orgasm from the overload of input. I almost regretted it when Ivy had turned onto our street.

Now, with a finger, I pushed the last bit of cheese onto the spoon, ignoring Jenks's pig noises from the ladle hanging over the center island. I hadn't stopped eating since losing my fur, but as I'd had only carrots for the last three and a half days, I was entitled to a little binge.

Setting the empty container aside on the dirty plate before me, I wondered if it hurt more or less to transform if you were a human. From the muffled, masculine groan of pain that had emanated from the bathroom before the shower started, I'd say it hurt just about the same.

Though I had scrubbed myself twice, I thought I still smelled mink under my perfume. My torn ear throbbed, my neck had red-rimmed punctures where Baron had bitten me, and my left leg was bruised from falling into the exercise wheel. But it was good to be a person again. I glanced at Ivy doing the dishes, wondering if I should have taped up my ear.

I still hadn't brought Ivy and Jenks entirely up to speed on my last few days, telling them only about my captivity, not what I had learned during it. Ivy had said nothing, but I knew she was dying to tell me I had been an idiot for not having a backup plan for escape.

She reached for the tap, turning it off after she rinsed the last glass. Setting it to drain, she turned and dried her hands on the dish towel. Seeing a tall, thin, leather-clad vamp doing dishes was almost worth the price of admission to my crazy life. "Okay, let me get this straight," she said as she leaned against the counter. "Trent caught you red-handed, and instead of turning you in, he put you in the city's rat fights to try and break you so you'd agree to work for him?"

"Yup." I stretched to reach the bag of frosted cookies next to Ivy's computer.

"Figures." She pushed herself into motion to get my empty plate. Washing it, she set it next to the glasses to drip. Apart from my dishes, there had been no plates, silverware, or bowls. Just twenty or so glasses, all with a drop of orange juice in the bottom.

"Next time you go up against someone like Trent, can we at least have a plan for when you get caught?" she asked, her back to me and her shoulders tense.

Annoyance pulled my head up from my bag of cookies. I took a breath to tell her she could take her plans and use them for toilet paper, then hesitated. Her shoulders were as tight as her stance was rigid. I remembered how worried Jenks said she was, and what she had said about how me flying off the handle jerked her instincts into play. Slowly my breath slipped out. "Sure," I said hesitantly. "We can have a fail-safe plan for when I screw up, as long as we have one for you, too."

Jenks snickered and Ivy flicked a glance at him. "We don't need one for me," she said.

"Write it out and post it by the phone," I said casually. "I'll do the same." I was halfway kidding, but I wondered if in all her anal-retentive glory she just might do it.

Saying nothing, Ivy, not content to let the glasses and plates drain by themselves, began to dry them. I crunched my gingersnaps, watching her shoulders ease and her motions lose their hair-trigger quickness. "You were right," I said, thinking I owed her at least that much. "I've never had anyone I could count on before. . . ." I hesitated. "I'm not used to it."

Ivy turned, surprising me with the relief in her stance. "Hey, don't sweat it."

"Oh, save me," Jenks said from the utensils rack. "I think I'm going to puke."

Ivy snapped her towel at him, her lips quirked in a wry smile I watched her closely as she went back to drying. Keeping calm and compromising made all the difference. Now that I thought about it, compromising had been how we got through our year working together. It was harder, though, to keep my cool when I was surrounded by all her stuff and none of mine. I had felt vulnerable and on edge.

"You should have seen her, Rachel," Jenks said in a loud, conspiratorial whisper. "Sitting day and night at her maps to find a way to get you free from Trent. I told her all we had to do was keep watch and help if we could."

"Shut up, Jenks." Ivy's voice was suddenly thick with warning. I shoved the last cookie in my mouth and rose to throw the bag away.

"She had this grandiose plan," Jenks said. "She swept it up from the floor when you were showering. She was going to call in all her favors. She even talked to her mother."

"I'm going to get a cat," Ivy said tightly. "A big, black cat."

I pulled the bag of bread from the counter and dug the honey out from the back of the pantry, where I had hidden it from Jenks. Taking it all to the table, I sat and arranged everything.

"Good thing you escaped when you did," Jenks said, swinging the ladle to send gleams of light about the kitchen. "Ivy was about to throw what little she has left after you—again."

"I will call my cat Pixy Dust," Ivy said. "I will keep it in the garden and not feed it."

My gaze shifted from Jenks's suddenly closed mouth to Ivy. We had just had a warm and fuzzy discussion without getting bit, vampy, or scared. Why did Jenks have to ruin it? "Jenks," I said with a sigh. "Don't you have something to do?"

"No." He dropped down, extending a hand into the stream of honey I was drizzling on a piece of bread. He sank an inch from the weight, then rose. "So, you gonna keep him?"

I looked blankly at Jenks, and he laughed.

"Your new bo-o-o-oyfriend," he drawled.

My lips pursed at the amusement in Ivy's eyes. "He's not my boyfriend."

Jenks hovered over the open jar of honey, pulling glistening strands up and into his mouth. "I saw you with him on that bike," he said. "Um, this is good." He took another handful, his wings starting to hum audibly. "Your tails were touching," he mocked.

Annoyed, I flicked my hand at him. He darted out of reach, then back. "You should have seen them, Ivy. Rolling around on the floor, biting each other." He laughed, and it turned into a high-pitched giggle. I slowly tilted my head as he listed to the left. "It was love at first bite."

Ivy turned. "He bit you on the neck?" she said, deadpan serious but for her eyes. "Oh, then it's got to be love. She won't let *me* bite her neck."

What was this? Pick on Rachel night? Not entirely comfortable, I pulled another piece of bread out to finish my sandwich and waved Jenks off the honey. He bobbed and weaved erratically, struggling to maintain an even flight as the sugar rush made him drunk.

"Hey, Ivy," Jenks said as he drifted sideways and licked his fingers. "You know what they say about the size of a rat's tail, don't you? Da longer da tail, da longer his—"

"Shut up!" I cried. The shower went off, and my breath caught. A surge of anticipation brought me up straight in my chair. I flicked a glance at Jenks, giggling-drunk on the honey. "Jenks," I said, not wanting to subject Baron to an intoxicated pixy. "Leave."

"Nuh-uh," he said, scooping up a handful. Peeved, I recapped the jar. Jenks made a small noise of distress, and I waved him up into the hanging utensils. With any luck, he would stay there until he threw off his drunk. That would be about four minutes, tops.

Ivy walked out, muttering about glasses in the living room. The collar of my robe was damp from my hair, and I tugged at it. I wiped the honey from my fingers, fidgeting in what felt like blind date jitters. This was stupid. I'd already met him. We had even had a rodent's version of a first date: a resounding stint at the gym, a brisk run from people and dogs, even a bike ride through the park. But what do you say to a guy you don't know who saved your life?

I heard the bathroom door creak open. Ivy jerked to a stop in the hall, her face blank as she stood with two mugs dangling from her fingers. I pulled my robe over my shins, wondering if I should stand up. Baron's voice eased past her and into the kitchen. "You're Ivy, right?"

"Um . . ." Ivy hesitated. "You're—uh—in my robe," she finished, and I winced. Great. He had her smell all over him. Nice start.

"Oh. Sorry." His voice was nice. Kind of resonate and rumbly. I could hardly wait to see him. Ivy seemed positively at a loss for words. Baron took a noisy breath. "I found it on the dryer. There wasn't anything else to wear. Maybe I should go put on a towel. . . ."

Ivy hesitated. "Um, no," she said, the unusual sound of amusement in her voice. "You're all right. You helped Rachel escape?"

"Yeah. Is she in the kitchen?" he questioned.

"Come on in." Her eyes were rolling as she preceded him into the room. "He's a geek," she mouthed, and my face froze. *A geek had saved my life?*

"Uh, hi," he said, standing awkwardly just inside the doorway.

"Hi," I said, too disconcerted to say more as I ran my gaze over him. Calling him a geek wasn't fair, but compared to what Ivy was used to dating, he might be.

Baron was as tall as Ivy, but his build was so sparse he seemed taller. The pale arms showing past Ivy's black robe had the occasional faint scar, presumably from prior rat fights. His cheeks were clean-shaven—I'd have to get a new razor; the one I'd borrowed from Ivy was probably ruined. The rims of his ears were notched. Two puncture marks on either side of his neck stood out red and sore looking. They matched mine, and I felt a flush of embarrassment.

Despite, or maybe because of, his narrow frame he looked nice, kind of bookish. His dark hair was long, and the way he kept brushing it from his eyes led me to think he usually kept it shorter. The robe made him look soft and comfortable, but the way the black silk stretched across his lean muscles kept my eyes roving. Ivy was being overly critical. He had too many muscles to be a geek.

"You have red hair," he said, shifting into motion. "I thought it would be brown."

"I thought you were—ah—shorter." I stood up as he approached, and after an awkward moment, he extended his hand across the corner of the table. Okay, so he wasn't Arnold Schwarzenegger. But he had saved my life. Maybe somewhere between a short, young Jeff Goldblum and untidy Buckaroo Banzai.

"My name is Nick," he said as he took my hand. "Well, it's Nicholas, actually. Thanks for helping me get out of that rat pit."

"I'm Rachel." He had a nice grip. Just the right amount of firmness without trying to prove how strong he was. I motioned to one of the kitchen chairs, and we both sat. "And don't mention it. We kind of helped each other out. You can tell me it's none of my business, but how on earth did you end up as a rat in the city fights?"

Nick rubbed a thin hand behind an ear and looked at the ceiling. "I—uh—was cataloging a vamp's private book collection. I found something interesting and made the mistake of taking it home." He met my eyes with a sheepish expression. "I wasn't going to keep it."

Ivy and I exchanged looks. *Just borrowing it. Ri-i-i-i-ight.* But if he had worked with vampires before, that might explain his ease around Ivy.

"He changed me into a rat when he found out," Nick continued, "then gave me to one of his business associates as a gift. He was the one who put me in the fights, knowing as a human, I'd have the smarts advantage. I made him a lot of money, if nothing else. How about you?" he asked. "How did you get there?

"Um," I stammered. "I made a spell to turn myself into a mink and got put in the fights by mistake." It wasn't really a lie. I hadn't planned it, so it was an accident. Really.

"You're a witch?" he said, a smile curving over his face. "Cool. I wasn't sure."

A smile crossed me. I'd run into a few humans like him who thought Inderlanders were merely the other side to the humanity coin. Every time it was a surprise and a delight.

"What are those fights?" Ivy asked. "Some sort of crime clearinghouse where you can get rid of people without getting blood on your hands?"

Nick shook his head. "I don't think so. Rachel was the first person I ran into. And I was there for three months."

"Three months," I said, appalled. "You were a rat for three months?"

He shifted in his chair and tightened the tie on his robe. "Yeah. I'm sure all my stuff has been sold to pay my back rent. But hey, I've got hands again." He held them up, and I noticed that though thin, they were heavily callused.

I winced in sympathy. In the Hollows it was standard practice to sell your renter's things if they disappeared. People went missing all too frequently. He didn't have a job anymore, either, seeing as he was "fired" from his last one.

"You really live in a church?" he asked.

My gaze followed his, roving over the clearly institutional kitchen. "Yeah. Ivy and I moved in a few days ago. Don't mind the bodies buried in the backyard."

He smiled a charming half smile. God save me, but it made him look like a little lost boy. Ivy, at the sink again, snickered under her breath.

"Honey," Jenks's tiny voice moaned from the ceiling, jerking my attention upward. He peered down from the ladle, his wings blurring to nothing when he noticed Nick. Flying unsteadily, he almost fell to the table. I cringed, but Nick smiled.

"Jenks, right?" Nick asked.

"Baron," Jenks said, stumbling as he tried to take his best Peter Pan pose. "Glad you can do something other than squeak. Gives me a headache. Squeak, squeak, squeak. That ultrasonic stuff goes right through my head."

"It's Nick. Nick Sparagmos."

"So, Nick," he said, "Rachel wants to know what it was like having balls as big as your head that drag on the floor."

"Jenks!" I shouted. *Oh, God help me.* Head shaking violently in denial, I looked at Nick, but he seemed to have taken it in stride, his eyes glinting as his long face grinned.

Jenks took a hasty breath, darting out of the way as I made a snatch for him. He was rapidly regaining his balance. "Hey, that's one bad-ass scar on your wrist," he said quickly. "My wife—she's a sweet girl—patches me up. She's a wonder with her stitching."

"Do you want something to put on your neck?" I asked, trying to change the subject.

"No. It's all right," Nick said. He stretched out slowly, as if he were stiff, abruptly straightening when there was a soft touch on my slippered foot. I tried not to be too obvious as I looked him over. Jenks was a lot more blunt.

"Nick," Jenks said, landing next to him on the table. "Have you ever seen a scar like this?" Jenks pushed his sleeve up to show a puckered zigzag from his wrist to his elbow. Jenks always wore a long-sleeved silk shirt and matching pants. I hadn't known he had scars.

Nick whistled appreciably, and Jenks beamed. "I got that from a fairy," Jenks said. "He was shadowing the same take my runner was. A few seconds at the ceiling with the butterfly-winged pansy, and he took his runner somewhere else."

"No kidding." Nick seemed impressed as he leaned forward. He smelled good: manly without dipping into Were, and no hint of blood at all. His eyes were brown. Nice. I liked human eyes. You could look at them and never see anything but what you might expect.

"What about that one?" Nick pointed to a round scar on Jenks's collarbone.

"Bee sting," Jenks said. "Had me in bed for three days with the shivers and jerks, but we kept our claim on the southside flower boxes. How did you get that one?" he asked, taking to the air to point at the softly welted scar ringing Nick's wrist.

Nick glanced at me and away. "A big rat named Hugo."

"Looks like he nearly took your hand off."

"He tried."

"Lookie here." Jenks tugged at his boot, yanking it off along with a nearly transparent sock to show a misshapen foot. "A vamp pulped my foot when I didn't dodge fast enough."

Nick winced, and I felt ill. It must be hard to be four inches in a six-foot world. Parting the upper part of his robe, he showed his shoulder and a hint of a curve of muscle. I leaned forward to get a better look. The light crisscrossing of scars appeared to be nail gouges, and I tried to see how far down they might go. I decided Ivy was wrong. He wasn't a geek. Geeks don't have washboard stomachs. "A rat named Pan Peril gave me these," Nick said.

"How about this?" Jenks let his shirt fall completely about his waist. I felt my amusement fade as Jenks's scarred and battered body came to light. "See here?" he said, pointing to a concave, round scar. "Look. It goes right through to the other side." He turned to show a smaller scar on his lower back. "Fairy sword. It probably would have killed me, but I had just married Matalina. She kept me alive until the toxins worked their way out."

Nick shook his head slowly. "You win," he said. "I can't beat that."

Jenks rose several inches in pride. I didn't know what to say. My stomach rumbled, and in the obvious silence afterward I murmured, "Nick, can I make you a sandwich or something?"

His brown eyes meeting mine were warm. "If it's not too much trouble."

I rose and shuffled in my pink fuzzy slippers to the fridge. "No trouble at all. I was going to make myself something to eat anyway."

Ivy finished putting the last of the glasses away and started cleaning the sink with scouring powder. I gave her a sour look. The sink didn't need cleaning. She was just being nosy. Upon opening the fridge, I silently assessed the take-out bags from four different restaurants. Apparently Ivy had been grocery shopping. Shuffling about, I found the bologna and a head of browning lettuce. My eyes went to the tomato on the windowsill and I bit my lower lip, hoping Nick hadn't seen it yet. I didn't want to offend him. Most humans wouldn't touch a tomato with a gloved hand. Shifting to block his view, I hid it behind the toaster.

"Still eating, are we?" Ivy murmured under her breath. "A moment on the lips . . ."

"I'm hungry," I muttered back. "And I'm going to need all my strength tonight." I stuck my head back in the fridge for the mayonnaise. "I could use your help if you have the time."

"Help with what?" Jenks asked. "Getting tucked into bed?"

I turned with my hands full of sandwich stuff and elbowed the fridge shut. "I need your help bringing in Trent. And we only have until midnight to do it."

Jenks's flight bobbled. "What?" he said flatly, every drop of humor gone.

I pulled my weary gaze up to Ivy. I knew she wasn't going to like this. If the truth be told, I'd been waiting until Nick was present, hoping that with a witness, she wouldn't make a scene.

"Tonight?" Ivy put the back of her wrist on her leather hip huggers and stared. "You want to make a run for him to-night?" Her eyes went to Nick and back to me. Tossing her rag into the sink, she dried her hands on a dish towel. "Rachel, can I talk to you in the hallway?"

My brow furrowed at her implied insult that Nick

couldn't be trusted. But then heaving a sigh of exasperation, I dumped everything in my arms onto the counter. "Excuse me," I said, giving Nick an apologetic grimace.

Peeved, I followed her out. I abruptly slowed at the sight of her standing halfway down to our rooms, her waspish outline looking dangerous in the dark hallway. The overpowering smell of incense in the close confines pulled me wire-tight. "What?" I said shortly.

"Letting Nick know about your little problem isn't a good idea," she said.

"He has been a rat for three months," I said, backing up. "How on earth could he be an I.S. assassin? The poor man doesn't even have any clothes, and you're worried about him killing me?"

"No," she protested, moving closer until I found my back against the wall. "But the less he knows about you, the safer you *both* will be."

"Oh." My face went cold. She was too close. Having lost her sense of personal space was not a good sign.

"And what are you going to accuse Trent of?" she demanded. "Keeping you as a mink? Putting you in the city's fights? If you go whining to the I.S. for that, you're dead."

Her speech had slowed to a sultry drawl. I had to get out of this hallway. "After three days with him, I have more than that."

From the kitchen came Nick's voice. "The I.S.?" he said loudly. "Are they the ones that put you in the rat fights, Rachel? You aren't a black witch, are you?"

Ivy jerked. Her eyes flashed to brown. Looking disconcerted, she backed up. "Sorry," she said softly. Clearly not pleased, Ivy returned to the kitchen. Relieved, I followed, to find Jenks on Nick's shoulder. I wondered if Nick had acute hearing or if Jenks had relayed everything to him. I was betting on the latter. And Nick's question about black witchcraft had been disturbing in its casualness.

"Nah," Jenks said, sounding smug. "Rachel's witchcraft is whiter than her ass. She quit the I.S. and took Ivy with her.

Ivy was their best. Denon, her boss, put a price on Rachel's head for spite."

"You *were* an I.S. runner," Nick said. "I get it. But how did you end up in the rat fights?"

Still on edge, I looked to Ivy, who was industriously scrubbing the sink again, and she shrugged. So much for keeping rat boy in the dark. Shuffling back to the counter, I pulled out six pieces of bread. "Mr. Kalamack caught me in his office looking for evidence of him moving biodrugs," I said. "He thought it would be more fun putting me in the rat fights than turning me in."

"Kalamack?" Nick asked, his large eyes going wider. "You're talking about Trent Kalamack? The councilman? He runs biodrugs?" Nick's robe had parted about his knees, and I wished he'd turn ju-u-u-ust a little more.

Smug, I layered two slices of bologna each on three slices of bread. "Yup, but while I was trapped I found out Trent isn't simply running biodrugs." I hesitated dramatically. "He's *making* them, too," I finished.

Ivy turned. Rag hanging forgotten in her slack grip, she stared at me from across the kitchen. I could hear kids playing tag next door, it was so quiet. Enjoying her reaction, I picked at the lettuce until I got to the green parts.

Nick was ashen-faced. I didn't blame him. Humans were terrified of genetic manipulation, for obvious reasons. And having Trent Kalamack dabbling in it was very worrisome. Especially when it wasn't clear which side of the human/Inderlander fence he was on. "Not Mr. Kalamack," the distraught man said. "I voted for him. Both times. Are you sure?"

Ivy, too, looked worried. "He's a bioengineer?"

"Well, he funds them," I said. *And kills them, and leaves them to rot on his office floor.* "He's got a shipment going out on Southwest tonight. If we can intercept it and tie it to him, I can use it to pay off my contract. Jenks, you still have that page from his datebook?"

The pixy nodded. "It's hidden in my stump."

I opened my mouth to protest, then decided it wasn't a bad spot. The sound of the knife was loud as I slathered mayonnaise on the bread and finished the sandwiches.

Nick pulled his head up from his hands. His long face was drawn and he looked pale. "Genetic engineering? Trent Kalamack has a biolab? The councilman?"

"You're going to love this next part," I said. "Francis is the one working the I.S. angle."

Jenks yelped, zipping up to the ceiling and down again. "Francis? You sure you weren't knocked on the head, Rache?"

"He works for Trent as sure as I just spent the last four days eating carrots. I saw him. You know those Brimstone takes Francis has been running? The promotion? *That car?*" I didn't finish my thoughts, allowing Jenks and Ivy to figure it out.

"Son of a pup!" Jenks exclaimed. "The Brimstone runs are distractions!"

"Yup." I cut the sandwiches in half. Pleased with myself, I put one on a plate for me and two on a plate for Nick; he was thin. "Trent keeps the I.S. and the FIB busy with Brimstone while the real moneymaker goes out on the other side of the city."

Ivy's motions were slow in thought as she washed her hands free of the scouring powder once more. "Francis isn't that smart," she said as she dried her fingers and set the dish towel aside again.

I went still. "No, he isn't. He's going to get himself tagged and bagged."

Jenks landed beside me. "Denon's gonna piss his pants when he hears this," he said.

"Wait up." Ivy's attention sharpened. The ring of brown in her eyes was shrinking, but it was in excitement, not hunger. "Who's to say Denon isn't on Trent's payroll, too? You'll need proof before going to the I.S. They kill you before helping you tag him. And catching him is going to take more than us two and an afternoon of planning."

My brow pinched in worry. "This is my only shot, Ivy," I protested. "High risk or not."

"Um." Nick's hand was shaking as he reached for a sandwich. "Why don't you go to the FIB?"

Ivy and I turned in a poignant silence. Nick took a bite and swallowed. "The FIB would go into a Hollow slum at midnight on a tip concerning bioengineered drugs—especially if Mr. Kalamack was being implicated. If you have any proof at all, they'll take a look."

I turned to Ivy in disbelief. Her face looked as blank as mine felt. *The FIB?*

My brow smoothed and I felt a smile come over me. Nick was right. The rivalry alone between the FIB and the I.S. would be enough to get them interested. "Trent will fry, my contract will be paid off, and the I.S. will look like a fool. I like it." I took a bite of my sandwich, wiping the mayonnaise from the corner of my mouth as I met Nick's eyes.

"Rachel," Ivy said warily. "Can I talk to you for a moment?"

I glanced at Nick, feeling my ire rise again. What did she want now? But she had already walked out. "Excuse me," I said, lurching to my feet and nervously tightening the tie on my robe. "The princess of paranoia wants a word with me." Ivy looked okay. It should be alright.

Nick brushed a crumb from his front, unperturbed. "You mind if I make some coffee? I've been dying for a cup the last three months."

"Sure. Whatever," I said, glad he wasn't insulted by Ivy's mistrust. I was. Here he came up with a great plan, and Ivy didn't like it because she didn't think of it first. "The coffee is in the fridge," I added as I followed Ivy into the hallway.

"What is your problem?" I said even before I reached her. "He's just some guy with sticky fingers. And he's right. Convincing the FIB to go after Trent is a heck of a lot safer than trying to get the I.S. to help me."

I couldn't see the color of Ivy's eyes in the dim light. It was getting dark outside, and the hallway was an uncomfortable black with her in it. "Rachel, this isn't a raid on the local vamp hangout," she said. "It's an attempt to bring down one of the city's most powerful citizens. One wrong word out of Nick and you'll be dead."

My gut clenched at the reminder. I took a breath, then slowly let it out. "Keep talking."

"I know Nick wants to help," she said. "He wouldn't be human if he didn't want to repay you somehow for helping him escape. But he's going to get hurt."

I said nothing, knowing she was right. We were professionals and he wasn't. I'd have to get him out of the way somehow. "What do you suggest?" I asked, and her tension eased.

"Why don't you take him up and see if those clothes in the belfry fit him while I book a seat on that plane?" she asked. "What flight did you say it was?"

I tucked a stray curl behind my ear. "Why? All we need to know is when it leaves."

"We might need more time. It's going to be close as it is. Most airlines will hold a plane if you tell them you have daylight restrictions. They blame it on the weather or a small maintenance issue. They won't take off until the sun isn't shining at 38,000 feet."

Daylight restrictions? That explained a lot. "Last flight to L.A. before midnight," I said.

Ivy's face grew intent as she fell into what I remembered as her "planning mode." "Jenks and I will go to the FIB and explain everything," she said in a preoccupied voice. "You can meet us there for the actual take."

"Whoa, wait a minute. I'm going to the FIB. It's my run."

Her frown was obvious in the dark of the hallway, and I stepped back, uncomfortable. "It's still the FIB," she said dryly. "Safer, yes. But they might tag you for the prestige of nailing a runner the I.S. couldn't. Some of those guys would love to kill a witch, and you know it."

I felt ill. "Okay," I agreed slowly, my mouth starting to water at the sound of gurgling coffee. "You're right. I'll stay out of it until you've told the FIB what we're doing."

Ivy's determined look shifted to one of shock. "You think I'm right?"

The smell of coffee was pulling me into the kitchen. Ivy followed me in, her footsteps soundless. I clasped my arms around myself as I entered the brighter room. The memory of hiding in the dark from fairy assassins quashed any feeling of excitement that the prospect of tagging Trent had given me. I needed to make some more spells. Strong ones. Different ones. Really different ones. Maybe . . . maybe black. I felt sick.

Nick and Jenks had their heads together as Jenks tried to convince him to open the jar of honey. By Nick's grin and continuous soft refusals, I guessed he knew something about pixies as well as vamps. I went to stand by the coffeemaker, waiting for it to finish. Ivy opened the cupboard and handed me three mugs, the question in her eyes demanding an answer as to why I was suddenly on edge. She was a vamp; she read body language better than Dr. Ruth.

"The I.S. is still spelling for me," I said softly. "Whenever the FIB moves to make a major play, the I.S. always follows to get involved. If I'm going to make a public appearance, I need something to protect myself from them. Something strong. I can make it while you're at the FIB, then join you at the airport," I said slowly.

Ivy stood at the sink, her arms crossed suspiciously. "That sounds like a good idea," she prompted. "Some prep work. Fine."

Tension pulled me tight. Black earth magic always involved killing something before adding it to the mix. Especially the strong spells. Guess I was about to find out if I could do that. Dropping my eyes, I arranged the mugs in a straight row. "Jenks?" I questioned. "What's the assassin lineup like outside?"

The wind from his wings shifted my hair as he landed by my hand. "Real light. It's been four days since you've been spotted. It's just the fairies now. Give my kids five minutes, and we'll distract them enough that you can slip out if you need to."

"Good. I'm going out to find some new spells as soon as I get dressed."

"What for?" Ivy asked, her tone going wary. "You have plenty of spell books."

I felt the dampness of sweat on my neck. I didn't like that Ivy knew it was there. "I need something stronger." I turned, finding Ivy's face curiously slack. Dread pulled my shoulders tight. I took a deep breath and dropped my eyes. "I want something I can use for an offensive," I said in a small voice. With one hand cupping an elbow, I put a hand over my collarbone.

"Whoa, Rache," Jenks said, his wings clattering as he forced himself into my line of sight. His tiny features were pinched in worry, doing nothing for my sense of well-being. "That's dipping kind of close to dark magic, isn't it?"

My heart was pounding, and I hadn't even done anything yet. "Dipping? Hell, it is," I said. I flicked a glance at Ivy. Her posture was carefully neutral. Nick, too, didn't seem upset as he rose, coming close at the promise of coffee. Again, the thought of him practicing black magic raced through me. Humans could tap into ley lines, though wizards and sorceresses were thought of as little more than a joke in most Inderland circles.

"The moon is waxing," I said, "so that will be on my side, and I wouldn't be making spells to hurt anyone in particular. . . ." My words trailed off. The silence was uncomfortable.

Ivy's relatively mild response was unnerving. "Are you sure, Rachel?" she asked, only the barest hint of warning in her voice.

"I'll be fine," I said as I looked away from her. "I'm not doing this out of malice but to save my life. There's a difference. . . ." *I hope. God save my soul if I'm wrong.*

Jenks's wings blurred in fitful spurts as he landed on the ladle. "It doesn't matter," he said, clearly agitated. "They burned all the black spell books."

Nick pulled the coffee carafe out from under the stream of

coffee and slipped a mug in its place. "The university library has some," he said as the hot plate sizzled against what spilled in the bare second it took.

We all turned to Nick, and he shrugged. "They keep them in the ancient book locker."

A wisp of fear tugged at me. *I shouldn't be doing this*, I thought. "And you have a key, right?" I said sarcastically, taken aback when he nodded.

Ivy exhaled in a puff of disbelief. "You have a key," she scoffed. "You were a rat an hour ago, and you have a key to the university's library."

He suddenly looked far more dangerous as he casually stood in my kitchen with Ivy's black robe hanging loose on his tall, lean body. "I did my work-study there," he said.

"You went to the university?" I asked, pouring myself a cup after Nick.

He took a sip of coffee, his eyes closed in what looked like bliss. "Full scholarship," he said. "I majored in data acquisition, organization, and distribution."

"You're a librarian," I said in relief. That's how he knew about the black spell books.

"Used to be. I can get you in and out, no problem. The lady in charge of us work-study peons hid keys to locked rooms near the doors so we wouldn't keep bothering her." He took another sip, and his eyes glazed as the caffeine hit him.

Only now did Ivy look worried, her brown eyes pinched. "Rachel, can I talk to you?"

"No," I said softly. I didn't want to go into that hallway again. It was dark. I was on edge. That my heart was pounding because I was afraid of black magic and not her would mean nothing to her instincts. And going to the library with Nick was a hindsight less dangerous than making a black spell—for which she didn't seem to have any care. "What do you want?"

She eyed Nick, then me. "I was only going to suggest you take Nick up to the belfry. We've got some clothes up there that might fit him."

I pushed myself from the counter, my untasted coffee tight in my grip. *Liar*, I thought. "Give me a minute to get dressed, Nick, and I'll take you up. You don't mind wearing a minister's hand-me-downs, do you?"

Nick's look of startlement eased into question. "No. That would be great."

"Fine," I said, my head pounding. "After you're dressed, you and I will go out to the library and you can show me all their black magic books."

I glanced at Ivy and Jenks as I walked out. Jenks was very pale, clearly not liking what I was doing. Ivy looked concerned, but what worried me most was Nick's casual ease with everything Inderlander, and now black magic. He wasn't a practitioner, was he?

Twenty-four

I stood on the sidewalk waiting for Nick to get out of the cab, estimating what I had left in my wallet before putting it away. My last paycheck was dwindling. If I wasn't careful, I'd have to send Ivy to the bank for me. I was burning it faster than usual, and I couldn't understand why. All my expenses were less. *Must be the cabs,* I thought, vowing to use the bus more.

Nick had found a pair of work-faded jeans up in the belfry. They were baggy on him, held up with one of my more conservative belts; our long-departed minister had been a large man. The gray sweatshirt with the University of Cincinnati's logo was equally outsized, and the gardening boots had been hopelessly too big. But Nick had them on his feet, clomping about like a bad Frankenstein movie. Somehow, with his tall height and casual good looks, he made slovenly seem attractive. I always just looked like a slob.

The sun wasn't down yet, but the streetlights were on since it was cloudy. It had taken longer to get the minister's small wardrobe into the wash than it had to get here. I held the collar of my winter coat closed against the chill air and scanned the headlight-illuminated street as Nick said a few last words to the cabbie. Nights could be chill in late spring, but I would have worn the long coat anyway to cover up the brown gingham dress I had on. It was supposed to go along with my old lady disguise. I had only worn it once before, to a mother-daughter banquet I was somehow roped into.

Nick unfolded himself out of the cab. He slammed the door shut and smacked the top of the car. The driver gave him a casual hand toss and drove away. Cars flowed around us. The street was busy in the hours of twilight when both humanity and Inderlander were in force.

"Hey," Nick said, peering at me in the unsure light. "What happened to your freckles?"

"Uh . . ." I stammered, fingering my pinky ring. "I don't have any freckles."

Nick took a breath to say something, then hesitated. "Where's Jenks?" he finally asked.

Flustered, I pointed across the street to the library steps with my chin. "He went ahead to check things out." I eyed the few people filing in and out of the library. Studying on a Friday night. Some people have an insatiable desire to ruin the curve for the rest of us. Nick took my elbow, and I tugged away from him. "I can walk across the street by myself, thank you."

"You look like an old lady," he muttered. "Stop swinging your arms, and slow down."

I sighed, trying to move slowly as Nick crossed in the middle of the street. Horns blew, and Nick ignored them. We were in student territory. If we had crossed at the intersection, we would have attracted attention. Even so, I was tempted to give a few one-fingered waves, but decided it might blow the old lady image. Then again, maybe not.

"Are you sure no one will recognize you?" I asked as we moved up the marble stairs and to the glass doors. Cripes, no wonder old people died. It took them twice as long to do anything.

"Yup." He pulled the door open for me and I shuffled in. "I haven't worked here for five years, and the only people working on Friday are the freshmen. Now hunch your back and try not to attack anyone." I gave him a nasty smile, and he added a cheerful, "That's better."

Five years meant he wasn't much older than I was. It was

about what I had guessed, though it was hard to tell under the rat-induced wear and tear.

I stood in the entryway to get my bearings. I like libraries. They smell good and are quiet. The fluorescent light in the entrance looked too dim. It was usually supplemented by the natural light coming in through the big windows running the entire two stories up. The gloom of sunset dampened everything.

My gaze jerked to a blur falling from the ceiling. It was headed right for me! Gasping, I ducked. Nick clutched my arm. Thrown off balance, my heels slipped on the marble floor. Crying out, I went down. Sprawled with my legs every which way, my face burned as Jenks hovered before me, laughing. "Damn it all to hell!" I shouted. "Watch what you're doing!"

There was a collective gasp, and everyone looked at me. Jenks hid himself in my hair, his merry laughter ticking me off. Nick bent and took my elbow. "Sorry, Grandmum," he said loudly. He gave everyone a sheepish look. "Grandmum can't hear very well," he said in a conspiratorial whisper, "the old bat." He turned to me, his face serious but his brown eyes glinting. "We're in the library now!" he shouted. "You have to be quiet!"

Face warm enough to make toast, I mumbled something and let him help me up. There was a nervous patter of amusement, and everyone returned to whatever they were doing.

An uptight, pimply-faced adolescent rushed up to us, worried about a lawsuit, no doubt. Amid more fuss than it warranted, he ushered us to the back offices, babbling about slippery floors, that they had just been waxed, and he would talk to the janitor immediately.

I hung on Nick's arm, moaning about my hip and playing the old lady to the hilt. The flustered kid buzzed us through a semisecure area. Red-faced, he fussed over me as he sat me down and propped my feet up on a swivel chair. The silver knife strapped to my ankle gave him a slight pause. I whispered faintly something about water, and he fled to find some. It took him three tries to get through the buzzed door. Silence descended as the door clicked shut behind him. Grinning, I met Nick's eyes. It wasn't exactly how we had planned it, but here we were.

Jenks came out from hiding. "Slicker than snot on a doorknob," he said, darting up to inspect the cameras. "Ha!" he exclaimed. "They're fake."

Nick took my hand and drew me to my feet. "I was going to take you down through the access in the employees' break room, but this will work." I looked blankly at him and he flicked his eyes to a gray fire door. "The basement is through there."

A smile curved over me as I saw the lock. "Jenks?"

"On it," he said, dropping down and starting to tinker. He had it sprung in three seconds flat. "Here goes . . ." Nick murmured as he turned the knob. The door opened to show a dark stairway. Nick flicked on the lights and listened. "No alarms," he said.

I pulled out a detection amulet and quickly invoked it. It stayed warm and green in my hand. "No silent alarms, either," I murmured, hanging it about my neck.

"Hey," Jenks complained. "This is first-year stuff."

We started down. The air was cold in the narrow stairwell, with none of the comforting smell of books. Every twenty feet a bare bulb burned, sending sickly yellow beams to show the dirt in the lee of the steps. A foot-wide band of grime made a stripe on the walls to either side of me at hand height, and my lip curled. There was a banister, but I wouldn't use it.

The way ended at an echoing dark hallway. Nick looked at me, and I glanced at my amulet. "We're clear," I whispered, and he flicked on the lights to illuminate a hallway with a low ceiling, the walls stark cinder block. Floor to ceiling wire gates ran down the length of the hall, doing nothing to hide the racks of books behind them.

Jenks buzzed confidently ahead of us. Heels clacking, I

followed Nick to a locked wire door. The ancient-book section. While Jenks flitted in and out between the diamond-shaped holes, I laced my fingers through the mesh and stood on tiptoe, all senses soaking it in. A frown pinched my brow. It was my imagination, of course, but it seemed I could smell the magic flowing out from the racks of books, all but visible as it eddied about my ankles. The feeling of old power emanating from the locked room was as different from the smell upstairs as a chocolate kiss is to a premium Belgium sweet. Heady, rich, and oh-so-bad for you.

"So where's that key?" I asked, knowing Jenks wouldn't be able to shift the heavy tumblers of the older, mechanical lock. Sometimes it's the older safeguards that work best.

Nick ran his fingers under a nearby shelf, his eyes glinting in a past frustration as his hand stopped. "Not enough seniority to go into the book locker, eh?" he muttered under his breath as he pulled out a key with a bit of sticky tack on it. Eyes tight, he looked at the skeleton key laying heavy in his hand before opening the wire-meshed door.

My heart gave a pound and settled as the door squeaked. Nick put the key in his pocket with an abrupt, determined motion. "After you," he said as he turned on the fluorescent lights.

I hesitated. "Is there any other way out of here?" I asked, and when he shook his head, I turned to Jenks. "Stay here," I said. "Watch my—back. . . ." I bit my lip. "Will you watch my back, Jenks?" I said, my stomach clenching.

The pixy must have heard the hint of a quaver in my voice as he lost his excitement and landed on my proffered hand. At eye level, he nodded. The sparkles in his black silk shirt caught the light, adding to the glow his blurring wings put out. "Gotcha, Rache," he said solemnly. "Nothing is going to come through here unless you know about it. Promise."

I took a nervous breath. Nick's eyes were confused. Everyone in the I.S. knew how my dad had died. I appreciated Jenks not saying anything, just telling me that he would be there for me.

"Okay," I said as I took off my detecting amulet and hung it where Jenks could see it. I followed Nick in, ignoring the creepy sensation of my skin tingling. Whether they contained black arts or white, they were just books. The power came from using them.

The door squeaked shut, and Nick brushed past me, gesturing me to follow. I took off my disguise amulet and dropped it into my bag, then undid the bun my hair was in and shook it all out. Fluffing it, I felt half a century younger.

I glanced at the passing titles as I passed them, slowing as the aisle opened up to a good-sized room hidden from the hallway by racks of books. There was an institutional-looking table and three mismatched swivel chairs that weren't even good enough for an intern's desk.

Nick strode unhesitatingly to the glass-door cabinet across the room. "Here, Rachel," he said as he pulled it open. "See if what you want is here." He turned, brushing the shock of black hair from his eyes. I blinked at the intent, sly look shadowing his long face.

"Thanks. This is great. I really appreciate it," I said as I dropped my bag on the table and came to stand beside him. Worry pinched me, and I pushed it aside. If the spell was too disgusting, I just wouldn't do it.

Carefully, I worked the oldest-looking book out. The binding had been torn off the spine, and I had to use two hands to manage the unwieldy tome. I set it at the corner of the table and dragged a chair up to it. It was as cold as a cave down here, and I was glad for my coat. The dry air smelled faintly like potato chips. Squelching my nervousness, I opened the book. The title page had been ripped out, too. Using a spell from a book with no name was disturbing. The index was intact, though, and my eyebrows rose. *A spell to talk to ghosts? Cool* . . .

"You aren't like most humans I've spent any time with," I said as I scanned the index.

"My mom was a single parent," he said. "She couldn't afford anything uptown and so was more inclined to let me play with witches and vampires than the kids of heroine addicts. The Hollows was the lesser of two evils." Nick had his hands in his back pockets and was rocking heel to toe as he read the titles of a row of books. "I grew up there. Went to Emerson."

I glanced at him, intrigued. Growing up in the Hollows would explain why he knew so much about Inderlanders. To survive, you had to. "You went to Inderland Hollows's high school?" I asked.

He jiggled the locked door of a tall free-standing closet. The wood looked red in the glow from the fluorescent lights. I wondered what was so dangerous that it had to be locked inside a closet, inside a locked vault, behind a locked door, at the bottom of a government building.

Picking at the heat-warped lock, Nick shrugged. "It was all right. The principal bent the rules for me after I got a concussion. They let me carry a silver dagger to get the Weres to back off, and rinsing my hair in holy water kept the living vamps from being too obnoxious. It didn't stop them, but the bad case of B.O. it gave me worked almost as well."

"Holy water, huh?" I said, deciding I'd stick with my lilac perfume rather than have a body odor that only vamps could smell.

"It was only the warlocks and witches that gave me trouble," he added as he gave up on the lock and sat in one of the chairs, his long legs straight out before him. I gave him a sideways smirk. I could well imagine the witches gave him trouble. "But the practical jokes stopped after I befriended the biggest, meanest, ugliest warlock in school." A faint smile played about his eyes, and he looked tired. "Turk. I did his homework for four years. He should have graduated a long time ago, and the teachers were glad to look the other way to get him out of the system. Because I didn't go whining to the principal all the time like the handful of other humans enrolled there, I was cool enough to hang with the

Inderlanders. My friends took care of me, and I learned a lot I might not have."

"Like that you don't have to be afraid of a vamp," I said, thinking it was odd a human would know more about vamps than I did.

"Not at noon, anyway. But I'll feel better once I take a shower and get Ivy's smell off me. I didn't know that was her robe, earlier." He clumped over. "What are you looking for?"

"Not sure," I said, nervous as he peered over my shoulder. There had to be something I could use that wouldn't send me too far down the wrong side of the "Force." A nervous amusement flashed through me. *You're not my father, Darth, and I'll never join you!*

Nick's eyes began to water at the strength of my perfume, and he backed off. We had driven over with the windows down. Now I knew why he hadn't said anything about it.

"You haven't lived with Ivy very long, have you?" he asked. I looked up from the index, surprised, and his long face went slack. "I, uh, sorta got the idea that you and she weren't . . ."

I flushed, dropping my eyes. "We aren't," I said. "Not if we can help it. We're just roommates. I'm on the right side of the hall, she's on the left."

He hesitated. "Do you mind if I make a suggestion, then?"

Mystified, I stared at him, and he went to sit on the corner of the table. "You might want to try a perfume with a citrus base instead of a flower."

My eyes widened. This was not what I had been expecting, and my hand crept up to cover my neck where I had dumped a splash of that awful perfume. "Jenks helped me pick it out," I said in explanation. "He said it covered Ivy's smell pretty good."

"I'm sure it does." Nick winced apologetically. "But it has to be strong to work. The ones based on citrus neutralize a vamp's odor, not just cover it up."

"Oh . . ." I breathed, recalling Ivy's fondness for orange juice.

"A pixy's nose is good, but a vamp's is specialized. Go shopping with Ivy next time. She'll help you pick out something that works."

"I'll do that," I said, thinking I could have avoided offending everyone if I had just asked for her help the first time. Feeling stupid, I closed the unnamed book and rose to get another.

I pulled the next book off the shelf, tensing when it was heavier than I thought it should be. It hit the table with a thump and Nick cringed. "Sorry," I said, pushing the cover straight to hide that I had torn the rotting binding. Sitting down, I opened the book.

My heart gave a thump and I froze, feeling the hair on my neck stand on end. It wasn't my imagination. Worried, I looked up to see if Nick had noticed it, too. He was staring over my shoulder at one of the aisles the book racks made. The eerie feeling wasn't coming from the book. It was coming from behind me. *Damn.*

"Rachel!" came a tiny call from the hall. "Your amulet went red, but no one's out here!"

I shut the book and stood. There was a flickering in the air. My heart pounded when half a dozen books in the aisle pushed themselves to the back of the shelves. "Uh, Nick?" I questioned. "Is there a history of ghosts in the library?"

"Not that I know of."

Double damn. I moved to stand beside him. "Then what the hell is that?"

He gave me a wary look. "I don't know."

Jenks flitted in. "There's nothing in the hallway, Rache. You sure that charm you gave me is working?" he asked, and I pointed at the disturbance in the aisle.

"Holy crap!" he exclaimed, hovering between Nick and me as the air started to take on a more solid form. As one, the books slid back to the front of the shelves. That was even creepier.

The mist turned yellow, then became firm. My breath hissed in through my teeth. It was a dog. That is, if dogs can be as big as ponies and have canines longer than my hand and tiny horns coming out of their heads, then it was a dog. I backed up a step with Nick, and it tracked us. "Tell me this is the library's security system," I whispered.

"I don't know what it is." Nick was ashen-faced, his slow confidence shattered. The dog was between us and the door. Saliva dripped from its jaw, and I swear it hissed when it hit the floor. Yellow smoke rose from the puddle. I could smell sulfur. What the devil was this thing?

"Do you have anything in your purse for this?" Nick whispered, stiffening as the dog's ears pricked.

"Anything to stop a yellow dog from hell?" I asked. "No."

"If we show no fear, maybe it won't attack."

The dog opened its jaws and said, "Which one of you is Rachel Mariana Morgan?"

Twenty-five

I gasped, my heart pounding.

The dog yawned with a little whine at the end. "Must be you," it said. Its skin rippled like amber fire, then it leapt at us.

"Look out!" Nick shouted, pushing me clear as the slavering dog landed on the table.

I hit the floor, rolling to a crouch. Nick cried out in pain. There was a crash as the table slid into the racks. It shifted back when the dog jumped off it. The heavy plastic shattered.

"Nick!" I cried, seeing him crumpled in a heap. The monster stood over him, nosing him. Blood stained the floor. "Get off him!" I shouted. Jenks was at the ceiling, powerless.

The dog turned to me. My breath caught. Its irises were red surrounded by a sickly orange color, and its pupils were slit sideways like a goat's. Never taking my eyes off it, I backed up. Fingers fumbling, I pulled my silver dagger from my ankle. I swear a doggy smile curved around its savage canines as I shrugged out of my coat and kicked off my old lady heels.

Nick groaned and moved. He was alive. A wash of relief swept me. Jenks was on his shoulder, yelling in his ear to get up.

"Rachel Mariana Morgan," the dog said, its voice black and honey sweet. I shivered in the basement's cold air, waiting. "One of you is afraid of dogs," it said, sounding amused. "I don't think it's you."

"Come find out," I said boldly. My heart was pounding, and I adjusted my grip on my dagger as I began to tremble. Dogs shouldn't talk. They shouldn't.

It took a step forward. I stared, mouth agape, as its front legs lengthened, pushing itself upward into a walking position. It thinned out, becoming manlike. Clothes appeared: artfully torn blue jeans, a black leather jacket, and a chain running from its belt loop to his wallet. It had spiked hair, colored red to match its ruddy complexion. Eyes were hidden behind black plastic sunglasses. I couldn't move from the shock of it as a bad-boy swagger came into its steps.

"I was sent to kill you," it said in a seedy London accent, still approaching as it finished turning into a cobbled-street gang member. "I was told to make sure you died afraid, sweet. Wasn't given much to go on. Might take a while."

I lurched back, only now realizing it was almost on me.

With motion almost too quick to be seen, its hand jerked forward like a piston. It hit me before I knew it had moved. My cheek exploded into a fiery agony, then went numb. A second blow to the shoulder lifted me. My stomach dropped, and I crashed backward into a book rack.

I struck the floor, books pummeling me as they fell. Shaking the stars from my vision, I rose. Nick had dragged himself between two racks of books. Blood ran from under his hair and down his neck. His face wore a look of awe and fear. He touched his head, looking at the blood as if it meant something. I met his eyes across the room. The thing was between us.

I gasped as it sprang, its hands grasping. I dropped to a knee. I swung my knife, lurching as it went right through it. Horrified, I scrambled out of its reach. It kept coming. Its entire face had gone misty, reforming as my knife passed through. *What the hell was it?*

"Rachel Mariana Morgan," it mocked. "I'm here for you."

It reached out and I turned to run. A heavy hand grabbed

my shoulder. It whipped me back around. The thing held me, and I froze as its other red-skinned hand folded into a murderous-looking fist. Grinning to show startling white teeth, it pulled its arm back. It was going for my middle.

I barely got my arm down to block it. Its fist hit my arm. The sudden shock of pain took my breath away. I fell to my knees, a scream ripping from me as I clutched my arm. It followed me down. Arm held close, I rolled away.

It landed heavy and hot to crush me under it. Its breath was steam upon my face. Its long fingers gripped my shoulder until I cried out. Its free hand snaked its way under my dress and up my inner thigh, roughly searching. My eyes widened in astonishment. *What the hell?*

Its face was inches before mine. I could see my shock mirrored in its sunglasses. A tongue slipped past its teeth. Warm and disgusting, it ran its tongue from my chin to my ear. Nails dug at my underwear. It savagely pulled at them, making them cut into me.

Jolted into action, I knocked the sunglasses askew. My nails dug at its orange irises.

Its surprised cry bought me a quick breath. In the instant of confusion, I pushed it off me and rolled away. A heavy boot smelling of ash lashed out, striking my kidney. Gasping, I huddled in a fetal position curved around my knife. That time I had gotten it. It had been too distracted to turn misty. If it could feel pain, then it could die.

"Not afraid of rape, sweet?" it said, sounding pleased. "You're one tough little bitch."

It grasped my shoulder, and I fought back, helpless against the long red fingers that pulled me stumbling up. My eyes flicked to Nick and the sound of heavy blows. He was hammering at the locked wooden cabinet with a leg from the table. His blood was everywhere. Jenks was on his shoulder, his wings red in fear.

The air blurred before me, and I staggered as I realized the thing had changed again. The hand now gripping my shoulder was smoothed. Panting, I looked up to see it had become a tall, sophisticated young man dressed in a formal frock and coat. A pair of smoked glasses was perched on its narrow nose. I was sure I had hit it, but what I could see of its eyes looked undamaged. Was it a vamp? A really old vampire?

"Perhaps you're afraid of pain?" the vision of an elegant man said, its accent now proper enough for even Professor Henry Higgins.

I jerked away, stumbling into a book rack. Grinning, it reached after me. It picked me up and threw me across the room at Nick, who was still hammering at the cabinet.

My back hit it with enough force to knock the air from me. The clatter of my knife on the floor was loud as my fingers lost their grip. Struggling to breathe, I slid down the broken cabinet, ending up half sitting on the shelves behind the shattered doors. I was helpless as the thing lifted me by my dress front.

"What are you?" I rasped.

"Whatever scares you." It smiled to show flat teeth. "What scares you, Rachel Mariana Morgan?" it asked. "It isn't pain. It isn't rape. It doesn't seem to be monsters."

"Nothing," I panted, spitting at it.

My saliva sizzled as it hit its face. Reminded of Ivy's saliva on my neck, I shuddered.

Its eyes went wide in pleasure. "You're afraid of the soul-less shadows," it whispered in delight. "You're afraid of dying in the loving embrace of a soulless shadow. Your death is going to be a pleasure for both of us, Rachel Mariana Morgan. Such a twisted way to die—in pleasure. It might have been better for your soul had you been afraid of dogs."

I lashed out, striking its face to leave four scratch marks. It didn't flinch. Blood oozed out, too thick and red. It twisted both my arms behind me, gripping my wrists with one hand. Nausea doubled me over as it pulled on my arm and shoulder. It pushed me up against the wall, crushing me. I got my good hand free and swung.

It caught my wrist before I could reach it. I met its gaze

and felt my knees go weak. The gentleman's frock had shrunk to a leather jacket and black pants. Blond hair and a lightly stubbled face replaced its ruddy complexion. Twin earrings caught the light. Kisten smiled at me, a red tongue beckoning. "You have a taste for vamps, little witch?" it whispered.

I twisted, trying to get away. "Not quite right," it murmured, and I struggled as its features shifted yet again. It grew smaller, only a head taller than I. Its hair grew long and straight and black. The blond stubble vanished, and the complexion paled to a ghost. Kisten's square jaw smoothed out to an oval.

"Ivy," I whispered, going slack in terror.

"You give me a name," it said, its voice becoming slow and feminine. "You want this?"

I tried to swallow. I couldn't move. "You don't scare me," I whispered.

Its eyes flashed black. "Ivy does."

I stiffened, trying to jerk away as it brought my wrist closer. "No!" I screamed as it opened its mouth to show fangs. It bit deep, and I screamed. Fire raced up my arm and into my body. It chewed at my wrist like a dog as I writhed, trying to pull away.

I felt skin tear as I twisted. I brought my knee up and pushed it away. It let go. I fell back panting, transfixed. It was as if Ivy stood before me, my blood dripping from her smile. A hand rose to brush the hair from its eyes, leaving a red smear across its forehead.

I couldn't . . . I couldn't deal with this. Taking a gasping breath, I ran for the door.

The thing snaked an arm out with a vampire's quickness and jerked me back. Pain flared as it slammed me against the cement wall. Ivy's pale hand pinned me. "Let me show you what vamps do behind locked doors, Rachel Mariana Morgan," it breathed.

I realized I was going to die in the basement of the university library.

The thing that was Ivy leaned close. I could feel my pulse pushing at my skin. My wrist tingled warmly. Ivy's face was inches from mine. It was getting better at pulling images out of my head. There was a crucifix around its neck, and I could smell orange juice. Its eyes were smoky with a remembered look of sultry hunger. "No," I whispered. "Please, no."

"I can have you anytime I want, little witch," it whispered, the gray silk of its voice twin to Ivy's.

I panicked, struggling helplessly. The thing that looked like Ivy grinned to show teeth. "You are so afraid," it whispered lovingly, tilting its head so its black hair brushed my shoulder. "Don't be so afraid. You'll like it. Didn't I say you would?"

I jerked as something touched my neck. A small sound escaped me as I realized it was a quick tongue. "You're going to love it," it said in Ivy's throaty whisper. "Scout's honor."

Images of being pinned to Ivy's chair flooded back. The thing holding me against the wall groaned in pleasure and nuzzled my head aside. Terrified, I screamed.

"Oh, please," the thing moaned as I felt the cool, icy sharpness of teeth graze my neck. "Oh, please. Now . . ."

"No!" I shrieked, and it drove its teeth into me. Three times it lunged with rapid, hungry motions. I buckled in its grip. Still fastened to me, we dropped to the floor. It crushed me under it against the cold cement. Fire burned at my neck. A twin sensation rose up my wrist, joining it in my head. Shudders racked me. I could hear it sucking at me, feel the rhythmic pulls as it tried to take more than my body could give.

I gasped as a tangy sensation broke over me. I stiffened, unable to separate pain from pleasure. It was . . . was . . .

"Get off her!" Nick shouted.

I heard a thump and felt a jarring. The thing pulled itself off me.

I couldn't move. I didn't want to. I lay sprawled on the floor, transfixed and numb under the vampire-induced stupor. Jenks hovered over me, the breeze on my neck from his wings sending tingling jolts through me.

Nick stood with blood dripping into his eyes. He had a book in his hands. It was so large, he was struggling with it. He was mumbling under his breath, looking pale and frightened. His eyes darted from the book to the thing beside me.

It melted back into a dog. Snarling, it leapt at Nick.

"Nick," I whispered as Jenks fanned pixy dust onto my neck. "Look out . . ."

"Laqueus!" Nick shouted, juggling the book against a raised knee as he flung out a hand.

The dog slammed into something and fell to the ground. I watched from the floor as it picked itself up and shook its head as if dazed. Snarling, it jumped at him again, falling back a second time. "You bound me!" it raged, melting from one form to another in a grotesque kaleidoscope of shapes. It looked to the floor and the circle Nick had made of his own blood. "You don't have the knowledge to call me from the ever-after!" it shouted.

Hunched over the book, Nick licked his lips. "No. But I can bind you in a circle once you're here." He sounded hesitant, as if he wasn't sure.

As Jenks stood on my outstretched palm and sifted pixy dust onto my ravaged wrist, the thing hammered against the unseen barrier. Smoke curled from the floor where its feet touched the cement. "Not again!" it raged. "Let me out!"

Nick swallowed hard and strode past the blood and fallen books to me. "My God, Rachel," he said as the book dropped to the floor with the sound of tearing pages. Jenks was dabbing at the blood on my face, singing a fast-paced lullaby about dew and moonbeams.

I looked from the broken book on the floor to Nick. "Nick?" I quavered, riveted to his silhouette against the ugly fluorescent lights. "I can't move." Panic washed through me. "I can't move, Nick! I think it paralyzed me!"

"No. No," he said, glancing at the dog. Settling himself

behind me, he pulled me up to sit slumped against him. "It's the vampire saliva. It will wear off."

Cradled in his arms and half in his lap, I felt myself start to go cold. Numb, I gazed up at him. His brown eyes were pinched. His jaw was clenched in worry. The blood ran from his scalp, making a slow rivulet down his face to soak his shirt. His hands were red and sticky, but his arms around me were warm. I started to shiver.

"Nick?" I quavered. My attention followed his to the thing. It was a dog again. It stood there, staring at us. Saliva dripped from it. Its muscles quivered. "Is that a vampire?"

"No," he said tersely. "It's a demon, but if it's strong enough, it has the abilities of whatever form it assumes. You'll be able to move in a minute." His long face screwed up in distress as he looked at the blood splattered about the room. "You're going to be all right." Still keeping me in the cradle of his lap, he used my silver knife to rip the bottom of his shirt. "You're going to be all right," he whispered as he tied the rag around my wrist and set it gently in my lap. I moaned at the unexpected bliss that rose from my wrist at the rough movement.

"Nick?" There were black sparkles between me and the lights. It was fascinating. "There aren't any more demons. There hasn't been a demon attack since the Turn."

"I took three years of Demonology as a Second Language to help me with my Latin," he said, stretching to reach my bag as Jenks tugged it out from the wreck of the table. "That thing is a demon." Keeping my head in his lap, he clattered through my things. "Do you have anything for pain in here?"

"No," I said dreamily. "I like pain." Face going slack, Nick's gaze shot to mine and then to Jenks's. "No one takes demonology," I protested weakly, wanting to giggle. "It's, like, the most useless thing in the world." My gaze drifted to the cabinet. The doors were still shut, but the panels had been broken by Nick's hammering and me being thrown into it. Beyond the splintered wood was an empty spot the size of the book on the floor beside me. *So that's what they hide in a locked cabinet, in a locked room, behind a locked door, in the basement of a government building.* I squinted at Nick. "You know how to call demons?" I questioned. God help me, but I felt good. All light and airy. "You're a black practitioner. I arrest people like you," I said, trying to run a finger down his jawline.

"Not exactly." Nick took my hand and set it down. Shaking the cuff of his sweatshirt past his hand, he used it to brush the blood from my face. "Don't try to talk, Rachel. You lost a lot of blood." He turned to Jenks, his eyes frightened. "I can't take her on the bus like this!"

Jenks's face looked pained. "I'll get Ivy." He dropped to my shoulder and whispered, "Hold on, Rache. I'll be right back." He flitted to Nick, the breeze from his wings sending more waves of euphoria through me. I closed my eyes and rode it, hoping it would never end.

"If you let her die here, I'll kill you myself," Jenks threatened, and Nick nodded. Jenks left with the sound of a thousand bees. The sound echoed in my head even after he was gone.

"It can't get out?" I asked, opening my eyes as my emotions swung from one extreme to the other and tears welled.

Nick shoved the big book of demon spells in my bag. His bloody handprints were all over both of them. "No. And when the sun rises, poof, it's gone. You're safe. Hush." He tucked my knife in my bag and stretched for my coat.

"We're in a basement," I protested. "There's no sun down here."

Nick ripped the lining from my coat and pressed it against my neck. I cried out as a pulse of ecstasy shot through me from the lingering effects of the vampire saliva. The bleeding had slowed, and I wondered if it was from Jenks's pixy dust. Apparently it could do more than make people itch.

"It's not sunlight that pulls a demon back to the ever-after," Nick said, clearly thinking he had hurt me. "It's something about gamma rays or protons. . . . Damn it, Rachel. Stop asking me so many questions. It was taught as an aid to understand language development, not to learn how to control demons."

The demon was Ivy again, and I shuddered as it licked its red lips with a bloodstained tongue, taunting me. "What grade did you get, Nick?" I asked. "Please tell me it was an A."

"Uh . . ." he stammered as he covered me with my coat. Looking frantic, he gathered me up in his arms, almost rocking me. My breath hissed in as my wrist throbbed in time with the pulses from my neck. "Easy," he shushed. "You'll be all right."

"Are you sure?" came a cultured voice from the corner.

Nick's head came up. Cradled in Nick's arms, I stared at the demon. It was back to wearing a gentleman's frock. "Let me out. I can help you," the demon said, all congeniality.

Nick hesitated. "Nick?" I said, suddenly frightened. "Don't listen to it. Don't!"

The demon smiled over its smoked glasses, showing flat, even teeth. "Break the circle and I'll take you to her Ivy. Otherwise . . ." The demon's brow furrowed as if it was worried. "It almost looks as if there's more blood outside of her than in."

Nick's gaze darted over the blood splattered on the walls and books. His grip on me tightened. "You were trying to kill her," he said, his voice cracking.

It shrugged. "I was compelled to. By binding me in your circle, you rubbed out the one that was used to summon me. With it went any compulsion to do his bidding. I'm all yours, little wizard." It grinned, and my breath came in a quick, fear-laced pant.

"Nicky . . ." I whispered as my blood-loss induced stupor was stripped away. This was bad. I knew this was bad. The remembered terror as it savaged me rose high. My pulse faltered as my heart tried to beat faster.

"Can you get us back to her church?" Nick asked.

"The one by the small ley line?" The demon's outline wavered as its expression turned startled. "Someone closed a circle with it six nights ago. The ripple it sent through the ever-after shook the cups on my saucers, so to speak." It tilted its head in speculation. "That was you?"

"No," Nick said weakly.

I felt ill. I had used too much salt. God help me. I didn't know demons could sense it when I drew on a ley line. If I lived through this, I'd never use them again.

The demon gazed at me. "I can take you there," it said. "But in return I want no compulsion put on me to return to the ever-after."

Nick's grip tightened. "You want me to let you loose in Cincinnati for the entire night?"

A power-filled smile edged over the demon. It exhaled slowly, and I heard the joints in its shoulder crack. "I mean to kill the one who summoned me. Then I'll leave. It smells over here." It looked over its smoked glasses, shocking me with its alien eyes. "You won't ever call me—will you, little wizard? I could teach you so much that you want to know."

Fear fought with the pain in my shoulder as Nick hesitated before shaking his head.

"You won't hurt us," Nick said. "Mentally, physically, or emotionally. You will take the most direct path and do nothing to endanger us afterward."

"Nick Nicky," the demon pouted. "One might think you didn't trust me. I can even get you there before her Ivy leaves if I take you through a ley line. But you'd better hurry. Rachel Mariana Morgan seems to be failing fast."

Through the ever-after? I thought in panic. *No!* That's what had killed my dad.

Nick swallowed, his Adam's apple bobbing. "No!" I tried to shout, squirming to get out of his grip. The stupor from its saliva was almost gone, and with the return of movement came pain. I welcomed the hurt, knowing the pleasure had been a lie. Nick was white-faced as he tried to keep me unmoving and hold the lining of my coat against my neck.

"Rachel," he whispered. "You've lost so much blood. I don't know what to do!"

My throat was too parched to swallow. "Don't—Don't let it out," I insisted. "Please," I pleaded as I pushed his hands off of me. "I'm fine. The bleeding has stopped. I'll be all right. Leave me here. Go call Ivy. She'll pick us up. I don't want to go through the ever-after."

The demon's brow furrowed as if it was concerned. "Mmmm," he mused gently, touching the lace at his throat. "Sounds like she's going incoherent. Not good. Tick-tock, Nick Nicky. Better decide quick."

Nick's breath hissed in and he tensed. His gaze roved over the pool of blood on the floor and then me. "I've got to do something," he whispered. "You're so cold, Rachel."

"Nick, no!" I shouted as he set me on the floor and lurched into a stand. Reaching out with a foot, he smeared the line of blood.

I heard a frightened wail. I covered my mouth as I realized it was coming from me. Terror pulsed through me as the demon shuddered. It slowly stepped across the line. It ran a hand across the bloodstained wall and licked its finger, never taking its eyes off of me.

"Don't let it touch me!" My voice was high-pitched. I could hear the hysteria in it.

"Rachel," Nick soothed as he knelt beside me. "It said it won't hurt you. Demons don't lie. It was in every text I copied."

"They don't tell the truth, either!" I exclaimed.

Ire flickered behind the demon's eyes, smothered in a wave of false concern for me before Nick could see. It came forward, and I struggled to push myself back. "Don't let it touch me!" I cried. "Don't make me do this!"

The fear in Nick's eyes was for how I was acting, not from the demon. He didn't understand. He thought he knew what he was doing. He thought his books had all the answers. He didn't know what he was doing. I did.

Nick gripped my shoulder and turned to the demon. "Can you help her?" he asked it. "She's going to kill herself."

"Nick, no!" I shrieked as the demon knelt to put its grinning face next to mine.

"Sleep, Rachel Mariana Morgan," it breathed, and I remembered no more.

Twenty-six

"**W**hat happened? Where is Jenks?" Ivy's voice penetrated my daze, close and worried. I could feel myself moving forward in a rocking motion. I had been warm, and now I was cold again. The smell of blood was thick. The memory of something more foul lingered in me: carrion, salt, and burnt amber. I couldn't open my eyes.

"She was attacked by a demon." It was terse and soft. Nick.

That's right, I thought, starting to piece everything together. I was in his arms. That's what that one good smell was, all masculine and sweaty. And that was his bloody sweatshirt pushing against my swollen eye, rubbing it even more sore. I started to shiver. Why was I cold?

"Can we get off the street?" Nick asked. "She's lost a lot of blood."

There was a warm touch on my forehead. "A demon did this?" Ivy said. "There hasn't been a demon attack since the Turn. Damn it, I knew I shouldn't have let her off the grounds."

The arms about me tensed. My weight shifted forward and back as he stopped. "Rachel knows what she's doing," Nick said tightly. "She isn't your child—in any sense of the word."

"No?" Ivy said. "She acts like one. How could you let her get mauled like this?"

"Me? You cold-blooded vamp!" Nick shouted. "You think I let this happen?"

My stomach clenched in a wave of nausea, and I tried to pull my coat over me with my good hand. I cracked my eyes, squinting in the glow of the streetlight. Couldn't they finish their argument after they put me to bed?

"Ivy," Nick said slowly. "I'm not afraid of you, so save the aura crap and back off. I know what you're up to, and I won't let you do it."

"What are you talking about?" Ivy stammered.

Nick leaned toward her, and I slumped unmoving between them. "Rachel seems to think you moved in the same day she did," he said. "She might be interested to know all your magazines are addressed to you at the church." I heard Ivy's quick intake of breath, and he added in an intent voice, "How long have you been living here waiting for Rachel to quit? A month? A year? Are you hunting her slow, Tamwood? Hoping to making her your scion when you die? Doing a little long-term planning, are we? Is that it?"

I struggled to turn my head from Nick's chest so I could hear better. I tried to think, but I was so confused. Ivy had moved in the same day I did, hadn't she? Her computer hadn't been hooked up to the net yet, and she had all those boxes in her room. How come her magazines had the church's address on them? My thoughts went to the perfect witch-garden out back and the spell books in the attic complete with alibi. God save me, I was a fool.

"No," Ivy said softly. "This isn't what it looks like. Please don't tell her. I can explain."

Nick lurched into motion, jostling me as he went up the stone stairs. My memory was returning. Nick had made a deal with the demon. Nick had let it out. It had made me go to sleep. It had made me go through the ley lines. Damn. The slam of the sanctuary door jolted me, and I moaned at the pulse of pain.

"She's coming around," Ivy said tersely, her voice echoing. "Put her in the living room."

Not the couch, I thought as the peaceful feeling of the sanctuary infused me. I didn't want to get my blood all over Ivy's couch, but then I decided it had probably seen blood before.

My stomach dropped as Nick crouched. I felt the gentle give of the cushions beneath my head. My breath hissed as Nick pulled his arms out from under me. There was the click of the table lamp, and I puckered my face at the sudden warmth and glare through my closed eyelids.

"Rachel?"

It was close, and someone gently touched my face.

"Rachel." The room got quiet. It was the hush that really woke me up. I opened my eyes, squinting to see Nick kneeling beside me. Blood still seeped from under his hairline, and a dried rivulet of it flaked from his jawline and neck. His hair was mussed and disheveled, and his brown eyes were pinched. He was a mess. Ivy was behind him, close in worry.

"It's you," I whispered, feeling light-headed and unreal. Nick leaned back with a relieved puff. "Can I have some water?" I rasped. "I don't feel so good."

Ivy leaned forward to eclipse the light. Her eyes rove over me with a professional detachment that cracked when she lifted the edge of Nick's makeshift bandage on my neck. Her eyes went puzzled. "It's almost stopped bleeding."

"Love, trust, and pixy dust," I slurred, and Ivy nodded.

Nick got to his feet. "I'll call an ambulance."

"No!" I exclaimed. I tried to sit up, forced back by fatigue and Nick's hands. "I'll get tagged there. The I.S. knows I'm alive." I fell back panting. The bruise on my face where the demon hit me pulsed in time with my heart. A twin throb came from my arm. I was dizzy. My shoulder hurt when I inhaled, and the room darkened when I exhaled.

"Jenks dusted her," Ivy said, as if that explained everything. "As long as she doesn't start bleeding again, she probably won't get any worse. I'll get a blanket." She rose with that eerie, fast grace of hers. She was going vampy, and I was in no condition to do anything about it.

I looked at Nick as she left. He seemed ill. The demon had tricked him. We had gotten home as promised, but now a demon was loose in Cincinnati when all Nick had needed to do was wait for Jenks and Ivy.

"Nick?" I breathed.

"What? What can I do?" His voice was worried and soft, tinged with guilt.

"You're an ass. Help me sit up."

He winced. With hands hesitant and cautious, he helped me inch my way up until my back was against the arm of the couch. I sat and stared at the ceiling while the black spots danced and quivered until they went away. Taking a slow breath, I looked at myself.

Blood splattered my dress where it showed past my coat draped over me like a blanket. Maybe now I could throw it away. A brown film of blood had stuck my nylons to my feet. My arm with the bite looked gray where it wasn't streaked with sticky blood. The hem of Nick's shirt was still tied around my wrist, and blood dripped wetly from it with the speed of a dripping faucet: plink, plink, plink. Maybe Jenks had run out of dust before he got to it. My other arm was swollen, and my shoulder felt like it was broken. The room got too cold, then hot. I stared at Nick, feeling myself go distant and unreal.

"Oh, shit," he muttered, glancing at the hallway. "You're going to pass out again." He grasped my ankles and slowly pulled me down until my head was supported by the arm of the couch. "Ivy!" he shouted. "Where's that blanket?"

I stared at the ceiling until it stopped spinning. Nick stood hunched in a corner with his back to me, one hand clenched about his middle, the other holding his head. "Thanks," I whispered, and he turned.

"What for?" His voice was bitter, and he looked ragged with dried blood on his face. His hands were black with it, the lines on his palms showing a stark white.

"For doing what you thought was best." I shivered under my coat.

He smiled sickly, his pale face going longer. "There was so much blood. I guess I panicked. Sorry." His gaze went to the hallway, and I wasn't surprised when Ivy strode in with a blanket over one arm, a stack of pink towels under the other, and a pan of water in her hands.

Unease overwhelmed my pain. I was still bleeding. "Ivy?" I quavered.

"What?" she snapped as she set the towels and water on the coffee table and tucked the blanket around me as if I was a child.

I swallowed hard, trying to get a good look at her eyes. "Nothing," I said meekly as she straightened and backed away. Apart from being paler than usual, she looked okay. I didn't think I could handle it if she vamped out on me. I was helpless.

The blanket was warm about my chin, and the light from the lamp piercing. I shivered as she sat on the coffee table and pulled the water closer. I wondered at the color of the towels until I realized pink didn't show old bloodstains.

"Ivy?" My voice edged into panic as she reached for the cloth pressed against my neck.

Her hand dropped, her perfect face going angry and insulted. "Don't be stupid, Rachel. Let me look at your neck."

She reached out again, and I shirked back. "No!" I cried as I jerked away. The demon's face flashed before me, mirroring hers. I hadn't been able to fight it. It almost killed me. Remembered terror soared high, and I found the strength to sit up. The pain in my neck seemed to cry out for release, for a return to that exquisite mix of pain and craving the vamp saliva had offered. It shocked and frightened me. Ivy's pupils swelled until her eyes went black.

Nick stepped between us, covered in drying blood and smelling of spent fear. "Back off, Tamwood," he threatened. "You're not touching her if you're pulling an aura."

"Relax, rat boy," Ivy exclaimed. "I'm not pulling an aura, I'm as mad as all hell. And I wouldn't bite Rachel right now even if she begged me. She stinks of infection."

That was more than I wanted to know. But her eyes were back to her normal brown as she wavered between anger and the need to be understood. I felt a flush of guilt. Ivy hadn't pinned me to the wall and bit me. Ivy hadn't taunted me, driving her teeth into me. Ivy hadn't sucked at my neck, moaning in pleasure as she held me down while I struggled. Damn it. It. Hadn't. Been. Her.

Still, Nick stood between us. "It's all right, Nick," I said, my voice trembling. He knew why I was afraid. "It's all right." I looked past him to Ivy. "I'm sorry. Please—look at it?"

Immediately Ivy seemed to lose her tension. She scooted closer with a quick, vindicated motion as Nick stepped out of the way. I let out my held breath as she gently worked at the soggy fabric. "Okay," Ivy warned. "This may tug a little."

"Ouch!" I cried as it pulled when she lifted, then I bit my lip to keep from doing it again. Ivy set the ugly wad on the table beside her. My stomach twisted. It was black with moist blood, and I swear there were bits of flesh sticking to the inside of it. I shivered at the cold feel of air on my neck. There was the shivery sensation of a slow flow of blood.

Ivy saw my face. "Get that out of here, will you?" she murmured, and Nick left with the soggy wad.

Face blank, Ivy put a hand towel across my shoulder to catch the renewed oozing. I stared at the black TV as she soaked a washcloth and rung it out over the pan of water. Her touch was gentle as she began to dab at the outskirts of the damage and worked her way in. Still, I couldn't help my occasional jerk. The threatened rim of black around my vision began to grow.

"Rachel?" Her voice was soft, and my attention darted to her, worried at what I would find. But her face was carefully neutral as her eyes and fingers probed the bite marks on my neck. "What happened?" she asked. "Nick said something about a demon, but this looks like—"

"It looks like a vampire bite," I finished blandly. "It made itself look like a vampire and did that to me." I took a shaky breath. "It made itself look like you, Ivy. I'm sorry if I'm a little flaky for a while. I know it wasn't you. Just give me some slack until I can convince my unconscious you didn't try to kill me, okay?"

I met her eyes, feeling a pulse of shared fear as understanding flashed over her. For all accounts, I had been ravaged by a vampire. I had been initiated into a club that Ivy was trying to stay out of. Now we both were. I thought about what Nick had said concerning her wanting to make me her scion. I didn't know what to believe.

"Rachel, I—"

"Later," I said as Nick came back in. I felt ill, and the room was starting to go gray again. Matalina was with him along with two of her children lugging a pixy-sized bag. Nick knelt at my head. Hovering in the center of the room, Matalina silently took in the situation, then took the bag from her children and bundled them to the window. "Hush, hush," I heard her whisper. "Go home. I know what I said, but I changed my mind." Their protests carried a horrified fascination, and I wondered how bad I looked.

"Rachel?" Matalina hovered right in front of me, moving back and forth until she found where my eyes were focusing. The room had gone alarmingly quiet, and I shivered. Matalina was such a pretty little thing. No wonder Jenks would do anything for her. "Try not to move, dear," she said.

A soft whir from the window pulled her up out of my sight. "Jenks," the small pixy woman said in relief. "Where have you been?"

"Me?" He dropped into my line of sight. "How did you get here before me?"

"We took a direct bus," Nick said sarcastically.

Jenks's face was weary and his shoulders were slumped. I felt a smile curve over me. "Is pretty pixy man too pooped to party?" I breathed, and he came so close I had to squint.

"Ivy, you gotta do something," he said, his eyes wide and worried. "I dusted her bites to slow the bleeding, but I've never seen anyone that was this white before and still alive."

"I am doing something," she growled. "Get out of my way."

I felt the air shift as Matalina and Ivy bent close over me. I found the idea of a pixy and a vamp inspecting the bloody mess of my neck reassuring. Since infection was a turnoff, I ought to be safe. Ivy would know if it was life-threatening or not. *And Nick,* I thought, feeling a faint need to giggle. *Nick would rescue me if Ivy lost control.*

Ivy's fingers touched my neck and I yelped. She jerked back, and Matalina took to the air. "Rachel," Ivy said worriedly. "I can't fix this. Pixy dust will hold you together for only so long. You need to be stitched. We have to get you to Emergency."

"No hospital," I said with a sigh. I had stopped shivering, and my stomach felt all funny. "Runners go in, but they don't come out." I gave in to my desire to giggle.

"You would rather die on my couch?" Ivy said, and Nick began to pace behind her.

"What is wrong with her?" Jenks whispered loudly.

Ivy stood up and crossed her arms to look severe and pissy. A pissy vampire. Yeah, that was funny enough to laugh at, and I giggled again.

"It's the blood loss," Ivy said impatiently. "She's going to yo-yo between lucidity and irrationality until she stabilizes or passes out. I hate this part."

My good hand crept up to my neck, and Nick forced it back under the blanket.

"I can't fix this, Rachel!" Ivy exclaimed in frustration. "There's too much damage."

"I'll make something," I said firmly. "I'm a witch." I leaned to roll off the couch and get to my feet. I had to go to the kitchen. I had to cook dinner. I had to cook dinner for Ivy.

"Rachel!" Nick shouted, trying to catch me. Ivy leapt forward, easing me into the cushions. I felt myself go white. The room spun. Wide-eyed, I stared at the ceiling, willing myself not to pass out. If I did, Ivy would take me to Emergency.

Matalina drifted within my sight. "Angel," I whispered. "Beautiful angel."

"Ivy!" Jenks shouted, fear in his voice. "She's getting delusional."

The pixy angel smiled a blessing on me. "Someone should go get Keasley," she said.

"The old lunker—uh—witch across the street?" Jenks said.

Matalina nodded. "Tell him Rachel needs medical help."

Ivy, too, seemed bewildered. "You think he can do something?" she asked, the edge of fear in her voice. Ivy was afraid for me. Maybe I should have been afraid for me, too.

Matalina flushed. "He asked—the other day—if he might have a few cuttings from the garden. There's no harm in that." The pretty pixy fussed with her dress, her eyes downcast. "They were all plants with strong properties. Yarrow, vervain, that sort. I thought perhaps if he wanted them, he might know what to do with them."

"Woman . . ." Jenks said warningly.

"I stayed with him the entire time," she said, her eyes defiant. "He didn't touch but what I said he could. He was very proper. Asked after everyone's health."

"Matalina, it's not our garden," Jenks said, and the angel grew angry.

"If you won't get him, I will," she said sharply, and she darted out the window. I blinked, staring at the spot where she had been.

"Matalina!" Jenks shouted. "Don't you fly from me. That's not our garden. You can't treat it as if it was." He dropped into my line of sight. "I'm sorry," he said, clearly embarrassed and angry. "She won't do it again." His face hardened, and he darted out after her. "Matalina!"

" 'S okay," I whispered, though neither of them were there anymore. "I say it's okay. The angel can ask anyone she wants into the garden." I closed my eyes. Nick put a hand on my head, and I smiled. "Hi, Nick," I said softly, opening my eyes. "Are you still here?"

"Yes, I'm still here."

"Good," I said. " 'Cause when I can stand up, I'm going to give you a bi-i-i-g kiss."

Nick's hand fell from me and he took a step back.

Ivy grimaced. "I hate this part," she muttered. "I hate it. I hate it."

My hand crept up to my neck, and Nick forced it back down. I could hear the faucet dripping again on the carpet: plink, plink, plink. The room began to revolve majestically, and I watched it spin, fascinated. It was funny, and I tried to laugh.

Ivy made a frustrated sound. "If she's giggling, she's going to be all right," she said. "Why don't you take a shower?"

"I'm okay," he said. "I'll wait until I know for sure."

Ivy was silent for three heartbeats. "Nick," she said, her voice thick with warning. "Rachel stinks of infection. You stink of blood and fear. Go take a shower."

"Oh." There was a long hesitation. "Sorry."

I smiled up at Nick as he edged to the door. "Go wash, Nick Nicky," I said. "Don't make Ivy go all black and scary. Take as long as you want. There's soap in the dish, and . . ." I hesitated, trying to remember what I was saying. ". . . and towels on the dryer," I finished, proud of myself.

He touched my shoulder, his eyes flicking from me to Ivy. "You should be all right."

Ivy crossed her arms before her, impatiently waiting for him to leave. I heard the shower go on. It made me a hundred times more thirsty. Somewhere, I could feel my arm pounding and my ribs throbbing. My neck and shoulder were one solid ache. I turned to watch the curtain move in the breeze, fascinated.

A loud boom from the front of the church pulled my attention to the black hallway. "Hello?" came Keasley's distant voice. "Ms. Morgan? Matalina said I could walk in."

Ivy's lips pursed. "Stay here," she said, bending over me until I had no choice but to look at her. "Don't get up until I get back, okay? Rachel? Do you hear me? *Don't get up.*"

"Sure." My gaze drifted past her to the curtain. If I squinted ju-u-u-u-ust right, the gray shifted to black. "Stay here."

Giving me a last look, she gathered up all her magazines and left. The sound of the shower drew me. I licked my lips. I wondered, if I tried really hard, could I reach the sink in the kitchen?

Twenty-seven

There was the rattle of a paper bag in the hallway, and I tilted my head up from the arm of the couch. The room held steady this time, and a fog seemed to lift from me. Keasley's hunched figure came in, Ivy close behind. "Oh, good," I whispered breathlessly. "Company."

Ivy pushed past Keasley and sat on the end of the chair nearest me. "You look better," she said. "Are you back yet or still in la-la land?"

"What?"

She shook her head, and I gave Keasley a wan smile. "Sorry I can't offer you a chocolate."

"Ms. Morgan." His gaze lingered on my exposed neck. "Have an argument with your roommate?" he said dryly as he ran a hand over his tightly curled black hair.

"No," I said hurriedly as Ivy stiffened.

He arched his eyebrows in disbelief and set his paper bag on the coffee table. "Matalina didn't say what I needed, so I brought a little of everything." He squinted at the table lamp. "Do you have anything brighter than that?"

"I've got a clip-on fluorescent." Ivy slipped to the hall and hesitated. "Don't let her move or she'll go incoherent again."

I opened my mouth to say something, but she vanished, to be replaced by Matalina and Jenks. Jenks looked positively incensed, but Matalina was unrepentant. They hovered in the corner, their conversation so fast and high-pitched I couldn't follow it. Finally Jenks left, looking like he was going to murder a pea pod. Matalina adjusted her flowing white dress and flitted to the arm of the couch beside my head.

Keasley sat down on the coffee table with a weary sigh. His three-day-old beard was going white. It made him look like a vagrant. The knees of his overalls were stained with wet earth, and I could smell the outside on him. His dark-skinned hands, though, were raw from an obvious scrubbing. He pulled a newspaper out from his bag and spread it open like a tablecloth. "So who's that in the shower? Your mother?"

I snorted, feeling the tightness of my swollen eye. "His name is Nick," I said as Ivy appeared. "He's a friend."

Ivy made a rude sound as she attached a small light to the shade of the table lamp and plugged it in. I winced, squinting as heat and light poured out.

"Nick, eh?" Keasley said as he dug in his bag, laying amulets, foil-wrapped packages, and bottles onto the newsprint. "A vamp, is he?"

"No, he's a human," I said, and Keasley peered mistrustingly at Ivy.

Not seeing his look, Ivy crowded close. "Her neck is the worst. She's lost a dangerous amount of blood—"

"I can tell." The old man stared belligerently at Ivy until she backed up. "I need more towels, and why don't you get Rachel something to drink? She needs to replace her fluids."

"I know that," Ivy said, taking a faltering step backward before turning to go into the kitchen. There was the clatter of a glass and the welcoming sound of liquid. Matalina opened her repair kit and silently compared her needles to Keasley's.

"Something warm?" Keasley reiterated loudly, and Ivy

slammed the freezer door shut. "Let's take a look," he said as he aimed the light at me. He and Matalina were silent for a long time. Easing back, Keasley let his breath slip from him. "Perhaps something to dull that pain, first," he said softly, reaching for an amulet.

Ivy appeared in the archway. "Where did you get those spells?" she said suspiciously.

"Relax," he said with a distant voice as he inspected each disk carefully. "I bought these months ago. Make yourself useful and boil up a pan of water."

She snuffed and spun about, storming back into the kitchen. I heard a series of clicks followed by the whoosh of the gas igniting. The taps ran full force as she filled a pan, and a faint yelp of surprise came from my bathroom.

Keasley had bloodied his finger and invoked the spell before I realized it. The amulet settled around my neck, and after looking me square in the eye to gauge its effectiveness, he turned his attention to my neck. "I really appreciate this," I said as the first fingers of relief eased into my body and my shoulders drooped. Salvation.

"I'd hold off on the thanks till you get my bill," Keasley murmured. I frowned at the old joke, and he smiled, crinkling the folds around his eyes. Resettling himself, he prodded my skin. The pain broke through the spell, and I took a sharp breath. "Still hurt?" he asked needlessly.

"Why don't you just put her out?" Ivy asked.

I started. Damn it, I hadn't even heard her come in. "No," I said sharply. I didn't want Ivy convincing him to take me to Emergency.

"It wouldn't hurt, then," Ivy said, standing belligerently in her leather and silk. "Why do you have to do things the hard way?"

"I'm not doing things the hard way, I just don't want to be put out," I argued. My vision darkened, and I concentrated on breathing before I put myself out.

"Ladies," Keasley murmured into the tension. "I agree sedating Rachel would be easier, especially on her, but I'm not going to force it."

"Thanks," I said listlessly.

"A few more pans of water, perhaps, Ivy?" Keasley asked. "And those towels?"

The microwave dinged, and Ivy spun away. What bee had stung her bonnet? I wondered.

Keasley invoked a second amulet and settled it next to the first. It was another pain charm, and I slumped into the double relief and closed my eyes. They flashed open as Ivy set a mug of hot chocolate on the coffee table, closely followed by a stack of more pink towels. With a misplaced frustration, she returned to the kitchen to slam about under the counter.

From under the blanket, I slowly pulled out the arm the demon had struck. The swelling had gone down, and a small knot of worry loosened. It wasn't broken. I wiggled my fingers, and Keasley put the hot chocolate into my grip. The mug was comfortingly warm, and the hot chocolate slid down my throat with a protective feeling.

While I sipped my drink, Keasley packed the towels around my right shoulder. Taking a squeeze bottle from his bag, he washed the last of the blood from my neck, soaking the towels. His brown eyes intent, he began to probe the tissue. "Ow!" I yelped, nearly spilling my hot chocolate as I jerked away. "Do you really need to do that?"

Keasley grunted and put a third amulet around my neck. "Better?" he asked. My sight had blurred at the strength of the spell. I wondered where he got such a strong charm, then remembered he had arthritis. It took one heck of a strong spell to touch pain like that, and I felt guilty that he was using his medicinal charm on me. This time I only felt a dull pressure as he poked and prodded, and I nodded. "How long since you were bit?" he asked.

"Um," I murmured, fighting off the drowsy state the amulet was instilling. "Sunset?"

"It's what, just after nine now?" he said, glancing at the clock on the disc player. "Good. We can stitch you all the way up." Settling himself, he took on the air of an instructor, beckoning Matalina close. "Look here," he said to the pixy woman. "See how the tissue has been sliced rather than torn? I'd rather stitch up a vamp bite than a Were bite any day. Not only is it cleaner, but you don't have to de-enzyme it."

Matalina drifted closer. "Thorn spears leave cuts like this, but I've never been able to find anything to hold the muscle in place while the ends reattach."

Blanching, I gulped my hot chocolate, wishing they would stop talking as if I was a science experiment or slab of meat for the grill.

"I use vet-grade dissolvable sutures, myself," Keasley said.

"Vet-grade?" I said, startled.

"No one keeps track of animal clinics," he said absently. "But I've heard the vein that runs the stem of a bay leaf is strong enough for fairies and pixies. I wouldn't use anything but catgut for the wing muscles, though. Want some?" He dug in his bag and put several small paper envelopes on the table. "Consider it payment for those slips of plants."

Matalina's wings colored a delicate rose. "Those weren't my plants to give."

"Yes, they were," I interrupted. "I'm getting fifty taken off my rent for keeping up the garden. I guess that makes it mine. But you're the ones tending it. I say that makes it yours."

Keasley looked up from my neck. A shocked stare came over Matalina.

"Consider it Jenks's income," I added. "That is, if you think he might want to sublet the garden as his pay."

For a moment there was silence. "I think he might like that," Matalina whispered. She shifted the small envelopes to her bag. Leaving them, she darted to the window and back again, clearly torn. Her fluster at my offer was obvious. Wondering if I had done something wrong, I looked over Keasley's paraphernalia laid out on the newspaper.

"Are you a doctor?" I asked, setting my empty mug down with a thump. I had to remember to get the recipe for this spell. I couldn't feel a thing—anywhere.

"No." He wadded up the water and blood-soaked towels, throwing them to the floor.

"Then where did you get all this stuff?" I prodded.

"I don't like hospitals," he said shortly. "Matalina? Why don't I do the interior stitching and you close the skin? I'm sure your work is more even than mine." He smiled ruefully. "I'd wager Rachel would appreciate the smaller scar."

"It helps to be an inch from the wound," Matalina said, clearly pleased to have been asked.

Keasley swabbed my neck with a cold gel. I studied the ceiling as he took a pair of scissors and trimmed what I assumed were ragged edges. Making a satisfied noise, he chose a needle and thread. There was a pressure on my neck followed by a tug, and I took a deep breath. My eyes flicked to Ivy as she came in and bent close over me, almost blocking Keasley's light.

"What about that one?" she said, pointing. "Shouldn't you stitch that first?" she said. "It's bleeding the most."

"No," he said, making another stitch. "Get another pot of water boiling, will you?"

"Four pots of water?" she questioned.

"If you would," he drawled. Keasley continued stitching, and I counted the tugs, my gaze on the clock. The chocolate wasn't sitting as well as I would have liked. I hadn't been stitched since my ex–best friend had hidden in my school locker pretending to be a werefox. The day had ended with us both being expelled.

Ivy hesitated, then scooped up the wet towels and took them into the kitchen. The water ran, and another cry followed by a muffled thump came from my shower. "Will you stop doing that!" came an annoyed shout, and I couldn't help my smirk. All too soon Ivy was back peering over Keasley's shoulder.

"That stitch doesn't look tight," she said.

I shifted uncomfortably as Keasley's wrinkled brow furrowed. I liked him, and Ivy was being a bloody nuisance. "Ivy," he murmured, "why don't you do a perimeter check?"

"Jenks is outside. We're fine."

Keasley's jaw clenched, the folds of skin on his jaw bunching. He slowly pulled the green thread tight, his eyes on his work. "He might need help," he said.

Ivy straightened with her arms crossed and black hazing her eyes. "I doubt that."

Matalina's wings blurred to nothing as Ivy bent close, blocking Keasley's light.

"Go away," Keasley said softly, not moving. "You're hovering."

Ivy pulled back, her mouth opening in what looked like shock. Her wide eyes went to mine, and I smiled in an apologetic agreement. Stiffening, she spun round. Her boots clacked on the wood floor in the hallway and into the sanctuary. I winced as the loud boom of the front door reverberated through the church.

"Sorry," I said, feeling someone ought to apologize.

Keasley stretched his back painfully. "She's worried about you and doesn't know how to show it without biting you. Either that or she doesn't like being out of control."

"She's not the only one," I said. "I'm starting to feel like a failure."

"Failure?" he breathed. "How do you stir that?"

"Look at me," I said sharply. "I'm a wreck. I've lost so much blood I can't stand up. I haven't done anything by myself since I left the I.S. except get caught by Trent and made into rat chow." I didn't feel much like a runner anymore. *Dad would be disappointed*, I thought. I should have stayed where I was, safe, secure, and bored out of my mind.

"You're alive," Keasley said. "That's no easy trick while

under an I.S. death threat." He adjusted the lamp until it shone right in my face. I closed my eyes, starting as he dabbed a cold pad at my swollen eyelid. Matalina took over stitching my neck, her tiny tugs almost unnoticed. She ignored us with the practiced restraint of a professional mother.

"I'd be dead twice over if it wasn't for Nick," I said, looking toward the unseen shower.

Keasley aimed the lamp at my ear. I jerked as he dabbed at it with a soft square of damp cotton. It came away black with old blood. "You would have escaped Kalamack eventually," he said. "Instead, you took a chance and got Nick out as well. I don't see the failure in that."

I squinted at him with my unswollen eye. "How do you know about the rat fight?"

"Jenks told me on the way over."

Satisfied, I winced as Keasley dabbed a foul-smelling liquid on my torn ear. It throbbed dully under the three pain amulets. "I can't do anything more about this," he said. "Sorry."

I had all but forgotten about my ear. Matalina flitted up to eye level, her gaze shifting from Keasley to me. "All done," she said in her china-doll voice. "If you can finish up all right, I would like to, um . . ." Her eyes were charmingly eager. An angel with glad tidings. "I want to tell Jenks about your offer to sublet the garden."

Keasley nodded. "You go right ahead," he said. "There's not much left but her wrist."

"Thanks, Matalina," I offered. "I didn't feel a thing."

"You're welcome." The tiny pixy woman darted to the window, then returned. "Thank you," she whispered before vanishing through the window and into the dark garden.

The living room was empty but for Keasley and me. It was so quiet, I could hear the lids popping on the pots of water in the kitchen. Keasley took the scissors and cut the soaked cotton off my wrist. It fell away, and my stomach roiled. My wrist was still there, but nothing was in the right place. No wonder Jenks's pixy dust couldn't stop it from bleeding. Chunks of white flesh were lumped into mounds, and little craters were filled with blood. If my wrist looked like that, what had my neck looked like? Closing my eyes, I concentrated on breathing. I was going to pass out. I knew it.

"You've made a strong ally there," he said softly.

"Matalina?" I held my breath, trying not to hyperventilate. "I can't imagine why," I said as I exhaled. "I've continually put her husband and family at risk."

"Mmmm." He put Ivy's pan of water on his knees and gently lowered my wrist into it. I hissed at the bite of the water, then relaxed as the pain amulets dulled it. He prodded my wrist and I yelped, trying to jerk away. "You want some advice?" he asked.

"No."

"Good. Listen anyway. Looks to me like you've become the leader here. Accept it. Know it comes with a price. People will be doing things for you. Don't be selfish. Let them."

"I owe Nick and Jenks my life," I said, hating it. "What's so great about that?"

"No, you don't. Because of you, Nick no longer has to kill rats to stay alive, and Jenks's life expectancy has nearly doubled."

I pulled away, and this time he let me go. "How do you figure that?" I said suspiciously.

The resonate *tang* of the pan hitting the coffee table was sharp as Keasley set it aside. He tucked a pink towel under my wrist, and I forced myself to look at it. The tissue looked more normal. A slow welling of blood rose to hide the damage, spilling over my wet skin to flow messily onto the towel.

"You made Jenks a partner," he said as he ripped open a

gauze pad and dabbed at me. "He has more at risk than a job, he has a garden. Tonight you made it his for as long as he wants. I've never heard of leasing property to a pixy, but I would wager it will hold up in a human or Inderland court if another clan challenged it. You guaranteed that *all* his children have a place to survive until adulthood, not just the few firstborn. I think that's worth an afternoon of hide-and-seek in a room full of lunkers to him."

I watched him thread a needle and forced my eyes to the ceiling. The tugs and pinches started up with a slow rhythm. Everyone knew pixies and fairies vied with each other for a good bit of earth, but I had no idea the reasons went so deep. I thought about what Jenks had said about risking death by a bee sting for a pair of measly flower boxes. Now he had a garden. No wonder Matalina had been so matter-of-fact about the fairy attack.

Keasley fell into a pattern of two stitches, one dab. The thing wouldn't stop bleeding. I refused to watch, my eyes roving over the gray living room until they fell upon the empty end table where Ivy's magazines had once sat. I swallowed hard, feeling nauseous. "Keasley, you've lived here awhile, right?" I questioned. "When did Ivy move in?"

He looked up from his stitching, his dark, wrinkled face blank. "The same day you did. You quit the same day, didn't you?"

I caught myself before I could nod my agreement. "I can see why Jenks is risking his life to help me, but . . ." I looked at the hallway. "What is Ivy getting out of this?" I whispered.

Keasley looked at my neck in disgust. "Isn't it obvious? You let her feed off you, and she won't let the I.S. kill you."

My mouth opened in outrage. "I already told you Ivy didn't do this!" I exclaimed, my heart pounding in the effort to raise my voice. "It was a demon!"

He didn't look as surprised as I would have expected. He stared at me, waiting for more. "I left the church to get a recipe for a spell," I said softly. "The I.S. sent a demon after me. It made itself into a vampire to kill me. Nick bound it in a circle or it would have." I slumped, exhausted. My pulse hammered. I was too weak to even be angry.

"The I.S.?" Keasley cut his needle free and glanced at me from under his lowered brow. "Are you sure it was a demon? The I.S. doesn't use demons."

"They do now," I said sourly. I looked at my wrist, then quickly away. It was still bleeding, the blood oozing from between the green stitches. I reached up to find my neck at least had stopped. "It knew all three of my names, Keasley. My middle name isn't even on my birth certificate. How did the I.S. find out what it was?"

Keasley's eyes were worried as he blotted at my wrist. "Well, if it was a demon, you won't have to worry about any residual vamp ties from your bites—I'd imagine."

"Small favors," I said bitterly.

He took my wrist again, pulling the lamp closer. He cupped a towel under it to catch the still-dripping blood. "Rachel?" he murmured.

Alarm bells rang in the back of my mind. I'd always been Ms. Morgan to him. "What?"

"About the demon. Did you make a deal with it?"

I followed his gaze to my wrist and went frightened. "Nick did," I said quickly. "He agreed to let it out of the circle if it got me back here alive. It took us through the ley lines."

"Oh," he said, and I felt myself go cold at his flat tone. He knew something I didn't.

"Oh, what?" I demanded. "What's the matter?"

He took a slow breath. "This isn't going to heal on its own," he said softly, setting my wrist on my lap.

"What?" I exclaimed, holding my wrist as my stomach churned and the chocolate threatened to come back up. The shower went off, and I felt a flash of panic. What had Nick done to me?

Keasley opened a medicated adhesive bandage and applied it over my eye. "Demons don't do anything for free," he said. "You owe it a favor."

"I didn't agree to anything!" I said. "It was Nick! I told Nick not to let it out!"

"It's not anything Nick did," Keasley said as he took my bruised arm and gently prodded it until my breath hissed in. "The demon wants additional payment for taking you through the ley lines. You have a choice, though. You can pay for your passage by having your wrist drip blood the rest of your life, or you can agree to owe the demon a favor and it will heal. I'd suggest the former."

I collapsed into the cushions. "Swell." Just freaking great. I'd told Nick it was a bad idea.

Keasley pulled my wrist to him and started winding a roll of gauze bandage around it. Blood soaked it almost as quickly as it went about my wrist. "Don't let it tell you that you don't have a say in the matter," he said as he used the entire roll, fastening the end with a bit of white medical tape. "You can dicker about how to pay for your passage until you both agree on something. Years, even. Demons always give you choices. And they're patient."

"Some choice!" I barked. "Agree to owe him a favor or walk around like I've got stigmata the rest of my life?"

He shrugged as he gathered his needles, thread, and scissors on his newspaper and folded it up. "I think you did pretty well for your first run-in with a demon."

"First run-in!" I exclaimed, then lay back panting. *First? Like there was ever going to be a second.* "How do you know all this?" I whispered.

He stuffed the newspaper in the bag and rolled the top down. "You live long enough, you hear things."

"Great." I looked up as Keasley pulled the heavy-duty pain amulet from around my neck. "Hey," I objected as all my pains started back in with a dull throbbing. "I need that."

"You'll do fine with just two." He stood up and dropped my salvation into a pocket. "That way, you won't hurt yourself by trying to do anything. Leave those stitches in for about a week. Matalina can tell you when to take them out. No shape shifting, meantime." He pulled out a sling and set it on the coffee table. "Wear it," he said simply. "Your arm is bruised, not broken." He arched his white eyebrows. "Lucky you."

"Keasley, wait." I took a quick breath, trying to gather my thoughts. "What can I do for you? An hour ago I thought I was dying."

"An hour ago, you were dying." He chuckled, then shifted from foot to foot. "It's important you don't owe anyone anything, isn't it?" He hesitated. "I envy you for your friends. I'm old enough not to be afraid to say that. Friends are a luxury I haven't indulged in for a long time. If you let me trust you, consider us even."

"But that's nothing," I protested. "Do you want more plants from the garden? Or a mink potion? They're good for a few days more, and I won't be using them again."

"I wouldn't count on that," he said, glancing into the hall at the sound of my bathroom door creaking open. "And being someone I trust might be expensive. I might call in my marker someday. Are you willing to risk it?"

"Of course," I said, wondering what an old man like Keasley could be running from. It couldn't be worse than what I was facing. The door to the sanctuary boomed shut, and I straightened. Ivy was done sulking and Nick was out of the shower. They were going to be at each other again in a moment, and I was too tired to play referee. Jenks buzzed in through the window, and I closed my eyes to gather my strength. All three of them at once might kill me.

Bag in hand, Keasley shifted as if to go. "Please, don't leave yet," I pleaded. "Nick might need something. He has a nasty cut on his head."

"Rache," Jenks said as he flew circles around Keasley in greeting. "What the devil did you say to Matalina? She's flitting over the garden as if she's on Brimstone, laughing and crying all at the same time. Can't get a straight word out of the woman." He jerked to a stop, hovering in midair, listening.

"Oh, great," he muttered. "They're at it again already."

I exchanged a weary look with Keasley as the muttered conversation in the hall came to an intent but quiet finish. Ivy walked in with a satisfied look. Nick was quick behind her. His scowl melted into a smile when he saw me upright and clearly feeling better. He had changed into an oversized white cotton T-shirt and a clean pair of baggy jeans fresh from the dryer. His charming half smile didn't work on me. The thought of why my wrist was bleeding was too real.

"You must be Keasley?" Nick asked, holding out his hand over the table as if nothing was wrong. "I'm Nick."

Keasley cleared his throat and took his hand. "Nice to meet you," he said, his words at odds with the disapproving look on his old face. "Rachel wants me to look at your forehead."

"I'm fine. It quit bleeding in the shower."

"Really." The old man's eyes narrowed. "Rachel's wrist won't quit."

Nick's face went slack. His gaze darted to me. His mouth opened, then shut. I glared at him. Damn it all to hell. He knew exactly what that meant. "It—um . . ." he whispered.

"What?" Ivy prompted. Jenks landed on her shoulder, and she brushed him off.

Nick ran a hand over his chin and said nothing. Nick and I were going to talk. . . . We were going to talk real soon. Keasley aggressively shoved his paper bag into Nick's chest. "Hold this while I get Rachel's bath started. I want to make sure her core temp is where it should be."

Nick meekly backed up. Ivy looked suspiciously between the three of us. "A bath," I said brightly, not wanting her to know anything was wrong. She'd probably kill Nick if she knew what had happened. "That sounds great." I pushed my blanket and coat off of me and swung my feet to the floor. The room darkened and I felt my face go cold.

"Slow up," Keasley said as he put a dark hand on my shoulder. "Wait until it's ready."

I took a deep breath, refusing to put my head between my knees. It was so undignified.

Nick looked sick as he stood in the corner. "Uh," he stammered. "You might have to wait for that bath. I think I used all the hot water."

"Good," I breathed, "that's what I told you to do." But inside I was withering.

Keasley harrumphed. "That's what the pans of water are for."

Ivy scowled. "Why didn't you say so," she grumbled as she walked out. "I'll do it."

"Mind that her bath isn't too hot," Keasley called after her.

"I know how to treat severe blood loss," she yelled belligerently.

"That you probably do, missy." Straightening, he backed a startled Nick into the wall. "You tell Ms. Morgan what she can expect concerning her wrist," he said, taking his bag back.

Nick nodded once, looking surprised by the short, innocuous-seeming witch.

"Rache," Jenks said, buzzing close. "What's going on with your wrist?"

"Nothing."

"What's going on with your wrist, Hot Stuff?"

"Nothing!" I waved him away, almost panting from the effort.

"Jenks?" Ivy called loudly over the distant sound of water flowing. "Get me that black bag on my dresser, will you? I want to put it in Rachel's bath."

"The one that stinks like vervain?" he called, rising up to hover before me.

"You've been in my stuff!" she accused, and Jenks grinned sheepishly. "And hurry up about it," she added. "The sooner Rachel is in the tub, the sooner we can get out of here. As long as she's all right, we need to see about finishing her run."

The recollection of Trent's shipment came flooding back. I looked at the clock and sighed. There was still time to get to the FIB and nail him. But I was not going to be taking part in it in any way, shape, or form.

Swell.

Twenty-eight

*B*ubbles, I thought, *ought to be marketed as a medicinal inducement for well-being.* I sighed, scooting myself up before my neck could slip under the water. Dulled by amulets and warm water, my bruises had retreated to a background throb. Even my wrist, propped high and dry on the side of the tub, felt reasonable. Faintly through the walls, I could hear Nick talking to his mother on the phone, telling her that work had gotten really hectic the last three months and that he was sorry he hadn't called. Otherwise, the church was quiet. Jenks and Ivy were gone. "Out doing my job," I whispered, my complacent mood going sour.

"What's that, Ms. Rachel?" Matalina piped up. The small pixy woman was perched on a towel rack, looking like an angel in her flowing white silk dress as she embroidered dogwood blossoms on an exquisite shawl for her eldest daughter. She had been with me since I got in the tub, making sure I didn't pass out and drown.

"Nothing." I laboriously lifted my bruised arm and drew a mound of bubbles closer. The water was going cold and my stomach was rumbling. Ivy's bathroom looked eerily like my mother's, with tiny soaps in the shape of shells, and lacy curtains over the stained-glass window. A vase of violets rested on the back of the commode, and I was surprised a vamp cared about such things. The tub was black, contrasting nicely with the pastel walls and rosebud wallpaper.

Matalina set her stitching aside and flitted down to hover over black porcelain. "Should your amulets get wet like that?"

I glanced at the pain charms draped around my neck, thinking I looked like a drunken prostitute at Mardi Gras. "It's okay," I breathed. "Soapy water won't dissolution them like saltwater does."

"Ms. Tamwood wouldn't tell me what she put in your bath," Matalina said primly. "There might be salt in it."

Ivy hadn't told me, either, and to tell the truth, I didn't want to know. "No salt. I asked."

With a small harrumph, Matalina landed on my big toe, poking above the water. Her wings blurred to nothing, and a clear spot formed as the bubbles melted. Gathering her skirts, she cautiously bent to dip a hand, to bring a drop up to her nose. Tiny ripples spread out from her touch on the water.

"Vervain," she said in her high voice. "My Jenks was right, there. Bloodroot. Goldenseal." Her eyes met mine. "That's used to cover up something potent. What is she trying to hide?"

I looked at the ceiling. If it took away the pain, I really didn't care.

There was a creak of floorboards in the hall, and I froze. "Nick?" I called, looking at my towel just out of reach. "I'm still in the tub. Don't come in!"

He scuffed to a halt, the thin veneered wood between us. "Uh, hi, Rachel. I was just, uh, checking on you." There was a hesitation. "I—um—need to talk to you."

My stomach clenched, and my attention fell upon my wrist. It was still bleeding through a wad of gauze an inch thick. The rivulet of blood on the black porcelain looked like a welt. Maybe that's why Ivy had a black tub. Blood didn't show up as well on black as it did on white.

"Rachel?" he called into the quiet.

"I'm okay," I said loudly, my voice echoing off the pink

walls. "Give me a minute to get out of the tub, all right? I want to talk to you, too—little wizard."

I said the last snidely, and I heard his feet shift. "I'm not a wizard," he said faintly. He hesitated. "Are you hungry? Can I make you something to eat?" He sounded guilty.

"Yeah. Thanks," I replied, wishing he would get away from the door. I was ravenous. My appetite probably had everything to do with that cakelike cookie Ivy made me eat before she left. It was as appetizing as a rice pancake, and only after I had choked it down did Ivy bother to tell me it would increase my metabolism, especially my blood production. I could still taste it on the back of my throat. Sort of a mix between almonds, bananas, and shoe leather.

Nick scuffed away, and I stretched with my foot for the tap to warm the water. The water heater was probably hot by now.

"Don't warm it, dear," Matalina warned. "Ivy said to get out once it went cold."

A wave of irritation swept me. I knew what Ivy had said. But I refrained from comment.

I slowly sat up and moved to sit on the edge of the tub. The room seemed to darken around the edges, and I abruptly wrapped a fluffy pink towel around myself in case I passed out. When the room stopped going gray, I pulled the plug on the tub and carefully stood. It drained noisily, and I wiped the mist from the mirror, leaning against the sink to look at myself.

A sigh shifted my shoulders. Matalina came to rest on my shoulder, watching me with sad eyes. I looked as if I'd fallen out of the back of a truck. One side of my face was welted with a purple bruise that spread up into my eye. Keasley's bandage had fallen off, showing a red gash following the arc of my eyebrow, to make me look lopsided. I didn't even re-member getting cut. I leaned closer, and the victim in the mirror mimicked me. Gathering my resolve, I pulled my damp, stringy hair away from my neck.

A sound of resignation slipped from me. The demon hadn't made clean punctures, but rather, three sets of tears that melted into each other like rivers and tributaries. Matalina's tiny stitches looked like a little railroad trellis running down to my collarbone.

The remembrance of the demon pulled a shudder from me; I had nearly died under it. Just that thought was enough to scare the hell out of me, but what was going to keep me awake at night was the niggling awareness that for all the terror and pain, the vampire saliva it had pumped into me had felt good. Lie or not, it had felt . . . staggeringly wonderful.

I gripped the towel closer around me and turned away. "Thank you, Matalina," I whispered. "I don't think the scars will be that noticeable."

"You're welcome, dear. It was the least I could do. Would you like me to stay and make sure you get dressed all right?"

"No." The sound of a mixer came from the kitchen. I opened the door and peeked into the hall. The smell of eggs was thick in the air. "I think I can manage, thanks."

The small pixy nodded and flitted out with her needlework, her wings making a soft hum. I listened for a long moment, and deciding Nick was safely occupied, I hobbled to my room, breathing a sigh of relief upon reaching it undetected.

My hair dripped as I sat on the edge of my cot to catch my breath. The thought of putting on pants made me cringe. But I wasn't going to wear a skirt and nylons, either. I finally settled on my "fat jeans" and a blue button-up plaid shirt that was easy enough to get into without bringing on too much pain from my shoulder and arm. I wouldn't be caught dead in such an outfit on the street, but it wasn't as if I was trying to impress Nick.

The floor kept shifting under my feet as I dressed, and the walls tilted if I moved fast, but eventually I emerged with my damp amulets clanking about my neck. I scuffed down the hallway in my slippers, wondering if I ought to try to cover my bruise with a complexion spell. Standard makeup wasn't going to cut it.

Nick blundered out of the kitchen, almost running me down. He had a sandwich in his hand. "There you are," he said, his eyes wide as he ran his gaze down to my pink slippers and back up again. "Do you want an egg sandwich?"

"No, thanks," I said, my stomach rumbling again. "Too much sulfur." The thought flashed through me how he had looked, that black book in his grip as he flung out his hand and stopped that demon dead in its tracks: frightened, scared . . . and powerful. I'd never seen a human look powerful. It had been surprising. "I could use some help changing my wrist bandage, though," I finished bitingly.

He cringed, thoroughly destroying the picture in my head. "Rachel, I'm sorry—"

I pushed past him and went into the kitchen. His steps were light behind me, and I leaned against the sink as I fed Mr. Fish. It was fully dark outside, and I could see tiny flashes of light as Jenks's family patrolled the garden. I froze as I saw that the tomato was back on the windowsill. A wash of worry hit me as I mentally cursed Ivy—then my brow furrowed. Why did I care what Nick thought? It was my house. I was an Inderlander. If he didn't like it, tuff toads.

I could feel Nick behind me at the table. "Rachel, I'm really sorry," he said, and I turned, bracing myself. My outrage would lose all its effect if I passed out. "I didn't know it would demand payment from you. Honest."

Angry, I brushed the damp hair from my eyes and stood with my arms crossed. "It's a demon mark, Nick. A freaking demon mark."

Nick folded his lanky body into one of the hard-back chairs. Elbows on the table, he dropped his head into the cup his hands made. Looking at the table, he said flatly, "Demonology is a dead art. I didn't expect to be putting the knowledge to practical use. It was only supposed to be a painless way to fulfill one of my ancient language requirements."

He looked up, meeting my eyes. His worry, the need for me to listen and understand, halted my next caustic outburst.

"I'm really, really sorry," he said. "If I could move your demon mark to me, I would. But I thought you were dying. I couldn't just let you bleed to death in the back of some cab."

My anger trickled away. He had been willing to take a demon mark to save me. No one made him do it. I was an ass.

Nick lifted the hair from over his left temple. "Look. See?" he said hopefully. "It stops."

I peered at his scalp. Right where the demon had hit him was a newly closed wound, red-rimmed and sore looking. The half circle had a line through it. My stomach clenched. A demon mark. Damn it all to hell, I was going to have to wear a demon mark. Black ley line witches had demon marks, not white earth witches. Not me.

Nick let his shock of dark hair fall. "It will vanish after I pay back my favor. It's not forever."

"A favor?" I asked.

His brown eyes were pinched, pleading for understanding. "It will probably be information or something. At least, that's what the texts say."

One hand clasped about my middle, I pushed my fingertips into my forehead. I really didn't have a choice. It wasn't as if Kotex made a pad for this kind of a thing. "So how do I let this demon know I agree to owe it a favor?"

"Do you?"

"Yes."

"You just did, then."

I felt ill, not liking that a demon had such a tie to me that it would know the moment I agreed to its terms. "No paperwork?" I said. "No contracts? I don't like verbal agreements."

"You want it to come here and fill out paperwork?" he asked. "Think about it hard enough and it will."

"No." My gaze dropped to my wrist. There was a small tickle. My face went slack as it grew to an itch and then a slight burning. "Where are the scissors?" I said tightly. He looked around blankly, and my wrist started to flame. "It's burning!" I shouted. The pain in my wrist continued to grow, and I pushed at the gauze, frantically trying to get it off.

"Get it off! Get it off!" I shouted. Spinning, I flipped the tap on full and shoved my wrist under the water. The cold water soaked through, quenching the burning sensation. I leaned over the sink, my pulse pounding as the water flowed, pulling away the pain.

The damp night air breezed in past the curtains, and I stared past the dark garden and into the graveyard, waiting for the black spots to go away. My knees were weak, and it was only the rush of adrenaline that kept me upright. There was a soft scraping sound as Nick slid a pair of scissors to me across the counter.

I turned off the tap. "Thanks for the warning," I said bitterly.

"Mine didn't hurt," he said. He looked worried and confused, and oh so bewildered. Grabbing a dish towel and the scissors, I went to my spot at the table. Wedging the blade through the gauze, I sawed at the soggy wrap. I flicked a glance up at him. Tall and awkward, he stood by the sink, guilt seeming to pour from his hunched posture. I slumped.

"I'm sorry for being such a crab, Nick," I said as I gave up on cutting it off and started to unwind it instead. "I would have died if it hadn't been for you. I was lucky you were there to stop it. I owe you my life, and I'm really thankful for what you did." I hesitated. "That thing scared the hell out of me. All I wanted was to forget about it, and now I can't. I don't know how to react, and yelling at you is very convenient."

A smile quirked the corner of his mouth, and he turned a chair so he could sit before me. "Let me get that for you," he said, reaching for my hand.

I hesitated, then let him pull my wrist onto his lap. He bowed his head over my wrist, and his knees almost touched mine. I really owed him more than a simple thanks. "Nick? I mean it. Thank you. That's twice you saved my life. This demon thing will be all right. I'm sorry you got a demon mark helping me."

Nick looked up, his brown eyes searching mine. I was suddenly very conscious of how close he was. My memory went back to feeling his arms around me, carrying me into the church. I wondered if he had held me all the way through the ever-after.

"I'm glad I was there to help," he said softly. "It was kind of my fault."

"No, it would have found me no matter where I was," I said. Finally the last wrap was gone. Swallowing hard, I stared at my wrist. My stomach twisted. It was entirely healed. Even the green stitches were gone. The raised white scar looked old. Mine was in the shape of a full circle with that same line running through it.

"Oh," Nick murmured, leaning back. "The demon must like you. It didn't heal me, just stopped the bleeding."

"Swell." I rubbed the mark on my wrist. It was better than a bandage—I guess. It wasn't as if anyone would know what the scar was from; no one had been dealing with demons since the Turn. "So now I just wait until it wants something?"

"Yeah." Nick's chair scraped as he stood up and went to the stove.

I propped my elbows up on the table and felt the air slip in and out of my lungs. Nick stood at the stove with his back to me and stirred a stewpot. An uncomfortable silence grew.

"Do you like student food?" Nick said suddenly.

I straightened. "Beg pardon?"

"Student food." His eyes went to the tomato on the sill. "Whatever's in the refrigerator over pasta."

Understandably concerned, I pushed myself upright and tottered over to see what was on the stove. Macaroni spun and rolled in the pot. A wooden spoon sat next to it, and my eyebrows rose. "Have you been using that spoon?"

Nick nodded. "Yeah. Why?"

I reached for the salt and dumped the entire canister into it.

"Whoa!" Nick cried. "I already salted the water. You don't need that much."

Ignoring him, I tossed the wooden spoon into my dissolution vat and pulled out a metal one. "Until I get my ceramic spoons back, it's metal for cooking and wooden for spells. Rinse the macaroni well. It ought to be okay."

Nick's eyebrows rose. "I would think you would use metal spoons for spells and wooden for cooking since spells don't stick to metal."

I made my slow way to the fridge, feeling my heart pound from even this little exertion. "And why do you suppose spells don't stick to metal? Unless it's copper, metal screws everything up. I'll do the spell crafting if you don't mind; you do dinner."

Much to my surprise, Nick didn't get all huffy and testosterone laden but only gave me that lopsided smile of his.

A jolt of pain broke through the amulets as I tugged the fridge open. "I can't believe how hungry I am," I said as I looked for something that wasn't wrapped in paper or plastic foam. "I think Ivy may have slipped me something."

There was a whoosh of water as Nick dumped the macaroni to drain. "Little cake thing?"

I pulled my head out and blinked at him. Had Ivy given him one, too? "Yes."

"I saw it." His eyes were fixed on the tomato, steam billowing around him as he rinsed the macaroni. "When I was doing my master's thesis, I had access to the rare-book vault." His brow pinched. "It's right next to the ancient-book locker. Anyway, the architectural designs of preindustrial cathedrals are boring, and one night I found a diary of a seventeenth-century British priest. He had been tried and convicted of murdering three of his prettiest parishioners."

Nick dumped the pasta back in the bowl and opened a jar of alfredo. "He made reference to such a thing. Said it made the vampire's orgies of blood and lust possible on a nightly basis. From a scientific point of view, you should consider yourself lucky. I imagine it's only rarely offered to someone not under their sway and compelled to keep their mouth shut about it."

I frowned in unease. What the devil had Ivy given me?

His eyes still on the tomato, Nick dumped the sauce over

the pasta. A rich smell filled the kitchen, and my stomach growled. He stirred it in, and I watched Nick watch the tomato. He was starting to look rather sick. Exasperated with humanity's groundless revulsion of tomatoes, I closed the fridge and hobbled to the window. "How did this get in here?" I muttered, pushing it through the pixy hole and into the night. It hit with a soft thud.

"Thanks," he said, taking a relieved breath.

I returned to my chair with a heavy sigh. One would think Ivy and I had a decaying sheep's head on our counter. But it was nice to know he had at least one human hang-up.

Nick puttered about, adding mushrooms, Worcestershire sauce, and pepperoni to the concoction. I smiled as I realized it was the last of my pizza fixings. It smelled wonderful, and as he plucked the ladle from the island rack, I asked, "Enough for two?"

"It's enough for a dorm room." Nick slid a bowl before me and sat down, curling his arm protectively about his bowl. "Student food," he said around a full mouth. "Try it."

I glanced at the clock above the sink as I dipped my spoon. Ivy and Jenks were probably at the FIB right now, trying to convince the front guy they weren't loons, and here I was, eating macaroni alfredo with a human. It didn't look right. The food, I mean. It would have been better in a tomato sauce. Dubious, I took a taste. "Hey," I said, pleased. "This is good."

"Told you."

For a few moments there was only the scraping of spoons and the sound of the crickets in the garden. Nick's pace slowed, and he glanced at the clock over the sink. "Hey, uh, I've got a big favor to ask," he said hesitantly.

I swallowed as I looked up, knowing what was coming. "You can crash here for the night if you want," I said. "Though there are no guarantees you'll wake up with all your fluids intact or even at all. The I.S. is still spelling for me. Right now it's just those tenacious fairies, but as soon as the word gets out that I'm still alive, we might be up to our armpits in assassins. You'd be safer on a park bench," I finished wryly.

His smile was relieved. "Thanks, but I'll risk it. I'll get out of your hair tomorrow. See if my landlord has anything left that's mine. Go visit my mom." His long face puckered, looking as worried as when he thought I was bleeding to death. "I'll tell her I lost everything in a fire. This is going to be a rough one."

I felt a stab of sympathy. I knew what it was like to find yourself on the street with only a box left of your life. "Sure you don't want to stay with her tonight?" I asked. "It'd be safer."

He went back to eating. "I can take care of myself."

I bet you can, I thought, my mind going back to that demon book he took from the library. It wasn't in my bag anymore, a tiny smear of blood the only thing to say it had ever been there. I wanted to come right out and ask if he worked black magic. But he might say yes, and then I'd have to decide what I was going to do about it. I didn't want to do that right yet. I liked Nick's easy confidence, and the novelty of seeing that in a human was decidedly . . . intriguing.

A part of me knew and despised that the attraction probably stemmed from my "hero rescuing the damsel in distress syndrome," but I needed something safe and secure in my life right now, and a magic-working human who could keep demons from tearing my throat out fit the bill nicely. Especially when he looked as harmless as he did.

"Besides," Nick said, ruining it, "Jenks will pix me if I leave before he gets back."

My breath slipped from me in bother. He was a babysitter. How nice.

The sound of the phone ringing echoed through the walls. I looked up at Nick and didn't move. I was sore, darn it.

He gave me that half smile of his and stood. "I'll get it." I took another bite as I watched his vanishing backside, thinking I might offer to go shopping with him when he bought himself some new clothes. Those jeans he had on were way too loose.

"Hello," Nick said, his voice dropping and taking on a surprisingly professional tone. "You've reached Morgan, Tamwood, and Jenks. Vampiric Charms Runner Service."

Vampiric Charms Runner Service? I thought. A little of Ivy, a little of me. It was as good as anything else, I suppose. I blew on a spoonful, thinking his cooking wasn't bad, either.

"Jenks?" Nick said, and I hesitated, looking up as Nick appeared in the hallway with the phone. "She's eating. You're at the airport already?"

There was a long pause, and I sighed. The FIB was more open-minded and eager for Trent than I had anticipated.

"The FIB?" Nick's tone had shifted to concern, and I stiffened as he added, "She did what? Is anyone dead?"

My eyes closed in a long blink and I set my spoon aside. Nick's concoction went sour in my stomach, and I swallowed hard.

"Um, sure," Nick said, the skin around his expressive eyes crinkling as he met my gaze. "Give us a half hour." The beep of the phone as he turned it off was loud. He turned to me and blew out his breath. "We have a problem."

Twenty-nine

I fell against the side of the cab as it made a tight turn. Pain broke past my amulets, and I clutched one-handed at my bag in misery. The driver was human, and he had made it painfully clear he didn't like driving out to the Hollows after dark. His constant muttering hadn't abated until he crossed the Ohio River and was back where "decent people kept themselves." In his eyes, my and Nick's only saving grace was that he had picked us up at a church and that we were going to the FIB, "A fine and decent establishment upholding the right side of the law."

"Okay," I said as Nick helped ease me upright. "So those fine and decent people at the FIB were harassing Ivy, playing good-cop/bad-cop. Someone touched her and—"

"She exploded," Nick finished. "It took eight officers to bring her down. Jenks says three are in the hospital for observation. Four more were treated and released."

"Idiots," I muttered. "What about Jenks?"

Nick put an arm out, bracing himself as we lurched to a stop before a tall stone and glass building. "They'll release him to a responsible person." His grin looked a tad nervous. "And in the absence of one, they said you would do."

"Ha ha," I said dryly. Peering up through the dirty glass of the cab, I read FEDERAL INDERLANDER BUREAU engraved deeply over the two sets of doors. Nick sidled out to the sidewalk first and extended a hand to help me. I slowly worked my way out and tried to find my bearings as he paid the cabbie with the money I slipped him. It was bright under the streetlights, and the streets themselves had remarkably light traffic for that hour. Clearly we were deep into the human district of Cincinnati. Looking up to find the top of the imposing building, I felt very much the minority and on edge.

I scanned the black windows around me for any sign of attack. Jax had said the fairy assassins left right after my phone call. *To get reinforcements, or to set up an ambush here?* I didn't like the idea that fairy catapults might be winching back as I waited. Even a fairy wouldn't be so bold as to tag me inside the FIB building, but on the sidewalk I was fair game.

Then again, they could have been taken off the run, seeing as the I.S. was sending demons now. I felt a flash of satisfaction, knowing the demon had ripped apart its summoner. They wouldn't send another any time soon. Black magic always swings back to get you. Always.

"You really ought to take better care of your sister," the driver said as he took the money, and Nick and I looked blankly at each other. "But I guess you Inderlanders don't care about each other as much as us decent folks. I'd pulp anyone who dared touch my sister with the back of his hand," he added before driving off.

I stared at his taillights in confusion until Nick said, "He thinks someone beat you and I'm bringing you in to file a complaint."

I was too nervous to laugh—besides, it would have made me pass out—but I managed a choking snicker, taking his arm before I fell over. Brow pinched, Nick gallantly pulled the glass door open and held it for me. A flash of angst went through me as I stepped over the threshold. I had put myself in the questionable position of having to trust a human-run establishment. It was shaky ground. I didn't like it.

But the sound of loud conversations and the smell of burnt coffee were familiar and soothing. Institution was written everywhere, from the gray tiled floor, to the chatter of loud conversation, to the orange chairs the anxious parents and unrepentant thugs sat in. It felt like coming home, and my shoulders eased.

"Um, over there," Nick said, pointing to the front counter. My arm was throbbing in its sling and my shoulder hurt. Either my sweat was diluting my amulets or my exertions were starting to cancel them out. Nick walked almost behind me, and it was bothersome.

The desk clerk looked up as we approached, her eyes widening. "Oh, sweetheart!" she exclaimed softly. "What happened to you?"

"I, uh . . ." I winced as I put my elbows on the counter to steady myself. My complexion charm wasn't enough to blur my black eye or stitches. Just what was I supposed to tell her? That demons were loose in Cincinnati again? I glanced behind me, but Nick was no help, turned away to the doors. "Um," I stammered. "I'm here to pick someone up."

She reached to scratch her neck. "Not the one who did that to you."

I couldn't help my smile at her concern. I was a sucker for pity. "No."

The woman tucked a strand of graying hair behind her ear. "I hate to tell you this, but you need to go to the Hillman Street office. And you'll have to wait until tomorrow. They won't release anyone after normal business hours."

I sighed. I hated the maze of bureaucracy with a passion, but I've found the best way to deal with it is to smile and act stupid. That way, no one gets confused. "But I talked to someone less than twenty minutes ago," I objected. "I was told to come here."

Her mouth made a round O of understanding. A wary expression settled around her eyes. "Ah," she said, looking at me sideways. "You're here for the—" She hesitated. "—pixy." She rubbed the beginnings of a small blister behind her neck. She'd been pixed.

Nick cleared his throat. "His name is Jenks," he said

tightly, his head lowered. Clearly he had heard the hesitation, thinking she had almost said "bug."

"Yes," she said slowly, leaning to scratch her ankle. "Mr. Jenks. If you would take a seat over there," she pointed, "someone will be with you as soon as Captain Edden is available."

"Captain Edden." I took Nick's arm. "Thank you." Feeling old and creaky, I angled to the orange monstrosities lined up against the lobby's walls. The woman's attitude shift wasn't unexpected. In a breath I had gone from honey to whore.

Though having lived openly with humans for forty years, tensions ran high at times. They were afraid, and probably for good reason. It's not easy waking up to find your neighbors are vampires and your fourth-grade teacher really was a witch.

Nick's eyes rove over the lobby as he helped me sit. The chairs were as unpleasant as I had expected: hard and uncomfortable. Nick sat beside me, perched on the edge with his long legs bent at the knees. "How are you doing?" he asked as I groaned while trying to find a halfway comfortable position.

"Fine," I said shortly. "Just dandy." I winced, tracking two uniformed men passing through the lobby. One was on crutches. The other's black eye was just starting to purple up, and he was scratching vigorously at his shoulders. *Thanks a heap, Jenks and Ivy.* My unease filtered back. How was I supposed to convince the captain of the FIB to help me now?

"You want something to eat?" Nick said, yanking my attention back. "I, uh, could go across the street for some Graeter's. You like butter-pecan ice cream?"

"No." It came out more brusque than I had intended, and I smiled to soften my words. "No, thank you," I amended, my worry settling in my belly to stay.

"How about something from the candy machine, then?

Salt and carbohydrates?" he prompted hopefully. "The food of champions."

I shook my head and set my bag between my feet. Trying to keep my breathing shallow, I stared at the scuffed tile floor. If I ate one more thing, I thought I was gonna ralph. I had eaten another bowl of Nick's macaroni before the cab picked us up, but that wasn't the problem.

"Amulets wearing off?" Nick guessed, and I nodded.

A pair of scuffed brown shoes came to a slow halt within my range. Nick slid to the back of his chair with his arms crossed, and I slowly pulled my head up.

It was a stocky man in a white dress shirt and khakis, trim and carrying the polish of an ex-marine gone civilian. He wore plastic-framed glasses, the lenses looking too small against his round face. There was the smell of soap about him, and his close-cropped hair was damp and stuck up like a baby orangutan's. My guess was he had been pixed and knew enough to wash before the blisters could start. His bandaged right wrist was in a sling identical to mine. Short black hair, short gray mustache. I hoped he had a long temper. "Ms. Morgan?" he said, and I straightened with a sigh. "I'm Captain Edden."

Great, I thought, struggling to stand up. Nick helped. I found I could look Edden right in the eye, making him rather short for all his official presence. I would almost say he had some troll blood in him if such a thing were biologically possible. My eyes lingered on the weapon holstered on his hip, and I spared a wish for my I.S.-issue cuffs. Eyes scrunched from my too strong perfume, he stuck out his left hand instead of the usual right, seeing as we were both unable to use them.

My pulse quickened as we shook left hands; it felt wrong, and I would rather use my bruised right arm than do it again. "Good evening, Captain," I said, trying to hide my nervousness. "This is Nick Sparagmos. He's helping keep me upright today."

Edden gave Nick a short nod, then hesitated. "Mr. Sparagmos? Have we met before?"

"No. I don't think so."

Nick's words were a shade too fast, and I ran my gaze down his carefully casual stance. Nick had been here before, and I didn't think it had been to pick up his tickets to the FIB's yearly fund-raising dinner.

"You sure?" the man questioned, running a quick hand over his bristly hair.

"Yeah."

The older man eyed him. "Yes," he said abruptly. "I'm thinking of someone else."

Nick's posture eased almost imperceptibly, piquing my interest further.

Captain Edden's gaze turned to my neck, and I wondered if I ought to try and cover my stitches with a scarf or something. "If you would come back with me?" the stocky man said. "I'd like to speak with you before I release the pixy to your custody."

Nick stiffened. "His name is Jenks," he muttered, just audible over the lobby noise.

"Yes. Mr. Jenks." Edden paused. "If you would come back to my office?"

"What about Ivy?" I asked, reluctant to leave the public lobby behind. My pulse was racing with just the effort to stand here. If I had to move quickly, I'd pass out.

"Ms. Tamwood will remain where she is. She's to be turned over to the I.S. for prosecution in the morning."

Anger overpowered my caution. "You knew better than to touch an angry vamp," I said. Nick's grip tightened on my arm, and it was all I could do to not try to jerk away from him.

A hint of a smile drifted over Edden. "It still remains that she assaulted FIB personnel," he said. "My hands are tied concerning Tamwood. We aren't equipped to deal with Inderlanders." He hesitated. "Would you come with me to my office? We can discuss your options."

My worry deepened; Denon would love to get Ivy incarcerated dead to rights. Nick handed me my bag, and I nodded. This was not good. It almost seemed as if Edden had goaded Ivy into losing her temper to get me to come down here with my hat in my hand. But I followed Edden to a glass-walled corner office off the lobby. At first it looked tucked out of the way, but with the blinds up, he would have a view of everything. Right now, they were closed to make his corner less of a fishbowl than it was. He left the door open, and the noise filtered in.

"Have a seat," he said, gesturing to the two green upholstered chairs opposite his desk. I gratefully sat, finding the flat padding marginally more comfortable than the plastic chairs in the lobby. As Nick stiffly lowered himself, I ran my eyes over Edden's office, noting the dust-covered bowling trophies and stacks of folders. File cabinets lined one wall, photo albums stacked on top of them to nearly the ceiling. A clock hung behind Edden's desk, ticking loudly. There was a picture of him and my old boss, Denon, shaking hands outside City Hall. Edden looked short and common next to Denon's vampire grace. They were both smiling.

I brought my attention back to Edden. He was slouched in his chair, clearly waiting for me to finish my evaluation of his office. If he cared to ask, I would have told him he was a slob. But his office had a cluttered efficiency about it that said real work was done here. It was as far from Denon's gadget-strewn, sterile office as my old desk was from a churchyard. I liked it. If I had to trust someone, I'd rather it be someone as unorganized as me.

Edden pulled himself straight. "I'll admit my conversation with Tamwood was intriguing, Ms. Morgan," he said. "As a former I.S. operative, I'm sure you know what bringing Trent Kalamack in under the suspicion of anything—much less manufacturing and distributing illegal bioproducts—could do for the FIB's image."

Right to the point. Snap my fingers if I wasn't starting to

like this guy. Still I said nothing as my stomach knotted. He wasn't done.

Edden put an arm on his desk, hiding his sling in his lap. "But you understand I can't ask my people to arrest Councilman Kalamack under the advice of a former I.S. runner. You're under a death threat, illegal or not."

My breathing quickened to match my whirling thoughts. I had been right. He had thrown Ivy into custody to get me down here. For one panicked instant I wondered if he was stalling me. If he had the I.S. on their way to tag me. The thought vanished in a painful rush of adrenaline. The FIB and the I.S. were in a bitter rivalry. If Edden was going to claim the bounty on my head, he'd do it himself, not invite the I.S. into his building. Edden had brought me down here to evaluate me. For what? I wondered, my worry tightening.

Deciding to take control of the conversation, I smiled, wincing as the swelling on my eye pulled. Giving up on my dazzle-them-to-distraction approach, I faced him squarely, pushing the tension from my shoulders down to my stomach, where he couldn't see it. "I'd like to apologize for my associate's behavior, Captain Edden." I looked at his bandaged wrist. "Did she break it?"

The barest wisp of surprise crossed him. "Worse. It's fractured in four places. They'll tell me tomorrow if I have to get a cast or simply wait for it to heal. Damn infirmary won't let me take anything stronger than an aspirin. It's a full moon next week, Ms. Morgan. Do you realize how far behind I will be if I have to take even one day off?"

This chitchat was going nowhere. My pain was starting to flow back, and I had to find out what Edden wanted before it was too late to move on Kalamack. It had to be more than Trent; he could have dealt with Ivy alone if that was all he wanted.

Steadying myself, I took off one of my amulets and pushed it across the desk. My bag was full of spells, but not one of them was for pain. "I understand, Captain Edden. I'm sure we can come to an agreement that would be mutually beneficial." My fingers left the small disk, and I struggled to keep my eyes from widening at the rush of pain. Nausea twisted my stomach, and I felt three times as weak. I hoped I hadn't made a mistake offering it to him. As witnessed by the desk clerk, few humans approved of Inderlanders, much less their magic. I thought it worth the risk. Edden seemed unusually open-minded. It remained to be seen how far.

His eyes showed only curiosity as he reached for the charm. "You know I can't accept this," he said. "As an FIB officer, it would be considered . . ." His face went slack as his fingers closed upon the amulet and the pain in his wrist was deadened. ". . . a bribe," he finished softly.

His dark eyes met mine, and I smiled despite my pain. "A trade." I arched my eyebrows, ignoring the pull of tape. "An aspirin for an aspirin?" If he was smart, he'd understand I was testing the waters. If he was stupid, It didn't matter, and I'd be dead by the end of the week. But if there was no way to convince him to act on my "tip," I wouldn't be sitting in his office.

For a moment Edden sat as if afraid to move and break the spell. Finally an honest smile came over him. He leaned to his open door and bellowed out into the hall, "Rose! Get me a couple of aspirin. I'm dying in here." He leaned back, grinning as he hung the amulet about his neck and hid it behind his shirt. His relief was obvious. It was a start.

My worry grew as a harried-looking woman walked in, her heels clicking on the gray tile. She visibly jerked at finding us in Edden's office. Pulling her eyes from me, she held out two paper cups, and he pointed to the desk. The woman's brow furrowed, and she set them next to his hand and silently left. Edden reached a foot out after her and kicked the door shut. He waited, shifting his glasses higher up his nose before crossing his good arm over his bad.

I swallowed hard as I reached for the two cups. Now it was my turn for trust. There might be anything in those tiny white pills, but finding relief from my pain was beyond expectation. The pills rattled as I brought the cup close and peered down at them.

I'd heard about pills. I'd had a roommate who swore by them, keeping a bottle of white tablets next to her toothbrush. She said they worked better than amulets, and you didn't have to stick your finger. I had watched her take one once. You were supposed to swallow them whole.

Nick leaned close. "You can palm it if you want," he whispered, and I shook my head. I quickly upended the cup with the aspirin, tasting the bitter bite of willow bark as I took a swallow of tepid water. I struggled not to cough as I felt the pills go down, clenching at the pain the sudden movement brought on. This was supposed to make me feel better?

Nick patted me hesitantly on the back. Through my watering eyes I could see Edden all but laughing at my ineptness. I waved Nick off and forced myself to sit up straight. A moment passed, then another. Still the aspirin didn't take effect. I sighed. Nothing. No wonder humans were so suspicious. Their medicines didn't work.

"I can give you Kalamack, Captain Edden." I glanced at the clock behind him. Ten forty-five. "I can prove he's dealing in illegal drugs. Both manufacturing and distribution."

Edden's eyes went alight. "Give me the proof, and we will go to the airport."

I felt my expression freeze. Ivy had told him nearly everything, and he still wanted to talk to me? Why hadn't he taken the information and brought some glory for himself? God knew it would be cheaper. What was he up to? "I don't have all of it," I admitted. "But I heard him discussing the arrangements. If we find the drugs, that's proof enough."

Edden pressed his lips together to make his mustache move. "I won't go out on circumstantial evidence. I've been a fool for the I.S. before."

I glanced at the clock again. Ten forty-six. His eyes met mine as I looked away, and I bit back a flash of annoyance. Now he knew I was in a hurry. "Captain," I said, trying to keep the imploring from my voice. "I broke into Trent Kalamack's office to get the proof but got caught. I spent the last three days as an unwilling guest. I overheard several meetings that substantiated my beliefs. He's a manufacturer and distributor of illegal biodrugs."

Calm and collected, Edden leaned back and swiveled his chair. "You spent three days with Kalamack and expect me to believe he was speaking the truth in front of you?"

"I was a mink," I said dryly. "I was supposed to die in the city's rat fights. I wasn't supposed to escape."

Nick shifted uneasily beside me, but Edden nodded as if I had confirmed his suspicions.

"Trent is running a rainbow of biodrugs out nearly every week," I said, forcing my hand down from playing with my hair. "Blackmailing anyone who can afford it and who is in the unfortunate situation of needing them. You could chart his hidden profits by plotting the I.S. Brimstone takes. He's using them as a—"

"Distraction," Edden finished for me. He hit the nearby file cabinet, leaving a small dent. Both Nick and I jumped. "Damn! No wonder we never catch a break."

I nodded. It was now or never. Whether I trusted him or not was irrelevant. If he didn't help me, I was dead. "It gets better," I said, praying I was doing the right thing. "Trent has an I.S. runner on his payroll who has been heading most of the I.S. Brimstone takes."

Edden's round face went hard behind his glasses. "Fred Perry."

"Francis Percy," I corrected him, a sudden flash of anger warming me.

Eyes narrowed, Edden shifted in his chair. Clearly he didn't like a bad cop any more than I did. I took a shaky breath. "A shipment of biodrugs is going out tonight. With me, you can nail them both. The FIB gets the credit for the tag, the I.S. looks like a fool, and your department quietly pays off my contract." My head hurt, and I prayed I hadn't just flushed my only chance down the toilet. "You could make it a consultant fee. An aspirin for an aspirin."

Lips pressed tight, Edden looked at the acoustic-tiled ceiling. Slowly his face calmed, and I waited, stilling myself as I realized I was clicking my nails together in time with the ticking of the clock.

"I'm tempted to bend the rules for you, Ms. Morgan," he said, and my heart gave a thump. "But I need more. Something the higher-ups can chart on their profit and loss statements that will show value for more than a quarter."

"More!" Nick exclaimed, sounding angry.

My head throbbed. *He wanted more?* "I don't have anything more, Captain," I said forcefully, frustration riding high in me.

He smiled wickedly. "But you do."

My eyebrows tried to go up, halted by the tape.

Edden glanced at his closed door. "If this works out—catching Kalamack, I mean . . ." A thick hand reached to rub his forehead. When his fingers dropped, the easy, self-assured confidence of an FIB captain was gone, replaced with an eager, intelligent gleam that set me back a pace. "I've been working for the FIB since I left the service," he said softly. "I worked my way up by seeing what was missing, and finding it."

"I'm not a commodity, Captain," I said hotly.

"Everyone is a commodity," he said. "My departments at the FIB are at a great disadvantage, Ms. Morgan. Inderlanders have evolved knowing human weaknesses. Hell, you're probably responsible for half our mental hang-ups. The frustrating truth is, we can't compete."

He wanted me to rat on my fellow Inderlanders. He should have known better. "I don't know anything you can't find in a library," I said, gripping my bag tightly. I wanted to get up and storm out, but he had me right where he wanted me, and I could do nothing but watch him smile. His flat teeth were startlingly human compared to the predatory gleam in his eye.

"I'm sure that's not entirely true," he said. "But I'm asking for advice, not a betrayal." Edden leaned back in his chair, seeming to collect his thoughts. "Occasionally," he said, "tonight with Ms. Tamwood, for example, an Inderlander comes to us seeking help or with information they don't feel—prudent—taking to the I.S. To be honest, we don't know how to deal with them. My people are so suspicious that they can't gain any useful information. On the rare occasion when we do understand, we don't know how to capitalize on it. The only reason we were able to contain Ms. Tamwood is because she agreed to be incarcerated once it was explained we would be more willing to listen to you if she did. Up until today we have reluctantly turned situations like this over to the I.S." His eyes met mine. "They make us look like fools, Ms. Morgan."

He was offering me a job, but my tension swelled instead of easing. "If I wanted a boss, I would have stayed with the I.S., Captain."

"No," he protested quickly, his chair creaking as he sat upright. "Having you here would be a mistake. Not only would my officers want my head on a pole, but it's against the I.S./FIB convention to have you on the payroll." His smile grew wicked, and I waited for it. "I want you as a consultant—occasionally—as the need demands."

I let my held breath out slowly, seeing for the first time what he was after.

"What did you say your firm was called?" Edden asked.

"Vampiric Charms," Nick said.

Edden chuckled. "Sounds like a dating service."

I winced, but it was too late to change it now. "And I get paid for these *occasional* services?" I asked, chewing on my lower lip. *This might work.*

"Of course."

Now it was my turn to stare at the ceiling, my pulse racing at the chance that I'd found a way out of this. "I'm part of a team, Captain Edden," I said, wondering if Ivy was having second thoughts about our partnership. "I can't speak for them."

"Ms. Tamwood has already agreed. I believe she said, 'If the little witch says yes, I'll go along with it.' Mr. Jenks expressed a similar feeling, but his exact words were substantially more—colorful."

I glanced at Nick and he shrugged uneasily. There was no guarantee, when all was said and done, that Edden wouldn't conveniently forget to pay off my contract. But something in his dry humor and honest reactions had convinced me he wouldn't. Besides, I had already made a pact with a demon tonight. This couldn't be any worse.

"Captain Edden, we have a deal," I said suddenly. "It's Southwest's 11:45 flight to L.A."

"Great!" His good hand hit the table with a thump, and I jumped again. "I knew you would. Rose!" he shouted to the closed door. Grinning, he leaned to open it. "Rose! Get a Brimstone dog team out to . . ." He looked at me. "Where's the Brimstone take?" he asked.

"Ivy didn't tell you?" I said in surprise.

"She may have. I want to know if she was lying."

"Main bus depot," I said, my heart hammering all the harder. *We were going to do this. I was going to tag Trent and get my death threat paid off.*

"Rose!" he shouted again. "The old bus depot. Who's pushing paper tonight who didn't go to the hospital?"

A feminine but robust voice cut over the accumulated clatter. "Kaman is here, but he's in the shower getting that bug dust off. Dillon, Ray—"

"Stop," Edden said. He stood, and, gesturing for Nick and me to join him, darted out of his office. I took a deep breath and lurched to my feet. Much to my surprise, my aches had retreated to dull throbs. We followed Edden down the hall, excitement making my pace quick. "I think the aspirin is finally working," I whispered to Nick as we caught up to Edden. He was hunched over a spotless desk, talking to the same woman who had brought me the pills.

"Call Ruben and Simon in," he said. "I need someone with a cooler head. Send them to the airport. Tell them to wait for me."

"You, sir?" Rose glanced over her glasses at Nick and me.

Her frown said it all. She wasn't happy having two Inderlanders in the building, much less standing behind her boss.

"Yes, me. Get the unmarked van around front. I'm going out tonight." He hoisted his belt up over his hips. "No mistakes. This one has to be done right."

Thirty

The floor of the FIB van was surprisingly clean. There was a faint odor of pipe smoke, reminding me of my dad. Captain Edden and the driver, introduced as Clayton, were up front. Nick, Jenks, and I were on the middle bench. The windows were cracked to dilute my perfume. If I'd known they weren't going to release Ivy until after the deal was done, I wouldn't have put it on. As it was, I reeked.

Jenks was on a rampage, his tiny voice scraping along the inside of my skull as he ranted, winding my anticipation to new heights. "Put a sock in it, Jenks," I whispered as I ran the tip of my finger around the bottom of my tiny cellophane bag of nuts for the last of the salt. When the aspirin had dulled my pain, my hunger kicked in. I'd almost rather have done without the aspirin if it meant not being famished.

"Go Turn yourself," Jenks snarled from the cup holder where I had put him. "They stuffed me into a water cooler. Like I was a freak on display! They broke my fringing wing. Look at it! Snapped the main vein. I've got mineral spots on my shirt. It's ruined! And did you see my boots? I'll never get the coffee off them."

"They apologized," I said, but I knew it was a lost cause. He was on a roll.

"It's going to take me a week to grow my damn wing back. Matalina is gonna kill me. Everyone hides from me when I can't fly. Did you know that? Even my kids."

I tuned him out. The tirade had started the moment they released him and hadn't quit yet. Though Jenks hadn't been charged with a crime—seeing as he'd been at the ceiling cheering Ivy on while she pummeled the FIB officers—he had insisted on poking about where he shouldn't until they put him in an emptied water jug.

I was beginning to see what Edden had been talking about. He and his officers hadn't a clue as to how to handle Inderlanders. They could have trapped him in a cupboard or drawer as he nosed about. His wings never would have gotten wet and become as fragile as tissue paper. The ten-minute chase with a net wouldn't have happened. And half the officers on the floor wouldn't have been pixed. Ivy and Jenks had come to the FIB willingly, and they still ended up leaving a trail of chaos. What a violent, uncooperative Inderlander might do was frightening.

"It doesn't make sense," Nick said loud enough for Edden in the front to hear. "Why is Mr. Kalamack padding his pocket with illegal gains? He's already independently wealthy."

Edden turned halfway around in his seat, his khaki nylon jacket sliding. He had a yellow FIB hat on, the only sign of his authority. "He must be funding a project he doesn't want to be found. Money is hard to trace when it's gotten from illegal means and spent on the same."

I wondered what it was. Something more going on in Faris's lab, perhaps?

The FIB captain brought his thick hand to his chin, his round face lit by the cars behind us. "Mr. Sparagmos," he questioned, "have you ever taken the ferry tour of the waterfront?"

Nick's face went still. "Sir?"

Edden shook his head. "It's the damnedest thing. I'm sure I've seen you before."

"No," Nick said, easing back into the corner of the seat. "I don't like boats."

Making a small sound, Edden turned back around in his seat. I exchanged a knowing look with Jenks. The small pixy made a sly face, catching on faster than I had. My empty bag of peanuts crumpled noisily, and I tucked it in my bag, not about to throw it onto the clean floor. Nick was shadowed and closed, the dim light from oncoming motorists blurring his sharp nose and thin face. Leaning close, I whispered, "What did you do?"

His eyes remained fixed out the window, his chest rising and falling in a smooth breath. "Nothing."

I glanced at the back of Edden's head. *Yeah, right. And I'm the I.S. poster girl.* "Look. I'm sorry I got you into this. If you want to just walk away when we get to the airport, I'll understand." On second thought, I didn't want to know what he had done.

He shook his head, giving me a quick flash of a smile. "It's all right," he said. "I'll see you through tonight. I owe you that for getting me out of that rat pit. One more week, and I was going to go insane."

Just imagining it gave me a chill. There were worse fates than being on an I.S. death list. I touched his shoulder briefly and eased back into my seat, surreptitiously watching him as he lost his hidden tension and his breath came easier. The more I knew about him, the larger his contrasts with most of humanity became. But instead of worrying me, it made me feel more secure. Back to my hero/damsel in distress syndrome. I'd read too many fairy tales as a child, and I was too much a realist not to enjoy being rescued once in a while.

An uncomfortable silence settled in, and my anxiety swelled. What if we were too late? What if Trent changed the flight? What if it had all been an elaborate setup? *God help me,* I thought. I had gambled everything on the next few hours. If this didn't happen, I had nothing.

"Witch!" Jenks shouted, jerking my attention to him. I realized he had been trying to get my attention for the last few moments. "Pick me up," he demanded. "I can't see jack from here."

I offered him a hand and he clambered up. "I can't imagine why everyone avoids you when you can't fly," I said dryly.

"This never would have *happened*," Jenks said loudly, "if *someone* hadn't torn my freaking *wing* off."

I set him on my shoulder, where we could both watch the outgoing traffic as we headed into the Cincinnati–Northern Kentucky International Airport. Most people just called it the Hollows International, or even more simply, the "Big H.I." The passing cars were briefly lit by the scattered streetlights. The lights became more numerous the closer we came to the terminals. A flash of excitement went through me, and I straightened in my seat. Nothing was going to go wrong. I was going to nail him. Whatever Trent was, I was going to get him. "What time is it?" I asked.

"Eleven-fifteen," Jenks muttered.

"Eleven-twenty," Edden corrected, pointing to the van's clock.

"Eleven-fifteen," the pixy snarled back. "I know where the sun is better than you know what hole to pee out of."

"Jenks!" I said, aghast. Nick uncrossed his arms, a wisp of his confidence returning.

Edden raised a restraining hand. "It's all right, Ms. Morgan."

Clayton, an uptight cop who didn't seem to trust me, met my eyes in the rearview mirror. "Actually, sir," he said reluctantly, "that clock is five minutes fast."

"See?" Jenks exclaimed.

Edden reached for the car phone and snapped on the speaker so we all could hear. "Let's make sure that plane is grounded and everyone is in place," he said.

Anxious, I adjusted my arm sling as Edden punched three numbers into the phone. "Ruben," he barked into it, holding it like it was a mike. "Talk to me."

There was a brief hesitation, then a masculine voice

crackled through the speakers. "Captain. We're waiting at the gate, but the plane isn't here."

"Not there!" I shouted, wincing as I yanked myself to the edge of the seat. "They should be boarding by now."

"It never came to the tunnel, sir," Ruben continued. "Everyone is waiting at the terminal. They say it's a minor repair and should only take an hour. This isn't your doing?"

I glanced from the speaker to Edden. I could almost see the ideas circulating behind his speculating expression. "No," he finally said. "Stay put." He broke the connection and the faint hiss disappeared.

"What is going on?" I shouted into his ear, and he gave me a black look.

"Get your butt back in your seat, Morgan," he said. "It's probably your friend's daylight restrictions. The airline won't make everyone wait on the tarmac when the terminal is empty."

I glanced at Nick, whose fingers were nervously tapping out the rhythm of an unheard beat. Still uneasy, I settled back. The landing beacon from the airport ran an arc across the underside of the clouds. We were nearly there.

Edden punched in a number from memory, a smile easing over his face as he took the phone off the speaker. "Hello, Chris?" he said, as I faintly heard a woman's voice answer. "Got a question for ya. Seems there's a Southwest flight stuck on the tarmac. Eleven forty-five to L.A.? What's up with it?" He hesitated, listening, and I found myself chewing on a hangnail. "Thanks, Chris." He chuckled. "How about the thickest steak in the city?" Again he chuckled, and I swear, his ears reddened.

Jenks snickered at something I couldn't hear. I glanced at Nick, but he was ignoring me.

"Chrissy," Edden drawled. "My wife might have a problem with that." Jenks laughed with Edden, and I tugged a curl, nervous. "Talk to you later," he said, and clicked the phone off.

"Well?" I asked from the edge of my seat.

The remnants of Edden's smile refused to leave him. "The plane is grounded. Seems the I.S. had a tip there's a bag of Brimstone on it."

"Turn it all," I swore. The bus was the decoy, not the airport. What was Trent doing?

Edden's eyes glinted. "The I.S. is fifteen minutes away. We could pull it right out from under them."

On my shoulder, Jenks started to swear.

"We aren't here for Brimstone," I protested, as everything started falling apart. "We're here for biodrugs!" Fuming, I went silent as a loud car approached us, heading back into the city.

"That one's above city code," Edden said. "Clayton, see if you can get a number off it."

Mind whirling, I waited for it to pass before I tried to speak again. The engine was racing as if the driver was doing thirty over the speed limit, but the car was hardly moving. The gears whined as it tried to shift in an all-too-familiar sound. *Francis*, I thought, my breath catching.

"That's Francis!" both Jenks and I shouted as I spun to see his broken taillight. My vision swam from the pain the quick movement started, but I half crawled to the far backseat, Jenks still on my shoulder. "That's Francis," I cried, my heart pounding. "Turn around. Stop! That's Francis."

Edden hit his fist into the dash. "Damn," he swore. "We're too late."

"No!" I shouted. "Don't you see? Trent is switching them. The biodrugs and Brimstone. The I.S. isn't there yet. Francis is switching them!"

Edden stared at me, his face alternating in the shadow and light as we continued up the long drive to the airport.

"Francis has the drugs! Turn around!" I shouted.

The van stopped at a traffic light. "Captain?" the driver prompted.

"Morgan," Edden said, "you're crazy if you think I'm going to pass up the chance to slip a Brimstone take right out from under the I.S. You don't even know if that was him or not."

Jenks laughed. "That was Francis. Rachel burned out his clutch right proper."

I grimaced. "Francis has the drugs. They're going out by bus. I'd bet my life on it."

Edden's eyes narrowed and his jaw clenched. "You have," he said shortly. "Clayton, turn around."

I slumped, letting out a breath I hadn't known I'd been holding.

"Captain?"

"You heard me!" he said, clearly not happy. "Turn around. Do what the witch says." He turned to me, his face tight. "You'd better be right, Morgan," he nearly growled.

"I am." Stomach churning, I settled back, bracing myself at the sharp U-turn. *I had better be right,* I thought, glancing at Nick.

An I.S. truck passed us on its way to the airport, silent with its lights flashing. Edden hit the dash so hard it was a wonder the air bag didn't come out. He snatched up the radio. "Rose!" he bellowed. "Did the dog team find anything at the bus depot?"

"No, Captain. They're on their way in now."

"Get them back out there," he said. "Who do we have in the Hollows in plainclothes?"

"Sir?" She sounded confused.

"Who's in the Hollows that I didn't move to the airport?" he shouted.

"Briston is at the Newport mall in plainclothes," she said. The faint ringing of a phone intruded, and she shouted, "Someone get that!" There was hesitation. "Gerry is backing her up, but he's in uniform."

"Gerry," Edden muttered, clearly not pleased. "Move them to the bus depot."

"Briston and Gerry to bus depot," she repeated slowly.

"Tell them to use their ACGs," Edden added, shooting a glance at me.

"ACGs?" Nick asked.

"Anticharm gear," I said, and he nodded.

"We're looking for a white male, early thirties. Witch. Name is Francis Percy. I.S. runner."

"He's no better than a warlock," I interjected, bracing myself as we came to an abrupt halt at a red light.

"The suspect is probably carrying spells," Edden continued.

"He's harmless," I muttered.

"Do not approach unless he tries to leave," Edden said tightly.

"Yeah." I snorted as we lurched into motion again. "He might bore you to death."

Edden turned to me. "Will you shut your mouth?"

I shrugged, then wished I hadn't as my shoulder started to throb.

"Did you get that, Rose?" he said into the phone.

"Armed, dangerous, don't approach unless he tries to leave. Gotcha."

Edden grunted. "Thanks, Rose." He flicked the radio off with a thick finger.

Jenks yanked on my ear, and I let out a yelp.

"There he is!" the pixy shrilled. "Look. Right ahead of us."

Nick and I leaned forward to see. The broken taillight was like a beacon. We watched as Francis signaled, squealing his tires as he lurched into the bus depot. A horn blew, and I smirked. Francis had nearly been hit by a bus.

"Okay," Edden said softly as we circled to park on the far side of the lot. "We have five minutes until the dog team gets here, fifteen for Briston and Gerry. He will have to register the packages with the front desk. It will be a nice proof of ownership." Edden undid his seat belt and spun his bucket chair as the van halted. He looked as eager as a vamp with that toothy grin of his. "No one even look at him until everyone gets here. Got it?"

"Yeah, I got it," I said, jittery. I didn't like being under someone else's direction, but what he said made sense. Nervous, I slid across the seat to press my face to Nick's window and watch Francis struggle with three flat boxes.

"That him?" Edden said, his voice cold.

I nodded. Jenks walked down my arm and stood on the sill of the window. His wings were a blur as he used them for balance. "Yeah," the pixy snarled. "That's the pancake."

Glancing up, I realized I was almost in Nick's lap. Embarrassed, I put myself where I belonged. The aspirin was starting to wear off, and though my remaining amulet would be good for days, the pain was starting to break through with an unsettling frequency. But it was the fatigue I was really worried about. My heart was hammering as if I had just finished a race. I didn't think it was just from the excitement.

Francis kicked his car door shut and tottered into motion. He was the picture of self-importance as he strutted into the depot in his loud shirt with the turned-up collar. I smirked as he smiled at a woman coming out and got a quick brush-off. But on remembering his fear while sitting in Trent's office, my contempt took on a shade of pity for the insecure man.

"Okay, boys and girls," Edden said, pulling my attention back. "Clayton, stay here. Send Briston in when she arrives. I don't want anyone out of plainclothes in sight of the windows." He watched Francis go through the double doors. "Have Rose move everyone in from the airport. Looks like the witch, er, Ms. Morgan was right."

"Yes sir." Clayton reluctantly reached for the car phone.

Doors started to open. It was obvious we weren't your typical group of bus patrons, but Francis was probably too stupid to notice. Edden stuffed his yellow FIB hat into a back pocket. Nick was a thin nobody; he looked like he belonged. But my bruises and sling drew more attention than if I had a bell and a card that said, "Will work for spells."

"Captain Edden?" I said as he slipped out and stood waiting. "Give me a minute."

Edden and Nick looked wonderingly back at me as I rummaged in my bag. "Rachel," Jenks said from Nick's shoulder. "You've got to be kidding. Ten makeup charms couldn't make you look better right now."

"Go Turn yourself," I muttered. "Francis will recognize me. I need an amulet."

Edden watched with interest. Feeling the press of adrenaline, I awkwardly rummaged with my good hand in my bag for an aging spell. Finally I dumped the bag onto the seat, grabbed the right charm and invoked it. As I set it around my neck, Edden made a sound of disbelief and admiration. His acceptance—no, approval—was gratifying. That he had taken my pain amulet earlier had a lot to do with me agreeing to owing him a favor or two. Whenever a human showed any appreciation for my skills, I got all warm and fuzzy. *Sucker.*

Jamming everything away in my bag, I creakily eased myself out of the van.

"Ready?" Jenks said sarcastically. "Sure you don't want to brush your hair?"

"Shove it, Jenks," I said as Nick offered me a hand. "I can get down by myself," I added.

Jenks made the jump from Nick to me, settling on my shoulder. "You look like an old woman," the pixy said. "Act like it."

"She is." Edden grabbed my shoulder to keep me from falling as my vamp boots hit the pavement. "She reminds me of my mother." His eyes scrunched as he made a face and waved his hand before his nose. "She even smells like her."

"Shut up, all of you," I said, hesitating as my deep breath made me light-headed. The jarring pain from my landing had gone straight up my spine and into my skull, settling itself for a long stay. Refusing to let my fatigue get a foothold, I jerked away from Edden and hobbled to the doors. The two men followed, three paces behind. I felt like a slob in my fat jeans and that awful plaid shirt. Carrying the illusion of being old didn't help, either. I tugged at the door, unable to open it. "Someone open this door for me!" I exclaimed, and Jenks laughed.

Nick took my arm as Edden opened the door and a gust of overheated air billowed into us. "Here," Nick said. "Lean on me. You look more like an old lady that way."

The pain I could deal with. It was the fatigue that overwhelmed my pride and forced me to accept Nick's offered arm. It was either that or crawl into the bus station.

I shuffled in, a stir of excitement quickening my pulse as I scanned the long front counter for Francis. "There he is," I whispered.

Almost hidden behind a fake tree, Francis was talking to a young woman in a city uniform. The Percy charm was having its usual effect, and she looked annoyed. Three boxes were on the counter beside him. My continued existence was in those boxes.

Nick pulled gently on my good elbow. "Let's sit you down over here, Mother," he said.

"Call me that again and I'll take care of your family planning for you," I threatened.

"Mother," Jenks said, his wings fanning my neck in fitful spurts.

"Enough," Edden said softly, a new hardness in his voice. His eyes never left Francis. "All three of you are going to sit over there and wait. No one moves unless Percy tries to leave. I'm going to make sure those boxes don't get on a bus." His gaze still on Francis, he touched the weapon hidden behind his jacket and casually made his way to the counter. Edden beamed at a second clerk before he even got close.

Sit and wait? Yeah, I could do that.

I gave in to Nick's gentle pull and moved toward the bank of chairs. They were orange, same as at the FIB, and looked equally comfortable. Nick helped me ease down into one, taking the chair next to mine. He stretched out and pretended to nap, his eyes cracked to watch Francis. I sat stiffly with my bag on my lap, clutching it as I had seen old ladies do. Now I knew why. I hurt all over, and I felt like I would fall apart if I relaxed.

A kid shrieked, and I took a quick breath. My eyes drifted from Francis, busy making an ass of himself, to the other patrons. There was a tired mom with three kids—one still in diapers—arguing with a clerk over the interpretation of a coupon. A handful of businessmen absorbed in their business, striding importantly, as if this was only a bad dream and not the reality of their existence. Young lovers pressed dangerously close, probably fleeing parents. Vagrants. A tattered old man caught my eye and winked.

I started. This wasn't safe. The I.S. could be anywhere, ready to tag me.

"Relax, Rache," Jenks whispered as if reading my mind. "The I.S. isn't going to nack you with the captain of the FIB in the same room."

"How can you be so sure?" I said.

I felt the wind on my neck as he fanned his useless wings. "I'm not."

Nick opened his eyes and sat up. "How are you doing?" he asked quietly.

"I'm fine," Jenks said. "Thanks for asking. Did you know some lunker at the FIB snapped my freaking wing off? My wife is gonna kill me."

I managed a smile. "Hungry," I answered Nick. "Exhausted."

Nick glanced at me before returning his gaze to Francis. "You want something to eat?" He jingled the coins in his pocket, left over from the cab fare to the FIB. "You have enough for something out of the machine there."

I let a faint smile come over me. It was nice to have someone worried about me. "Sure. Thanks. Something with chocolate?"

"Chocolate," Nick affirmed, standing up. He glanced from the vending machines across the room to Francis. The snot was leaning halfway across the counter, probably trying to get her phone number. I watched Nick walk away. For someone so thin, he certainly moved with grace. I wondered what he had done to have gotten hauled into the FIB.

"Something with chocolate," Jenks drawled in a high falsetto. "Ohhhh, Nick. You're my hero!"

"Get stuffed," I said, more out of habit than anything else.

"Ya know something, Rache," Jenks said as he settled himself further on my shoulder. "You're going to make one really weird grandma."

I was too tired to come back with anything. I took a deep breath, making it slow so nothing would hurt. My eyes flicked from Francis and back to Nick, anticipation making my stomach feel tight. "Jenks," I said, watching Nick's tall shape as he stood before the candy machine, his head bowed over the change in his hand. "What do you think about Nick?"

The pixy snorted, then seeing I was serious, settled down. "He's okay," he said. "Won't do anything to hurt you. He's got this hero complex thing going, and you seem to need rescuing. You should have seen his face when you were flat out on Ivy's couch. I thought he was going to turn up his toes to the daisies. Just don't expect him to have your ideas of right or wrong."

My eyebrows pinched, hurting my face. "Black magic?" I whispered. "Oh God, Jenks. Don't tell me he's a practitioner?"

Jenks laughed, sounding like wind chimes. "No. I meant he doesn't have a problem stealing library books."

"Oh." I thought back to his unease in the FIB office and then in the van. Was that all it was? Somehow, I didn't think so. But pixies were known for their judge of character, no matter how flighty, flaky, or mouthy they were. I wondered if Jenks's opinion would change if he knew about my demon mark. I was afraid to ask. Hell, I was too afraid to show it to him.

I looked up as Francis laughed, writing something down on a paper and pushing it toward the ticket lady. He wiped a hand under his narrow nose and gave her a ratty grin. "Good girl," I whispered when she crumpled it up and tossed it over her shoulder as Francis headed for the door.

My heart seemed to catch. He was headed for the door! *Damn.*

I glanced up for help. Nick was struggling with the machine, his back to me. Edden was deep in conversation with an official-looking man in a bus uniform. The captain's face was red, and his eyes were fixed to the boxes behind the counter. "Jenks," I said tersely. "Get Edden."

"What? You want me to crawl over there, maybe?"

Francis was halfway to the door. I didn't trust Clayton outside to be able to stop a dog from taking a leak. I stood, praying that Edden would turn around. He didn't. "Get him," I muttered, ignoring Jenks's outrage as I plucked him from my shoulder and set him on the floor.

"Rachel!" Jenks shouted as I hobbled as fast as I could, trying to get between Francis and the door. I was too slow, and Francis cut ahead of me.

"Excuse me, young man?" I warbled, my pulse racing as I reached out for him. "Would you tell me where the baggage area is?"

Francis spun on a quick heel. I struggled not to show my alarm that he might recognize me and my hatred for what he had done. "This is the bus depot, lady," he said, his thin lips twisted in annoyance. "There is no baggage area. Your stuff is on the curb outside."

"What's that?" I said loudly, mentally cursing Edden. *Where the hell was he?* I grabbed Francis arm in a tight grip, and he looked down at my spell-wrinkled hand.

"It's outside!" he shouted, trying to tug away, reeling as my perfume hit him.

But I wouldn't let go. From the corner of my sight I saw Nick beside the candy machine, staring blankly at my empty seat. His gaze rove over the people, finally catching mine. His eyes widened. He darted to Edden.

Francis had tucked his papers under his arm and was using his other hand to try and pry my fingers from him. "Lemme go, lady," he said. "There's no baggage claim."

My fingers cramped, and he jerked away. Panicking, I watched him tug his shirt straight. "Freaky old bat," he said with a huff. "What do you old hags do, swim in your perfume?" Then his mouth dropped open. "Morgan," he hissed, recognizing me. "He told me you were dead."

"I am," I said, my knees threatening to buckle. I was up on adrenaline alone.

His stupid grin told me he had no idea what was going on. "You're coming with me. Denon will give me a promotion when he sees you."

I shook my head. I had to do this by the book or Edden would be ticked. "Francis Percy, under the authority of the FIB, I am charging you with conspiring to willfully run biodrugs."

His grin vanished as his face went white under his ugly stubble. His gaze darted over my shoulder to the counter. "Shit," he swore, turning to run.

"Stop!" Edden cried out, too far back to be any good.

I lunged at Francis, grabbing the back of his knees. We went down in a painful thump. Francis squirmed, kicking me in the chest as he tried to get away. I gasped, hurting.

A whoosh of air streaked over us where my head had been. I jerked my attention up. Stars crossed my vision as Francis struggled to escape.

No, I thought as a blue ball of flame smashed into the far wall and exploded. *Those stars were real.*

The ground shook at the force of the blast. Women and children screamed, falling back to press against the walls. "What was that?" Francis stammered. He twisted under me, and for a heartbeat we watched, mesmerized, as the flickering blue flame plastered itself in a sunburst across the ugly yellow wall until it folded back in on itself and vanished with a pop.

Frightened for the first time, I turned to look behind me. Standing confidently by the hallway to the back offices was a short tidy man dressed in black, a red ball of ever-after in his hand. A wisp of a woman dressed the same blocked the main doors, her hand on her hip and her white teeth grinning. The third was a muscular man the size of a VW bug by the ticket counter.

It looked like the witch conference at the coast was over. Swell.

Thirty-one

F rancis's breath came in a gulp of understanding. "Let me go!" he shrieked, fear making his voice high and ugly. "Rachel, let me go! They're going to kill you!"

I dug my fingers into him as he struggled. Jaw gritted, I grunted in pain as his effort to flee pulled my stitches out. Blood flowed, and I fumbled in my bag for an amulet, watching from the corner of my sight as the short man's lips moved and the ball in his hand turned from ever-after red to blue. *Damn.* He was invoking his charm.

"I don't have time for this!" I muttered, angry as I lay half atop Francis, trying to tag him.

People were running now. They scattered into hallways and unhindered past the woman and into the parking lot. When witches dueled, only the quick survived. My breath hissed in through my nose as the man's lips stopped moving. Pulling his arm back, he threw the spell.

Gasping, I yanked Francis up and before me.

"No!" he shrieked, his mouth and eyes ugly in fear at the incoming charm.

The force of it slid us across the floor and to the chairs. His elbow jammed into my bruised arm and I grunted in pain. Francis's scream cut off in a frightening gurgle.

My shoulder turned to agony as I frantically pushed him off me. He sagged to the floor, senseless. Scooting backward, I stared. A pulsing blue sheet filmed him. A thin smear of it was on my sleeve. My skin crawled as the haze of blue ever-after reality slid from my sleeve to join that coating Francis. He was convulsing, covered in it. Then he went still.

Breath fast, I looked up. All three assassins were speaking Latin in tandem, their hands making unseen figures in the air. Their motions were graceful and deliberate, looking obscene.

"Rache!" Jenks shrilled from three chairs away. "They're making a net. Get out! You gotta get out!"

Get out? I thought, looking at Francis. The blue had vanished, leaving his arms and legs sprawled in unnatural angles on the floor. Horror flashed through me. I had made Francis take my hit. It had been an accident. I hadn't meant to kill him.

My stomach clenched, and I thought I might vomit. I pushed my fear aside, using my anger to get to my knees. I grasped for an orange chair, pulling on it to lever myself upright. They had made me make Francis take my hit. *Oh God. He was dead because of me.*

"Why did you make me do that?" I said softly, turning to the short man. I took a step forward as the air started to tingle. I couldn't say that what I'd done was wrong—I was alive—but I hadn't wanted to do that. "Why did you make me do that?" I said louder, anger swelling as the sensation of pinpricks broke over me like a wave. It was the beginnings of the net. I didn't care. I scooped up my bag as I passed it, kicking my uninvoked amulet out of the way.

The ley line witch's eyes grew wide in surprise as I came at him. Face going determined, he started chanting louder. I could hear the other two whispering like an ash-laden wind. It was easy to move in the center of the net, but the closer I got to the edge, the harder it became. We stood in a blue-tinted bowl of air. Past it, Edden and Nick struggled, trying to push their way in.

"You made me do that!" I shouted.

My hair lifted and fell in a breath of ever-after as their net went solid. Jaw clenched, I spared a glance beyond the haze of blue, seeing the muscle-bound mountain of a man outside it, keeping it in place even as he threw ley line spells at the hopelessly outclassed FIB officers who had swarmed in. I didn't care. Two of them in here with me. They weren't going anywhere.

I was angry and frustrated. I was tired of hiding in a church, tired of ducking splat balls, tired of dunking my mail in saltwater, and tired of being scared. And because of me, Francis was lying on the dirty cold floor of a cruddy bus depot. Worm that he was, he hadn't deserved that.

I swung my bag forward as I limped toward the short man. I reached unseeing, feeling the notches of the amulets for a sleep charm. Mad as hell, I wiped it across my neck, letting it go to dangle from the cord. His lips started moving, and those long hands of his began sketching patterns. If it was a nasty spell, I had four seconds. Five, if it was strong enough to kill me.

"Nobody!" I exclaimed, staggering forward by will alone. His eyes widened as he saw my demon scar as I made a fist. "Nobody makes me kill anyone!" I shouted, swinging.

We both staggered as I connected with his jaw. Shaking my hand from the pain, I hunched into myself. The man stumbled back, catching himself. The gathering of power abruptly lessened. Furious, I gritted my teeth and swung again. He hadn't expected a physical attack—not many ley line witches did—and he raised his arm to block me. Grabbing his fingers, I gave them a backward twist, breaking at least three.

His scream of pain was echoed by the woman's cry of dismay from across the lobby. She started forward at a run. Still gripping his hand, I swung my foot up, yanking him forward to smack into it. His eyes bulged. Clutching his stomach, he fell back. His watering gaze tracked someone behind me. Still not breathing, he dropped and rolled to the right.

Gasping, I hit the ground and rolled to the left. There was a boom, and my hair blew back. I pulled my head up from the floor as the ball of green ever-after spread itself on the wall and down the hallway. I turned. The wisp of a woman was still coming, her face tight and her mouth going non-stop. A red ball of ever-after in her hand swelled, streaked with her own green aura as she tried to bend it to her will.

"You want a piece of me?" I shouted from the floor. "Do ya?" Staggering, I rose to put a hand to the wall to stay upright.

The man behind me said a word. I couldn't hear it. It was too alien for my mind to understand. It rolled into my head, and I struggled to make sense of it. Then my eyes opened wide and my mouth dropped in a silent scream as it exploded inside me.

Clutching my head, I fell to my knees, screaming. "No!" I shrieked, clawing at my scalp. "No! Get out!" Black-crusted red slashes. Squirming maggots. The sour taste of decayed flesh.

The memory of it burnt itself out from my subconscious. I looked up, panting. I was spent. There was nothing left. My heart pounded against my lungs. Black spots danced at the edges of my sight. My skin felt tingly, as if it wasn't mine. *What the hell had that been?*

The man and the woman stood together, her hand under his elbow as she supported him hunched over his broken hand. Their faces were angry, confident—and satisfied. He couldn't use his hand, but clearly he didn't need it to kill me. All he had to do was say that word again.

I was dead. The more-than-usual kind of dead. But I would take one of them with me.

"Now!" I heard Edden shout faintly as if through a fog.

All three of us started as the net went down. The shadow of blue hazing in the air fell into itself and vanished. That big witch outside the net was on the floor with his hands laced behind his head. Six FIB officers ringed him. Hope twanged through me, almost painful.

A darting shape drew my eye. Nick. "Here!" I shouted, grasping the cord of the invoked sleep charm from the floor where I had dropped it and winging it to him.

The assassin turned, but it was too late. White-faced, Nick dropped the loop over the head of the woman and backpedaled. She crumpled. The man fumbled for her, easing her to the floor. Mouth agape in surprise, he darted his glance over the room.

"This is the FIB!" Edden shouted, looking awkward in his sling and with his weapon held in his left hand. "Put your hands behind your head and stop moving your mouth or I'll blow it the hell off!"

The man blinked, shocked. He glanced at the woman at his feet. Taking a breath, he ran.

"No!" I cried. Still on the floor, I dumped my bag. I grabbed an amulet, smacked it against my bleeding neck, and threw it at his feet. Half the charms in my bag were tangled in it. Like a bola, it flew through the air at knee height. It hit him, wrapping around his leg like he was a cow. Tripping, he went down.

FIB personnel swarmed over him. Breath held, I watched, waiting. He stayed down. My charm had dropped him into a sweet, helpless sleep.

The noise of the FIB personnel beat at me. With a single-minded purpose, I crawled to Francis lying alone by the chairs. Fearing the worst, I rolled him over. His sightless eyes stared up at the ceiling. My face went slack. *God, no.*

But then his chest moved, and a stupid-ass smile quirked his thin lips as they shifted in whatever dream he was in. He was alive and breathing, deep under a ley line spell. Relief poured through me. I hadn't killed him.

"Tag!" I screamed into his unconscious, narrow, ratty face. "Do you hear me you sodden sack of camel dung? Tag! You're it!" *I hadn't killed him.*

Edden's scuffed brown shoes scraped to a halt beside me. My face went tight, and I wiped a blood-smeared hand under my eye. *I hadn't killed Francis.* Squinting, I ran my gaze up Edden's creased khakis and his blue arm sling. His hat was on, and I couldn't seem to take my eyes off the blue letters spelling out FIB glowing against the yellow background.

A satisfied harrumph came out of him, and his wide grin made him look even more like a troll. Numb, I blinked as my lungs pressed against each other. It seemed to take an awful amount of effort to fill them.

"Morgan," the man said happily, extending a thick hand to help me up. "You okay?"

"No," I croaked. I reached for him, but the floor tilted. As Nick gasped a warning, I passed out.

Thirty-two

"**L**isten!" Francis shouted, spittle flying from him in his fervor. "I'll tell you everything. I want a deal. I want protection. I was only supposed to do Brimstone takes. That's all. But someone got spooked and Mr. Kalamack wanted the drops switched. He told me to switch the drops. That's all! I'm not a biodrug runner. Please. You gotta believe me!"

Edden said nothing, playing the silent bad cop as he sat across from me. The shipping papers Francis had signed were under his thick hand as an unspoken accusation. Francis cowered in a chair at the end of the table, two chairs down from us. His eyes were wide and frightened. He looked pathetic in his bright shirt and polyester jacket with the sleeves rolled up, trying to live the dream he wanted his life to be.

I carefully stretched my sore body, my gaze falling on the three cardboard boxes stacked ominously at one end of the table. A smile curved over me. Hidden under the table and in my lap was an amulet I'd taken from the head assassin. It glowed an ugly red, but if it was what I thought it was, it would go black when I was dead or in the event the contract on my life had been paid off. I was going home to sleep for a week as soon as the little sucker went out.

Edden had moved Francis and me into the employees' break room to stave off a repeat of the witch attack. Thanks to the local news van, everyone in the city knew where I was—and I was just waiting for fairies to crawl out of the ductwork. I had more faith in the ACG blanket draped over me than the two FIB officers standing around to make the long room seem cramped.

I tugged the blanket closer around my neck, appreciating its minor protection as much as its warmth. Spiderweb-thin strands of titanium were woven into it, guaranteed to dilute strong spells and break mild ones. Several of the FIB officers had yellow coveralls made out of a similar fabric, and I was hoping Edden would forget to ask for it back.

As Francis babbled, my eyes ran over the grimy walls decorated with sappy sentiments about happy workplaces and how to sue your employer. A microwave and a battered fridge took up one wall, a coffee-stained counter took up another. I eyed the decrepit candy machine, hungry again. Nick and Jenks were in the corner, both trying to stay out of the way.

The heavy door to the break room opened, and I turned as an FIB officer and a young woman in a provocative red dress slipped in. An FIB badge hung around her neck, and the yellow FIB hat perched on her overstyled hair looked like a cheap prop. I guessed they were Gerry and Briston from the mall. The woman's face scrunched up and she whispered a derisive, "Perfume." My breath puffed out. I'd love to explain, but it would probably do more harm than good.

The whispers of the FIB officers had lessoned dramatically after I'd ditched the old lady disguise and turned into a battered twenty-something with frizzy red hair and curves where they ought to be. I felt like a bean in a maraca, and with my sling, my black eye, and the blanket draped around me, I probably looked like a disaster refugee.

"Rachel!" Francis cried urgently, drawing my attention back to him. His triangular face was pale, and his dark hair had gone stringy. "I need protection. I'm not like you. Kalamack is going to kill me. I'll do anything! You want Kalamack; I want protection. I was only supposed to do Brimstone. It's not my fault. Rachel, you've got to believe me."

"Yeah." Tired beyond belief, I took a deep breath and looked at the clock. It was just after midnight, but it felt like nearly sunrise.

Edden smiled. His chair scraped as he got to his feet. "Let's open 'em up, people."

Two FIB officers eagerly stepped forward. I clutched the amulet in my lap and anxiously leaned to see. My continued existence was in those boxes. The sound of ripping tape was loud. Francis wiped his mouth, watching in what looked like a morbid fascination and fear.

"Sweet mother of God," one of the officers swore, backing away from the table as the box opened. "They're tomatoes."

Tomatoes? I lurched to my feet, grunting in pain. Edden was a breath ahead of me.

"It's inside them!" Francis babbled. "The drugs are inside. He hides the drugs in tomatoes so the custom dogs can't smell them." White-faced behind his stubble, he pushed his sleeves up again. "They're in there. Look!"

"Tomatoes?" Edden said, disgust crossing him. "He ships them out in tomatoes?"

Perfect red tomatoes with green stems stared back at me from their cardboard packing tray. Impressed, my lips parted. Trent must have wedged the vials into the developing fruit, and by the time it was ripe, the drug was safely hidden inside a faultless fruit no human would touch.

"Get over there, Nick," Jenks demanded, but Nick didn't move, his long face ashen. At the sink, two officers who had opened the boxes were violently scrubbing their hands.

Looking like he was going to be sick, Edden stretched to pick a tomato up, examining the red fruit. There was not a blemish or cut on the perfect skin. "I suppose we probably ought to open one up," he said reluctantly, setting it on the table and wiping his hand on his pants.

"I'll do it," I volunteered when no one spoke up, and someone slid a tarnished table knife across the table at me. I picked it up with my left hand, then remembering my other hand was in a sling, I looked for some help. Not one FIB officer would meet my gaze. Not one was willing to touch the fruit. Frowning, I set the knife aside. "Oh well," I breathed, raising my hand and bringing it down on top of the fruit.

It hit with a sodden splat. Red goo splattered over Edden's white shirt. His face went as gray as his mustache. There was a cry of disgust from the watching FIB officers. Someone gagged. Heart pounding, I took the tomato in one hand and squeezed. Pulp and seeds squirted from between my fingers. My breath caught as a cylinder the size of my pinky pressed against my palm. I dropped the mass of pulp and shook my hand. Shouts of dismay rose as the red flesh splattered against the table. It was only a tomato, but one would think I was pulping a decaying heart by the noise the big, strong FIB officers were making.

"Here it is!" I said triumphantly, picking out an institutional-looking vial gooped in tomato slime and holding it aloft. I'd never seen biodrugs before. I had thought there'd be more.

"Well, I'll be," Edden said softly, taking the ampule in a napkin. The satisfaction of discovery had overwhelmed his abhorrence.

A wisp of fear tightened Francis's eyes as his gaze darted from me to the boxes. "Rachel?" he whimpered. "You'll get me protection from Mr. Kalamack, right?"

Anger stiffened my back. He had betrayed me and everything I believed in—for money. I turned to him, the gray edging my sight as leaned over the table and I put myself in his face. "I saw you at Kalamack's," I said, and his lips went bloodless. Grabbing the front of his shirt, I left a red smear across the colorful fabric. "You're a black runner, and you're gonna burn." I pushed him back into his chair and sat down, my heart pounding from the effort—satisfied.

"Whoa!" Edden said softly. "Someone arrest him and read him his rights."

Francis's mouth opened and closed in alarm as Briston pulled her cuffs from her hip and snapped them around his wrists. I reached into my sling and awkwardly un-hooked my charm bracelet. I tossed it to land next to her—just in case Francis had something nasty in his rolled-up sleeves—and at Edden's nod, she laced it on Francis's wrist as well.

The soft and certain pattern of the Miranda flowed out in a reassuring cadence. Francis's eyes were wide and fixed to the vial. I don't think he even heard the man at his elbow.

"Rachel!" he cried as he found his voice. "Don't let him kill me. He's going to kill me. I gave you Kalamack. I want a deal. I want protection! That's the way it works, right?"

My eyes met Edden's and I wiped my hand free of the last of the tomato on a scratchy napkin. "Do we have to listen to this right now?"

A wicked, not so nice smile came over Edden. "Briston, get this bucket of crap into the van. Put his confession on tape and paper. And read him his rights again. No mis-takes."

Francis stood, his chair scraping the dirty tile. His narrow face was drawn and his hair had fallen into his eyes. "Rachel, tell them Kalamack is going to kill me!"

I looked at Edden, my lips pressed tight. "He's right."

At my words, Francis whimpered. His dark eyes looked haunted, as if unsure whether he should be happy or upset that someone was taking his worries seriously.

"Get him an ACG blanket," Edden said in a bothered tone. "Keep him secure."

My shoulders eased. If they got Francis tucked out of sight quick enough, he'd be safe.

Briston's gaze flicked to the boxes. "And the—uh—tomatoes, Captain?"

His grin widened as he leaned over the table, careful to keep his arms out of the splattered mess. "Let's leave that for the evidence crew."

Clearly relieved, Briston gestured for Clayton. "Rachel!" Francis babbled as they pulled him to the door. "You're going to help me, right? I'll tell them everything!"

All four of the FIB officers roughly escorted him out, Briston's heels clicking smartly. The door snicked shut, and I closed my eyes at the blessed silence. "What a night," I whispered.

Edden's chuckle pulled my eyes open. "I owe you, Morgan," he said, three paper napkins between his fingers and the tomato-slimed white vial. "After seeing you with those two witches, I don't know why Denon was so set on bringing you down. You're a hell of a runner."

"Thanks," I whispered around a long sigh, stifling a shudder as my thoughts returned to trying to fight two ley line witches at once. It had been close. If Edden hadn't jarred the concentration of that third witch to break the net, I would have been dead. "Thanks for getting my back, I mean," I said softly.

The absence of the FIB officers had pulled Nick from the corner, and he handed me a foam cup of something that might have once been coffee. He carefully lowered himself into the chair beside me, his gaze flicking between the three boxes and the tomato-smeared table. It seemed seeing Edden touch one had given him a measure of courage. I flashed him a tired smile and cupped my good hand about the coffee, taking advantage of its warmth.

"I'd appreciate it if you would inform the I.S. you're paying off my contract," I said. "Before I set foot out of this room," I added, tugging the ACG blanket closer.

Edden set the vial down with a reverent slowness. "With Percy's confession, Kalamack can't buy his way out of this." A smile played about his square face. "Clayton tells me we got the Brimstone at the airport, too. I ought to get out from behind my desk more often."

I sipped my coffee. The bitter swill filled my mouth, and I reluctantly swallowed. "How about that call?" I said as I set the cup down and looked at the red amulet glowing in my lap.

Edden sat up with a grunt and took out a slim cell phone. Cradling it in his left hand, he hit a single digit with his thumb. I looked at Jenks to see if he noticed. The pixy's wings blurred, and with an impatient look, he slid from Nick and walked stiffly down the table to me. I raised him up to my shoulder before he could ask. Levering himself close to my ear, Jenks whispered, "He's got the I.S. on speed dial."

"How about that," I said, the tape pulling on my eyebrow as I tried to raise it.

"I'm going to wring every drop of gloat out of this one," Edden said, slouching back in his chair as the phone rang. The white vial stood out before him like a tiny trophy. "Denon!" he shouted. "Full moon next week. How you doing?"

My jaw dropped. It wasn't the I.S. Edden had on speed dial. It was my old boss. And he was alive? The demon hadn't killed him? He must have had someone else do his dirty work.

Edden harrumphed, clearly misunderstanding my surprise, before turning his attention back to the phone. "That's great," he said, interrupting Denon. "Listen. I want you to call off the run you have on a Ms. Rachel Morgan. Maybe you know her? She used to work for you." There was a slight pause, and I almost caught what Denon said, it was so loud. On my shoulder, Jenks fanned his wings in agitation. A sly smile came over Edden.

"You *do* remember her?" Edden said. "Great. Call your people off. We're paying for it." Again a hesitation, and his smile grew. "Denon, I'm offended. She can't work for the

FIB. I'll move the funds when the accounts open in the morning. Oh, and could you send one of your trolleys out to the main bus depot? I've three witches needing extradition to Inderlander custody. They were making a ruckus, and since we were in the neighborhood, we downed them for you."

There was a spate of angry conversation from the other end, and Jenks gasped. "Ooooh, Rachel," he stammered. "He's ticked."

"No," Edden said firmly, sitting straighter. He was clearly enjoying this. "No," he said again, grinning. "You should have thought about that before you set them on her."

The butterflies in my stomach wanted out. "Tell him to dissolution the master amulet keyed to me," I said, setting the amulet to clatter onto the table like a guilty secret.

Edden put a hand over the phone, drowning out Denon's irate voice. "A what?"

My eyes were fixed on the amulet. It was still glowing. "Tell him," I said, taking a slow breath, "I want the master amulet keyed to me dissolutioned. Every assassin team spelling for me has an amulet just like this one." I touched it with a finger, wondering if the tingle I felt was imagined or real. "As long as it's glowing, they won't stop."

His eyebrows arched. "A life-sign monitoring amulet?" he said, and I nodded, giving him a sour smile. It was a courtesy from one assassin trio to the next so no one would waste time plotting to murder someone already dead.

"Huh," Edden said, putting the phone to his ear. "Denon," he said cheerfully. "Be a good boy and dunk the charm monitoring Morgan's life signs so she can go home to bed."

Denon's angry voice was loud through the small speaker. I jerked when Jenks laughed, vaulting himself up to sit in the swing of my earring. Licking my lips, I stared at the amulet, willing it to go out. Nick's hand touched my shoulder, and I jumped. My eyes fixed back onto the amulet with a hungry intensity.

"There!" I exclaimed as the disk flickered and went out. "Look! It's gone!" Pulse hammering, my eyes closed in a long blink as I imagined them going out all over the city. Denon must have had the master amulet with him, wanting to know the exact moment the assassins were successful. He was one sick puppy.

Fingers shaking, I picked it up. The disk felt heavy in my hand. My gaze met Nick's. He seemed as relieved as I was, the smile on his face reaching his eyes. Exhaling, I fell back against the chair and slipped the disk into my bag. My death threat was gone.

Denon's angry questions echoed through the phone. Edden grinned all the wider. "Turn on your TV, Denon, my friend," he said, holding the speaker away from his ear for a moment. Drawing it close, he shouted, "Turn on your TV. I said, turn on your TV!" Edden's eyes flicked to mine. "Bye-bye, Denon," he said in a mocking falsetto. "See you at church."

The beep as the circuit broke was loud. Edden leaned back in his chair and crossed his good arm over the one in the sling. His smile was one of satisfaction. "You're a free witch, Ms. Morgan. How's it feel to come back from the dead?"

My hair swung forward as I looked down at myself, every scratch and bruise complaining for attention. My arm throbbed in its sling, and my face was one solid ache. "Great," I said, managing a smile. "It feels just great." It was over. I could go home and hide under my covers.

Nick stood and put a hand on my shoulder. "Come on, Rachel," he said softly. "Let's get you home." His dark eyes rose to Edden's briefly. "She can do the paperwork tomorrow?"

"Sure." Edden rose, taking the vial cautiously between two fingers and dropping it into a shirt pocket. "I'd like you to be at Mr. Percy's interrogation, if you could manage it. You have a lie-detecting amulet, don't you? I'm curious to see how they compare to our electronic devices."

My head bobbed, and I tried to find the strength to rise. I didn't want to tell Edden how much trouble it was to make those things, but I wasn't going to go spell shopping for at least a month, to give the charms aimed at me a chance to filter out of the marketplace. Maybe two months. I looked at the black amulet on the table and stifled a shudder. *Maybe never.*

A soft boom of sound shifted the air and the floor trembled. There was a heartbeat of absolute silence, then the faint noise of people shouting filtered through the thick walls. I looked at Edden. "That was an explosion," he breathed, a hundred thoughts racing behind his eyes. But only one struck me. *Trent.*

The door to the break room flung open, smashing into the wall. Briston fell into the room, catching herself at the chair Francis had recently occupied. "Captain Edden," she gasped. "Clayton! My God, Clayton!"

"Stay with the evidence," he said, then darted out the door almost as fast as a vamp. The sound of people shouting drifted in before the door majestically closed. Briston stood in her red dress, her knuckles white as she clenched the back of the chair. Her head was bowed, but I could see her eyes welling up in what looked like grief and frustration.

"Rachel." Jenks prodded at my ear. "Get up. I want to see what happened."

"Trent happened," I whispered, my gut clenching. *Francis.*

"Get up!" Jenks shouted, tugging as if he could yank me up by my ear. "Rachel, get up!"

Feeling like a mule at the plow, I rose. My stomach lurched, and with Nick's help, I hobbled out into the noise and confusion. I hunched under my blanket and held my injured arm tight to me. I knew what I'd find. I'd seen Trent kill a man for less. Expecting him to sit idle as a legal noose slipped around his neck was ludicrous. But how had he moved so quickly?

The lobby was a confusing mess of broken glass and milling people. Cool night air came in through the gaping hole in the wall where glass once hung. Blue and yellow FIB uniforms were everywhere, not that they were helping matters. The stench of burning plastic caught at my throat, and the flickering black and orange of a fire beckoned from the parking lot where the FIB van burned. Red and blue lights flashed against the walls.

"Jenks," I breathed as he tugged on my ear to urge me on. "You keep doing that and I'll squish you myself."

"Then get your sorry little white witch behind out there!" he exclaimed in frustration. "I can't see squat from here."

Nick fended off the well-meaning efforts of good Samaritans who thought I'd been hurt in the explosion, but it wasn't until he scooped up an abandoned FIB hat and set it on my head that everyone left us alone. His arm curved around my waist, supporting me, we haltingly crunched over the broken glass, stepping from the yellow lights of the bus station into the harsher, uncertain come-and-go lights of the FIB's vehicles.

Outside, the local news was having a field day, sequestered in their little corner with bright lights and excited gestures. My stomach twisted as I realized that their presence had likely been responsible for Francis's death.

Squinting at the heat coming from the fire, I made my slow way to where Captain Edden stood quietly watching, thirty feet back from the flaming van. Saying nothing, I came to a standstill beside him. He didn't look at me. The wind gusted, and I coughed at the black taste of burnt rubber. There was nothing to say. Francis had been in there. Francis was dead.

"Clayton had a thirteen-year-old," Edden said, his eyes on the billowing smoke.

I felt as if I had been punched in the gut, and I willed myself to remain upright. Thirteen was not a good age to lose your father. I knew.

Edden took a deep breath and turned to me. The dead expression on his face chilled me. Flickering shadows from the fire pulled the few lines in his face into sharp relief. "Don't worry, Morgan," he said. "The deal was you give me Kalamack, the FIB pays off your contract." Emotion crossed his face, but I couldn't tell if it was rage or pain. "You gave him to me. I lost him. Without Percy's confession, all we have is a dead witch's word over his. And by the time I get a warrant, Kalamack's tomato fields will be plowed under. I'm sorry. He's going to walk. This . . ." He gestured to the fire. "This wasn't your fault."

"Edden—" I started, but he held up his hand.

Pulling away from me, he walked away. "No mistakes," he said to himself, looking more beaten than I felt. An FIB officer in a yellow ACG coverall rushed up to him, hesitating when Edden didn't acknowledge him. The crowd swallowed them up.

I turned back to the sudden bursts of gold and black, feeling ill. Francis was in there. Along with my charms. Guess they weren't so lucky after all.

"This wasn't your fault," Nick said, putting his arm around me again as my knees threatened to buckle. "You warned them. You did everything you could."

I leaned into his support before I fell over. "I know," I said flatly, believing it.

A fire engine wound between the parked cars, clearing the street and drawing an even larger crowd with its sporadic whoops of siren. "Rachel." Jenks tugged on my ear again.

"Jenks," I said in a bitter frustration. "Leave me alone."

"Blow it off your broomstick," the pixy snarled. "Jonathan is across the street."

"Jonathan!" Adrenaline rushed painfully through me, and I pulled from Nick. "Where?"

"Don't look!" Nick and Jenks said simultaneously. Nick put his arm back around me and started to turn me away.

"Stop!" I shouted, ignoring the pain as I tried to see behind me. "Where is he?"

"Keep walking, Rachel," Nick said tightly. "Kalamack might want you dead, too."

"Damn you all back to the Turn!" I shouted. "I want to see!" I went limp in an effort to make Nick stop. It sort of worked as I slipped from him and hit the pavement in an untidy pile.

Twisting, I scanned the opposite street. A familiar, hurried gait drew my attention. Darting between emergency personnel and rubberneckers was Jonathan. The tall, refined man was easy to spot, standing head and shoulders above most of the crowd. He was in a heap of hurry, headed for a car parked before the fire engine. Stomach clenching in worry, I stared at the long black car, knowing who was inside.

I swatted Nick out of the way as he tried to get me upright, cursing the cars and people who kept getting in my line of sight. The back window rolled down. Trent met my eyes and my breath caught. By the light of the emergency vehicles, I could see his face was a mass of bruises and his head was bandaged. The anger in his eyes clenched my heart. "Trent," I hissed as Nick crouched to grip me under my arms and help me up.

Nick froze, and we both watched from the ground as Jonathan came to a halt beside the window. He bent to listen to Trent. My pulse raced as the tall man abruptly straightened, following Trent's gaze across the street to mine. I shivered at the hatred pouring from Jonathan.

Trent's lips moved, and Jonathan jumped. Giving me a final glare, Jonathan walked stiffly to the driver's door. I heard the door slam over the surrounding noise.

I couldn't take my eyes from Trent. His expression remained angry, but he smiled, and my worry tightened at the promise in it. The window went up and the car slowly drove away.

For a moment I could do nothing. The pavement was warm, and if I got up, I would only have to move. Denon hadn't sent the demon after me. Trent had.

Thirty-three

I bent to get the paper from the top step of the church's stoop. The smell of cut grass and damp pavement was almost a balm, filling my senses. There was a sudden rush on the sidewalk. Pulse pounding, I fell to a defensive crouch. The small-girl giggle following the pink bike and tinkly bell down the sidewalk was embarrassing. Her heels flashed as she peddled like the devil was after her. Grimacing, I slapped the paper against the palm of my hand as she disappeared around the corner. I swore, she waited for me every afternoon.

It had been a week since my I.S. death threat was officially nulled, and I was still seeing assassins. But then, more than the I.S. might want me dead.

Exhaling loudly, I willed the adrenaline from me as I yanked the door to the church closed behind me. The comforting crackle of newsprint echoed off the thick support beams and stark walls of the sanctuary as I found the classifieds. I tucked the rest of the paper under an arm and made my way to the kitchen, scanning the personals as I went.

"'Bout time you got up, Rache," Jenks said, his wings clattering as he flew annoying circles around me in the tight confines of the hall. I could smell the garden on him. He was dressed in his "dirt clothes," looking like a miniature Peter Pan with wings. "Are we going to go get that disc or what?"

"Hi, Jenks," I said, a stab of anxiety and anticipation running through me. "Yeah. They called for an exterminator yesterday." I laid the newsprint out on the kitchen table, pushing Ivy's colored pens and maps away to make room. "Look," I said, pointing. "I've got another one."

"Lemme see," the pixy demanded. He landed squarely on the paper, his hands on his hips.

Running my finger across the print, I read aloud, " 'TK seeking to reopen communication with RM concerning possible business venture.' " There was no phone number, but it was obvious who had written it. Trent Kalamack.

A weary unease pulled me to sit at the table, my gaze going past Mr. Fish in his new brandy snifter and out into the garden. Though I had paid off my contract and was reasonably safe from the I.S., I still had to contend with Trent. I knew he was manufacturing biodrugs; I was a threat. Right now he was being patient, but if I didn't agree to be on his payroll, he was going to put me in the ground.

At this point I didn't want Trent's head; I wanted him to leave me alone. Blackmail was entirely acceptable, and undoubtedly safer than trying to get rid of Trent through the courts. He was a businessman, if nothing else, and the hassle of disentangling himself from a trial was probably greater than his desire to have me work for him or see me safely dead. But I needed more than a page out of his daily planner. Today I would get it.

"Nice tights, Jenks," came Ivy's weak croak from the hall.

Startled, I jumped, then changed my motion to adjusting a curl of hair. Ivy was slumped against the doorframe, looking like an apathetic grim reaper in her black robe. Shuffling to the window, she shut the curtains and slumped against the counter in the new dimness.

My chair creaked as I leaned back in it. "You're up early."

Ivy poured a cold cup of coffee from yesterday, sinking down into a chair across from me. Her eyes were red-rimmed and her robe was tied sloppily about her waist. She listlessly fingered the paper where Jenks had left dirty footprints. "Full moon tonight. We doing it?"

I took a quick breath, my heart thumping. Rising, I went to dump out the coffee and make more before Ivy could drink the rest. Even I had higher standards than that. "Yes," I said, feeling my skin tighten.

"Are you sure you feel up to it?" she asked as her eyes settled on my neck.

It was my imagination, but I thought I felt a twinge from where her gaze rested. "I'm fine," I said, making an effort to keep my hand from rising to cover the scar. "Better than good. I'm great." Ivy's tasteless little cakes had made me alternatingly hungry and nauseous, but my stamina returned in an alarming three days rather than three months. Matalina had already removed the stitches from my neck to leave hardly a mark. Having healed that fast was worrisome. I wondered if I was going to pay for it later. And how.

"Ivy?" I asked as I got the grounds out of the fridge. "What was in those little cakes?"

"Brimstone."

I spun, shocked. "What?" I exclaimed.

Jenks snickered, and Ivy didn't drop my gaze as she got to her feet. "I'm kidding," she said flatly. Still I stared at her, my face cold. "Can't you take a joke?" she added, shuffling to the hall. "Give me an hour. I'll call Carmen and get her moving."

Jenks vaulted into the air. "Great," he said, his wings humming. "I'm going to go say good-bye to Matalina." He seemed to glow as a shaft of light pierced the kitchen as he slipped past the curtains.

"Jenks!" I called after him. "We aren't leaving for at least an hour!" It didn't take that long to say good-bye.

"Yeah?" came his faint voice. "You think my kids just popped out of the ground?"

Face warming, I flicked the switch and started the coffee brewing. My motions were quick with anticipation, and a glow settled in to burn in my middle. I had spent the last week planning Jenks's and my excursion out to Trent's in painful detail. I had a plan. I had a backup plan. I had so many plans I was amazed they didn't explode out my ears when I blew my nose.

Between my anxiety and Ivy's anal-retentive adherence to schedules, it was exactly an hour later that we found ourselves at the curb. Both Ivy and I were dressed in biker leather, giving us eleven feet, eight inches of bad-ass attitude between us—Ivy most of it. A version of those assassin life-monitoring amulets hung around our necks, tucked out of sight. It was my fail-safe plan. If I got in trouble, I'd break the charm and Ivy's amulet would turn red. She had insisted on them—along with a lot of other things I thought were unnecessary.

I swung up behind Ivy on her bike, with nothing but that fail-safe amulet, a vial of saltwater to break it, a mink potion, and Jenks. Nick had the rest. With my hair tucked under the helmet and the smoked faceplate down, we rode through the Hollows, over the bridge, and into Cincinnati. The afternoon sun was warm on my shoulders, and I wished we really were just two biker chicks headed into town for a Friday afternoon of shopping.

In reality, we were headed for a parking garage to meet Nick and Ivy's friend, Carmen. She would take my place for the day, pretending to be me while they drove around the countryside. I thought it overkill, but if it pacified Ivy, I'd do it.

From the garage, I would sneak into Trent's garden with the help of Nick playing lawn-service guy, spraying the bugs Jenks had seeded Trent's prize rosebushes with last Saturday. Once past Trent's walls, it would be easy. At least, that's what I kept telling myself.

I had left the church calm and collected, but every block deeper into the city wound me tighter. My mind kept going over my plan, finding the holes in it and the "what ifs." Everything we had come up with seemed foolproof from the safety of our kitchen table, but I was relying heavily upon Nick and Ivy. I trusted them, but it still made me uneasy.

"Relax," Ivy said loudly as we turned off the busy street

and into the parking garage by the fountain square. "This is going to work. One step at a time. You're a good runner, Rachel."

My heart thumped, and I nodded. She hadn't been able to hide the worry in her voice.

The garage was cool, and she wove around the gate, avoiding the ticket. She was going to drive right on through as if using the garage as a side street. I took my helmet off upon catching sight of the white van plastered with green grass and puppies. I hadn't asked Ivy where she had gotten a lawn-care truck. I wasn't going to, either.

The back door opened as Ivy's bike lub-lub-lubbed closer, and a skinny vamp dressed like me jumped out, her hand grasping for the helmet. I handed it to her, sliding off as her leg took my place. Ivy never slowed the bike's pace. Stumbling, I watched Carmen stuff her blond hair under the helmet and grab Ivy's waist. I wondered if I really looked like that. Nah. I wasn't that skinny. "See you tonight, okay?" Ivy said over her shoulder as she drove away.

"Get in," Nick said softly, his voice muffled from inside the van. Giving Ivy and Carmen a last look, I jumped into the back, easing the door shut as Jenks flitted inside.

"Holy crap!" Jenks exclaimed, darting to the front. "What happened to you?"

Nick turned in the driver's seat, his teeth showing strong against his makeup-darkened skin. "Shellfish," he said, patting his swollen cheeks. He had gone further in his charmless disguise, dying his hair a metallic black. With his dark complexion and his swollen face, he looked nothing like himself. It was a great disguise, which wouldn't set off a spell checker.

"Hi, Ray-ray," he said, his eyes bright. "How you doing?"

"Great," I lied, jittery. I shouldn't have involved him, but Trent's people knew Ivy, and he had insisted. "Sure you want to do this?"

He put the van into reverse. "I've an airtight alibi. My time card says I'm at work."

I looked askance at him as I pulled off my boots. "You're doing this on company time?"

"It's not as if anyone checks up on me. As long as the work gets done, they don't care."

My face went wry. Sitting on a canister of bug killer, I shoved my boots out of sight. Nick had found a job cleaning artifacts at the museum in Eden Park. His adaptability was a continual surprise. In one week he had gotten an apartment, furnished it, bought a ratty truck, got a job, and took me out on a date—a surprisingly nice date including an unexpected, ten-minute helicopter tour over the city. He said his preexisting bank account had a lot to do with how fast he had found his feet. They must pay librarians more than I thought.

"Better get changed," he said, his lips hardly moving as he paid the automated gate and we lumbered out into the sun. "We'll be there in less than an hour."

Anticipation pulled me tight, and I reached for the white duffel bag with the lawn care service logo on it. In it went my pair of lightweight shoes, my fail-safe amulet in a zippy bag, and my new silk/nylon bodysuit tightly packaged into a palm-sized bundle. I arranged everything to make room for one mink and an annoying pixy, tucking Nick's protective, disposable paper overalls on top. I was going in as a mink, but I would be damned if I was going to stay that way.

Conspicuous in their absence were my usual charms. I felt naked without them, but if caught, the most the I.S. could charge me with was breaking and entering. If I had even one charm that could act on a person—even as little as a bad-breath charm—it would bump me up to intent to do bodily harm. That was a felony. I was a runner; I knew the law.

While Nick kept Jenks occupied up front, I quickly stripped down to nothing and jammed every last bit of evidence that I had been in the van into a canister labeled TOXIC CHEMICALS. I downed my mink potion with an embarrassed haste, gritting my teeth against the pain of transformation. Jenks gave Nick hell when he realized I'd been naked in the back of his van. I wasn't looking forward to changing back, suffering Jenks's barbs and jokes until I managed to get in my bodysuit.

And from there it went like clockwork.

Nick gained the grounds with little trouble, since he was expected—the real lawn service had gotten a cancellation call from me that morning. The gardens were empty because it was the full moon and they were closed for heavy maintenance. As a mink, I scampered into the thick rosebushes Nick was supposed to be spraying with a toxic insect killer but in actuality was saltwater to turn me back into a person. The thumps from Nick tossing my shoes, amulet, and clothes into the shrubs were unbelievably welcome. Especially with Jenks's lurid running commentary about acres of big, pale, naked women as he sat on a rose cane and rocked back and forth in delight. I was sure the saltwater was going to kill the roses rather than the aggressive insects Jenks had infected them with, but that, too, was in the plan. If by chance I was caught, Ivy would come in the same way with the new shipment of plants.

Jenks and I spent the better part of the afternoon squashing bugs, doing more than the saltwater to rid Trent's roses of pests. The gardens remained quiet, and the other maintenance crews stayed clear of Nick's caution flags stuck around the rose bed. By the time the moon rose, I was wound tighter than a virgin troll on his wedding night. It didn't help that it was so cold.

"Now?" Jenks asked sarcastically, his wings invisible but for a silver shimmer in the dark as he hovered before me.

"Now," I said, teeth chattering as I picked my careful way through the thorns.

With Jenks flying vanguard, we skulked from pruned bush to stately tree, finding our way in through a back door at the commissary. From there it was a quick dash to the front lobby, Jenks putting every camera on a fifteen-minute loop.

Trent's new lock on his office gave us trouble. Pulse pounding, I fidgeted by the door as Jenks spent an entire, unreal five minutes jigging it. Cursing like a furnace repairman, he finally asked for my help in holding an unbent paper clip against a switch. He didn't bother to tell me I was closing a circuit until after a jolt of electricity knocked me on my can.

"You ass!" I hissed from the floor, wringing my hand instead of wringing his neck like I wanted. "What the hell do you think you're doing?"

"You wouldn't have done it if I had told you," he said from the safety of the ceiling.

Eyes narrowed, I ignored his snarky, half-heard justifications and pushed open the door. I half expected to find Trent waiting for me, and I breathed easier upon finding the room empty, lit dimly from the fish tank behind the desk. Hunched with anticipation, I went right for the bottom drawer, waiting until Jenks nodded to tell me it hadn't been tampered with. Breath tight, I pulled it open to find—nothing.

Not surprised, I looked up at Jenks and shrugged. "Plan B," we said simultaneously as I pulled a wipe from a pocket and swabbed everything down. "To his back office."

Jenks flitted out the door and back. "Five minutes left on the loop. We gotta hurry."

I bobbed my head, taking a last look at Trent's office before I followed Jenks out. He buzzed ahead of me down the hallway at chest height. Heart pounding, I followed at a discreet distance, my shoes silent on the carpet as I jogged through the empty building. The fail-safe amulet about my neck glowed a nice, steady green.

My pulse increased and a smile curved over me as I found Jenks at the door to Trent's secondary office. This was what I had missed, why I had left the I.S. The excitement, the thrill of beating the odds. Proving I was smarter than the bad guy. This time, I'd get what I came for. "What's our clock?" I whispered as I came to a halt, pulling a strand of hair out of my mouth.

"Three minutes." He flitted up and then down. "No cameras in his private office. He's not there. I already checked."

Pleased, I slipped past the door, easing it closed as Jenks flew in behind me.

The smell of the garden was a balm. Moonlight spilled in, bright as early morning. I crept to the desk, my smile turning wry, since it now had the cluttered look of one that was being used. It took only a moment to find the briefcase beside the desk. Jenks jimmied the lock, and I opened it up, sighing at the sight of the discs in neat, tidy rows. "Are you sure they're the right ones?" Jenks muttered from my shoulder as I chose one and slipped it into a pocket.

I knew they were, but as I opened my mouth to answer, a twig snapped in the garden.

Pulse hammering, I jerked my thumb in the "Hide" gesture to Jenks. Wings silent, he flitted up to the row of light fixtures. Not breathing, I eased down to crouch beside the desk.

My hope that it might be a night animal died. Soft, almost inaudible footfalls on the path grew louder. A tall shadow moved with a confident quickness from the path to the porch. It took the three steps in one bound, moving with a content, happy motion. My knees went weak as I recognized Trent's voice. He was humming a song I didn't recognize, his feet moving to a spine-tingling beat. *Crap,* I thought, trying to shrink farther behind the desk.

Trent turned his back to me and rummaged in a closet. An uncomfortable silence replaced his humming as he sat on the edge of a chair between me and the porch, changing into what looked like tall riding boots. The moonlight made his white shirt seem to glow past his close-cut jacket. It was hard to tell in the dim light, but it looked as if his English riding outfit was green, not red. *Trent bred horses,* I thought, *and rode them at night?*

The twin thumps of his heels into his boots were loud. My breath coming faster, I watched him stand, seeming far taller than the extra inch the boots gave him. The light dimmed as a cloud passed before the moon. I almost missed it when he reached under the chair he had been sitting on.

In a smooth, graceful motion, he pulled a gun and trained it on me. My throat closed.

"I hear you," he said evenly, his voice rising and falling like water. "Come out. Now."

Chills raced down my arms and legs, setting my fingertips to tingle. I crouched beside the desk, not believing he had sensed me. But he was facing me squarely, his feet spread wide and his shadow looking formidable. "Put your gun down first," I whispered.

"Ms. Morgan?" The shadow straightened. He was actually surprised. I wondered who he had expected. "Why should I?" he asked, his mellow voice soothing despite the threat in it.

"My partner has a spell right over your head," I bluffed.

The shadow that was Trent shifted as he glanced up. "Lights, forty-eight percent," he said, his voice harsh. The room brightened, but not enough to ruin my night vision. Knees turning to water, I rose from my crouch, trying to look as if I had planned this as I leaned against his desk in my silk and spandex bodysuit and crossed my ankles.

Gun tight in his grip, Trent ran his gaze over me, looking disgustingly refined and smart in his green riding outfit. I forced myself to not look at the weapon pointing at me as my gut tightened. "Your gun?" I questioned, sending my gaze to the ceiling where Jenks waited.

"Drop it, Kalamack!" Jenks shrilled from the light fixture, his wings clattering in an aggressive noise.

Trent's stance eased to match my own tension-laced, casual poise. Motions sharp and abrupt, he took the bullets from the gun and tossed the heavy metal to my feet. I didn't touch it, feeling my breath come easier. The bullets clattered dully into a pocket of his riding jacket. In the stronger light, I could see evidence of his healing demon attack. A yellowing bruise decorated his cheekbone. The end of a blue cast poked beyond the cuff of his jacket. A healing scrape showed on his chin. I found myself thinking that despite it all, he looked good. It wasn't right that he should look so confident when he thought he had a lethal spell hanging over him.

"I only need to say one word, and Quen will be here in three minutes," he said lightly.

"How long do you take to die?" I bluffed.

His jaw clenched in anger, making him seem younger. "Is that what you are here for?"

"If it was, you'd already be dead."

He nodded, accepting that as truth. Standing wire-tight across the room, his gaze flicked to his open briefcase. "Which disc do you have?"

Feigning confidence, I brushed a strand of hair out of my eyes. "Huntington. If anything happens to me, it will go to six papers and three news studios along with the missing page of your planner." I pushed myself off from his desk. "Leave me alone," I threatened flatly.

His arms hung unmoving at his sides, his broken one at an angle. My skin pricked, though he made no move, and my veneer of confidence slipped. "Black magic?" he mocked. "Demons killed your father. Shame to see the daughter go the same way."

My breath hissed in. "What do you know of my dad?" I said, shocked.

His eyes slid to my wrist—the one with the demon scar—and my face went cold. My stomach knotted as I remembered the demon killing me slowly. "I hope it hurt you," I said, not caring that my voice quavered. Maybe he'd think it was in anger. "I don't know how you survived it. I almost didn't."

Trent's face went red and he pointed a finger at me. It was nice to see him act like a real person. "Sending a demon to attack me was a mistake," he said, his words sharp. "I don't deal in black magic, nor do I allow my employees to do so."

"You big fat liar!" I exclaimed, not caring if it sounded childish. "You got what you deserved. I didn't start this, but I'll be damned if I don't finish it!"

"I'm not the one with the demon mark, Ms. Morgan," he

said icily. "A liar as well? How disappointing. I'm seriously considering withdrawing my offer of employment. Pray I don't, or I won't have any reason to tolerate your actions any longer."

Angry, I took a breath to tell him he was an idiot. But my mouth stopped. Trent thought I had summoned the demon that had attacked him. My eyes went wide as I figured it out. Someone had called two demons—one for me, one for him—and it hadn't been anyone at the I.S. I'd stake my life on it. Heart pounding, I reached out to explain, then shut my mouth.

Trent went wary. "Ms. Morgan?" he questioned softly. "What thought just percolated through that head of yours?"

I shook my head, licking my lips as I took a step back. If he thought I dealt in black magic, he'd leave me alone. And as long as I had proof of his guilt, he wouldn't risk killing me. "Don't back me into a corner," I threatened, "and I won't bother you again."

Trent's questioning expression hardened. "Get out," he said, moving from the porch in a graceful movement. Shifting as one, we exchanged places. "I'll give you a generous head start," he said as he reached his desk, snapping his briefcase shut. His voice was dusky, as rich and abiding as the scent of decaying maple leaves. "It may take ten minutes to reach my horse."

"Excuse me?" I asked, confused.

"I haven't run down two-footed prey since my father died." Trent adjusted his hunter-green coat with an aggressive motion. "It's the full moon, Ms. Morgan," he said, his voice thick with promise. "The hounds are loosed. You're a thief. Tradition says you should run—fast."

My heart pounded and my face went cold. I had what I came for, but it would do me no good if I couldn't escape with it. There was thirty miles of woods between me and the nearest source of help. How fast did a horse run? How long could I go before I dropped? Maybe I should have told him I hadn't sent the demon.

The distant sound of a horn lifted through the black. A baying hound answered it. Fear struck through me, as painful as a knife. It was an old, ancient fear, one so primal it couldn't be soothed with self-induced delusions. I didn't even know where it came from. "Jenks," I whispered. "Let's go."

"Right behind you, Rache," he said from the ceiling.

I took three running steps and dove off Trent's porch. I landed in a rolling crouch in the ferns. There was an explosion of a gun. The foliage beside my hand shattered. Lunging into the greenery, I bolted into a sprint.

Bastard! I thought, my knees almost giving way. What happened to my ten minutes?

Running, I fumbled for my vial of saltwater. I bit through the top and soaked my amulet. It flickered and went out. Ivy's would turn and stay red. The road was less than a mile. The gatehouse was three. The city was thirty. How long would it take Ivy to get here?

"How fast can you fly, Jenks?" I panted between foot strikes.

"Pretty damn fast, Rache."

I stuck to the paths until I reached the garden wall. A dog bayed as I climbed over it. Another answered. *Shit.*

Breathing in time with my strides, I ran over the manicured lawn and into that eerie wood. The sound of the dogs fell behind me. The wall was giving them trouble. They'd have to go around. Maybe I could do this. "Jenks," I panted as my legs began to protest. "How long have I been running?"

"Five minutes."

God, help me, I silently pleaded, feeling my legs begin to ache. It felt like twice that.

Jenks flew ahead, pixy dust sifting from him to show me the way. The silent pillars of dark trees loomed and vanished. My feet thumped rhythmically. My lungs ached and my side hurt. If I lived through this, I promised myself I was going to run five miles a day.

The calling of the dogs shifted. Though faint, their voices

sang sweeter, truer, promising they'd soon be with me. It struck like a goad. I dug deeper, finding the will to keep to my pace.

I ran, pushing my heavy legs up and down. My hair stuck to my face. Thorns and brambles ripped my clothes and hands. The horns and dogs grew closer. I fixed my gaze on Jenks as he flew before me. A fire started in my lungs, growing to consume my chest. To stop would mean my death.

The stream was an unexpected oasis. I fell into the water and came up gasping. Lungs heaving, I pushed the water from my face so I could breathe. The pounding of my heart tried to outdo the hoarse sound of my breathing. The trees held a frightened hush. I was prey, and everything in the forest was silently watching, glad it wasn't them.

My breath rasped at the sound of the dogs. They were closer. A horn blew, pulling fear through me. I didn't know which sound was worse.

"Get up, Rachel!" Jenks urged, glowing like a will-o'-the-wisp. "Go down the stream."

I scrambled up, lurching into a slogging run in the shallows. The water would slow me down, but it would slow the dogs down, too. It would only be a matter of time before Trent would split the pack to search both sides of the stream. I wasn't going to get out of this one.

The pitch of the dogs singing faltered. I surged out onto the bank in a panic. They had lost the scent. They were right behind me. Visions of being torn apart by dogs spurred me on though my legs could hardly move. Trent would paint his forehead with my blood. Jonathan would save a lock of my hair in his top dresser drawer. I should have told Trent I hadn't sent that demon. Would he have believed me? He wouldn't now.

The burble of a motorbike brought a cry from me. "Ivy," I croaked, reaching out to support myself against a tree. The road was just ahead. She must have already been on her way. "Jenks, don't let her go past me," I said between gasps for air. "I'll be right behind you."

"Gotcha!"

He was gone. I stumbled into motion. The dogs were baying, soft and questing. I could hear the sound of voices and instructions. It pushed me into a run. A dog sang clear and pure. Another answered it. Adrenaline scoured through me.

Branches whipped my face and I fell into the road. My skinned palms stung. Too breathless to cry out, I forced myself up from my knees. Staggering, I looked down the road. A white light bathed me. The roar of a motorbike was an angel's blessing. Ivy. It had to be. She must have been on her way before I broke the amulet.

I got to my feet, listing as my lungs heaved. The dogs were coming. I could hear the thump of horses' hooves. I started a jolting, weaving jog toward the approaching light. It rushed upon me in a sudden surge of noise, sliding to a halt beside me.

"Get on!" Ivy shouted.

I could hardly lift my leg. She pulled me up behind her. The engine thrummed under me. I gripped her waist and struggled not to fall into the dry heaves. Jenks buried himself in my hair, his tight grip almost unnoticed. The bike lurched, spun, and leapt forward.

Ivy's hair flew back, stinging as it hit me. "Did you get it?" she shouted over the wind.

I couldn't answer. My body was trembling from the abuse. The adrenaline had spent itself out, and I was going to pay for it in spades. The road hummed under me. The wind pulled my heat away, turning my sweat cold. Fighting back the nausea, I reached with numb fingers to feel the reassuring bump of a disc in a front pocket. I patted her shoulder, unable to use my breath for anything other than breathing.

"Good!" she shouted over the wind.

Exhausted, I let my head rest against Ivy's back. Tomorrow I'd stay in bed and shake until the evening paper came. Tomorrow I'd be sore and unable to move. Tomorrow I'd put bandages on the welts from the branches and thorns. Tonight . . . I'd just not think about tonight.

I shivered. Feeling it, Ivy turned her head. "Are you all right?" she shouted.

"Yeah," I said into her ear so she could hear me. "Yeah, I am. Thanks for coming to get me." I pulled her hair out of my mouth and looked behind me.

I stared, riveted. Three horsemen stood on the ribbon of moonlit road. The hounds were milling about the horses' feet as they pranced with nervous, arched necks. I had just made it. Chilled to the core of my soul, I watched the middle rider touch his brow in a casual salute.

An unexpected pull went through me. I had bested him. He knew and accepted it, and had the nobility to acknowledge it. How could you not be impressed by someone that sure of himself. "What the hell is he?" I whispered.

"I don't know," Jenks said from my shoulder. "I just don't know."

Thirty-four

Midnight jazz goes very well with crickets, I thought as I sprinkled the chopped tomato on the tossed salad. Hesitating, I stared at the red globs among the leafy green. Glancing out the window at Nick standing before the grill, I picked them all out and tossed the lettuce again to hide what I had missed. Nick would never know. It wasn't as if it would kill him.

The sound and smell of cooking meat pulled at me, and I leaned past Mr. Fish on the sill to get a better look. Nick was wearing an apron that said "Don't stake the cook, cook the steak." Ivy's, obviously. He looked relaxed and comfortable as he stood at the fire in the moonlight. Jenks was on his shoulder, darting upward like fall leaves in the wind when the fire spurted.

Ivy was at the table, looking dark and tragic as she read the late edition of the *Cincinnati Enquirer* in the light of a candle. Pixy children were everywhere, their transparent wings making shimmering flashes when they reflected the moon, three days past full. Their shouts as they tormented the early fireflies broke into the muted roar of Hollows' traffic, making a comfortable mix. It was the sound of security, reminding me of my own family's cookouts. A vamp, a human, and a posse of pixies were an odd sort of family, but it was good to be alive in the night with my friends.

Content, I juggled the salad, a bottle of dressing, and the

steak sauce and backed out the screen door. It slammed behind me, and Jenks's kids shrieked, scattering into the graveyard. Ivy looked up from the newsprint as I set the salad and bottles beside her. "Hey, Rachel," she said. "You never did tell me how you got that van. Did you have any trouble taking it back?"

My eyebrows rose. "I didn't get the van. I thought you did."

As one, we turned to Nick, standing at the grill with his back to us. "Nick?" I questioned, and he stiffened almost imperceptibly. Full of a questioning speculation, I grabbed the steak sauce and eased up behind him. Waving Jenks away, I slipped an arm around Nick's waist and leaned close, delighted when his breath caught and he gave me a look of surprised speculation. *What the heck. He was a nice guy for a human.* "You stole that truck for me?" I asked.

"Borrowed," he said, blinking as he remained carefully unmoving.

"Thank you," I said, smiling as I handed the bottle of steak sauce to him.

"Oh, Nick," Jenks mocked in a high falsetto. "You're my hero!"

My breath slipped from me in bother. Sighing, I let my hand drop from around Nick's waist and stepped back. From behind us came Ivy's snort of amusement. Jenks made kissing noises as he circled Nick and me, and fed up, I darted my hand out.

Jenks jerked back, hovering in surprise as I almost got him. "Nice," he said, darting off to bother Ivy. "And how's your new job going?" he drawled as he landed before her.

"Shut up, Jenks," she warned.

"Job? You have another run?" I asked as she shook open the newsprint and hid behind it.

"Didn't you know?" Jenks said merrily. "Edden arranged it with the judge to give Ivy three hundred hours of community service for taking out half his department. She's been working at the hospital all this week."

Eyes wide, I went to the picnic table. The corner of the paper was trembling. "Why didn't you tell me?" I asked as I angled my legs past the bench and sat across from her.

"Maybe because they made her a candy striper," Jenks said, and Nick and I exchanged dubious looks. "I saw her on her way to work yesterday and followed her. She has to wear a short pink and white striped skirt and a frilly blouse." Jenks laughed, catching himself as he fell off my shoulder. "And white tights to cover her perky little ass. Looks real good on her bike."

A vampire candy striper? I thought, trying to picture it.

A chortle slipped from Nick, quickly turned into a cough. Ivy's knuckles as she gripped the paper turned white. Between the later hour and the relaxed atmosphere, I knew it was hard for her to keep from pulling an aura. This wasn't helping.

"She's at the Children's Medical Center, singing and having tea parties," Jenks gasped.

"Jenks," Ivy whispered. The paper slowly dropped, and I forced my face into a careful impassivity at the black hazing her.

Wings a blur, Jenks grinned and opened his mouth. Ivy rolled the paper. Quicker than sound, she slammed it at him. The pixy darted up into the oak, laughing.

We all turned at the creak of the wooden gate by the front walk. "Hello-o-o-o. Am I late?" came Keasley's voice.

"We're back here!" I shouted as I spotted Keasley's slow moving shadow making its way across the dew-wet grass past the silent trees and bushes.

"I brought the wine," he said as soon as he was closer. "Red goes with meat, right?"

"Thanks, Keasley," I said, taking the bottle from him. "You didn't have to do that."

He smiled, extending the padded envelope tucked under his arm. "This is yours, too," he said. "The delivery man didn't want to leave it on the steps this afternoon, so I signed for it."

"No!" Ivy shouted, reaching across the table to intercept it. Jenks, too, dropped from the oak, his wings making a harsh clattering. Looking annoyed, Ivy snatched it out of his grip.

Keasley gave her a dark look, then went to see how Nick was doing with the steaks.

"It's been over a week," I said, peeved as I wiped my hand free of the condensation from Keasley's wine. "When are you going to let me open my own mail?"

Ivy said nothing, pulling the citronella candle closer to read the return address. "As soon as Trent stops sending you mail," she said softly.

"Trent!" I exclaimed. Worried, I tucked a strand of hair behind my ear, thinking about the folder I'd given Edden two days ago. Nick turned from the steaks, his long face showing concern. "What does he want?" I muttered, hoping they couldn't tell how agitated I was.

Ivy glanced up at Jenks, and the pixy shrugged. "It's clean," he said. "Open it up."

"Of course it's clean," Keasley grumbled. "You think I'd give her a spelled letter?"

The envelope felt light in my grip as I took it from Ivy. Nervous, I slid a freshly painted nail under the flap, tearing it. There was a bump inside, and I shook the envelope over my hand.

My pinky ring slid out and fell into my grip. My face went slack in shock. "It's my ring!" I said. Heart pounding, I looked at my other hand, frightened to not see it there. Eyes rising, I took in Nick's surprise and Ivy's worry. "How . . ." I stammered, not remembering even having missed it. "When did he—Jenks, I didn't lose it in his office, did I?"

My voice was high, and my stomach tightened when he shook his head, his wings going dark. "You didn't have any jewelry that night," he said. "He must have taken it afterwards."

"Is there anything else?" Ivy asked, her tone carefully neutral.

"Yeah." I swallowed, and slipped my ring on. It felt odd for a moment, then comfortable. Fingers cold, I pulled out the thick slip of linen paper smelling of pine and apples.

" 'Ms. Morgan,' " I read softly in unease. " 'Congratulations on your newfound independence. When you see it for the illusion it is, I'll show you true freedom.' "

I let the paper fall to the table. My thick feeling of disquiet that he had seen me sleeping broke apart in the knowledge that that was all he did. My blackmail was tight. It had worked.

Slumping, I put my elbows on the table and dropped my forehead into my hands in relief. Trent had taken the ring from my sleeping finger for one reason only. To prove he could. I had infiltrated into his "house" three times, each one more intimate and unguarded than the last. That I could do it again whenever I wanted was probably intolerable to Trent. He had felt the need to retaliate, to show that he could do the same. I had gotten to him, and that went a long way toward ridding myself of my angry, vulnerable feeling.

Jenks darted down to hover over the note. "The sack of slug salt," he said, and angry pixy dust sifted from him. "He got past me. He got past me! How the hell did he do that?"

Steeling my face, I picked up the envelope, noticing the postmark was the day after I had escaped him and his dogs. The man worked fast. I'd give him that. I wondered if it had been him or Quen who did the actual pilfering. I was betting it was Trent.

"Rache?" Jenks landed on my shoulder, probably concerned at my silence. "You okay?"

I glanced at Ivy's worried expression across from me, thinking I ought to be able to get a laugh out of this situation. "I'm gonna get him," I bluffed.

Jenks flitted up and away, his wings clattering in alarm. Nick turned from the grill, and Ivy stiffened. "Whoa, wait a moment," she said, flicking Jenks a look.

"No one does that to me!" I added, clenching my jaw so I wouldn't smile and ruin it.

Keasley's brow furrowed. Eyes pinched, he sat back.

Ivy went paler than usual in the candlelight. "Slow down, Rachel," she warned. "He didn't do anything. He just wanted to get the last word. Let it go."

"I'm going back!" I shouted, standing to put some distance between us in case I was yanking her chain too hard and she came after me. "I'll show him," I said, waving an arm. "I'll sneak in. I'll steal his freaking glasses and mail them back to him in a freaking birthday card!"

Ivy stood, her eyes going black. "You do that, and he'll kill you!"

She actually thinks I'd go back? Was she nuts? My chin trembled as I tried not to laugh. Keasley saw it, and he chuckled, reaching for his unopened wine.

Ivy spun with a vamp quickness. "What are you laughing about, witch?" she said, leaning forward. "She's going to kill herself. Jenks, tell her she's going to kill herself. I'm not going to let you do this, Rachel. I swear, I'll tie you to Jenks's stump before I let you go back!"

Her teeth were a gleam in the moonlight and she was wound tight enough to pop. One more word, and she might make good her threat. "Okay," I said lightly. "You're right. I'll leave him alone."

Ivy froze. A heavy sigh slipped from Nick at the grill. Keasley's gnarly fingers were slow as they pulled the foil from the top of his bottle. "Oooh doggies, she got you, Tamwood," he said, laughing low and rich. "She got you good."

Ivy stared, her pale, perfect face marred with shock and the sudden realization that she'd been had. A stunned bewilderment, quickly followed by relief and then bother, crossed her. She took a breath. Holding it, her face went sullen. Eyes tight and angry, she dropped back down to the picnic table's bench and shook out the paper.

Jenks was laughing, making circles of pixy dust to sift down like sunbeams to glitter on her shoulders. Grinning, I rose and went to the grill. That had felt good. Almost as good as stealing the disc. "Hey, Nick," I said, slipping up behind him. Those steaks done yet?"

He gave me a sideways smile. "Coming right up, Rachel."

Good. I'd figure everything else out later.

A Fistful of Charms

Kim Harrison

There's no rest for the wicked, even when the taint on your soul isn't your fault.

It would be wise for witch and bounty hunter, Rachel Morgan, to keep a low profile right now. Her new reputation for the dark arts has piqued the interest of Cincinnati's night-prowlers, who despise her and long to bring an end to her interference, one way or another.

Nevertheless, Rachel must risk exposure. Her ex-boyfriend, Nick, has stolen a priceless Were artefact, and, as tempting as it may be to let the Weres tear him apart, Rachel feels obliged to attempt a rescue. But other sinister forces also covet the relic Nick has hidden. Some who desire it so badly, they will take the city – and everyone in it – apart to wield its frightening power.

ISBN-13: 978-0-00-723613-8
ISBN-10: 0-00-723613-1

The Good, the Bad and the Undead

Kim Harrison

During the last few months, former bounty-hunter Rachel Morgan has been rather busy. Having escaped relatively unscathed from her corrupt former employers, she's acquired a vampiric room-mate – called Ivy, faced were-wolf assassins; battled shape-shifting demons, found the time to pick up a boyfriend (even if he is only human), and has opened her very own runner agency.

But cohabiting with a vampire, however reformed, has its dangers. Ivy's evil vampire ex-boyfriend has decided that he wants her back, and views Rachel as a tasty side-dish. To make matters worse, Rachel's demon mark is the ultimate vamp-aphrodisiac – one that works both ways.

The stakes are high, and if Rachel is to save herself and her room mate she must challenge the criminal master vampire and confront dark secrets she's kept hidden even from herself.

ISBN-13: 978-0-00-723611-4
ISBN-10: 0-00-723611-5

Every Which Way But Dead

Kim Harrison

If you make a deal with the devil, can you still save your soul?

To avoid becoming the love-slave of a depraved criminal vampire, bounty-hunter and witch, Rachel Morgan, is cornered into a deal that could promise her an eternity of suffering.

But eternal damnation is not Rachel's only worry. Her vampire roommate, Ivy, has rediscovered her taste for blood and is struggling to keep their relationship platonic, her boyfriend, Nick, has disappeared – perhaps indefinitely, and she's being stalked by an irate pack of werewolves. And then there's also the small matter of the turf war raging in Cincinnati's underworld; one that Rachel began and will have to navigate safely before she has the smallest hope of preserving her own future.

ISBN-13: 978-0-00-723612-1
ISBN-10: 0-00-723612-3